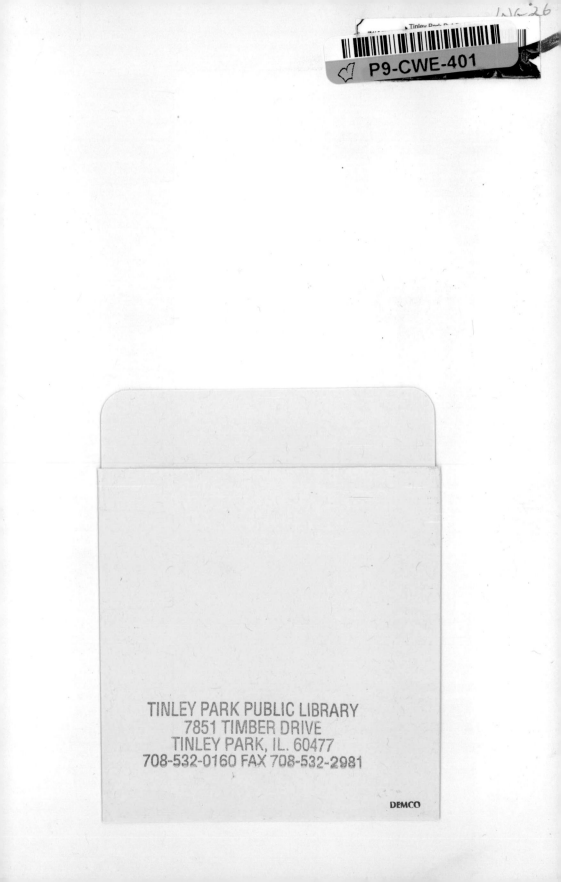

──THE──
HOUSE OF
THE STAG

BOOKS BY KAGE BAKER

THE COMPANY SERIES

In the Garden of Iden
Sky Coyote
Mendoza in Hollywood
The Graveyard Game
Black Projects, White Knights: The Company Dossiers
The Life of the World to Come
The Children of the Company
The Machine's Child
Gods and Pawns
The Sons of Heaven

ALSO BY KAGE BAKER

The Anvil of the World
Dark Mondays
Mother Aegypt and Other Stories

THE HOUSE OF THE STAG

KAGE BAKER

TOR®

A TOM DOHERTY ASSOCIATES BOOK
NEW YORK

THE HOUSE OF THE STAG

Copyright © 2008 by Kage Baker

A Tor Book
Published by Tom Doherty Associates, LLC
175 Fifth Avenue
New York, NY 10010

www.tor-forge.com

Tor® is a registered trademark of Tom Doherty Associates, LLC.

ISBN-13: 978-0-7653-1745-2
ISBN-10: 0-7653-1745-1

First Edition: September 2008

Printed in the United States of America

0 9 8 7 6 5 4 3 2 1

In loving memory of
MARQUE SIEBENTHAL
Actor—Acrobat—Fool
Gone where the oaks are green

THE
HOUSE OF
THE STAG

the speaking rock

There are figures painted on the rock. They are hard to see, because time has faded them with rainfall and sunlight. Stick figures with spears, things that seem to be both beasts and men, geometric shapes, spirals, rayed stars. This stick figure with its innocent male appendage, this other beside it depicted as female, with its two little globes and outdomed belly: they are lovers, clearly. Their voices have been lost to time.

But watch them: they will come to life. Some echo of the chanted words will come back, and the little figures will move.

———

The girl was pregnant by the boy. Their names were Ran and Teliva; they belonged to a tribe of forest people.

It was hot under the orchid canopy, it was thunder weather and the sky was leaden. With the baby crowding under her heart, Teliva couldn't breathe. Ran led her along the green trail, an easy-climbing path, up to the bare, high, cooler, open places on the mountain. Where water came down like a white veil into a pool, they swam and drank spray. But above the thunder of the falls they heard another noise, and ventured forth dripping and timid to see who cried so in the twilight.

They found the boy, only minutes old, howling and striking with fists at the empty air. He lay alone on the bare rock, in blood, with no footprint to show who had dropped him there.

Teliva took him up in her arms, and as she did, she felt the first sharp pain of her own deliverance. When she came down the trail again by morning light, she carried two little boys, with Ran walking beside to steady her.

They called their own son Ranwyr, and they called the foundling Gard, which meant "big" in their language.

Nobody knew who had left him there on the mountain; there were no other people in the world, except for the demons. Demons came out of rock and light and air, born of the elements as people were born from wombs. Sometimes they took the shape of people. Sometimes they came down to the dances and lay with women and men. Still, no one had ever seen a child made that way.

The people made a song about it, one of their long songs of complicated melodies, though the words were always simple. A song might say only *I love you and want you,* or *The river runs very high today.* The song they made about Gard ran, *Where did the boy come from?*

They put the desolate cries of the abandoned baby in it, and the cries of Teliva in her labor, and the wailing of Ranwyr as he drew his first breath. And the refrain, repeated 555 times was *Where did the boy come from?*

But no one ever found out.

Despite there being no fire, nor clothes or possessions, the people lived in a complicated world. Gard and Ranwyr must learn, as they grew, all the different names for weather, and the colors of the river and what they meant, and the smells of the forest and what they meant too. And they must learn right and wrong.

It was wrong to pull green fruit from a tree, or to interrupt a singer. It was wrong to be angry, wrong to grab for what you wanted or stare angrily into another's eyes. *Two people can walk one trail, if they are patient,* was the rule.

It was right to help Ran when he gathered fruit, and to be a big strong son carrying it back. It was right to shade the little new girl from the sun with big leaves, when Teliva set her down in a nest of grass; and, later, it was right to keep the little girl from going near the white angry river.

They had just begun to learn the names of the stars when the strangers came.

One night, Gard and Ranwyr lay at the edge of the dancing green, keeping watch over their sister. The dancers moved in their two lines on the wide lawn, which was starred with white flowers. Pairs of lovers had crept away into the bowers, all around, and now and then through the music Gard could hear the noises they made as they coupled.

"We're almost old enough to do that," he said, sitting up to peer out across the green.

"No, we're not," said Ranwyr. "Pyelume only danced this year for the first time, and she's three years older than we are."

"I wasn't talking about dancing," said Gard, with exaggerated patience.

"Neither was I."

Gard scowled, trying to see through the moving thicket of adult legs. "Boys are ready first, though. Ran told me so. It's already standing up on its own, sometimes."

"That's nothing. Mine does too," said Ranwyr.

"Oh, it does not."

"It did! You just didn't see. But we have to be older. Three more summers, and then I'm going into the bowers with Melilissu," announced Ranwyr.

"Melilissu already went into the bowers with Nole," Gard informed him. "And they made a baby."

"Oh," said Ranwyr, crestfallen. "Did they? Where is it?"

"Hasn't bloomed yet," said Gard. "Remember how long it took before Luma came out?"

"I don't want to make a baby yet anyway," said Ranwyr.

"I could," said Gard. "I'd like to be one of the fathers." He looked out at the bowers again. "I wonder why Ran and Teliva still go there. They already have us. And Luma."

"Oh, look! The moon is rising," said Ranwyr. They watched it rise, full and silver, and heard the singer's voice saluting the light in silver notes. The black shadows of the dancers were long and sharp-edged now.

At first they thought the drummers had been joined by new men and were starting a new cadence; they had no idea what hoofbeats were. But then there were new black shadows against the moon, moving fast, and there was screaming. The singer fell silent. Gard and Ranwyr cowered together, and behind them the little girl woke in her nest and began to wail.

The riders were circling, circling and screaming. The people milled together, frightened, and one man broke and ran for the edge of the trees; but a rider rose in the saddle and whirled something over his head. It screamed too, and spun out across the night air and tangled the man's legs. He fell heavily.

Teliva came running. Ran was close behind her, and close behind them came a rider in pursuit, silhouetted so high up on his mount! His eyes gleamed, his teeth gleamed. He was still screaming, but Gard realized he was laughing too. The rider raised his arm. He clutched a tangle of—vines? Round and round he swung them—

Gard felt anger like a white river in his whole body. He jumped up shouting right under the beast's hooves, and it reared back. The rider slid off and fell. Ran and Teliva passed him, flying into the darkness under the trees, stopping only to scoop up the little girl. The boys followed them. They ran a long way into the darkness, until the screams were distant.

"What was that?" cried Ranwyr. "What just happened?"

But Ran only shook his head, taking the baby from Teliva's arms. "I don't know."

The strangers did not look like the people, nor did they look like demons. The pictures on the rock won't tell you what they looked like: stick figures sketched in and then cut across with vicious lines, circled each with a black nimbus. Does it symbolize their strangeness, or is it an attempt to enclose their power, shut it away like a layer of pearl around a lump of grit? Their eyes stare. Their teeth are bared.

No one knew where they had come from, either. One day they were just *there*, building shells of stone in the wide plain east of the river, where lightning had struck fire and opened square miles to the sky. Between the black stumps pointing up they piled stones, or dug square-sided holes, or tore the earth up in long stripes.

The old life was broken, and nothing could be understood anymore. The strangers rode through the forest, slaughtering or kidnapping anyone they could catch.

The older people died first. Some of them stubbornly behaved as though the world hadn't changed, and walked into danger. Some children died, too young to know better or too old to listen to warnings. Some fathers died, not quiet or careful enough when they crept out to pick fruit. Some mothers died, taking too long to dig out roots.

The ones who were taken alive were later seen in the strangers' fields, tethered together, weeping as they pulled the plows, and the strangers beat them. At night they were herded back into pits under the walls and made to build more walls. When they died, their bones were thrown out to the edges of the fields they made.

Ran and Teliva found a hole under the roots of a tree, in the bank above a stream. It was as dark inside as the pits where the slaves were kept, but from its mouth there was a good view of the open meadows on the other side of the stream. Above it, the forest was so dense no riders could get through without making a lot of noise.

The children grew up in that place, learning to be quiet. Gard was broad-chested and tall; Ranwyr was thin, with bright eyes and clever hands. Gard learned well, but it was Ranwyr who discovered how to make bowls from gourds, who discovered how to weave reeds into baskets. The girl Luma was pale and small. She couldn't remember a time when things had been any different.

One night in winter the wind howled across the open fields, funneling like ice water into the hole under the tree. Ran and Teliva huddled to-gether, and their children with them, looking out at the blue night and white stars. Suddenly a dark shape was against the stars, a body scram-bling through. Gard threw himself forward, got his strong arms around the shape and wrestled it to the ground.

The other gnashed his teeth, struggled in silence. Ran crawled for-ward and peered at him. "Let go! Let go, he's one of us."

Gard released the man, who sat upright and gulped breath. "I know you. Ran from by the River. Aren't you?"

"I was," said Ran. "By the dark stream, now. Forgive my son. Here's a drink for you."

"That's all right." The other accepted the water gourd, looked at it in surprise a moment before tilting it to drink. He spilled a little and sat turn-ing the gourd in his hands. "Do you remember me? Shaff from the pear trees. I was; no trees there anymore. These times we live in! Eh?"

"This isn't time," said Ran. "Time's broken. What are you doing here?"

"I've been trying to get out," said Shaff.

"Out?" said Ranwyr. "Out where?"

Shaff turned and looked in his direction. "How many of you are there?"

"All of us," said Ran. "Where's your family?"

"Gone."

They were silent for a moment. Then, Ranwyr asked, "Have you found a way out?"

"Not yet," said Shaff hoarsely. "I went up the mountain to get away, but I couldn't go far. It's too cold, up high, and I couldn't breathe. I looked down on the world and saw the Riders' places, all their houses and fields, where we used to live. I saw the mountains stretching all the way around the round world.

"I saw the River going away, and I thought I'd go that way too. I went down and followed the River by night, swimming, hiding in the reeds by day.

"At last the River went under a mountain, and I couldn't go under with it. So I turned around and followed it back in the other direction. At last I couldn't go any higher, but I saw where the River came from, tears running from a green cold eye in a white mountain. The cold burned my feet; I was lame for three days and three nights.

"But I met a demon as I lay up there. He told me there are places on the other side of the mountains."

"Places on the *other* side?" said Teliva.

"Who's that?" Shaff leaned forward, staring into the dark. "Oh, a woman—I haven't seen a woman since—"

He stopped.

"How can there be other places?" said Ranwyr at last.

Shaff licked his dry lips. "The demon said, if you could get over the mountains, you'd see everything like it used to be. The green trees and the dancing greens. No Riders! No houses or pits. It's warm, and rains more. Every tree bears fruit! That's what he told me.

"So I'm going back, to see if I can find a way through the mountains."

"Did the demon know how to go there?" asked Gard.

"He only laughed at me," said Shaff. "Demons can fly. Demons can walk in the high places where we'd die. They're not even afraid of the Riders! He told me, he's eaten one."

Shocked silence greeted this news. "What are you doing here?" said Ran at last.

"Looking for a place to sleep tonight," said Shaff. He turned longing eyes to Teliva.

He stayed with them that night. Out of politeness, and pity too, Teliva lay down with him. In the morning he went on, to search for a way through the edge of the world. They never saw him again.

———

Ranwyr grew tall. Gard grew taller. They were good sons, silent when they walked out, careful at spotting snares and hiding their tracks. Now and then they met others of their people, hurrying through the night. They heard that the rumor had spread, that there was a safe place outside the world.

There was a song made, the first new one since the strangers had come, about the stars that sailed above the smoke of the Riders' houses. It was never sung aloud, but only passed in whispers from one night walker to another. The song told how the stars crossed the fields of the sky and left no tracks; the stars crossed behind the mountains at night, escaping into the sweet green place where everything was just as it had used to be. The refrain was *Oh, that we were stars.*

Ranwyr and Gard sat in the doorway, keeping watch when Ran slept. They turned their faces to the mountains always, wondering how to get out.

————

Life became harder, as the seasons rolled. The strangers cut down the trees, pushed their fields closer, so Ran must lead his sons farther and farther from the door to find food. There was plenty growing in the fields, and some of the people took it; but they left tracks, and the Riders came hunting and killed them or captured them.

One night Ran and his sons went gathering melons. On their way home they crossed a meadow open to the sky, taking a short way because the melons were heavy. Gard heard the hoofbeats first, as the Rider spurred toward them by starlight. He heard the whirling of the net in the air, and dropped what he carried and ran for his life.

From the corner of his eye he saw Ranwyr running too and heard Ran, not so swift, running behind. He heard the cry, the impact of the weighted stones that dropped the net; heard Ran crying out for him to run.

But Gard disobeyed, he spun and stopped, saw the Rider's beast rearing up and the Rider's weapon striking down at Ran, who lay sprawled in the net. And then, not knowing how he'd crossed the ground between, Gard was by the Rider and wrenching the weapon away, and the Rider fell from its beast's back and struck at him as it fell. Gard hit it with the weapon, battered it to the ground again, and again, and at last it stopped trying to rise.

Gard stood there gasping, with the weapon in his hand. Ranwyr was beside him, though he hadn't seen him come back, crouched over Ran and pulling the net free. Ran's arm bled, its sinews cut. The beast stood and stamped, with mad frightened eyes, and foam dripped from its jaws.

They bound Ran's arm up with leaves, gripped it tight, wound with cord cut from the net.

"Run home," said Ran, "run home, before it wakes!"

"It won't wake," said Gard. He kicked it, and its head lolled.

Ranwyr looked on it in horror. "You killed it."

"It was easy," said Gard, in wonder. "Look how weak its arms are! Look how the point went through, just like through a rotten apple. Why should *they* kill *us*?"

"This is unclean," said Ran, clutching his wounded arm. "Come away from this unclean thing. Let it lie! And wash yourself. Its blood stinks."

No word but reproach. Gard took the rebuke across his shoulders, looked down.

"Father," said Ranwyr, "there might be others—and they'll see the body and know—"

"I'll stay behind," said Gard. "I'll hide it. You go home; I'll wash before I come back."

———

Alone in the night, Gard looked at the weapon in his hand. It was the first spear he had ever seen, bronze-pointed, the haft wound around with strips of skin. But it balanced light in the hand and had seemed to think for him as it had struck, finding the places to stab out the Rider's life.

Gard set it aside and searched the body. The Rider had had knives, bronze leaf-blades with a good edge, and he took those too. The other things he left alone, the stinking harnesses and hair, the matted stuff that it had worn on its thighs. Its beast stood there still, as though afraid to move. Gard rose and looked at it, saw the tight-pulled straps that bound and cut it. These he sliced away with the knife, and pulled them off and let them drop. The beast started and raised its neck.

It leaped away, staggering a little, as though it had forgotten how to run. It tossed its head, spiking the stars with its antlers, feeling no cruel pull in its mouth. Now it took a few tentative steps and now it trotted, gathering speed. It stretched its legs and ran at last, it bounded, it soared! Up it went toward the mountains and vanished on the high slopes.

Gard stared after it, wondering, his mind full of new things. He bent and dragged away the stinking body of his enemy.

———

Ran's wound healed, but the arm withered. He lay in fevers a long time, became querulous, became thin. Gard and Ranwyr bore it all on their shoulders now, hunting, watching by the dark stream that dried in the summer heat. Yellow muck over stones, unwholesome, and even the river low in its bed.

One night Ranwyr and Gard took water gourds and climbed the hills, hoping to find water running from the mountains. In a high place they found the white torrent leaping out of the rocks. There they drank and filled the gourds; there they heard the voice and lifted their heads and listened.

"Someone's singing," murmured Ranwyr. They took the gourds and crept in search of what they'd heard. In a high place where the stones reared against the stars, they found the singer. Under glowing stars, with starlight in his hair, he sang stars down the sky. His face was young. Silver ran from his eyes.

He stopped singing and regarded them.

"Who are you, singing in this high place? Come down! The Riders will hear," said Ranwyr.

The man replied:

I was their quarry, and I am not found.
Their swift steeds cannot run me down.
Their long lances cannot pierce my flesh.
I am not slain. And I sing.

"No singing now, not in this sorry world; the songs are whispered, and we hurry in the dark. Come down, poor fool, before they catch you there," said Gard.

"No Riders can catch me. I came to this high place to sing; a thousand stars fell, and two burned out my eyes, as I sang. I was blinded, but I knew a thousand new Songs, and with them saw better than with my eyes.

"I went down this mountain to sing to my love, but she was taken, she was taken, while I sang in my high place. I went heedless to the slave pits, climbed those black walls to free her.

"But she was dead. She was dead, and I am not dead. I wept in the dark places; the guards did not hear me. A child wept near me; he had fetter sores on his skin. To comfort him, I sang the first Song. His sores were healed.

"I walked among them all: bred mothers and children, broken men, all, and healed them all. Sores, the wound of the ax and plowshares, the stripes of the lash, I healed. Fevers I took away, and the galling of chains. When day came, I walked out unseen, unstopped. In my arms I carried a child. 'My sister lived by the waterfall,' said her mother. 'Oh, Healer, take her my girl!' And so I freed that child.

"Now I go and come to them all, in the pens, in the fields. I am never slain, though Riders hunt me. I am never slain."

Gard shook his head. "Friend, come down; the sorrow has made you sick! Come shelter with us. We have a safe place; your mind will heal."

But the singer smiled at him. "I never will be healed, until the people are free. Though I will come soon to all your safe places, I never will be sheltered. Go down, and tell them to come up to me. I will heal all our poor race, here on this mountain of stars, down in the blackness of the pit. Go down and tell them!"

His voice was strange and wild, the crying of birds, far up on an autumn sky. He resumed his song. With one last long troubled stare, Gard took up his water gourd and left. Ranwyr followed after, joyful.

"Now he's come, the bright one, the beloved! He'll heal the world!"

"No man can do that," said Gard.

"But he wore a crown of stars," said Ranwyr. "You saw that he was holy, you heard the stars burning silver in his voice!"

"I saw a poor mad fool in pain. They will be kind spears, that get him," said Gard.

Soon the stories began.

There had been a little girl, screaming, her foot pierced through by thorns of bronze in a spring-jawed trap. Somehow she'd been freed beneath the Riders' very noses, and carried back to her father's shelter. A smiling stranger had blessed her. Her wounds closed without scar.

In dark security a family stifled and burned with fever, mother and children, father. A star-eyed stranger brought them bitter herbs in water; they drank and were healed.

A brother and sister had been tracked by Riders, but heard a voice singing to call them on. Just ahead of the spear points they ran, following the voice, hearts beating loud, the hooves behind them beating louder. Then, a miracle: the trees themselves had closed behind them, hiding the hunted, bewildering the hunters.

So the stories ran, and on the speaking rock the Star appears here: a figure drawn with rayed stars for eyes, silvery ash used to make a cloud of light about him. His raised hands bless. He is in many places.

Ranwyr told the stories over in the dark, all he heard, to give them hope. The little girl listened wide-eyed, Teliva listened and wrung her hands in longing; Ran listened and shook his head. Gard sat apart, arms folded, impatient.

"Let's go out and look for him then, your Star," he said. "We know where to find him to see if he's still singing up there, waving his blind hands. You'll see the truth!"

So they climbed the hills, Gard and Ranwyr, when the smoke of the Riders' halls was carried up past them on high wind. Under bright stars burning, they climbed and met others climbing the trail: men and women they had not seen in years, many they had supposed were dead. Their hearts were high to see so many together, though the people moved like ghosts through the night, and many hobbled or crawled.

"Where are you going?" Gard asked a woman.

"To find the Star!" she answered.

"You've heard the stories too?" asked Ranwyr.

"Everyone has heard them," said a man who passed them on the trail.

"So many of us!" said Ranwyr, with his eyes shining. He stared upward as he climbed, looking for the line of stones against the stars that marked where they had met the man. Gard turned often as he climbed to look back, uneasy, mindful of the Riders. From so high he could look out on the world they had taken with their spears, where they sat planted now at their ease; and the displaced people floated up toward the stars like bubbles or smoke, chasing a fantasy. It made his heart wild, white like the wild river.

Then he heard the singer again, the voice in the night. All around him people moaned and rushed forward. He saw the wave of them break around the high stone where the singer was, and on all sides they stretched up their arms to him.

Smiling, the Star held out his hands. "Welcome."

"Help us," cried the people, their voices braided out of longing and despair. "Oh, Star, help us, heal us! *Make my leg straight again.* Make my baby strong. *Bring my father out of the pit.* Take away this fever. *Sing to us, Bright One, and make the old days come again!* Give us our youth back, before we knew what evil was! *Oh, let everything be as it used to be.*"

The Star shook his head. "Your old ways are lost. I can never sing back the child into the womb, the leaf into the bud. I cannot take this stain from the face of the sun. But, my people, I can ease your pain!

"Listen and be comforted, no more scattered in lurking isolation, no more slaves slaughtered and forsaken. Learn what I have learned! Come and let me teach you, and you will walk, as I walk, unfearing in the light. With a song, I close wounds; I know the songs of the flowers of the field, and all their properties. I know songs to clean poisoned waters, songs to hear the speech of beasts and all birds of the air.

"Come and learn from me! I can teach you to endure, as the earth endures, until we may be free. I can give you strength."

"Good!" said Gard, standing up among them all. "Give us strength, then, Star. For every wound you close, the Riders open a new one; for every snare you loose, the Riders set another. Do you know songs to drive them out? Teach them to me! Help us make spears, to open wounds! Help us weave snares, to catch the strangers!"

But the Star held up his hands. "I have no songs that kill, no power to wound. Listen well, all you who have despaired: the snare you make for another will catch your own feet. The Riders can't kill us all, unless we become what they are. That way we lose ourselves, beyond hope."

Gard spoke in anger then, drawing his brows together. "You lost your mate to the Riders! Who are you to say we shouldn't fight? Once we were like flowers, and we were trampled down. I won't be trampled anymore!"

The Star replied, "I tell you that a flower will be our deliverance! That flower will lead us from this valley; but let us go in innocence. I would not walk to freedom with blood upon my feet, over the bodies of the dead!"

"Then others will walk over your body," said Gard, and in white anger he turned and strode away down the mountain. Ranwyr watched him go, hesitant to speak. Resolved, he raised his voice:

"Holiest of men, I know you have the power to do wonders. Is there no song to open a way through the mountains? We all know there are fair groves far away, where no Riders can follow. Sing to make the stones crack, the earth shift, and where it opens, lead us through! There we'll live in innocence, ourselves and free."

But the Star answered, "I have no song to break the mountains. Until the deliverer comes to us, we must endure, Ranwyr, as the mountains endure."

Ranwyr bowed his head, and in his heart hope fell low like a spring of water receding; but still he said. "Teach me, then, Bright One, that I may teach others. Let me walk in your path."

Now others crowded up, begging to be taught too. They sat at the Star's feet, and he taught them the first of the Songs. He promised a way to step from time as a man steps from a trail. He promised a way to open eyes, that they might see the truth of light and matter. He promised a way to weave light and matter like a net, the pattern in control, seen all perfect from outside of time.

Some listened and understood. Some listened and thought they understood.

―――――

Soon there were disciples. Ranwyr was the first, but, eager as he was, he could not learn the tricks that cloaked the others in stars and night. He could not safely walk in the Riders' pens and carry out the children of slaves, though others did, nor walk unseen among the fields and leave no track. He learned the names of herbs and their properties, what cooled a fever or eased pain; but he could not save Ran or heal his withered arm.

Ran would not believe in the Star, though Teliva sat beside him pleading. His heart dried in him like the dark stream, and one night he turned his face down to the earth and listened for its heartbeat. Then Ran slept and never woke again, though Teliva sat beside him weeping.

"Will you never open your eyes to me again? Once you walked with me in the long grass, where little lilies poked through and opened their bright throats, and the white mist was on the hillsides and concealed us when we lay down; and your eyes looked into mine.

"Will you never speak to me again? Once you lay with me in the summer groves, and the blossoms drifted over us and the branches bowed with fruit down to my lips, and the long red sunlight of summer dappled the forest floor; and you sang all night long.

"Will you never lift your head again? Once you rose, you moved without tiring, and on the dancing green under stars you were light-footed, and through the red and yellow leaves that drifted you were the swiftest in the chase, and brought me down, best of all the young men; and you rose above me high and strong.

"Will you never hear my call again? Once I sang like a bird, no heartbroken note, once I sang and you heard me over meadows, over valleys, over mountains and groves; once you came to my voice, dropping down swift from where you soared. You heard if I turned in my sleep, you woke if I murmured in my dreams.

"But you have been unfaithful, you have listened to the earth's voice, you have despaired, gone down into sleep and left me to my grief. How will I go after you and leave your children unprotected? Who will care for us now, Ran?"

Gard and Ranwyr gave Ran to the earth. Afterward they spoke together, debating what they ought to do; for Ran's stream was dry, and Ran's refuge no longer was a safe home. The Riders' fields now stretched to the edges of his grove.

"There are high caves in the rock," said Ranwyr, "and He and His disciples keep safe places there for widows, for orphans. It's cold, no flowers bloom there; but the water is fresh and clean, and no Riders climb so high."

Gard bent his black brows, grumbling, "Who is He, has He become a god? If He's so high, let Him free us all."

But Gard looked narrowly at the girl Luma, saw that she was growing breasts; saw the lines that marked Teliva's face, and how she thirsted for any kind of hope, and so he agreed. Teliva went one last time to gather flowers, blooms of late summer, all she could find, blowing to feather and seed, to lay in the old place. They moved on. The Star welcomed the women, granted them shelter in his high places.

Gard would not stay with them on the mountain, to look down on the wide land where his people had lived. His anger ran like the white torrent, and so he went down again, into the trees beyond the Riders' fields.

Now those who were dark rumor in the past were themselves haunted by darker rumors still. Something stalked and slaughtered in the wood beyond their fields. Lone hunters, overseers wandering too far from the plowed edge, travelers, vanished without trace. Now among the sheep, a bull; now among the roses, one black thorn to shed the Riders' blood.

Gard had watched his enemy and learned well. He dug pits, deeper than the strangers ever made, more cunningly hidden than theirs. He set snares, lined with sharpened stakes, tempered in slow fire struck from flint, to bite deep and hold fast. He did more than his enemies could do: walked unseen on the trail behind to catch, rose from the running water to drown, dropped from the high tree branch to strike in silence.

And Gard plundered the Riders he struck down. He stored up what he took: long knives and daggers, spears with barbed heads, coiled black whips and heavy-weighted nets, jewelry in heaps. Now openly he wore an arm ring made of bronze, a silver collar worked with grinning skulls, taken from a Rider. The bodies he sank in the wide marsh; the heads he kept, a pyramid of bone, the best of all his treasures.

One night Gard saw a fire burning, so tall it licked the underside of the clouds. He crept as close as he could to the Riders' halls, lying flat in the plowed furrow, and watched one of their houses burn. Before the sun rose he had retreated to the trees, but still he watched; and at sunrise saw a procession coming out, four Riders together. Before them they drove one of their own, prodding his old back with spears. When he stumbled and fell, they laughed; when he struggled to rise, pushing himself up with bound hands, they spit on him and struck him with the butts of their weapons.

Amazed, Gard fell back and watched from a hiding place as they came on into the trees. Where the woods were thickest, they halted, dismounting. One took a rope and threw it over a tree branch, tied it tight; he looped it through the binding on the old one's wrists and hauled him up. The old one hung there, feet just barely touching the earth. His escorts laughed at him and rode away, back to their houses, while he screamed after them. He was bloodied, had been stripped naked of the hides the Riders wore.

Gard sat watching a long while after they had gone, as the old one's cries faded to mutters of outrage. At last Gard climbed a tree and looked from that high vantage, to see whether the Riders had doubled back; but they had abandoned their victim.

He scrambled down and vaulted from the low branch, landing before the old Rider. The man screamed again and spat at Gard. He hissed long words in the Riders' speech, venomous sounds.

Gard hefted his spear. "I wonder why they left you, old piece of filth."

"Eeh?" The old Rider broke off cursing and peered at him. "You speak slave?"

Gard was astonished. None he had ever killed had spoken to him in his own tongue. "I'm not a slave."

"No," the old Rider agreed. "You not them. You have hair-face; the sire slaves, they smooth-face same as dams. You too big. What you be, monster?"

Gard touched his beard a little self-consciously. Ranwyr had no beard; none of the men among the people had them either. "You speak our language badly."

"Only slave language," said the old Rider, looking contemptuous. "Not worth learn better. Listen, monster: you cut me loose, I give you many presents. Eeh? Many dam slaves to fuck."

"I won't cut you down," said Gard, with white anger rising high. "You Riders killed my father! And I'll kill you. I've killed a lot of you!

"See my silver collar? I got it from one of your proud hunters. He came looking for me, arrogant shit, thinking he'd slaughter me. I drew him on, through my trees; soon the fool was lost, far from his meek slaves and his high house. What a surprise when I leaped out to face him!

"He tried to run me down, laughing, with his sharp lance aimed at my heart. Oh, but I got him then! My spear went through him and pinned him to a tree. His beast fled from under him and he hung howling. Then it was *my* laugh, old fucker! I sawed away his head and had his silver collar.

"And this, my arm ring with pictures: see this? The beasts run round it, and little hunters chase, but never catch them. Seen this before? I caught the overseer who wore this. All one afternoon I lay in wait, all one afternoon I watched him use his whip across my people's backs. I got him when he went into the woods to make filth. I made him suffer before I split his head, like a rotten melon, in two pieces.

"You think we're all slaves, all weak, all weeping, all frightened of you! Not me!"

The old Rider listened to him in amazement, studied him as he spoke. He licked his dry lips and managed to smile.

"But only you. Only *one* of you brave. All the rest, slaves who cry like babies. No big words from *them*, only 'Oh! Oh! Spare me! Please!'"

"There'll be others," said Gard. "Other free people will join me. We'll kill you all and we'll take our land back!"

The old Rider grinned through his blood. "Eehhhh? Big brave slaves join you? I think no. Just you, big slave with hairy face. Just you alone fight. What for?"

"For my people!" shouted Gard, and struck him in the face.

The Rider's head rolled; he spat out blood and laughed. "Your *people*. You think people thank you? They never thank you." The Rider turned his furious gaze toward the fields, toward the houses beyond and the smoke still going up from his burning home. "I was Leader, there. I was wise. I was strong. When we lost old land, *I* found my people this new place. Good fields here. Good hunting. Many slaves. We grew big.

"Eehhhhh . . . shitten little boys be young men soon. My child fight me. My child! Stronger than me now. The old man goes down, pah! And the young man take his animals, and his wives, and his gold. Burn his house. He say, 'Die, old man!' and my *people* say, 'Die, old man!' No one speak for me.

"Put me out here for monsters like you to kill. You Leader fight for them, you give them good things, *your people*. Eehhhhh, but you see some- day: long time come, they throw you out too. No speaking for you, no thanking you.

"And why? People be shitten, monster. All people. Old man tells you so, young monster. Old man knows. Kill them all, all . . ."

"I'll kill *you*," said Gard sternly. "You're evil."

And he stabbed the old man through the throat, because he was sick of the sound of his voice, and stove in his head with a rock, because he didn't want it as a trophy. He walked away feeling angry and miserable, as though he wanted to wash.

He went home, climbing up the mountain where the shrill wind whistled around the stones, and the scree slid down. The sun glared in the hard bright sky, throwing his shadow stark and black. He looked down on the soft green lands, a long stone's throw away, but to his people so lost they might have been on the sun. He turned his face to the place of exiles, the dark cave mouths in the high rock.

Gard went in at the door where his family sheltered; sat and lay his long spear across his feet. Teliva, old woman, smiled for him as she pounded something in a bowl. The girl Luma ducked her head, shy. Ranwyr hardly noticed him, tired eyes like broken eggs, mouth bruised with mantras, mumbling prayers.

Gard watched, dissatisfied, a taste of poison in his mouth. Luma's long fingers worked, twisted seed-pod fiber into thread. After an hour she had a skein of fine yarn; and Ranwyr had nothing to show for that hour but whispered syllables.

Gard looked about and saw no stores of food. Teliva went to the water gourds, but they were empty; she picked two up and shuffled for the door. "No." Gard rose to his feet, took the gourds from her. "I'll go for water, Mother. Ranwyr! You come help me."

Ranwyr opened his eyes, bewildered. "No, no!" said Teliva. "He works so hard. He was up all night, studying. Let him be."

So Gard went alone to the spring, fetching back water. He went out again to the meadows and dug roots and gathered acorns; he came back and filled the storage baskets in the cave. Teliva smiled at him. But when she dippered out the evening meal, she first served beardless Ranwyr.

Gard ate in silence, scowling. The old Rider sat at his side and mocked him, as only the dead may do; he took away the savor of Gard's meal. At last Gard rose and took his spear, and now Ranwyr saw and rose to follow him out.

"Thank you," said Ranwyr. "I hadn't noticed the gourds were empty. I meant to fetch water, but I didn't realize it was so late."

"That's because you're a fool," said Gard, "and lazy. You sit there all day with your eyes closed! And the Riders still ride, thanks to cowards like you."

He strode off into the night.

———————

Ranwyr went to the Star in his high place, where he sang under the milky stars.

"Bright One, bring me peace," said Ranwyr. "I can't learn the Songs. I shame my mother, my sister. Why do I fail? My brother walks in the abyss, he reeks of blood, he's made of rage. Yet his trees bear, and mine die in the blossom."

The Star turned his eyes upon him, broken lights shining from two sunken caves.

"No. Hoarded skulls will not ransom us, Ranwyr; still all our race will rise proud and free. Sunset does not make the dawn false! Don't think our sun will never rise again."

"I would give my life to make it rise," said Ranwyr.

Silence, under the silver mist burning; the shattered eyes were dim. The Star spoke at last:

"Be steadfast, Ranwyr. Soon enough, our people will require all you have. No one will call you a coward, when your moment comes."

Ranwyr went home, without peace.

———

Low gray stubble in the fields of the strangers, raw earth littered with dead yellow leaves, a sickle hanging on a fence; birdcall, the lines of marsh fowl streaming off slowly, deserting.

Down in the black slave pens, plague and death came. Packed against the walls, the slaves in stewing torpor rotted. The Star walked among them, bringing starlight and clean air, healing with a cool touch. Five of his disciples walked in his steps, unseen, unknown by the Riders who feasted above in the high halls.

But the wind came up from the valley and brought death, even to the cold clean places where the free still lived. Ranwyr himself felt the thorn in his throat, the coals behind his eyes. He himself sank, and gasped, drowning in flame of fever. Teliva couldn't wake him; she screamed for Gard, who came and laid aside his spear.

He turned his uneasy hand to healing. All he knew to do was fetch water and wipe away sick sweat, but he did, and raised his dark uncertain voice in song. He thought the fever would spread like fire, eating through his family.

"Go to the Star," he told Luma. "Go up and save yourself; live and bear children."

Luma ran weeping, ran to the Star himself as he returned from the slave pens. He came quick, without a word, though he had been three days and nights without rest. In Teliva's shelter he found Gard still well, holding down Ranwyr, who raved and fought as Teliva mourned. Cool air came in with the Star; soft light came in with him; water-distilling mist came in with him and quenched the fire that burned Ranwyr.

Luma helped the Star, doing as he instructed her to do. He praised the skill of her hands and her quick understanding. All the while he stayed, she remained beside him, brought him all he required. She watched his cool hands and wished they would touch her heart, ease her pain.

When Ranwyr's fever broke, when the Star went back to his high place—then Luma went with him. She begged to be taught the Songs, and he welcomed her into his service.

Ranwyr opened sunken eyes at last to see Gard sitting by the door, his spear across his feet. Ranwyr sat up, looking in wonder at the old woman sleeping deathlike. Quick and bitter was the memory of young Teliva's face, radiant, flowers in her hair. He saw no sister. He looked his question at Gard; his tongue was too swollen in his mouth to speak.

"The girl has gone," said Gard. "They call your Star the Comforter of Widows, and so he is; they ought to call him Comforter of Maidens too. Drink! Here's the water gourd. Don't you die, or Mother will follow you. Be brave, for once in your life."

"You never got sick?" Ranwyr asked.

Gard shook his head. "My luck. If you can call it luck, to live here now. Your Star can free as many as he likes from out the slave pens; what's the use, when sickness reaches out to kill us here? This is one more thing they've done to us, the Riders, with the dirty way they live. We never knew sickness until they came." And Gard spat out the door.

Ranwyr laid his head down. He dreamed of flying over the mountains to green groves.

Teliva woke and tottered back and forth as she fetched water, as she prepared meals. Her talk was all of hope. Gard listened and forbore to argue.

Ranwyr lay dull and listless, watching the light on the wall. When he rose, Teliva praised him for his strength, and every word she spoke burned him. Why should he be praised for anything, who had failed in everything? He walked out into the flat sunlight and looked at the empty world. He walked a long way, not meaning to go anywhere.

He slept out in the open that night, heedless of the danger, in wild despair flinging his heart against the night sky, a bloody rag to catch the notice of the stars. By morning all his tears were gone.

Ranwyr woke upon a grim and stony heath, far up a mountainside. Numb, he crawled to a little stream, bathed his face, and lay there for a while. He had been staring at a withered stump for some few minutes when it moved, became a twisted wrinkled thing, pulling long mustaches. Ranwyr leaped to his feet. The thing laughed, cold and low.

"So you're the one who spent the night bleating and wailing on the cold hillside! Well, what's the matter? Not that I can't guess: some new offenses by the strangers, is it? More of the valley cut into squares and lines?" The speaker smiled and showed his saber fangs. He was a demon, of the kind that used to trade with Ranwyr's people.

Ranwyr spoke with caution, for he remembered well they were good neighbors only sometimes. Respectfully he said, "Pardon me, father, if I disturbed your rest. You guess rightly why I wept. Things go badly with my people now. It's not enough that they should make us slaves; the Riders have defiled the very earth, maybe past all hope of cleanness. I think we will all die."

The demon yawned, considering his words. "Now, there's a pity. I remember when your people came along—pretty little things, pleasing to the eye, if cobwebs to the tooth. They kept to the forests and the shade; had lovely manners. The strangers, now, they know no courtesy at all. But they make lovely meat." He flicked his tongue, forked, over saw-edged teeth, and blinked in amusement.

"It was to be expected that a race as old and wise as yours would weather well, against invaders. But we pass lamenting from the world," said Ranwyr.

"Too bad. But so it is! You need teeth and claws to survive, teeth and claws and little tricks like this—" And in the sun the demon stretched. His lumpy shape ran and blurred, till golden on the grass a great cat sprawled. "Now let any fool with a spear walk in my path! Oh, don't fear: if I had wanted you, I'd have killed you by this time." For Ranwyr was shaking, but not with fear, not with fear.

"Long-lived father of the stony hills, if ever there was love between your race and mine, then help me now! For I see a way my people might be free, and all our sorrow ended."

"I do nothing out of love, my child. It's not my way. But let me hear what help you want from me; then we can bargain, though I promise nothing."

So on the bare hillside in morning light they sat: the youth intent and gesturing with hands spread wide, the demon peering out of time.

"Oh, father of the mountains, your mountains ring us round. We cannot escape through bitter cold, and ice, and rimy air. But if there were a way to get across without perishing of cold, we'd take that way and live in green places, just as we did long ago. Beyond the mountains there are groves where sorrow never comes; beyond the mountains age and death can't hunt us.

"And if we flew—if we could shift our shapes to bird and back again, then as a flock we'd soar above the mountains and the snow, and light in groves of everlasting peace. Teach me how to wear a raven's skin, storm-dark, scythe-winged! And I will pay you any price you name, so I may teach my people this."

A grimace split the demon's countenance. "You are a fool. Now, tell me what you have to pay me with, when I make my demand. A wreath of flowers? Drifts of pretty leaves? The smoothest river pebbles you can find? Or fruit and berries, yes, to give my teeth a rest from cracking fatty mar-rowbones? But that is all your wealth. Listen to me, boy! My price shall be your pain. I thrive on pain.

"Shape-shifting is no easy thing to learn, for such little cloud-creatures as you are. For you it will be mounded agony, and I will watch, and that will be my joy. But you will learn the discipline of mind that makes you master over bone and sinew, yes; you'll learn to realign the very cells that make yourself. You will ride on wings, young man, you have my oath on that. How you will teach your people I don't know. That's your concern. What do you say?"

"Suffering is nothing," said Ranwyr. "Give me wings."

Down from that place the days and nights went by. Ranwyr was given up for lost, taken or slain, and Gard scowled down his pride and thought about the Star. He meant to find Luma, whomever she lay with, and com-mend their mother into her care; he hoped grandchildren might ease grandmother's grief. Teliva wouldn't go, waiting by the door for Ranwyr's return.

One dim morning she woke with bright wonder in her eyes. "I dreamed last night I saw my son. Gard, come lead me out to some safe place where I may bathe, and there I'll pray, as the Star tells us to pray. He'll come home soon now, I know he will."

Gard, good son, did as his mother asked. He took her to a pool he knew, screened by reeds, warmed by sunlight, too high for hooves, un-known to any Rider. He left her there, telling her to stay; he promised he'd be back for her at sunset. Then he went down the mountain, on his business of blood, and lay in wait to cut a Rider's throat.

But mothers never act according to the plans of sons. Teliva at midday came back, fearful to be so long away from the cold and empty nest. There she wept, for its emptiness and her own, remembering how once her arms had been so full.

Across the doorway came a shadow; into her ears came the voice out of her dream. "Oh, Mother, forgive me! See, I've come back safe."

Ranwyr stood there smiling, thin and bent. Teliva in fresh flood of tears pressed close, she could not even speak, and clinging tight to him she trembled. He smiled and kissed her.

"I can't stay long. I came back to let you know where I'd gone, what I do. I'll tell you everything, but let me get a little sleep, only a little sleep or I will die. Just let me sleep . . ."

Teliva made him a bed, sweet straw new-shaken and red leaves, where he lay down and stretched out with a sigh. Then Teliva saw his back and screamed to see the sign, deep-cut and bleeding still: a scythe-winged raven, its outline scored into his living flesh.

"My child, my child! Who did this thing to you?"

Ranwyr caught her hands and pulled her close. "Don't touch it! No enemy did this, but a friend. I've shed my blood to give us wings, Mother! The pattern's only the sign of what I've learned, and what I'll teach. Do you remember Shaff, the traveler? Maybe he found no track across the mountains, but we won't need one. When this is done, we'll fly safe above them, to the forests on the other side."

Teliva did not understand, but saw the desperate hope in his eyes. She caught the spark, and her face lit with joy. "Now, blessed was the hour when I first felt you move under my heart! My son, my good and clever son, how brave you are! The Star himself will come and bless your name. Lie down again, take your rest. I'll fetch clean water to bathe you."

Teliva took the jug and hurried, dancing like a girl, and at the high pool met Gard searching for her, fearful of her harm. Her hair was wild, tears streamed down as she laughed; he thought she had broken under sorrow at last. She clapped her hands and cried, "Your brother, Gard, what a brother you have! My brave Ranwyr brings us such a gift! He's learning magic, and he'll set us free!"

Dark eyes narrowed under black brows. Gard said, "Then Ranwyr has come back?"

Teliva sang her words. "Yes, yes, alive and safe! He's resting now—I must draw water, I want to wash his dear feet—"

Gard put her from him, turned to stride down the track, his brow a thunderbolt; the white anger in his heart surged up, a fountain, a boiling torrent. He came to the shelter and saw Ranwyr there, dim in the shadows.

"Where have you been sulking all this time? Have you no shame, to tell our mother lies?"

Ranwyr lifted heavy eyes in stiff face, dull with sleep. Dazed, he mumbled, "I haven't told her lies."

Gard shouted back, "She broke her heart for you, to think that you were killed, you wretch! And you were hiding all the while, coward, useless coward, leaving me to watch her alone! Get on your feet, lazy fool!"

Ranwyr sat up, drew deep breath for pain, and put out both his hands. "I wasn't hiding. The thing I've done will save her life, and your life, all our lives. I went up to the empty places. We'll all be birds, my brother, and we'll fly away."

Gard seized Ranwyr's arm and pulled him up. "Magic! How stupid do you think I am? Will you stand on your feet, for once?"

"Don't shout at me! I feel so strange—the power's here, but wild, and I'm still incomplete—"

In his white anger and despair, Gard struck his brother soundly in the face.

Ranwyr opened his bleeding mouth and cried, "Shame!" Now horror was in his face, for he felt the power going wrong. It spun and twisted in him, out of his control. Inner parts broke and wrenched awry.

Even as he screamed a second time, "Shame!" his arms were fanning, spreading out. Upon him came a raven's form, agonized, distorted, black and huge. Now his third cry of "Shame!" became midword a croaking raven's cry. He beat his black wings, he took flight, shot forth and rose on the air. People heard him as he flapped and screamed, and heads turned up to see the wheeling thing that cried out in a raven's voice.

Teliva saw him, coming down the trail. She dropped the water jug; it broke, and from her heart the hope poured out and spilled upon the ground.

Three times Ranwyr circled, while his broken form and outline blurred, dissolving into smoke. At last he was the shadow of a raven, nothing more substantial. Now the Star, seeing him, lifted up his arms and sang a lament for Ranwyr son of Ran.

Cry sorrow for him, windy sky and rain!
In banks of milky cloud he finds no rest,
No peace or rest upon the driving wind.

Behold the shadow of the raven there, O people;
For your sake has Ranwyr come to this.
But he will brood forever over you,
And guard you down the ages of the world
In the dim air, and in the striped rain.

Gard stood horrified, staring at the sky; Teliva, shrieking, fell upon him there, a stranger now, a fury with hot eyes, and battered with her fists and did her poor best to kill him. Catching her wrists, he fended her off, held her back from him. He heard the word she had been screaming all this time, torn from her tight-locked throat: "Murderer!"

Now from the mountain meadows they came, to ring Gard round and judge him, all faces that he knew: the Star and his disciples, the men and women. Gard cried, "What happened here? What have I done? Mother—"

Teliva pulled away, standing straight, and spoke ice and venom. "I am no mother to the likes of you. You never shared the hollow of my womb with such a man as Ranwyr, my murdered son! You are some demon's child, dropped on the mountainside and left to die, and I wish you had! We saw you there, a howling foundling, on the very night my son was born. I put you to my breast; now may it wither, that it nourished you! For you have shown the thing you really are."

Gard had no words, but like a drowning man he fought for breath. A moment all was silent, as the earth spun; then the Star spoke.

"This day, Gard, you broke hope with your fist. People will die in chains, who had been free but for your white anger.

"But Ranwyr paid a price in love and pain, and he will not be cheated at the last; over all our people now the shadow of a raven spreads its wings. He'll carry her from the void, the promised deliverer; he will fetch her from dreams and bring her into the world."

"What will we do with Gard, the murderer?" Teliva cried, in misery and hate. "What punishment for him, you man of stars?"

Silver ran like rain from the Bright One's eyes. "Teliva, for the sake of lost Ranwyr, call down no death upon your foster son! His sorrow will outlast us all."

But she said, "We won't have him live among our kind! I cast him out! And if I may not wish him death, then here's my curse: long life to him indeed! Too long, till he is worn down as a stone with grief as great as mine."

The Star raised both his hands and cried aloud, "Now sorrow on sorrow! In this day of darkness we had griefs enough. Go forth, Gard, and seek another name."

Now without sound, and scanning slowly round the circle of sad eyes, Gard turned. Now he took up his dagger and his spear, and people drew back. He walked between them, walked toward the ridges and the south, until he was gone.

———————

The last pictures on the rock show stick figures in stiff posture of lament, all their arms lifted. Above them is the winged shape, neck bent back, re-curved to suggest its death agony. Rayed stars surround it, to signify that it has become sacred.

The figure walking away from them all has been drawn with staring animal eyes, black under black brows; to make him more monstrous still he has been drawn with four arms. One hand brandishes a spear, one brandishes a knife. One hand holds up a net. One hand is raised in a fist.

In defiance of all perspective, he has been drawn larger than the other figures.

1

the inventory

It's an immense and grand ledger: clasps plated in gold, cut jewels set along the spine, elaborate tooling to ornament the black stuff in which it is bound. All the same, it's a rather unpleasant-looking thing.

You can handle it, if you like, but you won't like the slightly clammy texture of the black stuff; you won't like the weight of the book in your hands, heavier than it ought to be.

You can open it, if you like, and try to read the iron-red text. You won't be able to read it, though, not without your eyes watering, and the disconcerting hieroglyphs will call to mind snakes, whips, thorns, claws. After a few pages you will notice the smell, which will disturb you to the foundation of your consciousness.

It is a slave registry.

It was not made by any crude band of conquerors, if that's your next question; no Riders with knives of bronze could have created anything this carefully made, nor would they have the meticulous patience to cut the point, dip the pen in—ink?—and write the history of each unfortunate soul . . .

———

4th day 3rd week 7th month in the 230th year from the Ascent of the Mountain. This day, flesh salvaged from the eastern face. Initially routed to Larder. Vitality detected; rerouted to Experimental Medicine and registered as Slave 4372301.

———

He opened his eyes to unrelieved blackness. Was he dead? He felt nothing. The last memory was of screaming air and blinding light, and a sense of regret as he'd fallen. He'd come so far up the ice wall, and before that so far through the passes, that it seemed a shame to die from simple clumsiness. But his frozen hands had failed him, and so . . .

Dead, then. Was this the womb of the earth? Not the way he had imagined it. He had thought it would be full of green and shifting lights, warm and humming. Not this, which was nothing. No light, no sound, no sensation of cold or heat.

The bleak thought surfaced: *Perhaps the earth would not have you.* Gard considered that prospect and resigned himself.

It was something of an anticlimax, then, when the light appeared. It flared, it danced like yellow leaves. He started, and every nerve in his body shrieked to life. He wept in pain as the light grew brighter. It was nearing him. He could hear, now, a clanking sort of noise, echoing, and the echoing of footsteps. Now and again the light paused, but always it came on again.

It resolved into a man. He wore the light in a thing like an openwork basket, mounted on his head. He was carrying a . . . water gourd? He wore a harness and woven stuff, like one of the Riders, but he did not look like a Rider. His skin was the color of a sunset. And now he was within arm's reach, if Gard had been able to move his arm.

He stopped and thrust his head in Gard's direction, in an interrogatory way. When he saw Gard looking back at him, he grinned.

"Hhhhnaaaii!" he said. Something popped into existence at his shoulder, the image of a burning child, and it moved its lips and spoke when he spoke again. "The big icicle is awake!"

Or, at least, that was what Gard understood him to say. Meaningless syllables sounded, but within his ear another voice spoke with meaning. Gard tried to answer him and could only sob.

"Yes, I daresay you would cry! I'd cry too, if I was in your condition. Cheer up, though; Magister Hoptriot thinks he will save your legs. Then you'll be lots of use. Always good to be of use, eh?" The man set down the— gourd? No, but it was like a gourd—and uncoiled a thing like a rope. He hooked its end into a wooden frame that held Gard's arm prisoner, and Gard felt a sting in his arm, a tiny spark out of the flaming pain that consumed him. He looked at himself by the light. All bandages, and stinking salve.

The man set the gourdlike thing down and looked Gard over. "Poor icicle. The medicine hurts, yes? Here's what you need." He pulled from a pouch at his waist a handful of leaves. They were green, nearly fresh, only a little limp with having been in the man's pouch. He thrust them between Gard's teeth. "You chew. Soon, you won't care about the hurt."

Gard did as he was told, rolling the leaves into a quid with his tongue.

Almost at once his tongue went numb, and then his mouth; the numbness spread down from there, merciful as cool water. The man squatted, watching him. He chuckled.

"There, now he's happy. Aren't you happy?"

"Am I dead?" said Gard thickly.

"No, not dead! By the grace of the masters, alive. You came a long way through the snow. What were you doing?"

Gard summoned memory. "Looking for a way through."

"Ahhh! To the cities on the other side?"

Gard looked at the man in incomprehension, wondering what *cities* might be, and the flaming child at the man's shoulder fretted and danced, and at last a tiny voice spoke in Gard's head: *Communities/villages/families of people.*

"Too bad. You're here now," said the man. He laughed and shook his head. "It's not so bad. I used to break my heart that I wasn't back there, and then one day I thought, what would I be doing if I was back there? Scrambling to find a crust to eat, a place to sleep. Don't have to do that, here. Food and a bed guaranteed, at least." He smacked his thighs and stood.

"Yes, you'll get better. You're strong. I heard they found you wrapped in a white bear's pelt! Did you kill it yourself?"

Bear? Gard had a hazy memory of the white thing that had come down the slope at him, an avalanche on four legs. He had run his spear down its throat and then leaped on its back and locked his arms about its neck . . . blood steaming on the snow, and how grateful he had been for the warmth of its carcass as he skinned it. A demon of the snows, he had assumed. Had that been a *bear?* The burning child bounced in place, affirmed the word.

"But of course you must have killed it yourself. Nice! One of the mistresses claimed that pelt, very pleased she was too. I heard that story, I said to myself, 'This is a strong one, he'll make it,'" the man chattered on.

"How are you talking in two voices?" Gard asked.

"Eh?"

"The fire-baby that talks in my head," said Gard, unable to point at it. "What is it?"

"That? Why, that's only a Translator. Clever, eh? Otherwise I shouldn't have any idea what your jungle talk meant, and I'll bet you never learned the speech of the Children of the Sun." The man grinned wide.

Children of the Sun? "Is that what you are?"

"Yes, of course!"

"Is that what the people here are?"

The man's grin faded. "No." He turned and looked over his shoulder into the darkness. "No, only a few of *us* here. And long, and so long since I've seen the sun. But it's better than dying, eh? Food and a bed, just as well, not so bad. How's your medicine doing, eh? All drained in?"

Too many new things to understand. And why bother to try, when the numbness and the blindness were so pleasant? Gard floated away into darkness and never felt the needle removed from his arm.

He felt nothing until a long while later, when there was brightness in his face again.

The pain returned with the light. He was being hoisted from the place where he lay, someone gripping him around the legs and someone catching him around the shoulders. He gulped for breath and gave a hoarse scream at the pain.

"Easy with him. Poor old icicle, I'll bet that hurt, eh? Can't give you the leaf for the pain, so sorry; Magister Hoptriot wants a look at you, and he wants you conscious. You be good and you'll have some later, eh? Old Triphammer promises you."

Gard looked around frantically as he was swung down to the floor. The man with the light towered above him; so did two dark giants who crouched, one at his head and one at his feet, and lifted him. He was slung between them on a litter, such as people used to drag the sick, the dying. He was carried forward through the darkness, as the man with the light trotted alongside. *Triphammer?* The burning child showed him a picture of the man with the light. Perhaps that was his name.

Now he could see, in the halo of light that traveled around him, that they were in a long corridor. Now and again they passed grottoes in the rock, shelves upon which other bodies lay. Some were bandaged. Some were unconscious. Some lay watching Gard pass, and their open eyes were glazed, listless, motionless. Others were bound and writhing, turning a restless, furious gaze on Gard as he passed, and they whined in their pain. They were kinds of people he had not seen before.

In his terror and disorientation, Gard opened and closed his hands, clutching for . . . what was there to save him? Not his spear, not his knife: gone down the ice wall forever. Not the strength of his body: melted away. Nothing left but his strength of will. Nothing in his power to do but die bravely. He clenched his fists. He gritted his teeth.

The whole jolting way he made no sound, though he thought his teeth might never unlock again; he endured. At last he was borne into a room that flared with brilliance painful to his eyes, and he closed them. He was raised, set down on something hard and cold.

Deft hands unwound the bandages from his legs and burned like hot iron in their touch. He opened his eyes, not wide, but enough to see Triphammer and two others, the ones who had carried him, standing in a line with their eyes lowered. The bearers were big, their skins the color of slate, their eyes like downcast moons.

His tormentor was robed in skin, the hair scraped off smooth; it was gloved and masked in skin too. The eyes domed out like an insect's. It murmured to itself as it examined him, but no burning child appeared to translate for it.

Gard chanced a look at his body. He saw his legs and feet blackened, shriveled, bent. He closed his eyes again, laid his head back, praying for death. Now the voice spoke in his ear: "Are you conscious?"

He opened his eyes again, saw the mask had turned toward him, with a burning child now dancing at its shoulder. "Yes," he said.

"'Yes, Master,' is what you're supposed to say," Triphammer told him hurriedly.

"Will he kill me if I won't call him Master?" said Gard.

Triphammer nodded, emphatic. The two big ones raised their eyes, stared at him.

"Then rot and eat filth, you slave," said Gard, to the masked one. The mask tilted toward him. There was the barest hint of a shrug; then it took a rag and dipped the rag in a bowl and daubed what was in the bowl on Gard's feet. The black skin smoked, peeled back, sloughed away. That was the last Gard saw before the darkness fell in on him again.

Four moons, lined up, were shining at him out of the starless night. Gard blinked at them, bewildered. The two at the left grew larger, and he felt hot breath in his face.

"Rahashpa, gotu," said a deep voice, and another of the burning children popped into view and lit the grotto. *Drink, brother.* The two litter bearers stood over him. One was leaning down to offer him a drinking gourd.

Gard drank, and gasped for breath. More fire. He hadn't thought fire could be liquid. But it warmed, rather than burned, and its aftertaste was pleasant. And the drinking gourd wasn't a gourd at all . . . it was the top of a skull. A laugh bubbled up out of his chest. He hadn't thought he'd ever laugh again.

"You called the master a slave," said the nearer of the two silver-eyed, grinning and showing a mouthful of fearsome teeth. "Your testicles are like two heads."

"The heads of enemies swinging at your belt," added the other.

"How we laughed in our hearts, when we heard your words."

"We said to ourselves, surely he is one of us."

"Are you?"

After a moment of confusion, Gard said, "Am I what?"

"One of our kind. But you must be one of our kind. If you were one of the Earthborn, you'd have died like a lily in the snow."

"But you are strong. We saw the skin of the beast you killed."

"What is Earthborn?" Gard asked.

The two looked at each other, puzzled. They looked at him. "You are a lost child, then."

Gard wondered what that meant. Lost child . . . yes, he had been, hadn't he? A foundling. No one's son. The one silver-eyed set aside the skull and leaned forward, nodding as though he understood.

"Ah, you were abandoned. It happens sometimes. Listen to me, brother: we are born of the Air. But when one of us takes flesh and mates with an Earthborn, or a Fireborn, there are children bred sometimes—"

"Earthborn are the slender things who live among the trees—"

"Triphammer, he's one of the Fireborn—"

"And you look a little like the Earthborn, but too big, too strong, and your heart is like ours. Welcome, lost child. Not to this filthy place; but to your own kind."

"Thank you," said Gard, trying to take in what they were telling him. He remembered the stories of his childhood. Were they demons, then?

The one with the skull bowl lifted it to Gard's lips again and then drew back suddenly, the silver moons blazing with emotion.

"By the Blue Pit! *The masters don't know his name!*"

The other one came close, leaned down too, spoke in an undertone, with urgency, "Little brother, have you told anyone your name?"

"No," said Gard.

They chortled with laughter, and the one beat his brother's arm so that the liquor in the skull slopped and smoked where it fell.

"Not your true name? But you were born in flesh. It would be the name you were given by the she that bore you," said the one with the skull bowl.

The memory of all that was past swirled by Gard, like a winter wind.

He shuddered and said, "I couldn't tell you the name of she who bore me, let alone the name she gave me, if she bothered."

The brothers rocked and hugged themselves.

"Oh, fortunate boy! Then no one knows, and there is no way you can be made a slave!"

"They may chain you. They may beat you. But unless the masters know your true name, *they may not own you.*"

"Even in this cell, you are free. Not like us. We must serve them. Poor old Grattur!"

"Poor old Engrattur! They called us down into flesh with promises of pleasure."

"They gave us food. They made us drunk."

"We were unwise. We told our names."

"Now we are slaves. Now they own our wills."

"Naming calls; naming owns."

"But *you* they'll never call. You they'll never own!"

"So you are Grattur and Engrattur?" said Gard, and they winced.

"Two fools, Grattur and Engrattur. If you could see the spells that bind us round, you would wonder how we even breathe."

"Trapped down here to serve them forever, and we cannot even die."

"They would only body us again, call us back by our names."

"Body you?" Gard asked.

"Make us bodies again, by craft, and lock us in them—," said Grattur. They heard footsteps, and then Triphammer looked into the grotto.

"What are you doing here? Icicle needs his rest. What is this, what is this? Are you making him drunk? Idiots!"

Grattur showed his teeth. Engrattur took a wad of leaves from a pouch and tucked them into Gard's mouth.

"He'll rest now, won't you, brother? Remember us, remember our fates. We're going, hothead!"

They shouldered their way out into the corridor. Triphammer looked after them angrily, then turned to hook the medicine into Gard's arm.

"Stupid demons," he muttered.

Am I a demon? Gard wondered, biting gratefully into the quid. The numbness came again, and the black bliss.

It was decided he would live, and so he was moved to a proper chamber; the grottoes, as Triphammer explained delicately, being more convenient to the Larder in case the seriously ill didn't pull through.

"But look what a fine cell you've been given!" said Triphammer, arranging the medicine rack above the new bed. "Dry as a bone. And look at all this fine bedstraw! Sweet as a summer meadow. I'll tell you, the masters must think you have great potential. My other patients would envy you. You don't often see slaves given such care, and that's a fact."

"I'm not a slave," said Gard.

Triphammer grimaced. "No need to be ungrateful. Here you lie, alive, and wasn't that their doing? And all your food and drink is their gift. You owe them service, really. After all. And it's not as though your future is so bleak. See, here's another gift for you!" Triphammer delved into a corner of the cell and held up two sticks, each with one end wrapped in rags. "Crutches! I'm to teach you to walk with them. Think of being able to get about on your own again, eh? Why, you might get a little wheeled cart, if you're diligent at your tasks.

"Perhaps even—" He dropped his voice. "There are special rewards for the best slaves, you know. Clever devices, all worked with spells. How'd you like a pair of *silver* legs, eh, to replace those poor withered ones? Set with gems, and strong enough to carry you across the world without tiring?"

The burning child had a lot of hopping and gesturing to do before Gard took in all Triphammer's meaning. But when he understood it at last, he looked scornful.

"That's a story for children. No men can make such things."

"Hai! And there you're wrong, my friend," said Triphammer, grinning. He pulled up a stool and sat. "I'll tell you a story, and no children's tale either, but the sacred truth, as I'm my mother's son.

"Long ago, when there were more gods than men, this black mountain rose up out of the earth. It was the tallest mountain in the world. It scraped the stars at night, raked up a plume of silver dust that trailed from its summit. Green lightnings crackled there, power hummed and danced there. And mages—who are drawn to the smell of power the way cats are drawn to stinking fish—went there and tried to find a way to take the power for their own and use it.

"From all corners of the earth they came, a long procession of mages going up hopeful, with their servants and their baggage and beasts; coming down broken, with their fine robes in rags, and their rich goods lost to the ice and snow. Every one of them it defeated. The power could not be taken. It would not be owned.

"And at last, the cleverest mage among them said, 'No one man can defeat the mountain. Yet, if two or three or ten went together, it might be done.'

"They came together and worked out a spell they thought would mine power from the mountain, as men mine ore from rock. Twenty of them met, twenty, and do you know how hard it is for so many mages to gather in one place, for one purpose? They're quarrelsome as cats. But the thought of so much power bound them to set aside their disputations, and one fine day they climbed the mountain, with their servants and their baggage and their beasts.

"They pulled themselves over the top, wading in snow, complaining. They drew the circle. They lit the braziers and cast on incense. They spilled blood, whose I don't know, and raised their chant. The power came at their call, it danced around them like green fire, and then—

"It bound them!

"It would not be bound, but bound them, all, with their servants and their baggage and their beasts, like a green bowl clamped down. They could not leave. They clawed and screamed at the wall that locked them in, till their fine robes were rags, and their rich goods were no use in the ice and snow. Miserable in the bitter weather they huddled there, and so at last to save their lives they dug into the mountain.

"They made tunnels, with their arts; caves and galleries, grand chambers at last, deeper and deeper always, and so in time made a grand palace under the rock. We are down at the mountain's roots, you and I, but if you went up, you'd see the fine rooms!

"And so they made the best of a bad bargain. Devised clever ways of growing food, in chambers lit by witchlight. Cut doors in the lower slopes, through which they still could not go, but other folk could be summoned and lured in to . . . to bring them things they needed. You have to admire them, don't you? Now they live like kings and queens, in this palace that might have been a prison. They are famed among mages."

Gard thought about this and could still not see so great a difference between mages and Riders. He saw clearly, though, that there was no use arguing with Triphammer. He said only, "And you came to serve them out of admiration, did you?"

Triphammer winced and looked away. "I was traveling. I lost myself, just as you did. Their servants found me and . . . I made myself useful. All for the best."

"So you came from the place on the other side of the mountains?"

"Long ago. Long ago. No use trying to go back now."

"Are there forests there?"

"Eh?" Triphammer looked up at Gard. "Forests? Big trees? Not where *we* live. It was open and warm, with good rock, and the blue sea . . . who'd want to live back in the woods? Nobody there but demons. You might walk for days and never see a living soul, just green leaves. *Brrrr!*"

10th day 5th week 4th month in the 231st year from the Ascent of the Mountain. This day, Slave 4372301 assigned to General Labor Pool, Class 3. Requisitioned by Magister Tagletsit.

Magister Tagletsit regretted the loss of the sun. He had come from a far desert country, where the sun was worshiped as a harsh lord, unquestioned master, king of dunes and stones and serpents, who withdrew his presence by night only that his trembling and shivering subjects might the better appreciate his return by morning.

So cruel a father must necessarily breed desperate love in his children. Magister Tagletsit, when he had found himself facing an eternity in stone-bound darkness, could not imagine life anywhere but under the blazing eye of his God. It nearly drove him to self-sacrifice; but then he had devised a means by which his discomfort was eased.

He lived in a great circular chamber, partitioned into rooms, the whole strictly aligned with the unseen points of the compass. All around its outer wall ran a tunnel. The tunnel wall was pierced through with many little windows into the rooms, through which shone the light and heat, at any given moment, of five hundred oil lamps.

The tunnel contained five thousand lamps, ranged in brass along its length, from east to west. One slave's duty was, each day, to consult the astronomical charts to determine at what precise spot on the horizon the unseen sun would rise, and when. He would enter the tunnel in felt slippers and move a golden peg to the corresponding point marked off on the tunnel wall.

Then he would return to his bed, for he was a valued slave with advanced clerical skills. Gard, unskilled cripple, must turn an hourglass and begin the daylong task of lighting each bank of lamps, east to west, one after another, extinguishing the first when the last had been lit. Then he would turn the glass and repeat the process on the next bank of lamps, thus working his way around the tunnel.

Each day he labored so, naked in the tunnel, while the sweat ran from his body, while the muscles in his arms screamed for hatred of his weight, and hatred of his useless legs that dangled between the crutches. Unthinkable to stop; for at each hour-mark a little cistern was mounted in the wall that would only discharge its drinking water for him if all the lamps to that point had been lit, and in the proper sequence too. The sweat of his body kept him faithful. The leather of his tongue in his dry mouth kept him faithful.

And if he was tempted, still, to die and never sweat or thirst again, one thought kept him still faithful: that there really were green forests beyond the mountains, and if he lived to escape, he might go there one day, even as Ranwyr might have gone. He might find a pass through the mountains into the valley and lead a weary people to freedom, even as Ranwyr might have led them.

And Magister Tagletsit was happy within his rooms, watching the angled light change with the passage of hours, basking in the warmth, and was able to pray in praise, "How great thou art, O Sun, whose eye pierces even into the depths of the earth! Truly thou art great, and none can hide from thee."

––––––––––––

"Not so bad, after all, is it?" said Triphammer, when he would come in to tend to Gard's legs at the end of every shift. "You've got a soft job, eh? Just you think about what they rescued you from. Just you remember that ice, and those banks of snow. That's what I do, when I get to feeling sorry for myself. There I was, lost in drifts over my head, and wasn't I grateful to be let inside here!"

Triphammer said the same thing always, reliable as the circling sun.

"Why weren't your legs frozen, like mine?" Gard asked him, one night.

"Because I had a proper pair of boots on when I ran away, didn't I? Wasn't a naked jungle-boy like you," said Triphammer, not unkindly. He took Gard's foot and bent his leg at the knee. "Here, now: push with your foot, try to straighten out your leg. Hard as you can. Good! Good boy!"

A rumble of wheels came from the corridor outside, the tramp of heavy feet approaching slowly. "Good boy!" a voice mocked them, high and shrill. "Isn't he just the best little cripple that ever was?"

A long-nosed, blind face came around the edge of the doorway, as though peering in. It was followed by the rest of the speaker, bulky body, big long arms, four small thick legs. It pulled a wagon that supported a pair of immense jars.

"Catering," the shrill voice announced. "Where's your bowl, cripple? Where's your pitcher? Going to make me hunt for them?"

"They're right by the door, where they're supposed to be!" said Triphammer in annoyance. "If you'd used your ugly nose instead of eaves-dropping on people, you'd have found them straightaway."

"Ugly, is it?" Big leathery hands groped, found Gard's meal dish and water pitcher. "Think I'll leave a big lump of something special in *your* bowl, hothead." Catering swung his arm backward and dipped the pitcher in one jar. He lifted it out and pretended to urinate in it.

"Just ignore him," said Triphammer to Gard.

Gard leaned up on his elbow to stare a threat, but saw Catering's empty eye-sockets. "Who put out your eyes, slave?"

The blind face grimaced, the head swung to and fro on its long neck.

"I was made without any," said Catering. He dipped Gard's bowl into the other jar and withdrew it brimming with dinner, into which he pre-tended to spit. "Here's your meal, cripple. May it poison you."

He slammed the bowl and the pitcher down and trudged on down the corridor. "He talks like that to everyone," said Triphammer. "All talk, though. Never you mind him."

Gard wondered what would frighten a creature so immense that it took refuge in threatening like a nasty-minded child.

———

Sometimes, as he struggled along the tunnel of the sun's path, Gard looked through the windows into Magister Tagletsit's rooms. At any hour he might see plump Magister Tagletsit in placid contemplation of a roll of paper covered in tiny black markings, or reclining on a bed cov-ered in rich woven stuff trimmed in gold, or pouring a bloodred drink for himself from a pitcher. The pitcher fascinated Gard. It seemed to be made of clear ice, cut and faceted in patterns, perilous beauty, and yet it never melted in the heat of the lamps. He wondered what it would feel like if he touched it.

One day, when Magister Tagletsit was away and the pitcher had been left on a table near a window, Gard reached through the window and touched it. He was surprised; it was no cooler than anything else in the room.

He paid a price to learn that much. Hobbling back to his cell when lamp-night had fallen, he was overtaken by Triphammer, who was scowl-ing.

"What'd you want to go lose a good job for, eh? Stupid icicle! Now we've both got to go report to Hodrash. No, not that way! Down this turning."

"Why?"

"Because you went and intruded, didn't you? Stuck your big, dirty jungle-paw through the window and left handprints all over the poor magister's nice pitcher!"

"But no one saw me," said Gard, astounded.

"You big fool, the magister's spirits saw you! These are *mages*. Didn't you know, they've got spirits you can't see, watching over all that belongs to them? But I suppose you didn't know, how could you know? I don't seem to have told you. The more blame to me. This way. Hurry! Don't make it worse for us."

Triphammer led him along an unfamiliar corridor in the rock. They turned in at last through a doorway. The chamber beyond was high-ceilinged, and to one side benches rose in stepped ranks, where a hundred might have sat without crowding. No one sat there now but three of the masters, in their fine robes, with a fourth entering in some haste. He bowed to the others, took his seat, and turned, all expectant, to watch.

On the floor of the chamber crouched a demon, golden-skinned, whose arms were great with muscle. He was amusing himself with a piece of intricately carved wood, a puzzle whose interlinking sections could be shifted to form different pictures. He set it aside when Gard and Triphammer entered and rose to his feet with a sigh. "Malefactors," he intoned in a bored kind of way.

"Reporting," said Triphammer briskly. "We acknowledge our sins and submit ourselves for discipline."

Gard, looking up, saw the masters lean forward in their seats. The demon went to the wall, where scourges of different sizes were hung, and looked over his shoulder at Triphammer. "Which of you is it to be first?"

"Me," said Triphammer, divesting himself of his tunic and hanging it neatly on a hook provided for that purpose. "My fault really, I should have explained better. And it's the boy's first time, Hodrash."

Hodrash nodded and selected a scourge. Triphammer went meanwhile to a post in the center of the floor. He stood on tiptoe to grasp hold of a bar at the top of the post. Gard watched, unbelieving, as Hodrash advanced and swung his big arm, and the scourge bit deep into Triphammer's back.

Triphammer grunted and set his face against the post. *Crack, crack, crack,* in quick succession the blows fell, businesslike. Gard remembered crouching hidden at the edge of a field, watching as an overseer had beaten a poor failing slave. White anger in his heart, then, and the resolve to die before he might ever be taken as a slave. And now—

"Hai," panted Triphammer, letting go of the bar and stepping back. Bright blood oozed from the stripes on his back. "Over and done, thank all the gods. Come on then, icicle. Your turn."

Icicle indeed; Gard stood frozen in his tracks. Hodrash looked at him in contempt, but there was pity in his face too, and he came to Gard saying loudly, "Not easy to move on those sticks, is it? Come along, boy." He hissed into Gard's ear, "Don't shame old Triphammer. If he endured, you should, a big lout like you."

So Gard let himself be led to the post, as though it were a nightmare and he had no power to resist, and let Hodrash help him to the bar, and Triphammer collected his crutches when they fell clattering to the floor.

————

"You didn't have to bellow like that," said Triphammer aggrievedly, as he washed Gard's back. "Though I suppose if it was your first time, it must have been a nasty surprise. You'll have a bit more self-respect next time, I hope."

"I will never be beaten for their amusement again," said Gard.

"That's the spirit! Resolve to be a better boy."

Gard opened one eye to look over his shoulder at Triphammer. He wanted to strike him; but Triphammer's own back was still bleeding, untended, and the same pain must still be throbbing in his skin.

"I never thought you'd do a stupid thing like that, else I'd have warned you," Triphammer went on, rubbing salve into Gard's cuts. It burned, though not so badly as the scourge. "But I did tell you they were mages, didn't I?"

"I didn't think they had any real power," said Gard.

"Ah! Thought they were street conjurors, did you? The kind who pull colored scarves out of their fists? No, no, boy."

"There was a man, among my people," said Gard slowly. "Everyone said he was so wonderful, so wise, that he was going to save us all. And he didn't. Things only got worse."

"Very likely, with your jungle shamans. But there is such a thing as real Power, you see? And the masters have it. You won't forget that now, I daresay."

"Never again," said Gard.

————

When Gard's back had healed, Triphammer took him down to his new job.

"It's not so bad, the Pumping Station," Triphammer said, as they approached a cavern mouth that glowed red with firelight. "You'll have lots of company, at least. You'll be off your feet too. And I'd find it a more satisfying kind of work if I were you, because after all, it's more important, isn't it? Keeping the air and water moving and all. If it wasn't for these fellows, we'd all freeze and die of thirst. So that's some compensation, eh? And it could be worse. You could have drawn cesspit duty."

Triphammer rambled on at greater length about how fortunate Gard was, but his voice was drowned out as they entered the cavern. The cavern echoed with noise.

In the center of it a great fire roared; in the roof of it great turning blades of fans were mounted, to send warmed air into the hypocaust. The fans were connected by a series of gears of increasing size to a long mechanism set in the floor, a row of a dozen handles at which eleven figures labored, cranking them, and the laborers sang as they worked, a deep plaintive repetitive chant.

Another bank of gears was at the far side of the cavern, with a dozen slaves laboring there, hard by where a black river emerged from rock and hurried to vanish over a precipice into darkness, from which mist rose. These gears lifted water to a turning screw that vanished into a shaft in the ceiling. The fire was fed by two demons who went back and forth with armfuls of some red stone, a mountain of which was piled at the back of the cavern.

The demons turned and stared as Gard entered with Triphammer.

"It's the free boy," yelled Grattur.

"It's the little brother," yelled Engrattur. They dropped the stones they had been carrying and advanced on Gard, grinning.

"You see?" shouted Triphammer. "You've friends here already. Won't that be nice? Mind you don't learn stupid habits from them, though. They had a nice secure job carrying litters for Magister Hoptriot, and what did they go and do?"

"Stole his elixirs to make ourselves drunk!" said Grattur proudly.

"Stole his powders to get ourselves stoned!" said Engrattur.

"What's he doing here? Not gear duty?"

"Not gear duty, a fine boy like this?"

"Well, you know—the legs," said Triphammer, gesturing at Gard's crutches.

"Ah. But we'd heard he'd pulled duty on the Big Lantern."

"So he did! A nice secure job, and he went and lost it by breaking the rules," said Triphammer. The brothers howled with laughter.

"Broke the rules!"

"Broke the rules! Ah, he's one of us!"

"Don't encourage him, you fools," said Triphammer, looking about nervously.

"We say what we like down here, hothead," said Grattur.

"As long as the gears keep turning, they don't care what we say," said Engrattur.

"Yes. Well. Maybe so, and maybe not," said Triphammer. He turned to Gard. "I'm off to see to my other patients. Got a poor fellow lost his arm to the Blood Entertainments. No end of work retraining. You take your place now, and work hard. You'll be grateful, come the end of your shift, for a good exercise session with your legs."

Triphammer left the cavern. The brothers pointed to the empty seat in the nearer bank of gears. "That's your place."

"Welcome to the Pumping Station!"

Gard hobbled to the gear bank and took his seat under the massed glare of the other workers. Their song had fallen off—not to say fallen silent, in the unceasing commotion of that place.

"Who's this big prick?" demanded the nearest. Gard scowled at him, then started as he saw the speaker had no legs. His body ended at the hips, in a smooth asexual curve. Looking along the line, Gard could see that most of the others had suffered the same fate.

"What happened to your legs?" blurted Gard.

"I was made without any," said the other. He jerked his head in the direction of his fellow workers. "Them too. No need for legs, in this job. They cheated us."

"Only half-bodied them," said Grattur, leaning down. "But they're just as trapped as we are. That's the masters for you, eh?"

"Lure a poor creature in with promises of fun, and then leave off the most important bits," said Engrattur.

"Grab your damned handle and help us," said the worker. Gard obeyed. Raggedly, from the other end of the line, the song began again.

Grattur and Engrattur took it up, as they kicked bits of dropped fuel into the fire. Gard listened a little while, and then he joined in too.

> *If I ever get out of here*
> *I will drink their blood*
> *It will be my wine.*
> *If I ever get out of here*
> *I will eat their hearts*
> *Roasted over slow fire.*
> *If I ever get out of here*
> *I will rape them all*
> *With a thunderbolt.*
> *If I ever get out of here*
> *I will fly so high*
> *On the smoke of their pyres.*
> *If I ever get out of here.*

Gard learned the song well, over the years, as his arms and shoulders thickened, as his beard grew out full. The shrunken muscles of his legs filled out again too, with Triphammer's patient work. The hour came when he was able to take a few tottering steps around the edges of his cell, leaning on the walls. The hour came when he hobbled to work with the aid of a cane only. The hour came when he walked unaided, but limped.

This caused some slit-eyed resentment among his fellow workers, but only for a little while. They soon had another focus for their dislike.

––––––

The hour came when Gard was returning to his cell, walking free, and was met by Triphammer running from the other direction.

"Hai, it's you! Hurry, hurry, get under cover!"

"What's happened?" Gard quickened his pace. Triphammer didn't answer, but grabbed him by the arm and hurried him to the cell. They were no sooner inside than Catering came trundling up, and so far as his face was able to express fear, it looked fearful. He didn't even stay for insult, just groped up Gard's pitcher and bowl and slopped them full, spilling half their contents putting them down again before he rushed on.

"We'll just sit in here and stay quiet," said Triphammer in a low voice. Gard, angry that he'd lost half his dinner, was grabbing for the bowl when an impact came that knocked him over. He sprawled on the floor, feeling it heave as though it were breathing. "Oh, oh," moaned Triphammer, hiding his face.

A noise like thunder came from somewhere far up overhead, and a long crack appeared in the rock wall. Then came three or four brief blasts of a sound Gard could not identify. There followed, unmistakably and terribly, the sound of many voices screaming.

Then there was silence. "What's happened?" Gard repeated in a hushed voice.

"A war," said Triphammer. The Translator at his shoulder sent an image into Gard's mind: fighting, chaos, death. "Sometimes the masters battle among themselves. Sometimes . . . but it never lasts long. Probably over now. Very hard on the poor demons, they don't know whose orders to follow, glad I'm not bound that way. Best thing for the likes of you and me to do is hide and take cover, yes, indeed."

Gard sat up cautiously. He pulled his dinner bowl close and shoveled down what little was left in it. There were no further explosions.

"Do you think it's over?"

"Might be," said Triphammer. "Might be. I've seen it over this soon, before. I'll have a lot of work to do, maybe. There'll be some executions. For a few weeks we'll have more meat in the stew than usual."

Gard stared down into his empty bowl. A thin smoke came curling along the corridor outside.

———

When he reported for his next shift, an uneasy trembling was still in the air. Grattur and Engrattur came and hit him on the shoulder, one after the other.

"Wondered if you'd made it. You're in the Western tunnels, aren't you?"

"That was right under the worst fighting, we heard. Do you know who won?"

"Do you know what it was about?"

Gard could only shake his head and take his place. A demon hurried in, walking on its knuckles. It was Chacker, who worked the station next to his. Chacker swung himself into his seat.

"They put out the fire in Western Level Three," he muttered to his neighbor on the other side.

"Five of them executed, I heard," said the neighbor. This drew smiles from all near enough to hear, and they began their song with an almost lighthearted intonation that morning:

If I ever get out of here
I will drink their blood
It will be my wine . . .

An hour into the shift, deafened by the song and the roar of the fans, Gard was startled to look up and see a pair of demons standing in the cavern mouth, one on either side of a young girl.

The demons wore armor. They carried spiked clubs and were in every way dreadful to look upon, but they seemed a little fearful, even embarrassed. The girl between them was slender and beautiful, beyond any doubt or conjecture, for she was naked save for the manacles she wore. She stood straight, with perfect composure, and smiled coldly at a point in the air somewhere miles from that place.

"By the Blue Pit," muttered Grattur.

"By the Blue Pit," echoed Engrattur, too astonished to come up with anything original. Gard stared openmouthed, until he felt his flesh rise to the occasion. He leaned forward, hoping to obscure matters. The song died off, all along the line, as the other laborers looked up and noticed the visitors.

"What's all this?" demanded Grattur, carefully addressing the guard on the right. The guard cleared his throat.

"This is the Lady Pirihine, Narcissus of the Void, of the line of Magister Porlilon, lately so unfortunate as to be crushed by the party of Magister Obashon. She has been sentenced to five years' labor here. We have delivered her to you, as we were commanded. We now withdraw."

The guard and his fellow took a step back and made what might have been interpreted as a bow in Lady Pirihine's direction—or perhaps not. They exited swiftly. Grattur and Engrattur exchanged a glance, not a happy one, and Grattur spoke with exquisite care to Lady Pirihine:

"Lady, we are bound creatures and must obey our orders to the letter. We will not exceed our charge. Please remember this, when you walk freely again."

"I will remember," she said, and her words hung in the air with such frost as to make Gard shiver.

He was elbowed sharply by Chacker. "Look at her! Look at those! Oh, oh, wouldn't I love to get my teeth in those! Come here, Princess, come here, high and mighty, I've got two hands for you anyway!"

"What are we going to do?" murmured Grattur.

"They'll tear her to pieces," said Engrattur.

"Here. You! Chacker. Leave your station. You're reassigned."

"Report up to Magister Thratsa. Icicle, you take his place."

Chacker pulled himself up from his seat with an expression of outrage, but he obeyed and went knuckling off, muttering to himself. Gard slid sidelong into Chacker's place. Grattur leaned down to him with an urgent look.

"We've treated you right, haven't we, little brother?"

"Now you do right by old Grattur and Engrattur."

"There'll be another war sometime."

"They fight among themselves all the time."

"She'll be out of here someday."

"Don't want her remembering us with spite, do we now?"

"Don't give her a reason to do that, little brother."

Gard nodded dumbly, wishing more than anything for a rag to cover himself. He did his best to arrange himself in a less conspicuous way, as Grattur and Engrattur turned to Lady Pirihine.

"Your place is here, Lady." They bowed and gestured toward the end-most seat. She stepped into it and sat and took hold of the handle without a word. Her manacles tinkled against the bar.

Gard averted his eyes. She worked away at the handle in silence beside him, and slowly, defiantly, the laborers at the far end took up their song again.

If I ever get out of here . . .

Gard felt the lady's thigh against his own.

"Is *that* why they call you Icicle?" inquired the Lady Pirihine, sounding amused.

Gard gulped and shook his head. He joined the song.

I will eat their hearts
Roasted over slow fire.
If I ever get out of here . . .

She joined in the song. Her voice was high and sweet. If frost ferns on frozen lakes had voices, they would sound like Lady Pirihine.

Gard now longed for the old days of labor, which, if they ground him to a powder of weariness each evening, were yet blessedly dull. Now, his days and nights were full of torment.

From Triphammer he borrowed a clout of bandage material one day and wound it around his loins, that they might not announce his every thought to the world. This made him the object of intense and hostile scrutiny when he took his place in the gear line, at the next shift.

"What's happened to it, Icicle?" demanded Trokka, who sat next to him these days. "Did it break off?"

"Did you go swimming in the White Pool, and one of Magister Bobna's pets had it off?" demanded Solt of the seat beyond, leaning over to see.

"No!" said Fosha, of the fourth seat down. "He wore it away, comforting himself at night. Now he's one of us, indeed!"

"Shut your muzzles, you lot," said Grattur.

"You're just jealous," said Engrattur.

"Don't you mind them, little brother," said Grattur.

"Ungrateful filth! You wouldn't want his seat," said Engrattur.

"Oh, wouldn't we?" cried several of the demons together.

Gard labored away in silence, thinking of new lyrics to the song, though it still began with *If I ever get out of here.* Presently came the tramp of boots in the corridor without, and Lady Pirihine was escorted to her seat by the guards. They almost-saluted and withdrew. She took hold of the gear handle and set to work. At once her gaze was drawn to the covering Gard wore. She smiled, but observed without comment awhile, as the song rose around them like a comforting prayer.

At last she leaned back from the handle and raised her hand. Everyone fell silent at once, as though a cord had closed each windpipe; everyone but Gard, and he sang on a verse or two before looking up. Lady Pirihine narrowed her eyes.

"You are not bound," she said in a tone of disapproval. She looked up at Grattur and Engrattur. "Slaves, I am not permitted raiment, not so much as a rag. Who is this piece of dirt to lord it over me?"

Grattur wrung his hands, and Engrattur clutched his head in dismay.

"The boy meant no offense, Lady," said Grattur.

"He'll divest himself at once, won't you, Icicle?" said Engrattur.

There was a strangling noise in the room, which would have been roars of laughter from the other demons, had the lady's gesture not bound them. Still they bared their teeth in merriment, crossed their eyes, and turned different colors. Even the little Translators seemed to burn green and blue.

Gard looked at Lady Pirihine sidelong, then rose in his seat. Turning from her, he unbound himself, letting the others down the line see well what they all lacked; at them he made a gesture that had meant extreme rudeness, among the forest people. Then he turned and sat down and resumed work.

He did not look at Lady Pirihine, but could feel her gaze burning into him. Presently she said, "What are you, slave, that you are not properly bound?"

"I am no slave," said Gard.

"Insolence! See where you are, and what you do. You are a slave. And you shall be a beaten slave when I may order it so."

"I am a prisoner here," said Gard. "If you live to order me beaten, then I will be beaten; but I am no slave."

"Or perhaps I shall order you killed."

Gard shrugged. "I don't care."

"I shall order you killed slowly, then."

"Pain is nothing new to me."

"This pain shall be, I promise you."

"I doubt it."

"You will beg me for permission to die."

"I will die when I choose."

All along the line the others listened to this, stifled in their delight. Grattur and Engrattur paced nervously, taking care they turned well away to grin. But now came another noise from the cavern's mouth, a rumbling of wheels, a heavy tread. The long-nosed face poked through first, sniffing the air with wide nostrils. Catering came in.

"What're you doing here?" said Grattur.

"You've no business here," said Engrattur.

"Got to fill my water tank, don't I?" said Catering. "Thirsty little slaves have drunk it dry."

"Why don't you fill it from the Kitchens cistern, then?"

"That's where you always fill it. What do you want here?"

Catering made a rude gesture at them and trundled his way across to the river's edge. There he filled his tank, with elaborate slowness. He was returning when he stopped short and swung his blind head from side to side. Once, twice, three times he snuffled the air.

"Why, what's this?" he exclaimed in badly acted surprise. "I smell a *female* down here! That couldn't be right, could it?" He approached Lady Pirihine's seat, groping before him.

"You've filled your tank, now get out," said Grattur.

"We're warning you, brother, don't be stupid," said Engrattur.

"But I'm only a stupid old Kitchen slave, aren't I?" said Catering with a sly smile. "And made without eyes, so I must feel my way about. Before I was a slave, I saw in all directions, like the sun. But now, by the wisdom of the masters, I'm only a poor blind slave."

Blind he may have been, but his hand found Lady Pirihine with no trouble and lingered on her.

"You will remove your hand at once," said Lady Pirihine. Catering obeyed, with pretended surprise. A second later his hand was on her again.

"What's giving me orders, in such a proud voice? It can't be a mistress! They wouldn't send one of their own down here, would they, where a low thing like me could play with her? Could a great lady really fall so far?"

"Remove your hand," said Lady Pirihine.

"I obey! And now I touch you again. How smooth you are."

"Stop it!" said Grattur in agony. Gard, who had looked on in disgust, pitied him.

"You fool!" said Engrattur.

Catering raised his face in their direction and sneered. "What are you afraid of? Didn't the masters send her down here as an example? Let her have a little taste of what we endure. We won't be punished."

"Take your hand away and keep it away," said Lady Pirihine.

"What, this hand? Of course, Lady! A poor slave must obey your *exact word*." Catering reached out the other hand and fondled her.

"I shall remember that you stood by and did nothing," said Lady Pirihine to Grattur and Engrattur.

"Lady, we are only slaves," they wept.

White anger rose up in Gard. He stood in his seat and grabbed Catering's hand, and wrenched the fingers backward so they broke. Catering screamed with pain, high and shrill as a mouse. He swung his other hand and caught Gard across the ribs, knocked him from his seat and very nearly into the great fire. Gard lay gasping, feeling his heart falter with the force of the blow. Catering clutched his broken hand, weaving his head to and fro, trying to pick up the scent of his enemy.

"Cripple!" he shrieked. "Be glad you'll never eat again!"

He came at Gard, his cart rumbling after him, and Gard rolled aside and staggered to his feet. He ran from the fire's edge. Catering swung around, sensing where he'd gone, and grabbed for him; but in doing so the cart swung into the fire and remained there. The demons began to roar, pounding their fists.

Having snatched Gard's shoulder, Catering clutched and pulled him close, gnashing broad yellow teeth.

Gard writhed out of his grasp. *I will kill him or he will kill me,* he thought, and became strangely calm, in spite of all the uproar, untroubled as a stone. Shame, guilt, and fear all dropped away. Even his white anger dropped away. There was only the moment. There was only the question: *Which of us will die?*

He leaped and got his arms around Catering's long neck and gripped close. This was the way he had killed the white demon of the snows. The *bear.* He hadn't known it was a bear. He hadn't known much of anything, then. How long ago had that been? How many years had gone by, as he labored here under black rock?

Catering choked and fought him, clawing at him with the unbroken hand, and now with a new urgency; for the cart was in flames. He lurched forward and swung the blazing cart from side to side, trying to shake it free. Water was flung out and hissed in the fire, sending up clouds of steam to the ceiling of the cavern. Grattur and Engrattur yelled in dismay and ran for armfuls of fuel lest the fire go out.

Gard released his grip and dropped, catching Catering's other hand as he fell. He twisted it and heard bone snapping. Catering screamed again and waved his arms in the air. "Filth in your *drink!* Filth in your *food!* Shit! Vomit! Piss!"

The fire had eaten as far as the traces of the cart now, and Catering danced madly to try to throw it off. The water tank went flying, shattering on the cavern wall. Gard scrambled out of the way and grabbed a potsherd, sharp as a flint blade. Running in under Catering's swung arm, he stabbed upward and cut across the throat.

Catering jerked. He made a clutching motion at his neck. He stumbled and fell sidelong, still kicking at the remains of the cart. Gard grabbed a piece of the broken cart and clubbed him with it, once and twice and again until he stopped moving, and thought only regretfully, *Now he is free.*

Gard dropped the club and staggered back, gulping painfully for breath. His fellow laborers were hooting, applauding, howling abuse at Catering. Lady Pirihine was watching him, rapt. Grattur came close and put a hand on his shoulder, as Engrattur stoked the fire.

"Oh, little brother, this is a bad business," Grattur said. "But it was well done."

"It was well done," said Engrattur. "But he was a useful slave."

"What are you feeling? You never shouted, you never snarled."

"Your face was as calm as though you were dreaming, the whole time."

"You'll be beaten for this, or worse."

"Still"—Engrattur leaned in close, dropping his voice, and jerked a thumb in the direction of Lady Pirihine—"that one will remember."

15th day 1st week 11th month in the 243rd year from the Ascent of the Mountain.
This day, Slave 4372301 reassigned to Blood Amusements.

"You must be mad," scolded Triphammer. "Raise your arms and take a deep breath. No pain now? . . . Good. The ribs are almost mended, you heal uncommon fast. There you were with that nice safe job, all you had to do was keep your head down and work hard and no one would ever have noticed you. Might have lived for years. Look at you now! You'll see a lot more of me, I can tell you that. Do you know what the life expectancy is, up here? It's measured in months."

"It's a nicer room," said Gard mildly. He had a raised bed on a pallet and had been brought far better food during his convalescence than ever Catering had carried. The air was warmer, for the hypocaust at which he had labored so many years down below was now sending its benefits up to him. He had even been given clothing.

"Nicer? Yes, of course it is, you fool. They want to keep you fit. Not much fun for them to watch a poor invalid stumbling about in the arena! Though to be truthful there are one or two who would . . . Well, it could be worse, I suppose. You might beat the odds. It's been known to happen," said Triphammer, unwinding bandages.

He tapped Gard's sides a few times, frowning. "Remarkable. Never have guessed they'd been broken at all. Magister Hoptriot would be interested to have a look at you, these days. You don't want his attention back on you, though. No, no. He'd only open you up to see what makes you different."

"Who's this Duke Silverpoint I'm to see, then?" said Gard. "Is he another of the masters?"

"The duke? Bless you, no!" Triphammer grinned. "He's one of *my* people. That is to say, we're not kindred or anything—hai, he's so far above me it makes my nose bleed even to think of it. Went into the mountains searching for an enemy of his noble family, I heard. Tracked the man for days to settle a blood debt, killed the bastard too, but then a blizzard came howling down and the masters found him.

"Now he's their weapons master. Quality just rises, you know. He'll train you. We're good at that, we Children of the Sun. You mind you pay attention to him! He'll have something useful to teach you. Not like those fool demons!"

Halfway along the corridor to the Training Hall, Triphammer looked over his shoulder, cleared his throat, and whispered to Gard, "You, er, should know that he isn't properly called duke down here. The masters don't like it. Took away his title, but they still can't make him a slave like the rest of us, ha ha!"

They emerged into a great hall. It was no raw stone cavern like the Pumping Station; the walls were dressed and finished stone, the ceiling a high barrel-vault. No fire pit, but three dozen oil lamps burned bright. Nor was the floor stone, but smoothed planks of wood, and a thick mat covered the center part of it.

At the far end of the room a man sat, making marks on a scroll. *That's writing*, thought Gard. He was a learned man, then. Beside him, Triphammer seemed to shrink as they approached the table where the man worked. Triphammer's smile grew ingratiating, he wrung his hands and bent low.

"My lord," he said. The man looked up. Though their skins were the same color Gard would not otherwise have known they were any kind of kindred, so little and wrinkled and grubby did Triphammer seem by comparison. "Here's the big greenie that's been sent up from downstairs, sir. Look at the arms on him, eh? You can do a lot with a promising fellow like this, I daresay. He's a good sort too, minds his manners, not like the demons. You'll like this one."

"Leave us, Triphammer," said Silverpoint.

"Yes, sir. Thank you, sir. And he heals fast, you'll be pleased to know, sir."

"Out, Triphammer."

"Just going, sir."

Gard turned and stared to watch Triphammer backing out of Silverpoint's presence, all the way down the hall. When Gard turned around again, Silverpoint was regarding him with a critical eye.

His face was aquiline and stern, smooth as though carved from stone, his gaze cold and thoughtful. When he stood, Gard saw that he was easily a head taller than Triphammer.

He came from behind the table and walked slowly around Gard, looking him over. "Raise your arms," he said. Gard obliged him. He studied Gard's chest a moment, nodding. He looked down at his legs. "These have been rebuilt. What happened to them?"

"They froze," said Gard, thinking that was an odd way to phrase it. "I was lame for a long time."

Silverpoint raised one eyebrow. "Any weakness now?"

"No."

Silverpoint nodded again. He stood back a few paces and studied Gard from that distance, frowning. "What race are you?"

Gard shrugged. "I was a foundling."

"Some mongrel, then. You heal like a demon, but you haven't the look in your eyes. Among what people were you raised?"

". . . We lived in the forest."

"I see."

After a pause, Silverpoint walked toward him again. Without warning, he struck Gard full in the face. Gard had him by the wrist before he could draw his hand back. Their gazes locked. "Why did you strike me?"

"To see what you'd do," said Silverpoint. Gard released him. Silverpoint withdrew to the table again. Sitting down, he took up his pen. "I was told you killed another slave."

"I did."

"Tell me about it, if you please."

Gard described his fight with Catering. Silverpoint listened closely, only taking his eyes from Gard's face now and then to note something down. When Gard had done, Silverpoint said, "I understand you killed a bear of the snows, also. Is this true?"

"Yes."

"Tell me about that."

Gard told what he could remember of killing the bear.

"And was that the first time you had killed?"

"No."

"Ah. Were you a great hunter among your people?" Silverpoint said with a degree of condescension as he wrote something down.

Gard felt a prickle of irritation, but kept it out of his voice. "Not of beasts, no. I killed men."

"Did you, now?" Silverpoint looked up. "And how did you come to be killing men?"

Gard drew a deep breath as he realized he hadn't thought of the past in years and didn't want to think of it now. But he told the story and did not leave out what he had done to Ranwyr. Silverpoint listened without writing, staring at him the whole while.

Gard finished his story and fell silent.

The silence dragged on a moment or two before Silverpoint leaned back in his chair. "Thank you." He took his pen and wrote a little while. Without looking up, he asked, "What weapon did you use the most?"

"My spear."

"What others?"

"Knives. And nets, sometimes."

"No swords?"

Gard blinked. The Translator showed him an image of the long knives he had seen the guards carrying. "No."

"Very well." Silverpoint wrote something more and underscored it; then laid aside the pen and looked up at Gard. "Listen closely, slave.

"Our *masters* are a mongrel pack drawn from the most degenerate races of the earth. They are cowardly and lazy—as mages tend to be—and, of late, somewhat inbred. Cruel, also. When not fighting amongst themselves for dominion over this wretched anthill, it amuses them to watch their slaves suffer death at one another's hands in the arena.

"Now, you would suppose that they would very shortly run out of slaves, living as they do in this remote spot. And so they would, if the majority of their slaves weren't demons they have bodied and bound to their service.

"A bound demon, cut to pieces, cannot escape its service; the masters merely summon its spirit back from the void and make it a new body. This diminishes the pleasure of the sport, as you might imagine, since a certain element of suspense is lacking.

"The demons, therefore, are given rewards for which they compete: new bodies more powerful, more attractive, better equipped to enjoy physical existence. And so they roar insults at each other as they wade across the sand, and boast of the terrible things they will do, and hack away at each other with something approaching enthusiasm.

"It is all depressingly theatrical and, on the whole, a disgusting way to live. But it is the only life they are permitted.

"And even this palls on our masters, in time.

"Accordingly, they reserve a special stable of fighters. Slaves, such as yourself, whom they did not body and have not bound to their service.

Slaves for whom there is no return to life, if they die in the arena. These have a greater incentive to fight well.

"You have heard all this and haven't so much as turned pale. What are you thinking, slave? Are you afraid?"

Gard thought about it. "No."

"Why not, slave?"

"I don't know."

"Do you wish for death, then? Perhaps for bringing such a death on your brother?"

Gard thought about that too. "No," he said at last. "I never meant to kill him. And if I die, I can never atone. I would rather live to get out of this place."

Silverpoint nodded. "I can train you. Yes, I think I can."

Training was as monotonous as working the gears in the Pumping Station, very similar really; Gard found he was expected to hold a weighted stick straight out at arm's length, and lunge, and retreat, in any one of several postures endlessly recited by Duke Silverpoint. Silverpoint sounded bored, almost sleepy the whole time, and no wonder; for the exercises dragged on for hours without change. Gard endured them.

He liked better the times when he was given a spear and permitted to attack a dummy stuffed with dead leaves, though it seemed a little silly. Silverpoint watched him closely at these times, saying little. After a month or so of observation Silverpoint began to request a particular angle of attack, or objective.

"How would you strike to disembowel your enemy? How to blind him? How to kill instantly? How to bring him to his knees in humiliation, but spare his life?"

Gard would oblige, and Silverpoint would nod and look thoughtful. Next he attached colored rags to various vital spots on the dummy and intoned for hour upon weary hour, "Red-*green*-yellow. *Red*-yellow. Red-yellow-*red*-green."

And Gard struck, and struck, and endured, though the dummy died a thousand deaths in a week. He thought of it as a Rider.

Sometimes other men would come into the great hall to practice, or to lounge and watch Gard as he strove with the dummy.

"Why are you wasting your time on this mongrel?" one of them said to

Duke Silverpoint one afternoon. Gard did not turn from his task, which was to bound from a standing start and, vaulting over the dummy, strike down through its shoulder to its heart. As he landed, however, he swung on his heel to regard the speaker.

It was a man of the same race as Silverpoint and Triphammer, bigger and younger than either. Gard had seen him a few times, practicing with a blade or staff.

"He shows promise," said Silverpoint. "You couldn't do so much, when you'd been six months in this hall."

"Is that so?" The fighter grinned at Gard. "But what *is* he? Some demon of the mountains jumped his mother, eh? I've never seen a greenie in clothes before. Looks damned funny. What, Greenie, you don't like my tone?"

Gard shrugged. He turned and killed the dummy three times in quick succession: through the heart, across the throat, through the kidneys.

"He reasons like a man," said Silverpoint. "And understands you, Quickfire."

"Really? Doesn't look intelligent. I suppose he's a Repeater?"

"No."

"A demon, and no Repeater? Hey, Greenie, are you a onetimer?"

"Am I permitted to talk?" Gard asked of Silverpoint.

Silverpoint nodded. "This is only a fighter, no higher in rank than you are."

"I take exception to that," said Quickfire.

"Then, Greenie, I don't like your tone," said Gard.

Quickfire blinked at him. "No, no—*you're* the greenie. You can't call me one. It isn't a generic insult, it's an ethnic one. If I call you a knuckle-dragging, sister-fucking, leaf-wearing branch-swinger, does that get the message across any more clearly?"

"He is trying to provoke you into fighting with him," said Silverpoint.

"Thank you, I had understood that," said Gard. "May I fight with him?"

"If you wish," said Silverpoint. "But you may not kill him."

Quickfire shouted with laughter at that. He went to a blade rack and selected two sabers and tossed one to Gard. Gard caught it and hefted it; it was an old practice blade. It balanced badly in the hand. A ragged edge on the guard was all too likely to open his knuckles. He shook his head and returned the saber to its place, selecting a better one.

"He has taken your measure, Quickfire," said Silverpoint with only a trace of amusement.

"What? I grabbed it up purely by chance," said Quickfire.

"You're a liar, whatever the color of your skin is," said Gard, and lunged at him.

Quickfire beat him back. "Wait for it! You're supposed to wait until the arms master says the fight can commence. What is this? Is he left-handed too, my lord?"

"No; but you are, and so he will fight you left-handed. He fights equally well with either hand," said Silverpoint.

"Or equally badly," said Quickfire, his bravado returning. "Well, come on!"

"You may begin," said Silverpoint, and he backed away a few paces and watched keenly as the fight commenced.

"Null point. Null point. Null point. Good, well done, but null. Point to Quickfire. Null point. Point to Gard! You see, Quickfire, how swiftly he learns?"

"'Gard'?" said Quickfire, panting as he dodged and cut. "What kind of name is that, *Gard*? It sounds like the noise you'd make choking on a fruit pit."

Gard ignored him and avoided the rain of quick, slicing cuts that followed and wondered if it was his opponent's habit to follow an insult with a sneak attack.

"Null point. Null. Null. Null. Gentlemen, you are welcome to watch, but you must remain beyond the yellow line. Null. Null. Point to Gard. Quickfire, you'll be beaten by a half-breed savage from the forest. Null point."

"If I had you home in Mount Flame City, *Gard*, you know what I'd do with you?" said Quickfire. "Geld you, so as to make you docile, and then I'd dress you up in servants' livery—just as though you were a man—and keep you in the front hall, to answer my door."

Quickfire stabbed and cut again, a twisting underhand move difficult to parry, and Gard thought, *Yes, an insult followed by a trick. Will he do it again?*

"Someone else may be gelded today, hothead," said a voice from the crowd that had gathered on the sidelines. It was a bass so deep Gard felt it vibrating in his bones. He did not glance at the speaker, but from the corner of his eye saw that one or two were standing there who towered above the others, and he had an impression of garish color.

"Null point. Null point," said the duke in an emotionless voice. "Gentlemen, remain beyond the yellow line. Null. Null point. Point to Quickfire. Focus or die, Gard."

"What, you mean I get to kill him?" said Quickfire, grinning.

"No. Null point. That was general advice. Shotterak, I will not ask you again. Null point, null point, null, null, null—"

"So, *Gard*, did it take you long to learn to walk on your hind—"

He's doing it again, thought Gard, and lunged.

"Point to Gard! Match."

There was a roar from the sidelines, general applause. Quickfire saluted with his blade and lowered it, smiling ruefully as he rubbed his shoulder. "He fights like a man, in any case. Clever beastie!"

Gard saluted, but did not put his blade down until Quickfire walked over and returned his own to the rack. "Very well done, really," said Quickfire, pleasantly enough. "Considering. You must have been a fighter before you came here, yes?"

"Yes," said Gard.

"Ah, well, and here I thought you a poor ignorant brute. No wonder my lord duke is investing such time in you! I do apologize. Dendekin Quickfire," he said, thumping Gard on the shoulder. "Where I come from, we have *two* names, you see? Seriously, what does your name mean?"

" 'Death,' " said Gard.

"Nice," said Quickfire. "Come and have a drink with me, Gard."

"He may not," said Silverpoint. "We have not finished here."

"Another time, then," said Quickfire, and thumped Gard once more on the shoulder, rather hard, and walked away.

Shotterak was a Repeater, a bound demon slain and rebodied weekly. Consequently it never mattered how well he fought; consequently he drank a great deal and took as many drugs as he could swallow, or inhale, or (in his case) shove under his carapace to be absorbed through his lubricating glands. Silverpoint had nothing but contempt for him.

Gard heard Shotterak rattling along behind him one day after a training session as Gard was on his way to Triphammer's cell.

"You. Gard. You're the one they used to call Icicle, eh?"

Gard stopped and turned. "Yes."

"I heard about you. Grattur and Engrattur. They said you're one of us. Only, you're not a Repeater? How's that?"

"I'm not bound." Gard watched Shotterak's face work as he tried to reason that through.

"Oh," said Shotterak at last. "Neat trick, that. How'd that happen?"

"No one knows my true name. Not even me."

"Oh." Shotterak lurched along beside Gard a moment, his lips moving in silence, then he broke into a broad grin. "Not even you! So you'll be out of here in one death! Oh, lucky bloody you."

"I hope so."

They were at the door of Triphammer's cell when Shotterak turned to Gard. "What was that trick, again?"

"No one can know my true name."

"Right. Right. Well, you did us proud, beating that little burn-arse. Good for you. Wish I had a few tricks like that."

"I just watched him," said Gard.

"Right. See, if I knew a few tricks, I'd fare better in the arena." Shotterak held up his arm, black blood oozing from the broken carapace. "Old Shotterak, he just goes in swinging, as seems natural, but there's always some bastard with a trick. And then, smash and hurt for old me, and they're all cheering for the bastard."

"What's this?" Triphammer looked up as they came in. "Evening, Icicle. Nine hells, Shotty, what is it this time?"

"Broke arm," said Shotterak, looking shamefaced.

"Nine hells. You can give us a minute, can't you, Icicle, while I paste him back together? Go for a nice soak in the hot pool. Come on, old crab, let's clean it out. You know what this comes of, don't you, Shotterak? This comes of fighting with a jawful of grass. And now I've got to give you another quid for the pain, so you'll never get clean of it, and I'll bet my mother's golden bones you'll be stoned the very next time you step out on the sand again, eh? Eh? And then you'll die again, and the rest of us get to force down crab stew for three weeks."

"Probably," said Shotterak with a guttural giggle.

"Because you'll never learn anything, and you know why? Because you're a stone-headed demon, that's why. No offense, Icicle. Never amount to nothing, Shotterak, because you have no self-control." Triphammer picked bits of broken carapace from the wound, shaking his head.

———

Gard sat in the pit below the arena, watching as sand scattered in kicked-up flurries. The dry sand, at least; the bloody sand stuck to the wall where it was thrown.

"It's easy," Triphammer assured him. "Well, so long as you're fast. And careful. You watch, see? Body part goes flying off, you jump up there, grab it with your hook, and sling it in here. Man goes down, you jump up, hook him by the collar, and same thing. Keep it clear for the fighters so nobody trips up, and they appreciate that. Most of them, anyway."

"Is this a punishment?" said Gard, watching as the two sets of legs circled each other. One pair looked as if they belonged to Shotterak; the other pair were scaly and a disagreeable shade of yellow. From high above them somewhere came a chanting, and a stamping, and an indefinable sound compounded of hunger and eagerness and rage.

"Punishment! No, no. When they punish you for something, you aren't in any doubt about it. No, this is more like *interning*, see? Your first real chance to get out there in the arena without risking your life. Usually." Triphammer dodged as a foot swept a wave of sand into the pit. "Haaiii! Shotterak, you ass. He's got no science, you see that? None at all. And he's smarter than Pocktuun, that one's got no brain at all hardly, he ought to be able to outthink him. But I'll bet you my next ten dinners Shotterak goes dow—"

There was a sickening *crack* and Shotterak's arm came spinning across the arena and landed trembling on the edge of the pit. Gard reached up and pulled it in. The stamping and chanting fell silent suddenly.

"What'd I say? Did I speak truth or what?" said Triphammer. "Pitch that in the bin that's going down to the Larder. The rest of him will follow in a minute, you wait and see."

Unpleasant sounds came from above, the most unpleasant being the chanting that rose again, a lustful encouragement. Gard strained on tiptoe to look up into the arena. A great roar from on high, and Shotterak's head came bounding across the sand toward him. Gard caught it and pulled it down.

Triphammer whistled. "Haaiii, poor ninny! What'd I tell him? Look at all that green around the jaws. Wouldn't listen, would you, eh?" he said, addressing the staring head. "Pitch it in the bin, Icicle. Now you'll have to go up and fetch what's left of him."

Gard shoved his hook up through the opening and scrambled after it gingerly. He found himself in stifling heat and blinding light. The sand burned his feet. Thirty paces away, Shotterak's body lay bleeding out black on the sand, twitching as though it too found the sand painfully hot. Beyond it, lumpen Pocktuun was exulting, stamping his feet and lifting his cleaver on high before lowering it to lick the blade.

Gard advanced with the hook held out before him on its long handle. He snagged Shotterak's corpse between the remaining arm and the shoulder and backed away hastily, dragging it toward the pit.

Doing so, he drew Pocktuun's attention. The tiny head turned, the eyes protruded on their stalks to focus on him. The immense lipless mouth grinned crazily. Pocktuun stalked toward Gard, swinging his cleaver. From above the chanting rose again, and laughter, and screams of encouragement.

"Come on, Icicle! Hurry!" cried Triphammer.

Encouraged by the applause, Pocktuun bounded forward, shaking the floor as he came. Gard raised the hook to fend him off. Pocktuun swung, and the cleaver cut the hook clean away, leaving only the long handle with its hewn end sliced on an angle. More laughter, more clapping, and the tight focus of massed attention.

Gard was aware of no fear, strangely, though a moment ago he had been sweating and terrified; only a sense of annoyance, and even that faded away under a crystalline calm. *Red-red-yellow-green.* He stabbed four times with the sharp point of the long handle, blows almost too quick to see. Pocktuun tottered to a halt, chuckling uncertainly, even as his body began to spurt blood like a slow fountain.

Again, the sudden breathless hush. Pocktuun dropped his cleaver and dabbled his thick fingers in the blood jets, peering down at them in wonder. He toppled slowly, as though going to kneel, and fell on his face in the sand.

Deafening noise. For the first time, Gard looked up beyond the glare of the lights. There in rows going up were people in rich-worked clothes, in colors for which he knew no names, yet, purple and peacock and ruby and midnight hues. Their faces were narrow or heavy, but all unnaturally smooth. Their eyes were glassy, fixed, alight with the curious emotion he had seen only twice before: when he had been beaten for their delectation, and when he had slain Catering before Lady Pirihine. Beyond, in the topmost stalls by the distant ceiling, slaves leaned down to watch, no less avid.

And they were cheering him. They were standing in their seats and shrieking. The masters were tearing things from their garments and flinging them down toward him, and the objects dropped into the glaring sand like rain all around Gard. He looked down in wonder. Buttons, and aglets, and pins and little ornaments, all of some yellow metal.

He looked up again, into the only calm face there. Duke Silverpoint sat alone in a booth on the lower wall, silent. He met Gard's gaze and nodded, only once, and made no sound at all.

"They want me to do it again?"

"You diverted them," said Silverpoint drily.

"You were a novelty," said Bhetla. He was the clerical slave whose duty it was to schedule the amusements in the arena; he was lean and dour and ancient, of an ancient race nearly gone from the world. "An armored champion taken down by a mere sand cleaner, practically unarmed, without one boast or challenge. Not only will they see it again, they will demand to see it fifteen or fifty times before they weary of the spectacle."

"But . . . does that mean I have to go up against the others with nothing but a broken pole too?"

"It does."

Gard clenched his fists. "I won't die for their amusement. I refuse."

"Then you must kill your opponents. Every time. I think you can," said Silverpoint.

"With respect, my lord, he was outrageous amazing lucky," said Triphammer in a trembling voice, as he kneaded Gard's shoulders. "Never seen the like. You can't ask the gods for luck like that a second time! 'Here, please deliver a pint of luck every third day, payment's under the loose brick next the doorstone.' They'll get affronted. He'll get himself killed and it'll be a sinful waste, if you ask me."

"I didn't," said Silverpoint. "And it wasn't luck. He knows that as well as I do. Don't you, Gard?"

Gard looked down, sullen. "Pocktuun was stupid. He was showing off, and he couldn't see very well. And he made the corpse hook a spear, and I know how to kill with a spear. That's all it was."

"Very good," said Silverpoint. "*Very* good. You will find it easy to do the same once or twice more. Then they will make it more difficult for you. Accordingly, we will step up your training. Eight hours a day. I will bring in specialists to spar with you."

"I suppose that's all we can do," said Triphammer mournfully. "Up in the Repeaters' dormitories, you should hear the challenges they're inventing for this boy. 'I will crush his skull and eat his liver for the honor of the Repeaters!' 'The Repeaters will avenge this insult! I myself will grind this tiny worm into the dust! He will beg for death by the time I've finished with him!' That sort of thing."

Bhetla made a scornful sound. "All talk and theatrics. The louder they are, the stupider."

"What were all those yellow things the masters threw down at me?"

"'Yellow things'! Hark at him! You big jungle booby, that was *gold!*" cried Triphammer. "That's the stuff you use to trade for food and drink and a soft bed, down in the cities! They were throwing it to you as an honor, on account of they were so impressed."

"Do I get to keep it?"

"Oh, gods, no. It's all been raked up and returned by now," said Triphammer, briskly pummeling Gard's upper back. "You're only a slave, after all."

———————

It fell out just as Bhetla had said: fifteen and more times the masters demanded to see Gard venture out with no more than a pointed stick, to face roaring titans. He killed them all, regardless of how loudly they declaimed or how garish the paint on their armor. Yet each time the applause grew a little fainter, ended more quickly. The last time, Gard found himself confronting a hurriedly rebodied Shotterak, who gave a half-hearted wave of recognition before he was slain again.

"I smell a change in the air," said Triphammer gloomily. He was watching from the sidelines as Gard trained. "They're getting bored. You ask me, they're going to want to see something really different, next time."

Gard, circling his practice opponent with a pair of matched blades, paid no attention. Fraitsha, his opponent, was lean and sinewy, with skin black as a grape and blades of differing lengths in each of his four hands. Gard ventured in, attacked, was beaten back.

Silverpoint nodded. "I think we can surprise them."

Fraitsha advanced, whirling his four blades in tight circles. Gard fell back, sprang sideways, flanked him, and nearly scored a hit on Fraitsha's lowermost right arm.

"*Something's* going to surprise them, if they don't open their eyes and ears," muttered Triphammer, with a curious choice of words, an idiom over which the Translator mopped and mowed before settling on the nearest explanation it could find: *secret or coded exchange for private hearing.*

Gard wondered what that meant. Silverpoint looked sharply at Triphammer. "That is none of our concern," he said, then added in the same peculiar idiom, "But if it were, we would wish them more blind and deaf, the filth."

"True enough," Triphammer sighed. "Still, it'll disrupt things. Oh, good one, Icicle! Fraitsha, he'll disarm you yet. Dis-arm you, eh?"

"Shut up," said Fraitsha, but Gard had circled him faster that he could turn and laid two quick cuts in succession on the high leather collar of his practice tunic.

"Fraitsha is slain. Well done, Gard," said Silverpoint, as Fraitsha lowered his blades in disgust. "Why were you distracted, Fraitsha? See what comes of eavesdropping on what doesn't concern you?"

"It concerns us all," said Fraitsha, rubbing his throat.

"We will not discuss this," said Silverpoint. Fraitsha shrugged and went to put his blades away. Gard slid the twin swords back into their scabbards, worn crossed on his back, and practiced drawing them again. Out, with a flourish, and back; out again, and thrusting. He was rather pleased with himself.

"Look at him!" said Triphammer. "You keep at it, Icicle. You'll get so you won't turn a hair, no matter what they send you up against. I just hope they don't want to see him fighting a onetimer like himself too soon. Or one of the women."

Gard dropped one of the blades. "Women?" he said, turning to stare.

Silverpoint gave him a keen look. "Ah. I perceive a weakness."

"I can't fight a woman!"

Triphammer got to his feet. "I'll just go up to the Convent and let them know you want one of them, shall I, my lord?"

"Madame Balnshik, I think," said Silverpoint.

———

"There *aren't* any women fighters," said Gard, not exactly stubbornly; he was sweating. "That would be wrong. How could I kill someone with a womb? And *breasts*? That would be . . . that would be . . . very wrong."

"Perhaps it was wrong in your tribe," said Silverpoint, condescension in his voice once more. "I expect your females were reserved for bearing young. Amongst civilized races, however, females have the right to engage in other careers. Some of them study warcraft."

"But . . . why? They have *breasts*," said Gard.

"To be sure, they do. Nonetheless, there are those amongst our masters who find the sight of women fighting one another intensely exciting, on some emotional level I do not care to examine in much detail," said Silverpoint, his condescension shading into irony. "Furthermore, there are those amongst our masters who enjoy being soundly beaten by a woman. I did mention they were a decadent collection of inbred cretins, did I not? In any case, you needn't worry about breaking any tribal taboos. In this godforsaken place, all women capable of bearing children are, in fact, forbidden to do much else.

"For the purpose of what I shall refer to as *violent delights*, however, our masters keep a stable of demonesses in suitable bodies. I think you would benefit from making the acquaintance of Madame Balnshik."

". . . But she has a womb," said Gard.

"In fact, she has not. She was bodied forth to be decorative; her original master was not concerned with breeding her," said Silverpoint. "Here comes the lady now."

Gard looked up in panic as a demoness entered the hall.

Decorative indeed. He had half-hoped she would be hideous, or spotted, or tusked. She was not. Dangerous-looking, yes. Tall and lithe and powerful, and she might have no womb, but she certainly had breasts. Silken skin the color of a thundercloud, and an easy, arrogant upright grace. She wore a fighting harness. And boots.

"Oh," said Gard.

Silverpoint inclined toward her. "Madame, how kind of you to come."

"My lord duke." She acknowledged him with a nod of her head. She swept Gard with a glance and smiled. "This would be your student?"

"It would," said Silverpoint. "I would like him to learn to fight women."

"I can't!" said Gard. "I can't . . . do any harm, to one so beautiful," he added, hoping that was the sort of thing she would like to hear. She smiled. Her hand flashed up and slapped him across the face.

"Don't talk nonsense, child. What makes you imagine you can harm me?"

"I shall leave him in your care, madame," said Silverpoint, and exited the hall.

"I am no child," said Gard, glaring at her.

"I have seen seven thousand summers come and go," replied Balnshik serenely. "To me, you are a child. Though a talented one, apparently. We in the Convent have heard of you, young Icicle; our people praise your strength. Come and prove it true." She went to the wall and selected a pair of blades.

"Couldn't I prove it in another way?" said Gard, trying to remember how men had spoken on the dancing green, when they were wooing a mate.

"Certainly not," said Balnshik, making an experimental cut through the air with one blade. "*Those* services are reserved for my owner, Magister Pread."

"What's he doing keeping you in fighting harness, then?" said Gard, watching the way her breasts moved as she swung the blades to and fro. "If you were mine, I'd—I'd make you a bed in the long grass and strew it with flowers."

"What a charming thought." Balnshik smiled, showing perfect white teeth. "However, my owner's pleasure is to watch me kill in the arena and then attend on him in his chamber, with whips. Not really very romantic, all things considered, but we do not choose our masters."

Gard blushed. "I would kill him for you."

"If you made any such attempt, I would be obliged to eat your liver," said Balnshik, with a sigh. "Do come on! Positions One through Ten, if you please. Now!"

And so they moved together, and sparks flew from their blades. From the first Gard experienced certain difficulties that made his footwork stiff and gravely impaired his concentration. Balnshik's eyes flashed, her full lips parted in a snarl with each succeeding point she scored; at last she stood back. "Well, really!" she said in exasperation. "Can't you think about anything else?"

"No," said Gard sadly.

"We won't accomplish anything with you in that state, you know."

"That's true," said Gard, daring to hope.

The lady lowered her blades and bowed her head a moment. She seemed to ripple like an image seen in water, and when she raised her eyes to his, they were eyes of flame in an horrific countenance. She bared long fangs, her tongue protruding between, and advanced on him with the speed and hungry purpose of a snake.

Gard shouted and leaped back. He fought for his life. His flesh gave over entirely its fond ambition. Three times Balnshik drove him up and down the hall, pursuing him relentless; she landed blows, but not so many as before. He scored killing points in his desperate defense before she fell back at last and resumed her more pleasing appearance.

"*Much* better," she said.

"Is that what you really look like?" said Gard, gasping for breath.

"This? Or the other?" said Balnshik. "It depends on what my master requires of me. No accounting for tastes, is there? This is the image I much prefer, of course."

Gard staggered to a bench and sat down. "But . . . what did you look like before?"

"Before I was bound? Ah." She came and sat beside him. "I would look, to your eyes, like a trail of blue smoke in the air. Or a banner in a high wind. Or possibly you'd perceive me as sound instead, and I might seem a run of notes on a harp, high to low. Or I might seem a trace of perfume, something between violets and ripe grapes, I'm told.

"If you were fully a demon, you would perceive more. You're a lost child, though; or so I hear. You were born to this shape, were you not?"

Gard nodded. "Grattur and Engrattur told you that?"

"My dear, we all talk amongst ourselves. They think very highly of you, you'll be pleased to know."

"That's nice," said Gard, daring to look at her sidelong. "Were you tricked into service, like them?"

"I? No! I'm quite old; it would take more than a few barrels of wine to lure me. No, my master's a diviner and got my name by arcane means. It took him years, I'm told." She shrugged. "He's persistent, even if he is a nasty little prick. Speaking of persistence, let us address your flaws in technique."

Gard scowled at the floor.

She was, in all, a kinder teacher than Silverpoint.

After the first month of training, Gard no longer flinched or delayed his killing strokes when sparring with her, nor with any other of the demonesses she brought down to assist in her efforts. He found he had but to summon the memory of the way her face had changed to drive any concern for her safety from his mind. He told her as much, one afternoon as they walked from the Training Hall.

"Oh, my dear," she said, looking at him with affection. "How very fortunate for you we're not lovers. You have no idea how one speaks to a woman, have you?"

"But I meant it as a compliment," said Gard. "It's the truth."

"The truth. I see. You haven't known many women, have you?"

"I had a mother. A foster mother, I mean. And a foster sister."

She was silent, staring at him, and he stammered, "And I knew Lady Pirihine, she that was condemned to work down in the Pumping Station when I was there."

Balnshik nodded. An unreadable expression crossed her face. "Yes, I knew about Lady Pirihine. But are you really telling me that before you came to this place, you had no mate? No lady companion of any kind?"

"I suppose I didn't, no," said Gard, irritable.

"The Blue Pit and the Red Dog," said Balnshik. "And his Little Green Tail too! How I wish you were mine to teach."

"But you are teaching me," said Gard, wishing she'd change the subject.

"Not in the way I'd like. This much I can teach you, lost child: truth is a fine wood, but no one appreciates being battered with a club made from it. Lies properly made are charming and wear well; kind lies will open locks and hearts. Illusion is more important still. It will serve you well to seem bigger than you are."

"What do you mean?"

"I'll give you an example," said Balnshik, tossing back her raven hair. "You are not weak; neither am I. But those who *are* weak love the appearance of power. How they worship it in others! When my lamentable master comes before me, he wishes to see a mistress of iron. If I wore silks and wept for love of him, he'd grumble and grow cold; but, oh, his eyes shine when my boot is on his throat, when I spit on him and flourish the scourge.

"You have amused them for a while, in the role they gave you: naked slave with a broken spear, defeating the pride of the warriors. But you will need to show them you are more than a dumb brute, my dear."

"I can do that, easily. I can kill any champion they send against me."

"And how modest and diffident you are! Yes, I know you can; but it will take more than skill at arms. You need an appearance that exceeds your truth."

"Should I wear painted armor, then, and boast?" said Gard, scornful.

Her eyes sparkled. "No, no," she said softly, looking him up and down. "Something simpler, and understated. That blank stare of yours has such potential; make the calm of your face suggest to them still water, dark water in which they will drown. They haven't noticed the grace of your body, though I have; let it suggest to them an animal striking in silence, among the buffoons in the arena.

"The battlers, the big clowns, wear scarlet and gold, they lime their hair into spikes, they scream and thunder and stamp. *You* be the unspoken threat, the never-raised voice, untouched, unmoved and implacable. The masters won't know what to make of you. They will fear you, without quite being aware they are afraid. Then they will admire you. Then they will desperately love you."

"I don't want their love," said Gard.

"Perfect!" said Balnshik, with a wry smile. "That's the way, my dear. Never *need* them. But you really do need a new costume. Something in black, I think."

———

She had a robe made for him, a plain garment of black, without the ornamentation he would have liked; dearly he wished he still had his collar of silver skulls. But when next the masters gathered for their fun, he stepped into the arena plain as a stroke of ink on a page, unarmored, with his two swords on his back.

There was applause at his entrance, with a buzz of excited muttering, presumably at his new appearance. He heard the massed intake of breath as one, and all in the seats leaned forward to stare at him, hungrily noting the robe, the two swords.

Gard looked up at them, unable to quite believe anything so trivial could hold their attention that way. For a moment the old anger, the white anger, rose in his heart; then it faded to a kind of impersonal sadness. There they were in their ranks above him, the ancient and the wise, powerful and learned mages all. What a bunch of idiots.

But he kept his face impassive, as Balnshik had advised; stood still as a stone and waited patiently for his opponent to enter the ring.

"Where is this slave? Where is this sand cleaner?" shouted someone from deep in the entry tunnel. With thundering steps he bounded out, a Repeater named Trathegost. His armor was steel enameled in purple, decorated all over with crimson skulls. It was painful to look upon; and for the first time Gard had an inkling of why Balnshik had pursed her lips and shaken her head when he had asked for some skulls, or perhaps a pattern of flames, on his fighting costume.

Trathegost smote the floor of the arena with a spiked mace and pointed his war-gauntleted hand at Gard. "You! Pathetic scavenger! Where's your broken stick? Who will scramble for *your* corpse when I scatter your entrails across these walls? Come and be punished for your insolence, onetimer!"

Gard said nothing in reply, but drew his blades. *Poor old battler,* he thought. *What kind of life is this? To feed their boredom, and then feed them again.*

Trathegost turned his face up to the audience. He roared as in fury, until the foam ran from the corners of his jaws, but desperation was in his eyes as he cried, "Now, do you see his disrespect? You see how he disdains to answer his betters? This is disrespect to *you,* my masters. Don't you long to see him punished?"

A few shouts of "Punish him!" came from the audience.

He is hungry for their attention, thought Gard. *They are hungry for the spectacle. I must not be hungry too.*

Trathegost lifted his mace and rushed Gard. Gard, calm, with pity in his heart, stepped up and sliced Trathegost's head from his shoulders, so quickly the blades were hardly seen to move.

"I never heard such cheering," said Triphammer, gleeful as he pounded Gard's back. "And, see what comes of giving them a good show? Look at all those presents! They sent those down because they're in love with you, be sure!"

Gard considered the basket of dainties, the bottles of wine, the blanket of purple worked with gold thread, the gold dish. "But they'd been yelling for me to be punished," he said.

"Well, so they were. Nobody loves you until you win, you see? But you're a *good* slave. You play along, Icicle, and there's nothing you can't have from them."

"Will they set me free?"

"Well, no, of course not! But, you know, women and all—well met, my lord," Triphammer concluded, hastily changing his tone.

Silverpoint surveyed the presents, with a curl of his lip. "Wine. And drugs. You can take those, Triphammer. You're not to touch them, Gard."

"Oh, my lord, that's a bit hard, isn't it? Let him enjoy what he's earned," said Triphammer.

"They'll weaken you, Gard," said Silverpoint. "Keep the blanket and the dish, if you like, but nothing else. You are in training."

"But he's trained now," said Triphammer.

"Training has only begun." Silverpoint looked into Gard's eyes. "You can't read, can you?"

"No," said Gard.

"Then you must learn. Two hours a day with Madame Balnshik."

"She teaches *reading*?" said Triphammer.

"Why?" said Gard.

"Because there are books I want you to study," said Silverpoint. "The masters will want to see if they can break you, now. Do you wish to be broken?"

"Not for them," said Gard.

"Then you won't be." Silverpoint left the room.

"Hardly seems fair," grumbled Triphammer. "Why shouldn't you enjoy a treat or two? That's *good* stuff they sent you. A cup of wine or a little dream won't do you any harm, I'm sure. I won't tell, if you'd like just a taste before I take it all away."

Gard shook his head. "This is no place to be weak."

So Gard met with Balnshik two hours each day, seated beside her at a table in Duke Silverpoint's own rooms, and she taught him the language of the Children of the Sun. Thigh to thigh they sat, and if her nearness and the pressure of her body tormented him with longing, that pain was soon eased by another kind of excitement entirely.

On his day of comprehension, when the little black characters suddenly spoke to him from the parchment, Gard learned that time and space could be stepped around.

He first read from a collection of travel essays by the scholar Copperlimb. The scholar was long dead, and the cities of the Children of the Sun an unimaginable distance away. Yet Gard left his body and walked there, in forgotten sunlight, beside the pleasant elder who opened his dead mouth and spoke with a living voice to describe for him the granaries of Troon, and the great houses of Mount Flame, and the barges moving slow on the river Baranyi. Best of all, he spoke of immense and ancient forests, though he had only seen a little way into their green darkness, for no roads ran through them.

The dead spoke, and Gard knew all these places, though he had never seen a city or any kind of watercraft; he saw them now stored in the characters on the page. To learn that such things were possible filled his heart with delight, surging higher than his old anger had ever risen.

He was given next a history of certain noble families among the Children of the Sun, who had slaughtered one another in great numbers over some deep insult. Gard was unable to understand just who had been insulted, or how, no matter how closely he read and reread the text; but valiant heroes had fought on both sides, and sometimes switched sides after being insulted by their own kinsmen. It was a great epic, full of song and sorrow. Still, the main thing Gard learned from it was that the Children of the Sun were quick to take offense.

After this he was given a book of poems that praised love, occasionally, but more often were about the joys of copulation. In particular the act of lying with another man's mate, without his knowledge or consent, was celebrated. To Gard this seemed shameful and rather silly. Moreover the detailed and repeated descriptions of the act of coupling made it difficult for him to read the poems with any composure, particularly with Balnshik sitting beside him.

He was therefore glad when they progressed to the next book, which was titled *The Perfect Warrior*. With keen pleasure he read through the chapters on attack and defense by sword and spear and staff, by warhammer and ax and mace. The diagrams were especially interesting. When he came to the second half of the book, however, Gard read in growing confusion, and then in bafflement, and finally in anger.

"This word, what's this word?" He pushed the open book across to Balnshik and pointed at it.

"That word is *meditation*," said Balnshik, and the Translator danced and fidgeted until it found a matching concept in Gard's understanding.

Gard drew his black brows together. "Then this part is stupid. *Meditation* is what fools and cowards do. They sit with their knees drawn up and mutter nonsense and pretend they can't hear you when you ask them to do some work. There's no magicking an enemy away by *meditation*. You'll end up with your head split."

"How strange, then, that so great an arms master as Prince Firebow devoted half his book to meditation," said Balnshik. "What a pity he didn't have your wisdom. I think you had better read on, all the same. It is just remotely possible the late prince knew a little more than you do."

With an ill grace Gard read on. At first he scowled and made scornful noises, but in time he grew silent and absorbed. Still frowning, he read, and more slowly. At last he closed the book and said, "I still think it's useless. What good will it do me to step outside myself as I fight? And *pretending* my fist can go through rock won't make it happen."

"You only say that because you don't think you can do it, yourself," said Balnshik.

"Of course I can do it, if it can be done. But this is all make-believe. Baby games. Thinking about a color, or saying a word over and over again. Stupid!"

"What is stupid?" said a voice from behind him, and Gard turned and saw Duke Silverpoint.

"Master Icicle has decided that Prince Firebow is a charlatan and a liar," said Balnshik.

"Has he, now? Why?"

"I didn't say that," said Gard hastily. "I just said that, er, *meditation* is stupid. And it doesn't belong in this book."

"You think so, do you?" Silverpoint came around the table and faced Gard. "You oblige me to defend the memory of my old teacher. Rise to your feet, please."

"I didn't know he was your teacher," said Gard, but he rose in instant obedience. "I'm sorry."

"Please seat yourself on the floor," said Silverpoint. "Are you comfortable?"

"Yes," said Gard, looking up uncertainly. Silverpoint drew a long knife and, leaning down, set its point between Gard's eyes.

"Very good. Be so good as to begin the First Breathing Exercise, as described in chapter six. I have no doubt you recall it with perfect clarity."

"Yes, sir." Gard closed his eyes, drew a deep breath, and held it a certain number of heartbeats before he let it out. Then he repeated the process. Then he did it again and continued as he wondered resentfully why so much importance was accorded to a vain and useless pastime.

He decided to hold an image in his mind, as *The Perfect Warrior* recommended. A star? A flower, opening its petals? A cloud? What possible use was an exercise like this, after all? It could only numb his mind with boredom. If this sort of thing wasn't a fraud, then surely poor Ranwyr, who had worked at it so diligently, who *believed*, would have gained powers enough to open a door through the mountains.

Gard saw again, so clearly, the valley where he had been born, the blue mountains ringing it round implacably. He felt the warmth of its earth under his bare feet. He tasted again the water of the dark stream, and the bitterness of green melons . . . they had been gathering green melons when the Rider had caught Ran.

He felt the spear in his hand, as he killed the Rider. Its mount stood before him. He knew, now, that it was called a *stag*. He cut away the cruel harness.

The night was dark. The stag was all he could see, glimmering under the stars. It looked calmly into his face, then turned and walked away from him. It looked once over its shoulder, as though to bid him follow, and so he followed it.

Its hoofprints filled with water, star-reflecting, easy to follow even through the dark wood. The green smell breathed out at Gard. He had forgotten the smell of woods. These were woods in spring. He could smell the little white flowers that had starred the dancing green. He had forgotten their scent too, but then it had been long years since they had bloomed anywhere. . . .

Dancers were on the green. He could hear the drumbeats. He could see their black shadows, now, under the stars. The stag walked straight through the dance and no one looked at Gard as he followed, for which he was grateful.

There at the edge, in the blossoming grove, Ran was just sitting down with a woman. But the woman was not Teliva, and as Gard stared, he saw that the man was not Ran, either. He did not know who they were. The woman was fair, with skin like the blossoms under the starlight, but she was a big-boned wench and he thought her face rather vacant. He walked past them impatiently, wondering where the stag was leading him.

It seemed to be proceeding up a trail between two steep high walls. They shone like the light of the moon, and at first Gard thought they were the ice walls under the mountains, where he had tried to climb and fallen. As he drew close, however, he could see that they were insubstantial. They were only a mist of starlight. The stag began to climb up through the starlight, and Gard strained to follow it and knew the only way to follow in such a place was to leave his heavy legs behind. He slipped free of them—of all his heaviness—and looked down at his poor limited body in surprise. How clumsy, how stupid he looked.

And how bright was the world around him, when he was not obliged to view it through a feeble lens set in a watery ball! True, he had lost any sensation of touch, he had lost the scent of springtime; but he saw perfectly, in all directions at once, and distance did not dim his perception. He saw that the bright void was filled with clouds of light in varied colors. They flew, they sped or lingered, and it could not be said they moved *up* or *down*, for neither of those concepts existed. Now and again they collided, and thunder roared out in the void and something like fire sprayed out.

It was familiar. When had he been here before?

Some other familiar thing pulled at his perception. It was a sound, an insistent call. He looked for its source and saw, far away, a darkness. By an act of will he crossed the distance without needing to travel, and saw . . . unbearable shadow and heaviness, crushing solidity, and yet shifting lights were trapped within it. One of the lights was calling him. It was a cloud of blue-violet. Its voice was beautiful.

Gard sent himself within the darkness without concern, for he knew he could always come out again. He was not bound to it, after all . . .

————

He opened his eyes with a start. He felt keenly the cold, and the pain of his stiff body. He put his hands up, trying to tear away the blinkers that limited his vision to a narrow pair of tunnels straight before him.

"No, no," said a gentle amused voice, as someone caught his wrists with a grip like steel. "You *need* those eyelids."

He scrambled to his feet and stared at Balnshik, at Duke Silverpoint.

Silverpoint was nodding. "Very good. Perhaps, now, you would be willing to admit that Prince Firebow was not entirely a fool?"

". . . Yes, sir," said Gard dazedly.

"He walked without flesh," said Balnshik. "The lost child caught a glimpse of his home, I think. Are you all right, my dear?"

Gard nodded his head. He felt somehow *bigger*, in a way he could not put into words. He felt wonder, and shame. More than anything he felt regret at the unfairness of it all: that he should learn, without any effort, what had been so difficult for Ranwyr.

"Here's our little pale scholar!" jeered Fraitsha, when Gard returned to the Training Hall. "Had a nice time ruining the sight of your eyes over a heap of books?"

"He did not," said Duke Silverpoint. "Put him through Ketta's Fourth Assault, if you please."

"Right." Fraitsha took down a mace, a spear, an ax, and a sword. He hefted them each, in his four hands, then leaped before Gard, swaying from side to side. "Come at me, Icicle."

Gard, armed with a spear and the two swords on his back, circled Fraitsha warily. Gard rotated the spear before him, trying to advance behind its wheel. Three or four other fighters entered the hall at that moment. He ignored them. Fraitsha thrust out with his spear and spoked the wheel, following swiftly with his mace to send Gard's spear flying into a corner of the hall, useless as a broomstraw. Gard retreated and drew his swords, but not before the ax whirred down and struck him lightly on the top of his head. It hurt.

"I have cloven your skull," Fraitsha announced. "Now I would sit and enjoy feasting on your brains. Clearly, reading did not fill them with anything that would stick in my teeth."

The other fighters laughed and applauded. They were onetimers, the elite, and Quickfire was among them. "Go and fetch your spear and begin again," said Silverpoint.

Gard felt irritation as he obeyed, embarrassment and discomfort; yet all these were somehow *wrong*. The emotions seemed like an outgrown garment, a note of music played off-key. Having retrieved the spear, he returned to his place and regarded grinning Fraitsha. Gard focused . . .

And time slowed. Gard saw himself as from outside, and Fraitsha as from behind; saw the deep red light pulsing through Fraitsha that was his real form, trapped in the four-armed flesh. He saw Duke Silverpoint, in whom a clear straight flame burned, and Quickfire burned indeed with high fleering bravado. The other fighters were likewise abstractions, points of colored light or pulsing animal forms.

Gard saw the way to defeat Fraitsha. It was simply a matter of being *here,* and *here* and *here* in this precise order, and at this particular speed. No more difficult than the old red-red-yellow game with the spear, the same principle in fact. He needed only to concentrate himself . . .

And it was done.

Fraitsha stood, blinking in amazement at his weapons, which were scattered before him on the floor. Gard stood behind him, an edged blade pressed to either side of Fraitsha's throat. There was a moment's shocked silence, before Silverpoint collected himself enough to say, "Fraitsha is be-headed."

A roar of applause followed his quiet words, as the elite fighters stormed forward.

"Give *me* a round with that demon," shouted one named Chint. He was wide and powerful and came of the same desert people as Magister Tagletsit. "How are you with the long blade, son of desolation?"

"He can fight with either hand," said Quickfire. "Take care."

Fraitsha was stepping to the side, looking from Gard to Duke Silver-point. "What have you done?" Fraitsha said to Silverpoint, but quietly.

"Why, forged a more perfect weapon," said Silverpoint, with a thin smile. "Was I not commanded so, by our lords and masters? And so I have. Gard, you may fight a round with Chint. Long blades."

Gard himself had been standing motionless all this while, no less sur-prised than Fraitsha. He turned to the other fighters, still with the sense of regarding them from some point near the ceiling of the hall. He drew a long blade from the racks and faced off against Chint.

Chint was right-handed. Chint was of a certain height, and a certain width across the shoulders, and his arms of a certain length, and now he was leading with the Shrattin Posture of Attack Number Seven, and so . . . defeating him was a matter of *these* moves . . .

Gard heard the blades ringing, rather than saw them strike, and then he was inside Chint's reach with the point of his blade at Chint's throat.

"To Gard," said Silverpoint unnecessarily. Another silence, but no cheer-ing this time, and then the fighters all began speaking at once.

"I see how he did it."

"Let me in there, I want to try that."

"Chint, where are your eyes? That's an old trick!"

Chint, still staring into Gard's face, slowly shook his head. Carefully Chint lowered his blade and stepped back. "Lord protect me. I would rather not fight you again, whatever you are."

He put his blade on the rack and walked away. Gard watched him go, a little confused.

"Silverpoint!" Vergoin stepped forward. He was tall, and arrogant; the rumor was he was one of the mages' own offspring, relegated to slave status some three or four civil wars back. "He and I, blade and net. This creature thinks we're brawlers like his idiot kinsmen, doesn't he?"

Silverpoint shrugged. "Blade and net, Gard. If you please."

Wondering, Gard went to the rack and drew the short blade and dragged a net from the barrel provided. The net was not large, but it was weighted, sewn with fluttering stuff to distract the eye. Vergoin drew another net from the barrel, not bothering to speak to Gard.

The work was all done with the net; the blade was merely for scoring the point once the net had fallen and snared one's opponent. Gard went to the center of the floor, turned to Vergoin, and saluted; Vergoin did not salute, but swung the net and brought it down in a high lazy arc.

Gard observed, detached, without anger. He saw himself dodging from under the net; he saw his own net floating up, with no conscious effort on his part, falling over Vergoin's head. It was the same maneuver he had used a hundred times against the Riders. The moment was one with all those other moments.

Now, as then, he dropped and dragged his opponent down . . . not from the back of a mount, but to the floor of the exercise hall. It took a little effort to stop the follow-through, but he saw himself refraining from punching his blade through Vergoin's heart a dozen times in quick succession, and only setting the point there. Vergoin cursed at him. "Get him off me!"

"To Gard," said Silverpoint.

"That was cheating!" said Quickfire. "Did you see his net? That was sorcery! He couldn't possibly have thrown that the way he did! Not *overhand*!"

"He didn't use sorcery," said Silverpoint.

"He didn't," said Vergoin, scrambling to his feet. He pulled off the net in disgust. "You think *I* wouldn't know a mage's trick? He's simply very fast. Animal cunning and speed. Not a bad job, Silverpoint. No wonder he's made mincemeat of the Repeaters."

Vergoin swept Gard with what was intended to be a coldly assessing stare. Back in its depths an emotion glinted, however. "Not a bad job," Vergoin repeated, and turned his back on Gard and walked from the hall.

"Do you find it difficult to control?" Silverpoint asked. "This seeing your-self from without? Does it disorient you?"

"No," said Gard. "At least, not much. It only happens if I'm fighting. Was this why you wanted me to learn to meditate?"

"In part." Silverpoint leaned back and studied him. "I wasn't certain you could do it. I hoped, to be sure. You understand what you must do, now?"

"Learn more?"

"Indeed you must. You know my language; now you must learn others, arcane and obscure. You will need them to read the other books I have in mind. They are for advanced students only. No one I have ever taught has got so far."

———

Two days later, Gard arrived at Silverpoint's quarters to find Vergoin and Bhetla there before him, deep in conversation with the duke. "You face less risk than any of us," Bhetla was saying. "You have only to do as you were bid, after all. No one will fault—" They broke off as Gard entered.

"And here's the creature himself," said Vergoin. "We won't keep you, Silverpoint. Just think about it, will you?" Vergoin stood and, with an ironical smile, bowed to Gard, and so took his leave. Bhetla nodded to Silverpoint and hurried after.

"Why were they speaking of me?" asked Gard.

"They admire your skill." Silverpoint pushed a book across the table to Gard. "Cutfile's *Use of the Hooked Blade*. Please give it your full attention, par-ticularly chapter six."

———

When next he stepped into the arena, Gard found himself confronted by no less than three grinning champions among the Repeaters. Pocktuun had been rebodied, and Trathegost likewise, and a rangy warrior who car-ried a flail.

"Yes," bellowed Trathegost, "it is I, puny shadow! You thought you'd vanquished me, didn't you? But I am come here to tell you that I will ex-tract my revenge! And I am not alone! See who has come along for sweet spite's sake! None other than *Pocktuun the Earth-Shaker!*" The masters ap-plauded and cheered wildly. Pocktuun turned in the lights, holding up his cleaver.

"But *I* will drink your blood first!" announced the newcomer. "I, Hrak-fafa, the Bitterness of Death!" He lashed out with the flail and so cut his applause, for the audience immediately leaned forward to see what would happen.

Gard sighed. A simple step back was enough to avoid the flail. *Three fighters, three different weapons.* He focused and saw the series of steps it would take to kill each of them. He took the necessary steps and watched himself sprinting forward, seizing Hrakfafa by the shoulders and somersaulting over him to pass between Pocktuun and Trathegost. Trathegost turned and swung with his mace, but missed Gard, striking Pocktuun instead. Pocktuun screamed in anger and went after Trathegost with his cleaver. Hrakfafa turned to see where Gard had got to, but Gard was behind him, beheading him at a stroke. Gard saw the red light that was Hrakfafa's true form flying free, vanishing upward.

Hrakfafa's body staggered forward between Pocktuun and Trathegost, straight into the swing of Trathegost's mace, and the corpse was hurled high up and struck the top of the arena wall, where it hung bleeding. Pocktuun got in a cleaver blow under Trathegost's lifted arm and half-severed his leg at the thigh.

Trathegost fell backward; as Pocktuun was bending over him with cleaver raised, Gard sprang to Pocktuun's back and beheaded him. A yellow light fountained out with the blood, rose, and was gone. Jumping clear from the body before it collapsed, Gard likewise beheaded Trathegost, who winked at him before his head rolled away and the twilight-colored essence soared free.

Gard looked up at the howling, cackling faces. Sweating and screaming, the masters shook their fists, leaped up and down in their seats. Some of the mistresses present had so far forgotten themselves as to tear open their bodices and expose their breasts to him. Some of them had black nipples. He had never seen black nipples before.

There in his customary place sat Duke Silverpoint. Vergoin sat beside him. They were not looking at Gard. They were looking up at the rest of the audience. Silverpoint was nodding his head.

——————

"It seems wrong," Gard said to Balnshik, as they bent over a grammar for an ancient and nearly forgotten language. "The Repeaters aren't my enemies. They're poor, and stupid, and they don't have a chance."

"They know that, my dear," said Balnshik. "They do not aspire to win. Only to amuse by dying as spectacularly as they may. For all the boasting and the insults, they are rather proud of you."

"I can see their spirits fly away, now, when I kill them."

"That is because you have learned to see as a demon sees. You have brought the two halves of yourself together, and so you are stronger. When you step outside yourself—when you float free of the shackles of time and space—then you are living as we live. When we are permitted to live."

"But . . . can't the others do that too? If Pocktuun or Shotterak can see outside themselves, as I can—it should be easy for them to win."

Balnshik sighed. "You have the advantage of a certain coherence they haven't got. You learned to live in a body of flesh. You are more, shall we say, *organized*.

"And, to be honest, they really are idiots."

————

"Another basketful of treats," said Triphammer cheerily. "Look at this! Fresh fruit! This is the stuff we poor slaves never get, you know."

"I got another golden bowl," said Gard. "It's inscribed. It says, 'For an esteemed slave.'"

"And aren't you glad you've got a good education now, so you can read it? That's someone of the mistresses sent you that, I daresay. They're mad for you. I can see it, peering up through the grate at them. Shouldn't think it'll be long before you're called on to perform some private services, eh?"

"What kind of services?"

"You know! Like for instance some fine lady will give you one of those hot-blooded stares, as who should say, 'Slave, I've got a loose bolt in my sedan chair; come and tighten it,' or maybe, 'Slave, come and put a fresh candle in my candlestick, and light my way to bed,' or maybe, 'Slave, I've got an itch that wants scratching, and it's where I simply cannot reach!'"

"Why should they do that?"

"He means they will invite you to copulate with them," said Duke Silverpoint.

"Oh."

The duke then said something further to Triphammer, which the Translator, after a bit of arm-waving, rendered as *archaic form of encoded speech*. Gard, however, was now fluent in the language of the Children of the Sun, and what he heard was "Thou art a rogue and a fool to tempt him thus. Desist, or it shall go hard with thee. He hath a great virtue in his present state, and look thou see it wasteth not."

"Worshipful duke, this slave meant no offense," Triphammer replied, with the same peculiar inflection. "Yet wherefore? Is not his flesh and all that to it pertaineth their property, and at their pleasure?"

"And canst thou say what their pleasure or their purpose may be? No? Therefore be mute, thou."

"Yes. Well," said Triphammer, and sniffed.

————

Now Gard learned what it was to become a hero. Bhetla was sending him out last at each entertainment. Deafening applause greeted his entrance into the arena; the tiers of seats were more packed than he had ever seen them. He wondered, gazing up past the lights, whether the whole population of the mountain stronghold were not crammed in this single stifling chamber. Surely all but the poor wretches who lay in darkness along the lowest corridors were here, and the laborers in the Pumping Station.

Night after night Gard went out and dispatched whole troops of armored brawlers with ridiculous ease. He found that with a very slight shift in concentration he could make his opponents' bodies betray themselves: a slip of the foot, a sudden weakness in a limb. A green corona hummed around his body at such times, hard to see, but he thought Duke Silverpoint noticed it.

Yet Gard despised his victories, that seemed no more than a child pushing over toys of clay and sticks.

Clay and sticks indeed; he was told that Magister Prazza, who oversaw the rebodying of captive demons, had had to call in more workers to sculpt replacement bodies, so pressed he was to supply them for the arena. Monotonous as the slaughter was, the masters had an infinite appetite for it.

Gard found he could now distinguish between certain families of the masters. Some groups had recognizable shared features: for example, the line of Magister Obashon, who had won in the last war, tended toward hooked noses and protruding eyes. Some family lines wore a predominant color, such as that of Magister Imriudeth, all sea green trimmed with scarlet. The black nipples, he learned, were done with paint and were an affectation of mistresses of a certain age, regardless of family allegiance.

The very young mistresses, and some of the younger masters too, had taken of late to wearing green tunics, crudely daubed with the likeness of a swart-bearded face. When Balnshik explained to Gard that the face was intended to be his own, his response was incredulous laughter.

"And is this not what I foretold?" she said. "You have made them love you."

"Love!" said Gard. "I don't want their love. I want to get out of here. You're trapped here, too; don't you want to be free?"

She smiled at him. "It's a question of patience, child. My master is a cobweb, a bubble, a troublesome minute in my long day. Seven thousand years passed before him, and seven thousand will pass after he is gone, and I will not so much as remember his name. But you . . . *you*, I think, could make good use of freedom. Let us hope for the best."

When the change came, it came swiftly.

Gard was standing ankle deep in blood, before a mountain of corpses, and looking wearily up at the audience when he heard an echo of tramping feet in the tunnel. He looked over and saw a party of men coming into the arena. They were, all, onetimers, decked out in their ceremonial armor. Quickfire led them.

A hush fell over the audience, and then an excited murmur. Quickfire drew his long blade and saluted the masters, turning under the lights, flashing a wide smile. There was some applause. The other fighters took up formal poses in a line to the right of him. Neither Chint nor Vergoin was among them.

Quickfire turned to Gard then and set his blade point-down in the mush of bloody sand.

"Gard, half-demon! Quite a name you've made for yourself in the arena," he shouted. "What hosts of the dead you've sent wailing from this pit! The mightiest of the mighty . . . such as they are . . . all laid low by you, and you haven't sustained so much as a scratch. Truly you are a famous slaughterer . . . of *Repeaters*.

"When such a mortal has proven himself with such distinction, it is customary to welcome him into our ranks. We, the elite, who have but one glorious death to offer the masters! We who *truly* risk our lives for their entertainment!"

More murmuring, and some anticipatory applause. Quickfire held up his gauntleted hand. "But," he said, in a voice like a brazen trumpet, "we will not welcome *you*, Gard!"

Dead silence, and then gasps of excitement from the audience. Gard, who had heard Quickfire out in silence, felt a certain chill. He kept his face impassive, however.

"Who is this trained savage, that he should enter our honored fraternity?" cried Quickfire. "That he has done so well, so far, is truly a credit to our esteemed weapons master." Quickfire bowed toward Duke Silverpoint. "But we weary of this farce and will end it. We challenge you,

Gard, to combat with your betters, in three days' time. Do you dare accept?"

Gard looked up at Silverpoint, who was in his customary seat, staring across the arena with a face of stone. He was gazing at Bhetla, who was in turn looking up at the audience, gauging its reaction. Bhetla was smiling.

Silverpoint hadn't known about this.

"I do accept," said Gard, and the breathless silence ended in tremendous cheers from the audience, but some catcalls too. Quickfire grinned. He stepped back and swept his hand at the row of fighters beside him.

"Then choose. Moktace the Chabian! Falma Hanidor! The elder Kamaton! Three fearless combatants, and all have sworn to take you down."

Gard spared not a glance at the sneering champions. He raised his hand, which wore no gauntlet, pointed straight at Quickfire, and looked straight into Quickfire's eyes. "I will fight *you*."

There was tumult from above them, and a certain frozen quality to Quickfire's grin. "Then it will be my pleasure to kill you," he said. "Go, Gard, and spend these three days praying to your forest gods."

"I have no gods," said Gard.

He went wearily down to his cell after the fight and found his chamber empty. He was pouring water to wash himself when Bhetla looked in at the door.

"There you are! You know, you should stay awhile in the arena, after the fighting. The masters would enjoy a better look at you. And they're always generous, after a good fight."

"I want nothing they can give me," said Gard.

"Is it so?" Bhetla grinned. "But you do hold their attention, these days. They speak of nothing else."

Gard shrugged. Bhetla stepped inside the cell, looking around. "Some presents, already, I see. You can expect more, over the next three days. I'd advise against eating or drinking anything you're sent, of course. There will be people betting on Quickfire."

"Will there?" Gard sluiced blood from his arms.

"Oh, yes. All the Children of the Sun, of course. Tell me, why did you pick that one? He's not the best of the onetimers, but now you'll have to do without a trainer."

"Why's that?"

"Akkati's Divine Mother, didn't you know?" Bhetla blinked at him.

"The only time the Children of the Sun stop killing one another is when a member of some other race attacks one of them. Then they all band together. Nobody likes Quickfire, but he's one of *theirs*, you see. Odd people. The rest of us aren't quite real, as far as they're concerned."

———————

Duke Silverpoint was not in the exercise hall, next morning, when Gard went in to practice. He put himself through the steps for working away stiffness, and when no one had shown up after two hours, he walked back to his cell. In the corridor he encountered Triphammer, carrying bandages to an injured fighter. Triphammer avoided his gaze, but shook his head and made sorrowful noises.

"What is it?" demanded Gard. Triphammer almost walked on, but he stopped and half-turned, not meeting Gard's eyes.

"Trouble, trouble. Oh, Icicle, what bad god possessed you? After all our hard work. As if I didn't have enough else to worry about! You might have won all kinds of favors. I'll weep, so I will, when they drag you away."

"Don't you think I'll win?"

Triphammer looked up at Gard in surprised pity. "*You?* Win against Quickfire? Don't be ridiculous. You're a fine fighter in your way, but you're . . . well, you're not a Child of the Sun. It stands to reason he'll beat you."

———————

Balnshik was in Gard's cell when he returned to it, setting up a folding cot.

"Hello," she said, looking up at him with a brief smile. "Would you be so kind as to hand me that bag?"

Gard gave her the bag. She withdrew a blanket and pillow and arranged her bed in a businesslike manner. He stood in the doorway, staring at her.

"Perhaps you're wondering why I'm here."

"I am, yes," said Gard.

"My master has been persuaded to bet that you will *not* be murdered before you step into the arena. Therefore I am sent to attend you, lest he lose his wager."

Gard scowled, feeling his face grow hot. "I don't need anyone to protect me."

"No, dear, of course not." Balnshik straightened up and shook back her long hair. "Though I did just think I'd remove the venomous serpent I found in your bed. And the poisoned pins stuck in the collar of your robe, and the plate of sweetmeats with broken glass in their centers some admirer sent you."

Gard stepped across his threshold carefully, sat slowly on the edge of his bed. "Yesterday I was their hero," he said in wonder. "Why do they hate me now?"

"It's a matter of looks, as far as I've ever been able to discern," said Balnshik. "As long as you were fighting warriors who were uglier than you were, you were the hero. But now you've challenged Quickfire, who is young and handsome and—perhaps most important—does not have a black beard. By all the rules of spectator sports, that makes you the villain. An audience has no brain, you see."

"I wasn't fighting to be their hero anyway. Will they still love Quickfire, once I've killed him?"

"I'm afraid so, my dear. To die, young and handsome, in the arena? The mistresses will weep over him and remember him. All fighters long for such glory."

"How stupid."

"Whyever did you pick him, over Moktace and the others? If you don't mind my asking?"

"Because he's my enemy. I don't know the others, but Quickfire will put thorns in my path if he can. And I know how he fights. I'll kill him."

Gard looked up at Balnshik. "I don't suppose you'd lie with me, lady?"

She sighed. "No, my dear. Only sleep with you."

———

She attended him faithfully, accompanied him to the exercise hall, and was in every respect a graceful and witty companion, cheering his heart as well as disposing of a couple of would-be assassins by night, discreetly, with no more than a muffled scream and a few telltale drops of blood by the door. But Gard's other need went unmet.

Now and again, as they walked from his room to the hall, they passed other slaves hurrying on errands. The demons among them grinned at Gard and made a curious gesture as they passed, as though they were lifting something to their mouths between finger and thumb.

"It's a good-luck sign," replied Balnshik, when Gard inquired what the gesture meant. "They wish you joy in eating the liver of your enemy."

"You mean someone actually hopes I'll win?"

"My dear, all your people will be cheering for you. We have never had a real champion before this." Balnshik hummed a phrase of music: *If I ever get out of here . . .*

My people, thought Gard. The idea felt strange, after so long.

He meditated the day of the fight, walking outside himself through the same country of stars, following the stag over the green lawn of his childhood. He saw again the couple he did not know, lying down together at the edge of the dance: the man he had thought was his father, and the unknown woman.

This time the stag led him past them and into dark tunnels, and he walked bodiless in his prison, saw Magister Tagletsit basking in the light of his false sun. Duke Silverpoint was writing, alone, in his chamber; Quickfire, cheered on by the other onetimers, was sweating as he practiced in the exercise hall. There was the Pumping Station, with its great central fire burning high, and sweat gleaming on the bodies of . . . all the folk who crowded into the cavern.

Why was there a crowd there? Why were they excited? Grattur and Engrattur were leaning down to listen intently to a man. Gard whirled his incorporeal point of view around to look into the man's face—and saw Vergoin.

But the stag walked on, and he was drawn to follow it. It went into a place he took at first to be the arena. No sand was on the floor; it was polished stone, inlaid with arcane designs. The stag struck fire there with its hooves; it put its antlers down and charged the black wall.

The wall exploded outward, fell with a roar. Sunlight streamed in, blinding, with a blue-green glimpse of ice, and white-flaring snow. The stag stood in the opening and turned to look at him.

But he was being called. Someone was pulling him by the hands. He had hands, again. He opened his eyes and peered at Balnshik, who was leaning down to him with a tender smile. "It's your hour, my dear," she said.

The halls were deserted, but she stayed with Gard all the way to the arena. She had put on her fighting gear too, harness and mail, as elegant as black velvet on her body.

"Are you planning on avenging my death?" he asked.

"I may do a little fighting today," she said lightly. "But I'm quite certain you won't die."

"What's that?" Gard nodded at a ribbon she had strung through a link of mail, a loop of vivid green.

She flicked it with her gloved finger. "Only a little token."

"Are you wearing it for me?"

"It looks that way, doesn't it?" said Balnshik. "You may see one or two others, tonight."

But when Gard stepped into the arena, to massed cheers and denunciation, he looked up and saw many green ribbons. The masters and mistresses who wore them sat huddled in groups together, at the far end from the main entrance to the tiers. Up in the slaves' gallery, some who wore nothing else wore green ribbons: around their necks, or from nose rings, or looped around tusks in quite a holiday fashion. They roared and hooted their approval of Gard. He gave them a wan smile and thought again, *My people.*

He swept the house with a long stare. Not a single seat was empty. With a start, he recognized Magister Hoptriot, of all people, wearing a green ribbon strung through his facial wrappings. And there in his customary place was Duke Silverpoint, and he too wore the ribbon, though he gazed straight before him and never looked once at Gard.

Again the echoing fanfare from the tunnel. Gard turned and faced its mouth, expecting the parade of champions once again; but only Quickfire walked forth.

There were cheers for him, applause loud as driving rain, and he held up his fists and flashed a grin at them. His grin faded a moment as he saw Silverpoint's green ribbon. He looked at Gard with keen hate. When the applause had died, he spoke loudly.

"Why, what a crowd has turned out to see you butchered, Gard! I was going to finish the job quickly, but it seems a shame not to put on a show for them, don't you think?"

Gard kept his silence, but, looking steadfastly at Quickfire, he drew his two blades. The crowd muttered gleefully, and some applauded.

Quickfire reached over his head and just as slowly drew a pair of blades. He grinned again. "Not a word for your fond followers? You surly misbegotten thing. Speech doesn't come easily for you, does it?" He began to circle Gard. Gard turned with him, eyeing him. Next would come the provocation . . .

"But then, your mother must have been silent too. Hard to talk, eh, through a muzzle and fangs?" Quickfire leaped in and swung at him, a round head cut with a right block.

Gard beat him back. The same pattern, then. But not quite the same style . . . what was wrong? It felt as though a layer of something, feltlike, was hanging in the air before Quickfire. It delayed Gard's impact, very slightly, but it did. He focused.

He saw from all directions, and it was as though Quickfire wore a wheel of flame on his chest. Under his cuirass was an amulet for protection. Gard watched himself swing for Quickfire's head and saw the spell in motion; yes, it did look like a cloth flung out, to snare and slow Gard's blade.

He saw, rather than felt, the white anger surge up, a distant thing. He resisted the urge to let it pull him down to that fighting floor.

The amulet must come off, therefore the cuirass must come off. And Quickfire was left-handed. Therefore . . .

Gard feinted and fell back, feinted and fell back, working himself around to Quickfire's right. Quickfire moved like his name, but he could not overcome his body's habit; all the attacks were staged from the left, with the right arm used only to block, the sword used like a shield.

Gard lunged forward, fighting through the barrier, driving the point deep into Quickfire's upper right arm and piercing the sinew there. Only one cut, but just where it needed to be. Quickfire dropped the sword, and he might have cried out, but the audience outcried him; their roar sent dust floating down from the ceiling, made the very sand underfoot vibrate.

Gard kicked the sword across the sand. It spun into the gutter and the edge, teetered there for a moment, and dropped into the salvager's pit. Was Triphammer in there, wringing his hands? Would he throw it back? Or was he wearing a green ribbon too?

Quickfire recovered himself and turned edge-on, presenting his left, and came at Gard with furious speed, with slashing head cuts. Gard beat them away, dancing to the left, always to the left, circling and circling to come at Quickfire's right side. Quickfire's right arm hung useless, but the small wound was hardly bleeding. Round and round Gard turned him, and then, without any signal, bounded away to the right and dropped low.

As Quickfire raised his blade for a head cut, Gard came in beneath and sliced upward, cutting through the side strap on the cuirass. It came at the price of a slash down Gard's cheek, slowed as he was by the amulet; he bounded away and circled again, disregarding the blood that welled at once and ran down, disregarding the yells of the crowd. They were shouting for Quickfire, young and handsome and brave, who showed no fear even when wounded.

"Oh, well done, *Gard*," shouted Quickfire, and gasped for breath. "You've wounded my armor. And I've spoiled your good looks, haven't I? So sorry. Shouldn't be a problem, though, should it? Don't you hump your females from behind? Not as though they have to look at you!" The audience shouted with laughter.

Gard let him talk, circling, evaluating. How did the shoulder of the cuirass fasten? How strong was the protection the amulet generated? He focused, went out of himself, and watched as he feinted toward Quickfire's heart. A veil of flame appeared, catching, delaying his blade point. Almost impossible to strike with a mortal wound there, then. He darted in toward the right side once more, aimed a scratch at the useless arm, and found the veil was not nearly so quick to materialize where the wound was not likely to be mortal.

It was all he needed to know. Gard circled again, parried an attack, then launched himself at Quickfire in the killing leap, bounding straight up. He struck downward with his left-hand blade, and the spell veil formed instantly over the vulnerable throat and neck. His blade's point slid away, struck instead his true target, the strap that closed the left shoulder of the cuirass.

It punched through, going into Quickfire's shoulder no more than an inch, nor was the wound deep. But it bit with painful force; Quickfire shouted and brought his fist up as Gard came down, and his blade stabbed upward through Gard's billowing robe and cut a trench in Gard's side from waist to shoulder. The point stopped just short of Gard's chin.

Gard hurled himself backward, ignoring this wound too. He watched Quickfire intently. Quickfire, enraged, started forward, flinging up his arm for a last head cut—

And his cuirass opened like a book and fell off him.

Gard sprang forward and knocked him down. Quickfire went sprawling, and how the crowd screamed and moaned in sympathy! There was a buzzing roar of wrath, like a disturbed hive, as Gard set his foot on Quickfire's chest. He leaned down and grabbed the amulet, breaking the cord from which it had hung. He held it up for the crowd to see.

Breath indrawn in a thousand throats. Gard felt the compass needle of their regard swing slowly round, as they recognized what it was he held, and what it meant.

Now they hated Quickfire. Howling, hooting, the audience sent their scorn on him in immense waves of sound, and he lay drowning in disgust with Gard's right blade an inch from his heart.

Gard looked down into his eyes. "I defeated you fairly. I am a better fighter than you are, and you knew it. You cheated because you were afraid of me, didn't you?"

"Oh, shut up and kill me," said Quickfire. Above them the audience was screaming, pounding their seats, and every pair of eyes was fixed on the point of Gard's sword.

"Should I kill you?" said Gard. "That would earn me the enmity of your kinsmen, wouldn't it? And then I'd need to look over my shoulder always, and wonder if the food or drink set before me had been poisoned. I don't think you're worth it."

"No!" Quickfire tried to rise, his eyes starting from his head in horror. "Don't do this to me! Give me a decent death!"

"No." Gard bore down on him with his foot. "Why should I, when your life was all talk and spite? I will be merciful and pardon you. Watch me."

Gard looked up at the audience and weighed the amulet in his hand; then he cast it into the sand cleaners' pit, in a gesture wide enough for all to see. A moan of anticipation came from the crowd. He turned and was just raising the point of his sword, and the moan was fading to a breathless silence—

Then, with a hollow *boom*, all four doors to the arena were flung open at once.

Armed figures ran in, dozens of them, and began to kill members of the audience. Gard looked up, astonished to see that those masters who had worn green ribbons were drawing weapons and joining in the massacre. Magister Obashon's family was slaughtered around him where he sat, and though he raised his arms and summoned explosions in red and blue and green to blind and blast his assailants, Balnshik herself leaped through the fires and cut away both his hands.

Vergoin was mercilessly dispatching some family group in cloth of gold livery. Magister Tagletsit, adorned with green ribbon, had prudently withdrawn to a seat against a pillar and waved an athalme in a threatening manner whenever the tide of the massacre drew too near for his comfort. Duke Silverpoint was on his feet and killing with efficiency the entire party of Magister Imriudeth, so that those he had not got to yet were shedding the colorful livery that marked them and running for the doors. Even so, none made it out alive.

A percussive shock, scattering flower petals, threw Gard to the sand. Lying there, he saw that Quickfire had rolled over and hidden his face.

Gard followed his example. There were more explosions, and much screaming. A fine mist of blood drifted down into the arena.

Gard rose cautiously when the screams had all but stopped. Quickfire remained on his face, sobbing.

All through the tiers of seats, bodies were slumped, though a crew of slaves were being directed in their removal by Magister Hoptriot. The living, most of whom wore the green ribbon, were moving among the dead stripping them of ornaments. Balnshik seemed to be kissing one of the masters; she rose with a languid motion and Gard saw the gaping wound in the master's throat, the white face with its eyes rolled back.

He was still staring at it when he heard the tunnel doors flung open. Someone was coming up the fighters' entrance. Gard turned to see who it was.

Lady Pirihine strode forth under the lights, naked as when he had seen her last, save for a green ribbon tied in a bow around her neck. Grattur and Engrattur flanked her, grinning. They, and she, carried blades no less naked and were splashed with blood in several colors. Lady Pirihine's eyes shone with cold triumph.

She raised her hand and pointed at Gard:

"I want him."

12th day 2nd week 10th month in the 246th year from the Ascent of the Mountain. This day, Slave 4372301 reassigned to Personal Service: allocated to Lady Pirihine, most puissant Narcissus of the Void, of the exalted line of Magister Porlilon.

"Bet you weren't expecting this," said Grattur.

"Bet you never imagined you'd be so lucky!" said Engrattur.

"You see? We *said* she wouldn't forget you!"

"Oh, you'll lead a sweet life now. Lucky bastard!"

Gard looked around them, slightly dazed. They had brought him to a suite of rooms up a long staircase. The rooms were splendid, all black and gold, draped and ornamented and rich beyond measure—and scrupulously clean, save for a long smear of blood where some faithful retainer's corpse had been dragged out.

"What is this place?"

"It was Magister Obashon's own chamber," said Grattur.

"*Was.* It'll be our lady's, now. Look at this!" Engrattur stuck his head through a doorway. "A bath, all polished stone and scented salts!"

"Look at this bed, all black silk and eiderdown!"

"Ooooh, lucky Icicle!" they chorused.

"I'll draw you a bath, she said you were to be washed."

"Look at this, you just open this bit and water runs out!"

"Bet you've never seen the like of this!"

"Bet you've never lain in such a bed!"

"Where is he? You big fools, there's a trail of blood all the way up here," said Triphammer, peering through the doorway.

"It's not from me," said Gard.

"That's something, anyway," said Triphammer, entering cautiously. He avoided Gard's gaze. "I've been sent to patch him up. All right are you, Icicle?"

"What's happened?" Gard sat on a padded bench—unbelievable softness—and let Triphammer come and inspect his hurts.

"Another war, what do you think?" said Triphammer.

"Surprise!" said Grattur.

"What fun we had!" said Engrattur.

"Idiots! It's a serious business!" said Triphammer. "Never good for the masters to fight amongst themselves. Always fewer of them, every time they have one of these little spats, and the bloodlines are getting thinned out. And it may have been all fun and games for you, but what about the poor devils who had to abide by their binding spells?"

"But that was the beauty of it," said Grattur.

"Our lady worked out a way around the spells," said Engrattur.

"She's clever with words, that one."

"We just had to obey *exactly* what she said."

"She put it in such a way we weren't *technically* disobeying the Great Order."

"We carried messages for her."

"We let the demons know, and her secret friends."

"But that's the end of the line of Magister Obashon," said Triphammer, dabbing something that stung on Gard's cheek. "Every last child of his, you slaughtered. And he was great and wise."

"Not wise enough," said Grattur cheerily.

"Should have killed our lady when he might," said Engrattur.

"Well, you two won something, anyway," said Triphammer. "Stand up, Icicle, let me see that long cut. *Sssssst!* But it's only bad here, and here. You'll need me to stitch those bits, and the cheek. She won't want your looks spoiled, eh?"

Triphammer rummaged in his kit for needle and thread and set to stitching Gard's cuts while Grattur filled a bath and scented it with perfumes. Engrattur, singing, flung back the silk sheets of the bed, scattered them with flower petals.

"That was a dishonor, what Quickfire did," Triphammer murmured softly, as he worked. "Wouldn't have thought it of him. Coward. You did right not to kill him. Sorry I couldn't . . . well, it's over and done now, eh? Lovely days ahead for you, that's certain. And you got to retire from the arena undefeated, do you realize that? They may even breed you, wouldn't that be fun?"

"What?" Gard thought with horror of raising children in that place.

"Don't be humble! They could use a little strong hybrid blood, especially now. It all works out for the best, see? It's like I always say to myself. 'Triphammer,' I say, 'what's so terrible, really, about being a slave? What were you when you were free but a beggar, a thief, never knowing where your next meal was coming from? Here, at least, you *amount* to something! You have a place!'

"And you, Icicle, where'd you be, if they hadn't rescued you from the snows? Worse still, what if you'd stayed in your jungle? You'd never have seen a beautiful room like this one, that's for certain. Or got to meet the likes of her ladyship, so refined and lovely. Or learned manners and reading and all from the duke. Know a stroke of good fortune when you see one, my friend."

"And now you'll be Mistress Pirihine's plaything!" said Grattur.

"You'll enjoy her. We can tell you, we have had the pleasure!"

"Lightning in a girl's skin, that one, hot snow, cool fire."

"'Give it to me, you big animals,' she said, and we had to obey."

They pounded each other, chortling. Gard watched them bleakly, wincing as Triphammer stitched his cheek closed. He was exhausted—and shaken by the slaughter he'd seen; but the prospect of easing his lusts after so long was beginning to glimmer through to him, like a hopeful dawn. He wondered if he might come to love Lady Pirihine, as a man ought to love a wife.

Triphammer remained until after Gard had bathed, that he might bandage the cuts. "Here's a set of clean clothes that I brought from your old room," he told Gard, pulling them from his bag. "She'll want you to wear her livery, of course, but you'll need something until then. And here's a quid for you, because you'll feel these hurts tomorrow, you know. But don't have a chew tonight, whatever you do! Her ladyship will be sore disappointed."

"She doesn't like being disappointed," said Grattur, chuckling.

"Hits you with her tiny little fists and screams abuse," said Engrattur, shaking his head with a fond smile.

"Let's hope she'll have a bit of patience with a weary fighter, eh? But you're strong, Icicle, you'll rise to the occasion." Triphammer gathered up his bag. "Cheer up, now! Just remember how lucky you are. Not such a bad life. Best thing, really."

Triphammer left; Grattur and Engrattur took their leave too, though only to stand outside the door with drawn blades. Gard sat alone, looking around at the fine things in the room. It was a warmer place, more ornamented than Duke Silverpoint's apartments. There were few books, and those immense and black, with jewels set in their spines.

He got up once, to follow the blood trail, and found that it led into a small spare antechamber with a narrow bed. Scattered on the floor were a jar of some oily stuff and a rag, and one ornamented boot with a curled toe. The luckless slave had been cleaning Magister Obashon's boots when they had come for him. Gard wondered where the other boot was.

He went back into the bedchamber and pulled down one of the books, to see if it was about weaponry. Written in one of the ancient tongues he had studied only briefly, it did not seem to be. Sounding out the characters (for he still moved his lips as he read), Gard felt the book begin to move in his hands, as though restless. He held it tighter and opened it to another section.

> To kill at a distance: this requires the sacrifice of a child of the same
> gender as the intended victim, dressed in every respect in the victim's
> habit, and in one of his or her garments if possible. Feed the child for
> three days and three nights on the following mixture . . .

Gard threw the book down in disgust. It snapped shut, seemed to shake itself, and began to crawl, batlike, to the shelf from which it had been taken. He heard the door open behind him and turned to see Lady Pirihine enter.

She was still naked, though her green ribbon was gone. She took in the grand room in a long traveling stare, smiling wide, nodded cursorily at Gard, and strode to Magister Obashon's jewel chest. It was locked; she uttered a word painful to hear and it sprang open. For some few minutes she amused herself by trying on such rings and necklaces as would fit her.

"Well, Icicle," she said at last, "here we are. Do you remember when I said I'd have you killed slowly?"

"I remember," said Gard.

"Perhaps I won't, after all. It was well done, to kill the beast that had laid hands on me against my will. And I owe you thanks, that you so held the attention of Obashon and all his party; they were much too caught up in the spectacle to pay attention to a little backstairs conspiracy." She dimpled as she found a great somber red stone, pendant from a chain of gold, and slipped it on so it hung between her breasts. "How nice I look! Don't you think I look nice?"

"You are beautiful, lady," said Gard, his body already testifying to that.

She turned to look at him and clapped her hands. "Ah, what a glorious monster you are! I'll have you right now." She hopped up on the bed and crouched, turning her hindquarters to him. "Do it! Do it exactly as you would with a she-creature in your forest tribe, do you understand?"

Gard was eager to oblige, though a little bewildered that she wanted no soft talk, no gentle touches first. He cleared his throat and began, hesitantly, to sing the Virgin's Song.

"What on earth are you doing?" She turned her head to look at him, scowling.

"This is how it was done with my people. I remember watching, when I was a boy. The song is for a virgin, and the man sings to the woman—"

"Imbecile! Do you really think I'm a virgin?"

Gard blushed, grimaced, and looked away. "Not you—I had no chances, where I lived—and then—"

But she had jumped from the bed and held her hand out in a commanding gesture. The red stone flashed. Her eyes widened. "Tulit's bones! *You're* a virgin!" she exclaimed.

"Yes," said Gard wretchedly. He watched a new expression come into her face, a new kind of lust entirely, and it made her look older, and hungrier, than did the simple desire to be pleasured.

She glanced down at his body with only fleeting regret. "Oh, what a fortunate day. I will have you, Icicle, but not like this; I won't waste such a gift. Go to the door; tell Grattur to send for Lord Vergoin. Draw me a bath, and see it's well scented."

So Gard spent the night of his victory in the narrow bed of the slave who had cleaned boots, listening as Vergoin and Lady Pirihine coupled in the next room.

When he was allowed to lie with her at last, it was not at all as he had thought it would be. There was no singing. No soft talk, no gentle touches either, and not even the gorgeous bed of black silk.

He was led, naked, into the chamber he had seen in his meditation, the high room with arcane designs set into its polished floor. Lady Pirihine bid him lie down in the circle at its center, flat on his back, and reach his arms and legs out to its edge. He felt his hands and feet gripped by something unseen. He fought back terror, thinking that he would be slain.

Lady Pirihine only smiled, and cast handfuls of incense on a brazier and chanted something in her sweet high voice. She moved around the edges of the room, lighting torches; only then did he see the robed and hooded figures massed in the shadows.

She knelt to anoint him with something that burned. Then she did what could not be described as love, not by any stretch of the truth.

It did not hurt him. It was rather wonderful, in respect to his long-pent-up desires. But when he looked up, in the throes of his fulfillment, he saw the masters all watching, with faces no less avid than when he had fought for his life in the arena.

Gard closed his eyes to shut them out. He tried, desperately, to summon the memory of the dancing green of his childhood, the tender couples kissing and murmuring together under the flowering trees. Here, again, he saw the couple at the edge: the man who resembled Ran, but was not, and the woman he did not know. . . .

The image stayed before him, even as the brazier exploded with green fire, even as the walls and floor ran with green and silver fire, so that the masters backed hurriedly away, and Lady Pirihine's triumphant laughter faltered as she drank in the power his initiation had generated.

He was weary and sore when he returned, at last, to his narrow bed in the antechamber. Lady Pirihine had summoned Vergoin once more, and Gard could hear them deep in conversation in the other room.

Something was on his pillow. He sat down and picked it up. A rose, perhaps from the masters' cavern gardens, dark red and sweetly perfumed. A small square of parchment was folded around its stem. Gard opened it and recognized Balnshik's handwriting.

My dear, I wish it had been me.

His service to the Narcissus of the Void was not, in most respects, unpleasant. Gard must wear her livery and sleep in her apartments on the narrow bed, though he was also bid to service her lusts when her lover Vergoin was otherwise occupied. His duties included tending to her wardrobe, locking away her jewels each night, and waiting her pleasure at table. He learned to carve and to pour without spilling, and how to fold napery into amusing shapes.

But he must also serve as her bodyguard, walking before her when she ventured forth to councils or amusements, with Grattur and Engrattur walking behind. They all three wore her livery of black and green, though Gard was also decked with a green-and-gold baldric, to remind all who saw him that Lady Pirihine's slave was an undefeated champion. He was given his two blades to wear, to underline the point.

Now Gard saw more of the masters' world, the Upper Tunnels and the great central cavern where they promenaded daily, in their finest robes, attended by other liveried slaves. Anyone seeing the Upper Tunnels might indeed think their builders were magnificent, for the floors were set with intricate mosaics, polished smooth, and the ceilings set with tiny glowing lamps to emulate stars. Opening off the tunnels were chambers cut into the living rock. Here were libraries, concert rooms, places where loot from the outside world was displayed for sale: jewelry, fine fabrics, carpets, wines and sweetmeats, musical instruments. These places were brilliantly lit, with a glamour of need sparkling on each least bauble.

Gard was struck with wonder at first, stopping to stare so often that Lady Pirihine took to carrying a small switch of braided leather, and with this she would strike him smartly to make him move on. As the weeks and months went by, however, and he learned Lady Pirihine's favorite progresses well enough to walk them blindfolded, Gard wearied of the place. Now he longed to seize the switch and goad on the Narcissus of the Void when she would stop in the great central cavern to gossip, or flirt with admirers, or listen to the petitions of those begging favors.

And all the while, below the elaborate artifice, the stifling warmth and glittering lamps, were the black passageways where half-bodied slaves toiled, and the sick and the dying lay in darkness. Gard remembered them well.

He was grateful to be released from the perfumed world a few hours each day, to the sanctuary of the training hall. Lady Pirihine desired her slave should not lose his fighting edge, and so he had the freedom of violence. Duke Silverpoint welcomed him back, with a courteous nod.

"You were one of Lady Pirihine's men?" Gard asked him.

"No. I merely kept silent about what I knew. And lent my hand in the final hour, of course."

"Why?"

Silverpoint gave one of his infrequent smiles. "There are now *seven* empty seats in the council chamber. With every quarrel, our masters diminish in numbers and strength. One must do what one can to help the process along."

Occasionally, now, Silverpoint did Gard the honor of sparring with him. By the third or fourth match, Gard realized that Silverpoint was still training him, though much more subtly. It was possible to strike Silverpoint; it was possible to defeat him. But Gard found that oftener than not blows did not connect, for the duke was inexplicably not where he had been when Gard had calculated the stroke and begun his follow-through; and yet Silverpoint had not dodged.

After one such match, Gard stepped back and lowered the point of his blade. "You're not using a spell. I'd see it, if you were. What are you doing?"

"It is a spell, if you like. But it involves no magic. What is the greatest danger to an accomplished fighter?"

"Overconfidence."

"And force of habit. You watch a particular opening and assume you know what I will do next. You have now fought so long, and so often, that your assumptions aren't even conscious; they're instinctive. I am tricking your instincts."

"How?"

"I refer you to Prince Firebow," said the duke, setting his blade back on the wall. "His last work, *The Fighting Mind*. He left it uncompleted at his death; I have the only copy and paid dearly for it. You may borrow it, however."

Gard pored over the manuscript in such late hours as he could keep a candle burning in his alcove. While magic was not involved in the techniques discussed, still a demon's power of sight was needed to make the most use of them; for an even greater degree of minute observation was called for, and swifter reflexes, and manipulation of the opponent. Methodically, Gard learned the mental tricks. Soon, in the training hall, he had mastered them.

It was a pity, he thought, that he would have no chance to use them in his new career.

———

"I shall attend a dinner party tonight," said the Narcissus of the Void, regarding her reflection in her mirror. "You will attend me, and taste each dish I am offered."

"Thank you, lady," said Gard.

She knit her brows in annoyance. "You big fool, you'll taste my food to see whether it's been poisoned. Really, sometimes I wonder whether we'll ever be able to wash the stink of the forest off you."

"Who would poison you, lady?"

"Nearly anyone on the council," she said with a sigh. "It is good to win the highest seat, but after that, it's nothing but a struggle to stay there. Now, I'll be dining with Magister Naryath, and I wish to impress him. Gatta's has a bottle of Sulemian wine in its window, just one; go down and buy it, and have it ready when I come back this afternoon. Have my black gown with the pearls laid out, and the green slippers. And a bath drawn; I like a bath when I've been to Blood Entertainments."

"I will not be required to escort you, lady?"

"No. Lord Vergoin's taking me. We'll use Grattur and Engrattur. I can't send *them* for the wine, of course. Imbecile demons. You do have that much in your favor, Icicle, you aren't quite as stupid as the others. Something to do with being a hybrid, no doubt. Ah! There's Vergoin."

They heard Grattur and Engrattur roaring forth the ceremonial challenge, with a great clashing of blades, and Vergoin's easy reply. A moment later he entered the bedchamber, smiling.

"Dread beauty, I have arrived," he said. "You won't want to miss the first match; Agoleth is going up against three fighters from the Convent."

"No!" exclaimed Lady Pirihine. "Icicle, fasten this clasp. Agoleth? Oh, they'll cut him to ribbons! We must see. The Sulemian wine, Icicle; forget it at your peril."

She departed with Vergoin, and Grattur and Engrattur marched proudly behind them.

Gard, a little sullenly, took gold from her household store and went down through the tunnels to the wine merchant's stall. There he purchased the bottle of Sulemian wine, with its lead seals and golden lettering. He wondered whether the wine had come from any land the scholar Copperlimb had visited, and whether he might taste the sunlight of a long-ago autumn, if he were to drink it.

Useless to wonder; useless to look thoughtfully at the mouths of certain tunnels as he passed them. He had learned enough to know that they led upward, and opened in sunlight on a trail that wound down between glaciers. But they were guarded at their far ends by bound demons, who suffered none to pass save those who were equally bound and so trusted to come back. Some three or four times each year a caravan went out, to return with luxuries for the masters.

It was by no means useless to plan, however. Gard had begun to compile a list in his head, of needful things he might acquire without arousing suspicion: thick boots proof against the snows, and warm clothing. Weapons he had in plenty, but he lacked knowledge. He meant, in time, to get acquainted with the caravan leaders and learn what paths led down to the lands below, where cities were. He meant, in time, to strike up a friendship with the demons who guarded the tunnels, and to see if he might make them unconscious with gifts of drugs or drink. *If I ever get out of here . . .*

Just now there was nothing to do but return to Lady Pirihine's apartments and do his best to get the jam spots out of her morning gown, and lay out the dinner gown she had requested, with her pearls and her green slippers.

He sat and meditated afterward. In his deep concentration Gard saw again the stag, leading him through the deep wood, and across the dancing green. The music had fallen silent. It seemed to Gard that this time, as he passed the couple on the edge, that the woman turned her face to him, seeming to see him.

He had not been long in the place of soaring lights when there came a flash, red light broken and shattered, and a sense of alarm. His attention was drawn down to a knot of darkness, where a white thing sped; a worm, screaming and spitting fire as it came, trailing a long ribbon of blood-stained silk. It was closely pursued by a second worm, and by a pair of blue lights moaning and lamenting. . . .

Coming back to himself, Gard heard the door flung open. He jumped to his feet and looked into the bedchamber as the Narcissus of the Void entered, and her afternoon gown had indeed been splattered with blood. Vergoin followed her, his face dark with anger.

"I don't care!" Lady Pirihine was saying. "This was a brand-new gown! Look where the lace is stained! Those stains will *never* come out."

"There will be talk, madam," said Vergoin. "It will be wondered whether one so unable to govern her temper is worthy of governing at all. He was a useful slave!"

"A slave is a slave," said Lady Pirihine. "How dare you! Icicle! What do you think you're doing, lurking there? You'd better have got me that wine!"

"I did, lady. Shall I draw the bath, now?"

"Do it!"

He attended her in her bath, marveling how the ugly look in her eyes was able to render quite charmless the beauty of her little pointed breasts and lush flanks. He helped her from the tub and into her black gown, clasped the pearls about her throat, and eased the green slippers on her feet, as Vergoin paced to and fro muttering.

They were still in a foul temper when, carefully bearing the Sulemian wine, he followed them out into the corridor. Grattur and Engrattur stood to attention to either side of the door. Gard was amazed to see their silver eyes streamed with tears.

There was little time to wonder about this, for Lady Pirihine minced away down the hall, refusing Vergoin's arm. He strode after her angrily. Gard must hurry after them, an awkward third to their party. Everyone was out of breath, and Lady Pirihine somewhat red-faced, when they arrived at last at the apartments of Magister Naryath.

Magister Naryath was tall, and portly, and affected a golden mask and the tone of an indulgent father.

"Little Pirihine! You are adorable, as always, but never more so than when you wear your hair in that charming fashion. Lord Vergoin, you are well met. I trust my poor table will not too gravely disappoint you."

"You must be joking," said Lady Pirihine. "Vergoin's been a slave, after all. I should imagine he's grateful for any scrap he gets."

Vergoin looked at her with venom.

Magister Naryath fluttered his hands. "Sweet Pirihine, we are all your slaves. Come now, children, don't quarrel. See where my table is set in your honor, with lilies of gold! Pray be seated."

"As you wish. I have brought a gift, dear Uncle Naryath," said Lady Pirihine.

Gard bowed and offered the Sulemian wine. Magister Naryath waved a hand and his demoness, a lithe creature who communicated by signing, came forth in silence. She received the bottle, gestured her thanks, and took it to the sideboard.

"How very kind of you, my child," said Magister Naryath.

"Oh, it's only a bottle of Sulemian," said Lady Pirihine, as Gard seated her. "Perhaps we'll just drink it ourselves, you and I, and not let Vergoin have any. Shall we? He's been so rude and cross with me, he really doesn't deserve better."

"So is good counsel rewarded," said Vergoin.

"I'm certain good fare will restore your customary affability," said Magister Naryath, as the demoness set the first of the dishes on the table. "Do try these, both of you! The eggs of sea dragons, gathered from the cliffs in far Salesh and pickled in wine of Dalith. I have found the flavor exquisite."

The Narcissus of the Void clapped her hands. She dipped up a spoonful.

"How delightful! Where's my big faithful Icicle? *He* shall have some. He never gets cross with me, do you, Icicle?"

Gard bent and allowed her to feed him from her spoon. The sea-dragon eggs looked like grapes. They tasted like fish, which startled him, but did not seem poisoned. Magister Naryath gestured with his little finger, and the demoness brought another spoon and carried away the one from which Gard had tasted.

"Let Uncle Naryath make peace between you, my dears," said the mage. "What causes little Pirihine to frown so?"

"A stupid slave got blood on my dress," said Lady Pirihine, pouting in what she imagined was an enchanting manner. "We had been to the Blood Entertainments, you know, and we had just the loveliest time—it was Agoleth the Unlucky, and he was pitted against three of the deadliest bitches from the Convent."

"Oh, how amusing that must have been!" said Magister Naryath.

"It *was.* They killed him by inches and then tossed his head back and forth like a ball. We laughed and laughed. I really was having the best time," said Lady Pirihine, allowing a little tremble into her voice, at the unfairness of it all. "And after it was over, of course I wanted to go down and claim his testicles. That's traditional, after all."

"An old and honored custom," agreed Magister Naryath.

"And we went down to that pit under the arena, and Vergoin *should* have held my train up off the sand, but he didn't, not that it mattered much because the stupid slave carrying away Agoleth's arms and legs tripped in the sand and all the parts went flying, and Agoleth's nasty old hand struck me right in the face, and his nasty old stumps got blood all over my best afternoon gown!"

"And so she had the slave killed on the spot," said Vergoin sourly.

"Well, I would have too," said Magister Naryath, leaning forward to pat Lady Pirihine's hand.

"He was a useful slave," said Vergoin, raising his voice. "He was Magister Hoptriot's assistant. Hoptriot will be offended, and, by the way, do you think *he's* going to lower himself to stitch up the fighters now? Triphammer won't be easy to replace."

"Oh, who cares?" said Lady Pirihine, with a toss of her head. "Nobody but you. Let's have some wine. Icicle, open the bottle."

Gard looked at her blankly. Triphammer had been killed?

Not such a bad life. Best thing, really. Food and a bed, just as well, not so bad. What's so terrible, really, about being a slave?

"Slave, your mistress has given you a command!" said Magister Naryath, and, hoping to distract his guests from their quarrel, rose in his seat and struck Gard in the face.

He could not strike back, he could not roar his wrath and sorrow; Gard only looked at Magister Naryath and wished him dead.

Magister Naryath gasped and shrank back; sweat boiled and ran from under his golden mask. A wine goblet shattered on the table. The Sulemian wine burst its seals, spurted like blood on the cloth. Pirihine's eyes were round with astonishment.

Vergoin was on his feet at once. "Peace! Gard, this is sad news for you, I know. Go into the kitchen, calm your mind a moment."

Gard turned from the table and went. The kitchen was small and dark, with Magister Naryath's demoness finding her way principally by touch. She was readying the main course as he entered, and looked at him in wonder. She pointed at him, ran her fingers down her cheeks as though following tear tracks, then turned her palms out in inquiry. *Why do you weep?* No Translator appeared for her, strangely.

"My friend has been killed," said Gard. "For nothing."

She put her arms around him. He leaned his face into her shoulder and wept out his sorrow and his wrath. All the while, quiet, urgent conversation was coming from the outer room. Gard caught the words "natural ability" and "stupid as a brick, but what power! If we could train him to work elementary spells . . ."

At last he lifted his face. "Thank you."

She signed, *That's all right.*

"Can't you speak?"

A negation, a gesture at her throat: *I was made without a voice. He likes silent women.*

Gard shook his head. He looked at the dish she was preparing. "Is your master planning on poisoning my mistress?"

She shook her head.

"What a pity."

She laughed at that. He had never seen anyone sign laughter before and was diverted.

———

"I have made a decision, dear Icicle," said the Narcissus of the Void. She looked up at him in her mirror, and her eyes were wide and her expression was one of childlike gravity. These past few days, in fact, she had played the little girl: all gaiety, laughter, and lisping talk, and many times she had asked for his assistance in opening some perfume vial or buttoning up some garment.

He only looked at her, now, and waited for her to speak. "I have never known a slave like you," she said, as though shyly. "You are so big, and strong, and yet so very clever! And Lord Vergoin feels that you might have it in you—if you were carefully trained, of course—to become a *mage!* Yes, just like one of us! Wouldn't that be wonderful?"

"Yes, lady." Gard waited to hear what else she would say.

"And so I said at once that I thought that was a wonderful idea. It has made me so proud to have an undefeated champion in my service, and if it turned out you were a natural mage too—why, I just think I'd scream, I'd be so very, very pleased with you." She turned and gave him a winsome smile.

"Really, lady?" said Gard, his face as blank as a wall.

"Yes." Lady Pirihine turned all the way around on her dressing-table stool and drew her legs up, and leaned forward conspiratorially. "Now, I'm going to tell you a secret. You mustn't tell the slaves, because—well, if everything goes as we hope, you won't be a slave anymore, will you? And they'd all be jealous of you.

"You must have heard the story, haven't you, of how the great families came to live here under the mountain?" She put her hand on his arm. Gard thought of telling her that he had heard the story from Triphammer, but he held his tongue and only nodded.

"And you may have heard that we're all trapped here—the mages and their children, and their children's children, forever. But it's not exactly true."

"No, lady?"

"No. You see, my own grandfather was the greatest mage of them all. Grand Magister Porlilon, that was his title. All the other mages were jealous of his power; that was why they so traitorously murdered him. But, just before he was killed, he was working on a spell of terrific power. It would have broken the mountain and freed us all, if he had lived to perform it.

"All this while, my family have preserved his workbook, with his last great spell written therein. Alas! We were none of us his equal. I'm a weak little thing on my own, the last of my great line. The other mages have studied it and thrown their hands up in despair. It would take a truly great mage to make that spell work. They know they haven't such power.

"But *you*—you, dear Icicle, have such strength! So you will be trained. You will become a mage. If you are good enough, you will be made free!

And perhaps you will be able to work Porlilon's last spell. Oh, such power you might have! Wouldn't you like that?"

"Yes, lady. I would like power very much."

3rd day 3rd week 9th month in the 248th year from the Ascent of the Mountain. This day, Slave 4372301 registered as an adept-in-training at the request of Lady Pirihine.

On a certain day, Gard was given a white loincloth to wear, and blindfolded, and led by Vergoin along several dank and echoing corridors. The tunnels slanted at first up and then down. In some parts the air was warm and steamy, and in others quite cold. At last they came into a place where echoes fell silent. Gard was stopped and felt Vergoin's hand drop from his shoulder.

There was a long, long silence then. Gard, annoyed with all the pretense, focused his attention and slipped out of himself a little. He perceived that he stood in a low and wide chamber in pitch-blackness. Along one wall was a long bench. Here were seated several hooded figures, and by each stood a slave robed and masked all in black, holding a dark lantern.

One of the hooded figures gestured in silence for his slave, who obligingly opened the lamp's shutter just far enough to allow a finger of light to glimmer out. By its illumination the hooded figure was able to peer at an hourglass, watching as the last grains ran out. He nodded and gestured an order at the slave. The slave closed the shutter once more, then reached up into the gloom and struck a gong.

When its single note died away, the nearest of the figures threw back his hood, just as his attendant slave opened his lantern's shutter. It bathed the master's face in an ominous and bloody light; his head seemed to be floating in fathomless darkness. A Translator popped up and added its light to the chamber.

"Unveil your eyes, slave," intoned the master. Gard pulled away his blindfold gladly and blinked a moment in the darkness. The effect of the floating head looked even sillier when seen through eyes of flesh.

Their power has dwindled, thought Gard. *Else they wouldn't need tricks with colored lanterns.*

"Is this the slave who calls himself Gard?"

Vergoin spoke, from somewhere behind Gard. "He is, master and mage."

"And he is brought before us as a candidate for initiation into our mysteries?"

"He is, master and mage."

"And who will speak for him? Who will testify that he is worthy?"

"I will, master and mage."

"And I," said another voice, hushed and trembling; Gard recognized it as Magister Naryath's.

"And I," said a woman's voice, Lady Pirihine's.

The red lantern was extinguished. A master on the far side of the room jabbed his lamp bearer rather impatiently, and a moment later the master's bald head appeared to be swimming forward in a pool of golden light.

"Three have spoken for you, candidate. Now you will be tested."

A slave hurried forward with his lantern, opening its shutter to throw light on a squat stone column that had been placed in the middle of the room.

"Bring water forth from the stone!"

Gard knit his brows. He looked for tricks, for hidden pipes, and saw none. He focused once again, went out of himself, and saw that the solid stone was no more than a mass of spinning lights. They moved in a certain pattern that made them appear as stone.

But . . . if they moved in a different pattern . . .

He surveyed the room, spotted a cup of water at the elbow of a palsied old master, who sipped from it frequently. The cup was a thin shell of lights flying in one pattern, but the lights it contained had their own dance. That was water.

He studied the dance, then turned his attention back to the stone. Could he make the lights change their pattern of movement? Only some of them . . . some of the lights would have to be discarded.

Gard reached out with his spirit self and, in a gesture that was like raking his hand through the lights but did not involve a hand or an arm, changed the lights' pattern.

The stone crumbled. Water rose from it in a jet, glittering in the light from the lamp. "He has done it!" murmured the palsied master, and there were indrawn breaths from the other masters, but one spoke with firm, raised voice:

"Now from the water and stone, bring forth earth."

That much would be easy, for the trick was obviously in the play of lights. Gard sent the water jet spurting up to the ceiling of the cavern, where it splattered and rained down. Of the stone, nothing was left but a handful of dry, sandy earth.

He saw the masters' concentration sharpen, now, and the bald-headed mage's eyes bulged with . . . fear? Eagerness?

"From the earth, now bring forth fire," the mage commanded.

Easier still to do. Gard looked on the mazy lights that were the discarded residue of the stone. He made them dance, and dance more quickly still. There was air, there was fuel, and in the friction of their dance now a spark. A little tongue of flame arose from the powdered earth.

Gard looked with contempt on the mages in their theatrical darkness, their concealed lamps. He made the flame seek out different elements in the powder; he divided the flames and sent them shooting out above the heads of the masters, balls of fire in red, in gold, in blue and green. There they hung burning, as the slaves exclaimed and the old men and women gasped for air. Gard heard Lady Pirihine clap her hands, he heard Vergoin murmur triumphantly, "I *told* you!"

And a voice murmured in his inner ear, gently mocking, *Show-off.* He turned, startled, and saw that one of the black-swathed slaves stood directly behind him. Black robes were not enough to disguise Balnshik's figure.

He let the lights burn out. There was a moment of silence. At last the bald mage said, "It is the judgment of this board that the slave is acceptable and will be trained."

Now his life became arduous once more, not least because the Narcissus of the Void seemed to desire his body's service more than ever. She invited rather than commanded, she prattled and teased and showered him with sweetmeats and trinkets. Even so, as he coupled with her in grim silence, he hated her, and the song ran again in his head: *If I ever get out of here . . .*

It ran in his head as Gard followed the course of study he had been set, for in all ways his work was monotonous as striking air with a pointed stick. He must learn to grind and compound incense; he must learn to cut and prepare herbs, and press oils, and distill waters and essences and attars.

He was apprenticed in turn to each of the masters, learning to detest each of them: Paglatha, the bald one, irritable and given to striking him across the knuckles when he made an error in General Thaumic Theory. Hoptriot, cold and enigmatic behind his skin mask, who taught him the dissection of corpses for the harvest of certain necessary parts. Flaktrey, blue-lipped, ancient and breathless, who was prone to stroking Gard's face as he taught him the correct pronunciation of certain spells. Pread, he who bore the mark of Balnshik's lash with smug content, who oversaw as Gard learned sums, then geometry, then algebra arcane, and at last Ipsissimal Calculus.

Sometime in these months, as he added to his store of languages arcane and modern, the Translators stopped appearing. He learned that they were drawn to ignorance and confusion, as fish are drawn to crumbs scattered on a pool, and he was no longer providing them with much of either.

He was granted, still, his two hours in the day for honing his skills in the fighters' hall, and was grateful. There Gard vented his sullen anger in violent exercise. All rage burned away, he was the better able to concentrate on his studies until day's end. Then, alone in his alcove once more, he meditated and let any residual anger drift away like vapor. So Gard heated and cooled, a tempering sword.

———

"And how is the young wonder of the world?" said a lazy voice behind him, one day when he had just run a practice dummy through the heart. He turned and saw Balnshik taking down a practice blade. "You're looking fit; I had expected you to be pale and nearsighted by this time."

"They aren't letting me near their books yet," he said, grinning at her. "Will you strive with me, madame?"

"I should love to," she said, and went on the attack. He blocked and beat back, focusing, and went out of himself. To his delight, she did the same. She appeared to him as a drift of blue smoke, shot through with violet sparkles. They circled slowly above their vaulting bodies, and no onlooker could have told their attention was anywhere but on the play of blade on blade.

My, my, you have learned. He heard her voice clearly, though it had not emanated from her throat.

Can you hear me? he inquired.

Of course I can, dear.

Can you see me, like this?

Oh, yes.

What do I look like?

Like leaf shadows and the light through leaves at high summer. If one subtracted the trees. And the sun. Quite nice, really.

Couple with me! Like this!

He felt rather than heard her laughter. *My dear child, one requires flesh for that particular act.*

Oh.

You see, now, why our people can be tempted into flesh and trapped there? I hear that you're getting a great deal of pleasure out of Lady Pirihine.

She's getting pleasure out of me. I hate her. She had Triphammer killed!

Poor little Triphammer. Yes, I saw that. But he's free now, at least.

Would I be able to see him again, like this?

No, dear. The Children of the Sun go on to another place when they disembody. Only we—which is to say demons—inhabit this place naturally. You, being what you are, may walk in both worlds. Only one of the qualities that make you so valuable to our masters, I suspect.

How did I come to be? Do you know?

How should I, dear? Other than the rather obvious fact that some demon found a man or maid of the Earthborn fair and took flesh to lie with them. Tell me, how were you found? Wrapped in a blanket and left where you'd be noticed quickly?

No. I was just—dropped. Like an animal. They found me by my crying.

Ah. Then I would say your father was the Earthborn, and your mother was the demon. Don't think the less of her for abandoning you; it would have taken all the flesh she could manifest to make you, and she'd have disembodied the moment you came into the world.

Couldn't she have taken on flesh again?

Only by eating you, dear.

Oh.

And now you are to become a mighty mage! Very unusual for our masters to share their knowledge, you know. They have never admitted a slave to their august ranks before. Don't you find that a little strange?

I am more powerful than they are. The learning is easy! I can see the spells, I can see the lights moving in things when the magic works, and they can't see them. Worn-out old fools, all of them.

And so concerned that you stay in the prime of physical health. Remarkable, isn't it? . . . Is it?

I would have said so, yes. Of course, I'm not in the habit of giving advice to such powerful and clever fellows as famous Gard the Icicle . . . but if I were, I might be inclined to tell him never to reveal to anyone that he can see spell structures. And to study any propositions made to him very, very carefully indeed.

Would you really?

I would. But I have not done so, for, if I did, I should disobey the command of silence laid on me by my master. And I never disobey his commands. And why should you need a warning from me? Doubtless you will rise to a seat on the high council one day, if you continue your astonishing progress.

I don't want a seat on their council. When I'm powerful enough, I'll escape from this place. I'll go back to the valley where I was born and I'll slaughter the Riders, all of them, at a blow, with fires of retribution! I won't leave a stone of their houses standing. My—my brother's people can live there in peace again.

Impressive. What will you do then?

I . . . perhaps they will welcome me, if I free them.

Perhaps they will.

A silence, while they beat back and forth, and lunged, and parried, and the bright steel rang like bells.

I will consider the warning you didn't give me.

Spoken like a wise child.

Gard progressed, over the months and following years, to ordeals by no means boring. In one trial, he must stay awake for seven days and nights together, watching a seething kettle the whole time, waiting for the seven-second interval in which the mixture turned a suspicious and livid blue, in order that he might plunge in his hand without hurt and draw forth a lump of blue ointment, and drop it at once in a basin of cold water and present the same to Magister Tagletsit. What Magister Tagletsit wanted with it, Gard was not told.

In his apprenticeship to Magister Karane, Gard was to memorize spells of a thousand words, then a thousand lines, then a thousand pages. Three mistakes Gard was permitted, but on the fourth Magister Karane seized a blade and cropped Gard's ears, as a punishment for not hearing better. Gard bore it without a word, though Lady Pirihine raged at his disfigurement. Gard mastered the trick of deep memory at last. The week after, Magister Karane most unwisely ate of a gift of sugared violets he had been sent by an unknown admirer and died in agony within minutes. The Narcissus of the Void was seen to smile, but did not notice that Gard's ears had already begun to grow back.

He mentioned it to Balnshik, the next time he met her in the Training Hall. She inspected his ears and smiled. "You're surprised? I thought you knew you were one of the Changeless. Surely the fact that you walk without crutches now gave you some idea?"

"No," said Gard. "What does Changeless mean?"

Balnshik gestured at her own body. "I am one. We wear this flesh by default, but as long as we wear it, it neither fades nor withers. The very oldest demons are Changeless, and I'm quite old. Half-breeds are all Changeless, for some reason. Rather lucky, given all their other disadvantages."

But Gard thought of Teliva's curse: *Long life to him indeed, so long, too long . . .*

Magister Hohnduhl taught him spells that were chanted or sung and congratulated him on his strong voice and perfect pitch. Gard wove complex nets of music that lit fires, that created illusions or broke targets.

He was proud of himself until the night he realized that this was what Ranwyr had striven so hard to learn, without success; and the truth had been simply that Ranwyr was tone-deaf. All the holiness in the world would not have made him an effective disciple of the Star's. The unfairness of this, and the growing awareness that the Star had not been entirely false after all, drowned Gard deep in black anger and sorrow.

Magister Paglatha taught him the spells that required sacrifices and led him down to the pens from which suitable victims were chosen. Now Gard must in horror choose between manacled slaves condemned to death and idiot children kept penned like animals. No demons were here, for only a true death imparted any virtue to a spell; and Magister Paglatha explained that careful discernment was required in the choice of a victim.

Magic, he explained, as any other endeavor, required certain expenditures. A fire must have fuel to burn, a child must have food to grow; so any spell must feed on thaumic energy. Energy might be generated in several ways, but the most reliable was by sacrifice. An object might be sacrificed. A virtue might be sacrificed. Best of all, in terms of the power it generated, a life might be sacrificed.

The slaves might be more robust, but brought only the crudest energy to spell work. The imbeciles, on the other hand, being of the masters' own noble blood, made a more perfect and poignant sacrifice. Moreover, said Magister Paglatha, their use in this way made for excellent thrift.

Gard could not bring himself to reach in among the children, where they mewled and rocked themselves to and fro. He pointed instead at the condemned slaves, and one was hauled forth for his use.

He was relieved when they apprenticed him at last to Magister Prazza, whose specialty was the summoning and embodiment of demons.

In Magister Prazza's casting chamber, a great book contained all the true names of demons bound to the mountain, with colored ribbons beside those that had lately been slain in the arena. Magister Prazza, who was small and bent and scarcely able to speak above a whisper, taught Gard the formulas for calling them back from their brief freedom.

Demons must be lured; they must be caught and held by certain signs. The more powerful ones must be cajoled and promised pleasures.

Before any such negotiation, bodies must be made ready for them, out of a certain dense clay brought up from the depths in great tubs. Gard learned to sculpt bone and sinew, organs and flesh, and was now grateful for what he had learned in Magister Hoptriot's dissecting chamber. Carefully he gave his figures strong limbs, eyes and tongues, anything he would not want to lack himself; bitterly he regretted his mistakes, when the clay transmuted and a new-bodied demon would limp away from him on legs of unequal length or gasp openmouthed for want of nostrils.

Overall, however, Gard showed great aptitude in this field. Magister Prazza grew cordial with so promising a student, and loaned him scrolls on the subject of advanced divination techniques for learning the true names of demons. By this means Balnshik, far too old and wise to be tricked into telling her name, had nonetheless been caught by her master, though her name was not in the Slave Inventory; Magister Pread jealously kept it secret. Gard took the scrolls back to his rooms—for he had now been granted a suite of his own, adjoining Lady Pirihine's—and studied them closely.

———

Late one night he retreated to his inmost room and improvised a casting chamber, muffling the walls with black drapes. Certain circles within circles he chalked on the floor; certain incense he cast on coals, prudently setting the brazier under a vent lest he die like a fool of asphyxiation. An offering of wine Gard set out. Last of all he took an athalme and gashed his arm, and let the blood drops fall on certain characters he had chalked within the circle.

He sat without the circle, focused, and went out of himself. Rising above, he called. Out across the void of light, he called, and the shifting star clouds heard him. Some echoed him. He called, insistent. At last one across the infinite distance turned, as though curious. Gard had no name for her, but he called with his shed blood, and that was enough to pull her to him; for the blood had once run in her own veins.

Gard opened his eyes. He saw the veiled light trapped within his chalked circle, spinning, shifting, a blur the color of blossoms and flesh. Now and again some of it coalesced into images: a hand, a hundred hands, an eye, teeth, a pair of legs, a profile. Gard caught his breath as he recognized the face. It resembled that of the woman he had seen, lying down with the man at the edge of the dancing green, at the start of his every meditation.

A deep-throated growling filled the room, though she had no throat with which to make the sound.

No, no, no, I don't want . . . how did you catch me? Who are you? What? What is it you want?

Gard mastered himself. *What is your name?*

A sparkle in the whirling lights suggested scornful laughter. *You think I'll tell you? Conjure away, little thing.*

No. Listen to me! You lay with an Earthborn man once.

Oooooohhhh, pleasure . . . no, I didn't. Wait, yes, I did. Pretty man. All alone where they danced. I saw what he wanted and I became her, ha ha, I made myself flesh out of the apple blossoms, wasn't I clever?

Yes, yes, you were clever.

And the lilies and the little, white, starry ones and the soft flesh of a doe carrying young and melons and the dew on the grasses. All sorts of things. I made a very nice body. We had delight. We had it for hours. I left him sleeping.

Who was he?

Who?

The man!

Some man, I don't know. An Earthborn.

You had a child by him.

What? No, of course I didn't. Oh! Wait. There was young. It kicked a lot. I was glad when it dropped.

I was that child.

You? No, silly, that was a baby. You're a man.

Time has passed. I grew. I am your son.

Son? . . . What's this wine for? Can I have some?

Gard looked at her, despairing. He tried again: *You are my mother.*

Mother? . . . What nice-looking wine.

Did you give me a name, Mother?

I don't remember. Maybe if I had some wine, I'd remember.

Gard sat back, exhaled. *Take the wine. But don't remember.*

The wine in the offering bowl smoked, it bubbled and hissed away into scented steam. Gard had been going to ask her to give him a name, if she had not done so in the hour of his birth; but he saw now what folly this would be.

When the wine was gone, the demoness seemed to sigh; she took more of a woman's shape, of beautiful hues like a meadow in spring.

Ahhh. I liked that. So you are the child I bore?

I am.

All grown-up now. You're handsome.

Thank you.

Well, what do you want?

Nothing, now.

I can kill someone for you, if you like. Fetch you something.

Thank you. Perhaps another time.

You are one of us. How are you able to do this? With the trapping circle?

I was born in flesh. I walk in both worlds.

How interesting. Well. Can I go now?

Yes.

Gard released her from his will, and she soared away, like a bird from his hand, like a fish into the river's current.

When he told Balnshik about it later, she patted his shoulder in sympathy, but shrugged. "I think she must be rather young," she said, tactful as ever.

————

9th day 4th week 5th month in the 250th year from the Ascent of the Mountain. This day, Slave 4372301 granted right of person. Assigned the name Gard, of the house of Magister Porlilon through affiliation. Registered as Adept, Magister-in-Training.

————

Gard stood again before the council of mages, but this time there was no business with colored lights or darkness; only full colorless light on a council of greedy-looking old men and women, gazing at him intently. He wore the red loincloth now. As he stood before them, Grattur came, bearing a red robe, and draped it across his shoulders.

"You have proven yourself able, Gard of Porlilon's house," said Magister Paglatha. "Worthy of your liberty, worthy of the great house that has lifted you from the dust. And, perhaps, worthy of our noble company. There remains but one test."

The Narcissus of the Void nodded. Engrattur stepped forth, looking rather nervous. He knelt before Gard, presenting him with a great book. It was blackened, as though it had been scorched, plain and battered-looking; no jewels set here, nor any letters of gold. But when Gard took it in his hands, he felt the power crackling and humming through it.

"This is the workbook of Most Exalted Magister Porlilon," said Magister Paglatha. "Study it well. Within you will find the notes for his last great composition, which is the spell that would have released us all from our captivity within this mountain, had he lived to perform it. Many great mages have attempted it; none have succeeded. If you are able to succeed where so many have failed, then you will indeed be worthy, not only of a seat on this council, but *the* seat, and you shall rule us all. Do you dare attempt this, Gard of Porlilon's house?"

Gard looked up at them, with the same quiet stare with which he had faced his opponents in the arena. His eyes were blank. One or two of them smiled in their sleeves, to think what a simple great beast he was, for all his power.

"Yes," he said.

"I think perhaps I should like to marry you, Gard," said Lady Pirihine, lounging back on his bed. Grattur and Engrattur, standing to attention to either side of her, exchanged uneasy glances.

"I am unworthy of such honor, lady," said Gard, not looking up from his work.

"Not before, but certainly *now*, don't you think? We ought at least to have a child together."

Gard remembered the imbecile children penned for sacrifice. "I do not think that is possible, lady."

"You never know. You're so splendidly vigorous, I'm sure I'd have a great lusty son. You've been practically adopted, as it is; we might make another Porlilon the Great. He'd grow up a prince, you know, because you'll rule the council after you work the Great Spell."

"What does Lord Vergoin think of this, lady?"

Lady Pirihine tossed her head. "He loves me like a brother and has always wanted what was best for me. And he has always wished *you* well. He'd be happy for us."

"Unfortunately, lady, the Great Spell requires that its practitioner remain celibate beforehand," Gard lied.

"It does?" Lady Pirihine sat up. "For how long?"

"As long as possible. The greater the period of abstinence, the stronger the chances of success," said Gard solemnly.

"Oh." Lady Pirihine looked at him, seemingly with genuine regret. "Then I really ought to leave you to your studies, oughtn't I?"

"It would aid my concentration, lady."

"And you must be able to concentrate, after all." The Narcissus of the

Void rose from his bed with a sigh. "Slaves, attend me in my private chamber."

Grattur and Engrattur grinned at each other, as they followed her out.

———

Whatever his descendants might be, Porlilon had been a great mage. His book was wound through with spells that rose above the open pages like fretwork of red and golden light, invisible to anyone else, but Gard saw them clearly; the more so when he went out of himself, to regard them with a demon's eye. Then the mage's whole intent stood forth in solid detail, a living design, magnificent.

Porlilon had written commentary in the margins, detailed notes on each spell, as though talking to himself, and all in a code that took Gard weeks to decipher. Gard worked through the simpler spells first, learning what thaumic energy was required to shatter a wall with a wave of his hand, or to deflect the flight of arrows.

He formed a grudging respect for the dead mage; for though he himself found the mechanism of the magic transparently obvious, no such insight had been granted to Porlilon. The old man had done every step of his spells blind, by calculation, with an exactitude that approached art. Gard discovered rows of figures in the margins too, carefully worked out to the last tiny fraction of energy expenditure.

———

In a late hour, though all hours looked the same under the mountain, Gard peered down at the last page of the Great Spell. He scowled; he rose from his chair to fetch a pair of candlesticks and set them by the guttering lamp beside which he had been reading, and ignited both with a gesture. By fresh white light he reread the last column of Magister Porlilon's figures.

"But that's wrong," he murmured to himself. He took paper and ink, and dipped his pen and copied the figures at the top of the column. He worked the sum through on his own, expecting any moment to find the decimal-point error that would make sense of what he had just read. Yet the result was unchanged. There was no error in the figures. The mistake must be greater, more fundamental, a flaw in the spell's very conception.

So accustomed had Gard grown to the precision and perfection of the old mage's work, he felt now the sort of dismay he might feel watching a dignified elder roll, drunk as a demon, in the dust.

The Great Spell could not possibly have worked. The energy it would require would be greater by a factor of ten than the amount stated in the opening conjecture.

Gard rose and paced, attempting to control his panic. Had Porlilon been a fraud? Or had his Great Spell been incomplete, at his murder?

He went to the book once more. No, the spell had been completed; for here underneath its last line was the mage's glyph, as he drew it under each completed spell, a bird of prey gripping a rose of five leaves in either foot.

But the right-hand rose was oddly truncated. . . .

The truth struck home. Gard snapped his pen in two pieces.

He concentrated, went out of himself, and saw the second spell laid over the page, the cloud that obscured the rose and what was written in the margin beside it and below. It had not been placed there by Magister Porlilon. Sweeping it back was as arduous as moving coiled chain, but it gave way to Gard's will, and he read thereunder what had been concealed from him.

Who among us would be willing? Anyone so great a fool as to miss the obvious would, alas, be incapable of the skill required to perform it. And they are selfish and fearful.

Perhaps our best hope is in the distillation of our blood through intermarriage. It may be that a few generations may produce some prodigy capable of working this with success. If the child is detected early and persuaded, from his earliest years, how glorious and necessary his self-sacrifice and death would be . . . indeed, persuaded that any other destiny were unthinkable for such a hero . . . perhaps promised a paradisal afterlife?

But it must be done in the very first bloom of his power, before said child is wise enough to sense the deception.

The room was, suddenly, much brighter. Gard looked up and saw that the force of his wrath had made the candle flames huge, so the wax was nearly all consumed. The fire was roaring high in the hearth, green and silver. He watched as, one by one, his lamp and then every drinking vessel in the room shattered.

His white anger subsided, froze into ice adamantine. Calmly he rose, fetched fresh candles, and lit them. He swept up the broken glass. Only then did Gard seat himself again, and turn the pages back to look once more at the opening prescription. Yes; here was the second spell, subtly altering the original figures for thaumic expenditure.

Gard sat a while in thought, his black brows knitted.

At last he found another pen. He opened his own workbook and placed it beside the one he had been studying all this while. He began to write.

Now and again he referred to the old book, copying out whole passages with exact faithfulness. Now and again he copied other passages and made significant alterations in them.

––––––––

Duke Silverpoint was extinguishing the lamps in the Training Hall when Gard entered. He turned, surveyed Gard, and raised his eyebrows.

"How might an old slave serve the redoubtable Gard, of the house of Magister Porlilon?"

Gard scowled in embarrassment. He held up the bottle of wine he had brought. "This is a vintage from the lands of your people. I would like to drink it with you."

"Would you?" Silverpoint took the bottle and looked at it. "Ah. Rare vintage, indeed. It's from the islands; some of them are nothing but stepped terraces of vineyards. At harvesttime the boats are decked with vine leaves, the black grapes are piled to the oarlocks, and the rowers sing as they ply the waters to and fro.

"You don't mean to get drunk, I hope. Those of your race lose all discretion, when they become drunk."

"I will not get drunk," said Gard, following the duke into his chambers.

Silverpoint nodded. He took down matched goblets, opened the wine, and poured. He offered one to Gard, with a slight ceremonial bow. They sat to either side of Silverpoint's hearth, speaking awhile of trivial things, and then:

"Did I ever tell you how much I enjoyed *The Fighting Mind?*" said Gard.

"You did not. I am gratified. It seemed to me that you, of all people, might make use of it."

"It is a shame the prince did not live to complete it."

"He had not written it out in full, at the time of his death, but he had indeed completed it. I sat with him, as I am sitting with you now, over a bottle of this same wine. He laid out for me the final chapter. We talked until nightfall, but I left him early, for my father disliked my late rising and would lock the house gate after the seventh hour.

"The next morning the prince went out on some matter of business and was set upon by retainers of House Beatbrass—they were old enemies, the Firebows and the Beatbrasses, you know. Four against one, and he took his death wound, but he slew them first.

"I can still recite his last chapter, so well I remember that night."

"Perhaps," said Gard, "in that case, you would explain something to me."

"And what would that be?"

Gard set his wine aside. "I noticed that the prince referred to a discipline he called the Second Mind. He implied that it could disguise a man's intention even from himself, misleading anyone who might see into his thoughts. It sounded as though it would have been explained in the last chapter."

"Yes."

"Did he teach you the Second Mind?"

Silverpoint swirled his wine in its goblet and tilted it up to drink deep. He set the empty goblet down. "At this moment, I must ask myself two questions. The first is, do you truly need to know?"

"I think I do. What's the second question?"

"Do *I* truly need for you to know?"

Gard looked into Silverpoint's eyes, then spoke to him in the language of the Children of the Sun, in the archaic form used for coded speech. "Thou hast prepared a weapon, all these years. Art thou now prepared to draw it and kill with it?"

Silverpoint smiled. "My son, it is thine hour. I have one last lesson for thee."

There at the table, he taught Gard the discipline of the Second Mind.

On the day he was to perform the Great Spell, Gard was awakened by a torrent of spiced fortified wine, dashed in his face. He sat bolt upright, sputtering, wiping his eyes.

"You clumsy fool!" he heard Grattur wailing.

"My lord Icicle, I'm sorry!" cried Engrattur.

"Wake him with a nice drink, our lady told you!"

"And here I've gone and drowned you with it! Oh, I'm sorry!"

"Jackass, fetch him a basin of water!"

"Here's water, my lord, here's soap and a towel!"

"It's all right," Gard told them. He felt curiously lighthearted, even disposed to laugh as he rose and washed sugared wine from his hair and beard. Grattur and Engrattur hovered close, wringing their hands.

"May we lay out your robes?"

"May we change your sheets and pillowcase?"

"I wouldn't bother about the bed," Gard said. "This is the day we go free, remember?"

"Oh! Never to sweep these floors again!" said Grattur joyously.

"Never to make these beds!" said Engrattur, recovering a little from his mortification.

"But you might lay out my clothes." Gard shivered as he dried himself. "Strange! I'm chilled through. Is something the matter with the hypocaust, do you think?"

Grattur and Engrattur looked at each other. "It seems all right to us."

"The Pumping Station crew are hard at work."

"Here are warm clothes in your wardrobe, my lord, trousers and boots."

"Here's a long shirt and a jerkin with a hood."

"He can't wear those under his robe, dolt, he'll be too warm!"

"He *said* he was chilled through, didn't he?"

"I'll wear them," said Gard. "The robe is light stuff, only made for show. Lay them out."

They dressed him, solicitous and ceremonial, and their fussing did not dispel his good mood. "Madame Balnshik sends her love, my lord."

"She told us to wish you luck."

"She isn't coming to watch?" Gard felt wistful a moment, before the sun of his happiness shone out again.

"She sends her regrets, but she has duties," said Grattur.

"Says she has to see to her master's goods," added Engrattur, and snorted with laughter.

"I'm sure I'll see her afterward," said Gard.

"Yes, she said you would."

"You're our hero, after all, you're *our* boy!"

He let them drape him in the magister's robe, to which he had been given only provisional right; but Gard felt confident of success. "What's the stick for, my lord?"

"What's the bag for? It's heavy!"

"The stick's for the spell," said Gard, taking it from Grattur. He tilted it down and showed them the lump of chalk at its end, bound there with leather strips. "See? I won't have to crouch on the floor to inscribe the circles and lines."

"Clever!"

"You always were a bright lad."

"And the bag is heavy with my casting apparatus, and the book of the Great Spell."

"Oh, that was a heavy book, I remember!"

"Shall we carry it for you?"

"No, no," said Gard, though as he took the bag, it was heavier than he had thought it would be. He shouldered it anyway, and took the chalking stick with his free hand. "Now, in the cupboard there you'll find eight bottles of good Sulemian wine. That's my gift, for faithful friends. Go drink to my success."

They wept their gratitude and prostrated themselves. As Gard strode forth, he heard the first of the bottles being opened.

He saw no one in the corridors, all the way to the great casting chamber, and when he entered it by the lower door, he saw why: half the population of the mountain was ranked upon the high seats above. All the surviving council, every scion of the great houses, the very cream of the mountain's society were all there, dressed in their heraldic colors. There was applause at his entrance, and he slung down his heavy bag and bowed to them all.

Their eyes glittered like diamonds. Gard remembered his time in the arena, when they had watched him like this. He felt proud, and happy, to think that he had progressed so far, risen so high.

He lit the braziers. He opened his bag. There on top was the box of incense, and just under it the book. He drew them forth. The incense to the braziers, the book to the lectern. He opened the book, noted well the necessary circles and inscriptions, and, taking up his chalk stick, marked them out on the floor.

A thoughtful mutter came from the galleries above. This inlaid floor was the very same where he had been deflowered, where the Narcissus of the Void had delighted in the power it had generated. He marveled, now, that it had so embittered him at the time. He looked up sidelong and spotted her, seated next to Vergoin. She gave him a nervous little smile. He smiled back.

Setting the chalk stick by the bag, Gard turned to the lectern and read for the preliminary incantation.

At once a green light appeared around him, ran from him like syrup and spread out across the floor. His audience gasped in admiration, leaned forward to see more clearly. With the first of the invocations, a spiral of red light came slowly down from the ceiling, a vortex of blood and fire, and hummed slowly as it spun above the floor.

One or two of those present applauded. They were struck to silence by their elders. Magister Paglatha had clenched his fists into boxes of bone; Magister Naryath was sweating again, so much his silent attendant took a kerchief and tucked it into his collar to catch the drops. He waved her away unseeing, intent on what was happening below.

With the second invocation a second vortex was formed, golden as the painful light of dawn, rotating about the other. There were no sounds in the chamber, now, but their droning song, and Gard's resonant voice as he read from his book.

He turned the page and saw at its top the four words he had written there:

You will awaken now.

His pleasant fog vanished instantly. He glanced up and saw what he had done so far; saw the massed gaze of his audience fixed on the whirling lights. With a cold and black satisfaction in his heart, he read aloud the next invocation, the one that he himself had written.

At first it seemed that nothing followed his words. There were little, flickering shadows high up; then they came streaming down, snakelike, and darkened. The droning noise changed. It took on a note of menace, of hunger.

"No, no," said Magister Tagletsit aloud. "That's wrong, surely—"

He was drowned out by the other mages, who began to shout.

"Idiot! You mispronounced something!"

"It's going wrong!"

"Gard! Break it off! Karrabant's Third Dismissal spell, quickly!"

Gard read on, only raising his voice as the howling began, and the bright colors faded and the vortex became a black wind full of knives. There were screams. Green lightning shot up from the floor and struck Magister Paglatha, and Magister Pread, and Magister Hoptriot, and last of all Magister Naryath, flicking aside his slave. Her flesh it ripped away, and a plume of rose-colored light sped forth from the shell, shouting for joy that it was free.

The four mages could not shout, as their lives were devoured by the spell. There was plenty of noise from everyone else, but Gard outcried them all.

"My masters all, pray keep your seats! You all knew it would take blood to break the mountain!"

And this was the last they heard, for there was an explosion then. Light streamed into the chamber, blinding bright. The roar of the black wind faded, but a thunder swelled louder still, made up all of the sound of stone cracking, tunnels falling in, galleries and chambers collapsing, and in a moment more nothing could be seen for the roiling cloud of black dust.

By that time Gard was gone, having grabbed up his chalk stick and his bag in the moment the chamber had broken open. He sprinted for the broken wall, leaped through, and kept running.

His boots were well-made, caravanner's boots that gripped the rocks and ice as he scrambled on. When he could no longer hear the sound of the mountain collapsing, he stopped long enough to open his bag. There, where he had hidden them away, were heavy gauntlets and a pair of snow goggles. Below was a warm cloak. At the bottom of the bag were packets of bread and dried meat.

Gard drew the clothing on, closed up the bag. Tilting the stick, he unwound the leather strip and the lump of chalk fell away, revealing the spear point glinting underneath.

Shouldering the bag once more, he ran on.

Low gray stubble in the fields of the strangers, raw earth littered with dead yellow leaves, a greening sickle hanging on a fence; birdcall, the lines of marshfowl streaming off slowly, deserting.

It was thunder weather and the sky was lead, no breath of air in the silent valley when he came down, the man; cloak as dark as a thundercloud, eyes as dark as death or stone. Retribution and death he brought with him, a gift in either hand, as he came though fields grown high with weeds.

No sound now, even the birdcry fallen silent. Beneath his boot a white skull turned. He kicked it from his path, to shatter on the steps of what had once seemed so high a hall; he saw it now for a miserable hut of piled stones. The great black door was standing open wide.

He mounted the steps, he looked in through the door, and there he saw the strangers fallen in their revelry. Bones, white bones lay in the banquet hall, still clutching cups. There upon a sagging couch bones coupled, the ribs a puzzle made of ivory.

He stepped over one who lay across the threshold, one whose skull was broken open by a mattock still in the hole, corroding and green. He descended the stairway to the pit and found it empty. Nothing was in the dark but dust, and smells. He left it by the gate where slaves went out to labor in the fields. No one labored there now. Only the wind cried there.

He crossed the fields, he walked across the land, and all he saw was sere and crumbling, derelict and old, empty, echoing, even the mountain caves. No bones there, nothing at all to reproach him or welcome him home.

Gard stood alone there, a long while.

2

the voice

She wears rags and feathers, with beads and bits of seashell braided in. Flowers are in her hair. Time has hunted her, caught her, torn her, and cast her away; but her voice, when she speaks to you, is still that of the young girl she once was. . . .

I was there that day, beside him. I saw what happened, that day in the wheat field, that day by the river. I saw his miracles. People tell so many lies now! But Meli was there too and we both loved him, and we saw everything.

I don't remember a time before the Beloved. We used to go up the mountain to listen to him teach when I was little, and even then I thought he was the most beautiful man I'd ever seen. His eyes were like silver rain and stars. He was gentle and kind, and his voice made you feel as though everything would be all right, even through the most terrible times.

He gave us fire. He taught us to make pots from clay, knives from flint. He, the Star, taught us to take the white fiber from the burst seedpod and spin it into thread, and he made the loom for us to weave on. He made ink, and brushes, teaching us how to keep our voices in the marks they made.

He came to us, once, when my mother had the fever, and he cured her with a kiss. He kissed her so sweetly, and she opened her eyes. She said afterward it was as though she'd been dying of thirst in cruel summer heat, when suddenly someone gave her spring rain to drink, and washed her soul clean with it too. For hours afterward, the hole we lived in smelled like a night in spring. I loved him then, I wanted to go with him and be with him always.

He saved Meli. She was born in the slave pits, the Riders had been cruel to her there; I think she saw her mother and father killed, but she'd never talk about that. She only said that one night she was crying, alone and afraid in the dark, when starlight and moonlight both came into the slave pit and *he* was there.

The Beloved sang and her chains dropped away. He took her in his arms and walked out with her, *right through a wall.* The overseers didn't see, they didn't hear. He carried her up the mountain to her mother's sister. They had a hiding place near ours.

Meli and I played together. We grew up together, we became sisters. All we wanted to do with our lives was follow the Star.

And so that was what we did, the year we were both fourteen. We climbed to the high place, up by the stars, where he met with his disciples to teach them. It was a long way to go, far past Teliva's Pool and along the ridge, but we could hear the Star singing and it guided us. We came at last out into that open place, where the Beloved sat among his disciples.

We knelt down at the edge, just happy to be there so close to him and listening. We didn't make a sound, but he saw us and smiled at us. I was crying, his song was so beautiful. It was only about the river and the wind, but hidden words in it took away sorrow.

When he stopped singing, all the disciples began to talk, asking him questions about the way some parts of the song went. One by one they went off to sit by themselves and practice it. When we thought it would be polite, we went to him, holding hands. We told him our names and said we'd like to be disciples.

Before he could answer, a disciple turned to us and said, "Little girls, the Star needs his rest. Go home to your mothers."

"No, no," said the Beloved, reaching out to us. "I know them, Lendreth. Come and be with me, Meli. Come and be with me, Seni. Let us talk awhile."

We were so thrilled! He sat with us, and we opened our hearts to him. I told him I'd be happy to do anything, whether it was wash the sores of the sick or walk down into the blackest of the slave pits, so long as I was allowed to wear the white robe. And Meli said the same, which was brave of her.

He told us those were no places for young girls, but he would teach us to care for our people; because, he said, that was what it meant to wear the white robe. We must love them as though they were our children, because we were all one family. We must help one another so that we would still be a strong and good people when the Child came to deliver us from our long sorrow.

We said we'd learn anything he cared to teach us, and hoped that he would take us as lovers too. He smiled and said we were his lovers even now, but still a little young for the cup of delight. Who knew, he said, but that before that cup filled we might not wish to share it with some other lover? And Meli said, and I said too, that we wanted no lover, ever, but only him.

He kissed us welcome, then. He asked whether we had told our families where we had gone. I was ashamed, because we hadn't. So he sent Lendreth down the hill to tell them we were safe. He told us that was our first lesson: that we must love everyone, and so we would never make sorrow for anyone. There was sorrow enough in the world.

———

We were all brothers and sisters together in the high place. No one was afraid, no one was angry, when the Beloved was there. Terrible things happened down in the world below, where the Riders were, and every night our brothers and sisters went down there with the Beloved to ease the poor slaves. They came back sometimes with orphans. We minded the little ones and played with them, just as we had done at home. We learned the songs to make them laugh, to make them forget the things they'd seen.

It was easy for me to learn the songs. It was a little harder for Meli, I don't know why. Power and violent force made her afraid; perhaps they made her remember her old life. Sometimes she woke at night weeping, heartbroken. When the Star came and spoke gently to her, only then were her nightmares banished.

Some of our brothers and sisters had learned to sing all the songs, had even made new ones of their own, and were proud that the Beloved had praised their skill and their power. Some brothers and sisters were better at finding the flowers of ease, the roots that took away fever, and the Beloved praised them too. Everyone had a gift, and no one—then—ever said one gift was better than another.

Every night, when the Beloved came back up to us, we brought water to wash him and kissed away his weariness; for he was only one man, and sometimes our sorrows were heavy enough to bend him down. Luma herself brewed his tea and brought it to him—yes, that one, Luma, who had been sister to Blessed Ranwyr. She was our sister now. I knew her. She had beautiful sad eyes, she was as graceful as a willow tree, and when the Beloved lay down with her, I longed to be her, but I was never jealous.

It was joyous when the Beloved sat in his high place under the stars, and all the people came up to listen to him. It was simple happiness when he'd take his rest among us and lie with his head in Luma's lap and tell us stories to make us laugh. You wouldn't have thought he was anyone then but our father, or our older brother, and we his loving family. Those are the times I remember best, those are the times I miss the most, when I think of how things are now.

One night, under the great tree, he leaned back in Luma's arms and smiled at us. "Time for a tale," he said. "Will you hear a story, my steadfast ones?"

"Please!" I cried, and the others gathered around and they cried too, "Please, Bright One, tell us a story."

"Then I'll tell you something from the old days of the world," he said.

"*Kingfisher was a proud and reckless bird. He prided himself on what a great hunter he was,*

and a fighter too, for he could catch fish and lizards, and beat them on the stones until he killed them.

But for all his courage, he was a dirty, slovenly lord in his own nest,

littered as it was

with fish scales and spoiled food. And he thought his appearance did not quite suit so great a lord among birds;

for he was rather small, and his garment was only a dusty black color.

How he envied Rook, who wore elegant feathers!

"*Oh, Rook's garments were striped in blue and white, he had a fine standing crest, and was tall,*

and had great wisdom besides, being able to speak

and travel between life and death. It happened one day that the weather was very hot. All the birds of the air panted in the shadows. Rook slipped out of his garment, and went to bathe in the river.

Kingfisher saw Rook's shed garment on the river bank, and wanted it; so he stole the fair garment, and pulled off his own, and left his there

for Rook to find.

"*But when Kingfisher dressed himself, he found the stolen garment was too big for him. The standing crest*

*flopped over loosely, and the long tail broke off short the first time he went into his
muddy den.*

And when Rook found his own garment stolen, he pulled on Kingfisher's,
for lack of anything better;
but it was too small, so that his face was left bare around the beak,
it fit him so tightly his walk was stiff and mincing.

*"Now when the other birds of the air laughed at Rook, he was wise enough to pay
them no mind;*
but when they laughed at Kingfisher, in his rumpled feathers
he was bitterly angry,
and dove beneath the water to hide himself. And so it is now: the Rook's serene
in his journey, and the souls he guides between life and death
do not mock his appearance. They are only grateful he is there
to lead them to the place of all rebirth. Lord Kingfisher
(for so he calls himself now)
wears his grand garment carelessly, and has stained his white breast with food.
His dark den still stinks for all the titles he gives himself.
Remember, then, children, the lesson, since I have given you garments:
you do not change your nature
with your robe."

Lendreth raised his hands and praised the Beloved; we all gave thanks.
Then some of them leaned forward eagerly, as they always did, to dispute
what the story meant.

"Are we the Rooks then, Beloved, and the Riders are the Kingfishers?"
said Jish.

"No, no, sister, the Beloved is more subtle than that," said Lendreth.
"And in any case the birds of the air are part of the natural world, as we
are, rooks and kingfishers both. The Riders are outside of nature, no part
of its shaping."

"I would have said the story is a warning against pride," said Shafwyr.
"And that we must perfect ourselves, before we presume to wear the white
robe."

"Or then again, perhaps the Rook is meant to be the Blessed Ranwyr,
and in that case the Kingfisher—," began Lendreth, then realized his dis-
courtesy: for Luma was present. How could anyone want to bring pain to
poor Luma, by reminding her of Cursed Gard? Lendreth was clever and
powerful, but seldom compassionate.

He coughed. "In that case, the Kingfisher represents the forces of ignorance and violence," he finished.

The Beloved only smiled, and taking Luma's hand, he kissed it. "Am I such a subtle man? Let's ask little Meli. What did the lesson mean, Meli, fair one?"

"That we do not change our natures with our robes," she said.

"And there you have it," said the Beloved.

I never understood why they made everything so complicated, the disciples. So many nights I would have been content to lie still and listen to the Beloved sing, under the stars; but there was always Lendreth or one of the others wanting to ask him questions.

"What is the nature of evil?" they wanted to know. I would have thought it was plain enough; evil was what the Riders did to us, hunting us and killing us, making us slaves. They burned the forests. They fouled the river. That was evil. Always the Star answered them simply, and plainly, and yet they could never seem to understand on one hearing.

Once, they disputed for months over whether it was right or wrong to plant things in the earth, since that was something the Riders had made us do. Were we not forcing the earth to give us something, rather than accepting the gifts she gave of her own accord? Was a scythe a wicked thing, since it did violence to the grain?

Or, which was the holier pastime, while we waited for the Promised Child to free us all: meditating and perfecting mastery of the Songs, or simply washing the sores of the sick, healing the wounded, caring for the orphans?

Or, had the Riders come among us as a secret gift, since by their cruelty we had been forced to a higher understanding of the world, whereas if they had never come, we might have continued in our ignorance of the Songs?

There was no truth but they could not cut it into tiny pieces, looking for hidden meanings.

Meli and I grew older, we grew tall, and at last the Star went to the bowers with us and we shared the cup of delight. I have had other lovers since, but none like my Beloved; and yet he was not mine only, but Meli's and Luma's and all the sisters'. Some of the brothers thought the less of us, that we so shared the Beloved's body. Yet I never knew such perfect peace as in his arms, I never felt so strong as when I walked out after having been with him.

And I needed strength. You weren't there, you don't know what it was like then; I walked in the slave pits beside him and saw the children born to women in chains. I walked beside him in the fields, unseen by the grace of his power, when we labored with our people to plant, to harvest, so the overseers would not flog them to death in the furrows where they worked.

Meli couldn't go down there at all. She tried once, she wanted to be brave. But when we came within sight of the Riders' high hall, black and squalid with its smoke going up pale in the starlight, she halted, trembled, could not bring herself to move or speak. I went back for her, but she looked at me with wild eyes and seemed to have taken root in the earth. The Beloved himself came and led her back up the mountain, and consoled her when she wept for shame at her fear.

I have heard some fools say the Star judged our poor people, that he only brought rescue to the innocent, the virtuous, and those who had sinned he left in their shackles. Oh, that's a wicked lie! He would have saved them all, if he had had the power. But there were limits to his strength, and he poured it out for us unselfishly.

I saw that, as the years went on. His back was bowed when he came up the mountain from the fields; the Star was tired when he lay down among us. Lendreth and the others would never let him rest, they wanted him to listen to their arguments, to answer their endless questions, though his eyes dimmed to hear them.

Perhaps that was how it started, when the others saw his limits too. I think it must have been around that time that Lendreth, and one or two others who had become masters and mistresses of the Songs, began to wonder whether they might not even surpass the Star in their power.

They never schemed against him. That would have been unthinkable. For all the horror of our days, we were a more innocent people then. But they did begin to think in terms of becoming his successors, should he ever leave us. They grew impatient when the Beloved dallied with us, or when he sang the songs meant only to make us laugh. How could we wreathe his hair with flowers, they wanted to know, when there was so much work to do? How could he tell us jokes when there was so much more to teach us that was important?

And Lendreth, who had a mind that moved in straight lines, came to him and proposed plans: how to better harvest and store the herbs we used, how to organize into shifts so that those who went down the mountain might get enough rest between times.

These changes were for the better, but there were other plans: Lendreth wanted to gather all the free people together and make a single place to live, one great cave or mountain field ringed around with sharpened sticks, so the Riders couldn't get in. He argued that the people would be safer in such places. The Beloved said only that the people would be no better kept in a pit on the mountain than they were kept in a pit in the valley.

Yet Lendreth went around talking to the free families, and some he persuaded to follow his plan. They left the tree hollows and caves and came up, and settled in a field above Teliva's Pool. Lendreth harangued others to come. They came, and stared awhile at the field in its ring of sharpened sticks, with its brushwood shelters under the open sun. Some stayed, unwilling to be impolite. Others faded back into the trees, in ones and twos, and did not come up again.

The next idea Lendreth had was that he, with the great power he had attained, might be able to find a way over the mountains. So he set off on the journey. The Beloved gave him a blessing, and Falena and Jish cut him a staff to help him where the way was rough. When you see all the wise trevanion now, these traveling teachers each with a staff, that was where it started. The Star never carried a staff, except at the end, when he needed one to walk.

Anyway Lendreth was gone a year and a season. He found his way back to us at last, thin and ragged, with a desperate look in his eyes. He spoke alone with the Star a long time. I heard Lendreth weeping, and I heard the Beloved speaking low, comforting him.

But I think Lendreth couldn't be comforted. An anger was in him, after that, a lack of patience. He studied harder, he meditated and fasted, he declined to lie with any of us. He presented the Beloved with new Songs. They were fine and useful Songs, except for the one that broke walls apart. The Beloved rebuked him, gently, over that Song. Why should we wish to break walls, when we could walk through them? The Riders were the ones who broke things.

There were long nights of discussion when Lendreth's voice got louder than anyone else's, and some among the brothers and sisters agreed with the things he said. Now he had disciples of his own, and they thought in straight lines.

But when the Child came to us, she did not come in a straight line.

A man of our people, named Kdwyr, was a prisoner in the slave pits. One summer day he was led out in his shackles to break the ground in a fallow field. The overseers chained him to a plow with two other men. They started them forward across the field.

It had been a dry summer. The earth was baked hard like stone. The two other men were ill with the fever of the pits, and they sweated and gasped as they struggled along. The overseers beat them. Kdwyr was a strong and compassionate man; he begged the overseers to uncouple the sick men from the plow, saying that he would plow the field himself.

The overseers jeered at him, but they let the sick men loose, to lie moaning in the heat of the sun. The overseers stood watching, meaning to laugh as Kdwyr strained to pull the plow.

Now this was the first miracle: the earth broke soft as though it were full of spring rain, and Kdwyr went ahead far down the field.

And this was the second miracle: though it had been hot clear weather, no cloud in the hard blue sky, no breath of wind, yet a sudden fog came up out of the river. It rolled over the field, it hid one man from another, and Kdwyr found himself alone.

And this was the third miracle: as Kdwyr stood looking about him, unable even to hear the overseers shout, his chains fell away from him and he stood free.

And this was the fourth miracle: before him on the ground appeared the shadow of a raven, though neither sun nor raven was to be seen. It was Blessed Ranwyr. The shadow moved away across the field and Kdwyr followed, a long way, crossing fields and meadows.

And the fifth miracle was the greatest, for the shadow of the raven led Kdwyr to a high meadow where lilies grew. In the midst of them was one great lily, with its petals just opened, and a fragrance that was all delight.

And in the lily lay the Child, the little girl newborn, the deliverance sent to us.

She was tiny, perfect, fairer than my poor words can tell. Serene, with the memory of the place from which she had come; but already the weight of the world was settling on her, with the petals bowing down to the earth.

Kdwyr put out his hands in wonder and caught her, before she fell. He put her to his shoulder and she did not cry, though he knew she would soon need milk. As he stood there wondering what to do, the raven's shadow floated on before him, leading him up the mountain.

Kdwyr followed, carrying the Child.

Now on that day the Beloved had not gone down the mountain to the slave pits, because the little blue lilies had just finished blooming, which is the best time to gather their bulbs for salve. He went with us to teach the younger sisters and brothers where to find them. Meli and I went too, and Luma, though Lendreth shook his head; he thought we were only going to take our pleasure with the Beloved.

We on the mountain saw the white mist filling the valley, sudden and haunted. The Beloved put up his hands, and said:

> Someone else has found a lily today,
> The flower we have longed for.
> Little sisters, little brothers, watch now;
> Who comes up the mountain, carrying light?

Luma saw first the raven's shadow, emerging from the mist, coming black and distinct across the summer grass. She knelt, weeping. The insubstantial shade hovered before her a moment. She said afterward she felt a kiss on her brow.

The rest of us watched as the man Kdwyr stepped out from the mist, blinking in the light of the sun. He knew no Songs. He had suffered in the darkness all his life. He was dirty with the filth of the pit, his shoulders were bowed with his labor; but he had found the Child, and in his hands she shone like a little star.

He came to us. Without a word he laid the Child in the waiting hands of the Beloved. Then he sat down and wept.

We did not see when the shadow passed, or where it went.

––––––––––

Of all the days of my life, that day was the best. I held her, these two arms of mine held the little Saint when she wasn't an hour old. We passed her from hand to hand and we wept for happiness, that she had come to us at last. When she woke from her first sleep and looked at us, her eyes were like the Beloved's, full of light; but where his ran with silver like tears, shimmered like the river, her eyes were clear and steady.

"What will happen now, Beloved?" asked Meli. Some of us had looked down into the valley, where the mist was all gone, half expecting the houses of the Riders would have vanished by now. But there they still stood, in the summer sunlight, sending up their smoke and reek.

"Now we will take her to the others," said the Beloved. "Let the free families see her and know that she is with us at last. Bring our brother Kdwyr."

"But my brothers are down there in the fields," said Kdwyr.

"They will soon be free men," said the Beloved. "Come and wash away your sorrows in Teliva's Pool."

We went back to the caves. I will always remember my Beloved as he walked that day in the sunlight, carrying the Child. I have seen statues since, of his smiling figure upright with the little one on his arm, her tiny hand raised in blessing. They never looked like that; on that bright day she was too little to sit up, let alone bless, and by the time she was old enough, he no longer stood so straight and tall.

But that was later. That day, that bright day, there was no sorrow.

The free women with milk in their breasts fed her, our Saint. We wrapped her in songs of praise. The little brothers ran to take the news to the disciples coming up the mountain. Lendreth came up, leading his shift, and when he saw the Child, he fell to his knees and wept, and rejoiced in the promised day.

And then he had questions. "What would she have us do now? How will we free ourselves?"

"I don't know," said the Star.

Lendreth started as though he had been struck in the face. "Don't know?" he repeated. "But you are the Star, and the Promised Child has come."

"She has come to us, yes," said my Beloved, looking down on the little girl where she slept in his arms. "Now it is her time to lead you. I cannot see, any more than you can, what her will is yet. We must wait and find out."

"But she is only a baby," said Lendreth. "Are we to wait until she can speak, to tell us what to do? I thought there would be miracles."

"And so there have been," said the Star. "And shall be. Trust her, Lendreth. Be patient. She has come a long way; let her rest awhile."

Lendreth fell silent, though I could tell from his face that he was disappointed. He wanted facts, he wanted dates and times precise, and he could not have them, because such things are only imaginary. So he sat and ate his heart out of vexation, in the midst of all our joy.

We sang under the sky that night, Meli and Luma and I holding hands together, and all the free people came up and joined us. The Beloved sang too. Our voices rose up to the stars; our voices ran down the mountain like springwater, like silver fire, and the earth throbbed with the power of it. The Child awoke and lay listening to us, and never cried.

In the gray light of morning the Star rose, with the little Saint in his arms. I was already awake. I shook Meli, who woke at once. Luma and the other disciples woke, sitting up one by one to hear what the Beloved would say.

"She is restless," he said quietly. "She knows they are suffering, down there. Lendreth, go ahead; tell them she is coming."

Lendreth jumped up and ran, his heart glad at last.

"Which of us will go with you, Beloved?" asked Luma.

"All are welcome to come with us," he said. "But it will be a long day. You will be weary by the end."

My heart was so light, I didn't see how I would ever be weary again, now that she was with us. We went down the mountain and the free people came too, leaving their caves and hiding places at last. Even Meli found the courage to come with us, now. Down through the forests, across the meadows, as the last stars faded, went my people.

No Riders came out of hiding to harm us. The whole world was silent, as though it were holding its breath. We could see the Riders' halls through the trees, but only one or two thin trails of smoke drifted up from their fires. When we came to the ford at the river, the Star turned and told the free people to wait on their side. There they stayed, in the shadows of the trees, watching us.

We waded across. As we came near the Riders' halls, it seemed to me they smelled worse than ever they had before. And they were quiet, when at this hour of the morning there should have been the noise of wood being cut to feed their fires, and grain being pounded to make their bread. Only, as we came up to the walls, we heard a sound of wailing, and voices raised in anger.

The Beloved walked straight for the wall of the slave pen. We went through, the wall parted like mist for us. Meli shook beside me, but this time she didn't hesitate to go back into that place she remembered. The Child made her brave.

There were gasps, hushed exclamations and sobs in the slave pen when we came through. All our chained people had been waiting, hardly able to believe Lendreth's message. Now they surrounded us, trembling, pushing to get a glimpse of her. In that black place she shone like a star. She exhaled the fragrance of rain, and white flowers.

The Beloved held her up. "She has come to you. She is your sister, your daughter, your mother. Let each one hold her."

The people passed her from hand to hand, stroking her cheek, kissing her brow. She did not fret or squirm or cry. I could see the grace around her like a silver veil, and a little of it lingered with each person who touched her, and they were illuminated. I saw gaunt mothers cradling their own thin children. I saw men worn down with age and sorrow, chain-scarred. I saw orphans, and widows, and people too far gone in fever to know whether they were dreaming this moment.

Where she passed, they sat up whole and well. Their sores closed. Now Lendreth had his miracle! That vile wound in the earth filled with peace, and all the hundreds packed in there were healed.

They did not ask, "When shall we be free?" or, "What shall we do now?" They had no questions for her. She was answer enough.

At last we heard the doors being opened above, and the overseers came down the ramp and started shouting orders. I saw them lift their heads and sniff the air. They looked frightened. Their fear made them cruel. They struck out with whips, needlessly, as our people obeyed them and filed up the ramp.

We walked with them. The overseers did not see us. They were shaking, sweating. We went out, and as we passed the door of the great hall, we heard lamentation. The smell was worse now, breathing out the door as from a sick mouth.

The sun was just rising as we were led to the fields by the river. The sky was hot, blue, and the air was clear and already warm. No wind moved the yellow wheat that bowed its heads.

The overseers roared, lashed out, and yet our people moved gentle and without resistance to their tasks, on their long chain lines. The men took sickles and cut the wheat; the woman followed a step behind, gathering it up, carrying baskets back and forth. The children went to and fro like mice, gleaning the grain that had been dropped. We worked beside them, as we had always done. The Beloved himself worked there, with the Child bound to his chest in a sling of white cloth.

I heard the overseers speaking among themselves, though I didn't know what they said. Fear was in their voices. One sat down in the shade of a tree and gasped. One waded into the river and stood there up to his neck. One wandered into the middle of a plowed field and began shouting at something only he could see. Others lay down. One vomited black stuff and lay still after that.

Some people have said that the Saint brought them pestilence. Even as her breath revived us and gave us strength, they say, it spread death among the Riders. I don't believe it. I think their dirtiness brought them down at last, as it would always have done, and her coming was our preservation against their death throes.

The overseers died, one after another, and yet we continued in eerie calm and stillness. There was only the sound of the chains clinking, as the people worked; only the noise of the sickles cutting through the stalks.

Then we heard the hoofbeats, and shrieks: not shrieking in fear but to frighten, the cry of the Riders as they hunted us. I looked and saw them coming around the great hall, urging on their mounts with cruel spurs. They were lords among the Riders, sick and drunk and mad, and they galloped toward us laughing and waving their knives.

"Stand fast," said the Star. "Be patient. They are dying men."

They came on. The children cried and tried to run in their shackles, and fell. In her sling, the little Saint twisted and struggled. She began to wail.

As her cry rose, there was a sharp sound, the crack and ring of metal. Chains were breaking, falling off. I saw the shackles dropping from ankles and wrists, springing away. People stood free, but did not move because they could not believe they were free. The Riders came on, swinging their weapons, stabbing at us with spears, and some of us they wounded.

I heard Lendreth shout, "You are slain if you disobey, and now you are slain if you obey! Defend yourselves!" He caught up a sickle and swung at the nearest Rider who careered close to him. The blade caught the beast in the throat. Blood shot out and drenched Lendreth's white robe, as the beast fell. The Rider thrashed under the animal. Then one man caught up the chain he had worn, and with it he began to beat the Rider.

I have seen horrors in my time, but never thought I would see my own people do such things as they did then. The killing spread like fire from that one spot in the field. I heard the harsh cries of my people, as they stabbed and battered the Riders to death. And the Star held up his hands, weeping; and the little Saint screamed and screamed.

One by one, as the Riders died, it stopped. The people looked at their bloody hands; they dropped the bloody sickles, the chains all foul with blood and brains and hair. They looked around as though they were waking from a dream. Lendreth raised his hands and shouted, "We have won! We are free!"

"Not free," said my Beloved, sorrowful.

On this day, in this field, your childhood ended
and your innocence went down in a spray of blood.
You gloried in your rage. You caught their pestilence,
more deadly than any fever; for you will live to justify this thing
and pride yourselves on what you did,
forgetting what you were before. You will become your enemies.
And so the future is set.
Oh, little Child, what labors, what troubles wait for you.

He did not speak to Lendreth, but walked across the field to where a child had been trampled and lay moaning in pain. He knelt by the boy and leaned down, setting the Child beside him. She touched the boy with her hand.

The boy was healed at once; but as my Beloved knelt by him, a dying Rider leaned up with a sickle, and struck at him and cut his foot to the bone. We ran to our Star, Luma and Meli and I, and saw the Rider stone dead, still gripping the sickle. We pushed him away and the blood welled from the Beloved's wound.

Luma tore her robe, she staunched the bleeding, and Meli and I begged him to let the Child heal his injury. He only shook his head.

Bind it up; but it will never heal.
So I will walk to freedom with blood upon my feet,
over the bodies of the dead; so doom fulfills at last.

We carried him from the field, back across the river, and the free people met him lamenting for his hurt. We stayed with him, we cleaned the wound and bound it up; Lendreth took the disciples to the outlying houses and fields, to find any of our people who might be hiding. They returned, pale and shaking at the things they'd seen, leading the last few who had been freed.

Lendreth was eager to atone for his lapse. He saw to it that bandages and salves were brought down from the mountain caves, and jars of water from the spring, for the river water was too fouled to drink. My Beloved lay quiet, holding the little Saint as though for comfort. She slept.

So we lay in the valley that night, without fear. For the first time I looked up and saw the stars from that place where our people had used to dance, so long ago. But the great trees were all dead, the dancing green a harrowed field. We were not the people we had been then. My Beloved had kept us alive, we had endured the chain and the lash in the innocence of our hearts; but he had lost us, even in the hour of his triumph.

Sometime in the night, the roofs of the houses across the river caught fire. We watched them burn.

When morning came, Lendreth knelt before my Beloved where he lay with us, and with downcast eyes asked what we were to do now. "We will leave this place," said the Star.

"Where are we to go?" asked Lendreth.

"We will follow the river," said the Star. "It will take us to the land beyond the mountains."

"Bright One, that is impossible," said Lendreth, raising his eyes. "I have been that way. I traveled as far as the mountain's wall and saw the river sink underground there. I tried to climb the wall, and failed. I searched for weeks and found no passes through, anywhere."

"You could not find them," said the Star. "And I could not find them. But the Child has come, and the world is new. She will make a way for us."

Lendreth bowed his head. "Then with respect, let us take the path of the sun, downriver, and not"—he lowered his voice—"Cursed Gard's way. I went that way too and saw nothing but cliffs of ice, and it is all climbing."

"The path of the sun, then," said the Star. "For we drift downstream."

We walked out of the land where we had been born. We sang farewell to the mountains that had been our refuge and our prison wall. We sang farewell to the great tree under which the Beloved had told us stories. We sang farewell to the ruined places that had been ours, where the Riders now lay in all corruption.

Lendreth had a litter made, and the poor lame Beloved sat in it and held the baby Saint, and we, his lovers, carried him. We put on our white robes and carried him proudly, we decked his litter with flowers.

Singing, we walked out of that land, and as we went, the spirits of our dead went with us. Some were white birds. Some were floating shadows. I saw them pouring up into the sky from the blackened beams of the Riders' houses, clouds and clouds of white butterflies, all who had died there in that black pit before the Child had come: their souls were released, and they followed us.

It was a long journey. We traveled slowly. The country was harsh, treeless, full of stones, and in places the river cut through steep gorges and foamed white and fast, uneasy footing. Sometimes we had to stop for days while Lendreth went out with the disciples to find streams of clean water to drink, so we could fill our carry-gourds. There was little to eat.

But the Beloved gave us heart. He told us the old stories, fresh and new now that they might be real, about the green warm forests on the other side of the mountains. He sang the old song "Oh, That We Were Stars," and it was not a sad song anymore but a hopeful one. We dreamed of orchards, and gardens, and sweet meadows.

He sang to the little Saint too, quietly, as we bore them along. It seemed to me that as he sang, something of him faded, and something of her brightened. He was in pain, for all we tried to ease him; the wound in his foot never did heal. His eyes dimmed, his voice grew faint.

But the Child sat up, she looked about her, she seemed to understand what she saw and heard. Sometimes I saw them singing together, as he held her before him. She watched his face, she moved her little lips as he did, as though she knew she must learn the Songs. She was a solemn baby.

———

We came at last to a high cold edge of land over which the river rushed. It fell far to break in white clouds below, where it shattered into a thousand streams and bled out across a marshy valley. At the other side of the valley the mountains rose steep and high, a sheer wall, no way through.

"This is what I tried to tell you," said Lendreth, coming close to speak quietly to the Star. "I went down there. I waded in muck like a heron through two moons, from one side of the valley to the other, and all I found was that the river drains away underneath. We cannot go farther."

The Star looked at him, sad. "We can. Have a little faith, Lendreth. The Child is with us, after all."

"But she's only a baby," said Lendreth.

My Beloved shook his head. He rose on the crutch we had made for him, and hobbling to the high place, he called for the little Saint. Luma brought her, from where she had been crawling in the sand at the river's edge. He brushed the sand from her, smiling, and set her in the crook of his arm. He bent down and whispered in her ear.

Then he raised his head. He sang a note of command. The river was disturbed in its bed, the gray water drew away from its banks and bubbled strangely, and weaving patterns formed in the torrent where it dropped over.

"You see, Lendreth? I am not strong enough. Yet, watch!" The beloved took the little girl's hand in his own, holding it up. He looked into her eyes and sang the note, softly. She opened her mouth and sang too, the same note, sustained. Their voices grew louder. He turned with her and looked out at the mountain wall.

Fools born since, who were not there, say they don't believe what happened next. They say we must have gone down and found some narrow hidden passage that led out, after long searching. That was not how it was. If you had been there as I was, you would never in your life forget.

I tell you the water trembled and rose in its banks, it raised its white neck up from the torrent and hung in the air, like a glass-bodied serpent. The wide water on the plain below drew together, closed like the fan of a bird's tail and pulled upward. Twisting and glittering in the sun, the water shot out with all its gathered force. It hurtled across the valley in midsky, roaring.

And the river struck the mountain so the mountain rang to its root. Chattering and gobbling, licking, hog greedy, it ate into the mountain, and stones and mud flew out and flowed down. Inward it bored and tunneled, making our way for us.

We lifted our hands and shouted, so heartened by this miracle after so many bitter days of traveling through bitter lands. My Beloved stood straight and motionless with the Child on his arm, and she never struggled, never moved to draw her hand from his, but watched steadily as the water thundered out across the void. The mountain was hidden in rainbows.

When the river had pierced through at last, and in sudden silence the rainbows vanished, only then did the Star sway where he stood. He called for us to come take the Child. Meli caught her as he staggered back, and Luma and I caught him as he fell.

The river fell too. It rained from the air and once more ran in its bed, hiding the wet rocks below in new mist. But we could see, now, the black cavern opened in the flank of the far mountain wall.

My Beloved did not move or speak, sick-pale, he did not open his eyes. Weeping we laid him in his litter, and the Child wept too. We set her beside him. He revived enough to put his arm about her. In a faint voice he told us to hurry. Lendreth shouted for us to follow no more than two abreast, and he led us down the steep slope and so along the edge of the marsh, the way he knew.

Half that day it took us, threading through perilous ways of black mud, but we came at last to the tunnel through the mountain and saw light at its distant end. We hurried through wet and echoing darkness, over rocks, splashing through pools of water, ducking under dripping gnarled roots.

It was just evening when we stepped out on the wet grass on the other side of the mountains. We looked down into a fair green land of forests, the place of our dreams. A new moon hung low in the sky, and one star.

―――――――

Sometimes I dream we are all back there, in the place we came through, and my Beloved is strong and sound, as he was in the old days. He sits under a great tree and he tells us stories, just as he used to, and jokes, and we love one another in the old way under the glowing lamps of the stars. Meli is happy, laughing. In my dream, he lies down with me in the sweet grass and delights me again. But now and again my dream ends badly, for I look up and see Lendreth there, shaking his head in disgust at us. . . .

The truth was nothing like my dream. The Star lay unconscious many hours. In the strong light of that place we saw that he looked worn and old, suddenly. The Child sat beside him, playing in the grass. Now and again she would crawl close and pat his sleeping face, and look questioningly at us.

When the Beloved woke at last, we tried to get him to take food, broths to bring back strength, such as we used to feed those newly rescued from the slave pits. He supped a little, but had no appetite. Lendreth reproached him, telling him it would be a shame if he couldn't enjoy our freedom for sickness.

"I am not ill, Lendreth," said the Star. "I am used up. My time is past. You have had an imperfect teacher, but she who has come is without imperfection. The time to come is her time."

We all wept, then, and begged him not to return to the earth. He smiled and said he would remain awhile yet, for the Child was still too little to lead us.

———

When he was strong enough, we put him in the litter and we traveled on, descending the slopes into the green trees. It was hot there. The air was clear and dry, with a glitter like crystal, even under the green shade canopy. Some of our people took off their garments and never put them on again, the air was so pleasant.

Under the trees we found the river, where it emerged from the mountain's root. We followed its bank, as we had done before. We found fruit trees, and many strange flowers. The Child ate gladly of the berries we brought her in a rolled leaf, filling her little fists and staining her mouth.

Months, we traveled. Our people became strong, even the children born in the pit put on flesh and laughed. And then we learned we were not alone in this fair country.

At a place where the river ran through a rock gorge, we saw a wonder: a high hill of rock, full of strange colors, on the edge of the water. Steps were cut into the rock, rising from the little beach. We were frightened. Even Lendreth turned to the Star with a pale face, thinking we had come to some place where Riders were.

The Beloved only held out his hands to calm us. He told us it was a place of fear for others, but we would come to no harm there, so long as we passed it by. I looked over my shoulder as we left it behind us and saw the steps going high up the face of the strange hill. They were neat and sharp cut, nothing like what the Riders had used to make; and demons build nothing, and anyway no one had seen a demon in years and years.

We knew nothing then about the Children of the Sun. The Beloved told us about them; he explained that they had come to this land even as we had, and we must share it with them. He said they were not an evil people, as the Riders had been, but a little stupid.

A week later we came to another falls, spilling down into a lake. Here the Beloved fell, struggling down the path beside the water, carrying our little Saint with him. We ran down lamenting, and Lendreth and Kdwyr dove in after them; but the Child was floating on the water, like a flower petal, unharmed, and in her tiny hand she held a corner of the Star's garment, so they found him easily and brought them both safe to the shore.

He lay ill on the bank a long while. The Child patted his face and kissed him, for she had learned to kiss by this time. At last he sat up and said that he must go on, for his time was short now.

One morning we woke and there was mist, thick and rolling above the surface of the water. One evening we saw a tide in the river rolling upward against the current, a white comber cresting, and we wondered at it.

On the next day we came to a fair green place, green meadows along the river's edge, green groves of cypress and oak, cool and wet. Purple herons stalked among the reeds and lit in far silver branches. Mist trailed low there. The air was filled with strange music, booming and sighing, and the crying of strange birds.

Here the Star begged us to set down his litter. Meli brought him the Child, and he kissed her fair brow and spoke softly in her ear. He set her down at his feet. Then he spoke to us all, our Beloved.

> This is the place of leave-taking. My light is gone, my strength
> is gone, my pain has burned it all away.
> But you will walk rejoicing in the light where the Child walks, for she will lead
>   you now. Be kind to her.
> Where I go now, I shall find ease at last, and long rest.

We wept to hear him say this. Yet our sorrow was mingled with joy: for the little Saint pulled herself up, grasping his robe. She stood on her two feet, steadily, and took her first steps there in that place, at that moment.

The Star laughed. "You see? The fair flower understands me."

But Meli threw herself at his feet, desperate, clawing the ground, begging not to be left behind. One or two others were like her, those who had suffered the worst in the old land. Luma knelt at his feet and said no word but stretched out her empty hands, she who had no family left but the Star.

He sighed, our Beloved. He bid us come to him one by one, and to each one he gave instruction. I saw Meli's face light with relief; I saw Lendreth looking grave, and Kdwyr too. The ones he chose went to the river's edge and stood there, expectant. To me they looked already like ghosts, half-transparent in the mist. Luma and Meli were among their number. I began to understand, but my heart broke.

When I came before my Beloved, he looked into my eyes. "My little Seni," he said, and kissed me. "You are one of the strong ones. You were always brave, and happy. Will you stay and help the little one care for our people? She will be grateful for your brave heart."

I could not speak, my throat ached so, but I nodded. He kissed away the tears that ran down my face, he put his hand on my brow and blessed me. Then I felt as strong as he said I was, and as brave.

He put the Child in my arms. Haltingly he went to the river's edge. We followed; Meli and I embraced and wept, we who had been little sisters together. The Child looked into the sorrowing faces and began to whimper, wide-eyed and fearful.

This was the last of his miracles, then: the Star lifted his hands and sang, and a white wave came rolling down the river. It bore a whiteness that seemed made of the foam, the mist, and the white wings of butterflies, and white birds. I didn't know then what it was.

A strong wind rose and the middle air grew clear, and we looked out on a silver expanse of water that glittered to the very end of the world. Scythe-winged birds floated and dipped above it, but they were not ravens; they were white as milk. The river flowed into it, rushing gladly as though to meet a lover.

My Beloved walked into the whiteness, and Luma followed him, and Meli, and those few other women and men he had chosen. The whiteness bore them. It moved away on the face of the water, taking them out to the glittering eternity.

For the first time in her life, the Child in my arms cried out in protest. She wailed and held out her little hands, staring after him. He turned and gazed on her, and raised his hand in a last blessing.

Our singing rose, our long lament drowning out awhile the roar of the long breakers on the shore.

She wears rags and feathers, with beads and bits of seashell braided in. Tears are on her face now, streaming from her eyes. The flowers in her hair have faded, for time has hunted her, caught her, torn her, and cast her away.

She looks up at the boat. It is no otherworldly vessel, no ship of crystal foam whose every line and spar runs with bright water. It is only a trading coracle with one mast, big enough for a few pilgrims and one or two bundles, brought by those who cannot quite leave their earthly possessions. But it is all her hope.

I did as he asked me. I stayed, I cared for the little Saint; we all cared for her. She grew tall. She grew beautiful and wise. She is still so, whatever the trevanion may say. They lie, they lie in their hearts to say otherwise. She triumphs over the darkness and is incorruptible, sinless, strong as the earth itself.

But I am weak now, and dream at night of a tree under stars and an innocent time. Waking and sleeping, I hear his voice. I have walked the cold sand yearning after him, and I cannot bear it anymore. Look, now! The tide and the wind favor us. I am already with my Beloved, in my heart.

Peace be with you.

3

the masks

Early evening over a crowded city of stone, still light in the west. One star hangs low in the sky.

Where the city slopes up into the hills there is an amphitheater, a half-circle of stone seats climbing the hillside, and a long, low building below. The platform in front of it is brilliantly lit by the glow from oil lamps cunningly magnified through lenses. Before the platform is a pit for musicians, who are already assembling there, and behind is a ramp leading to the shadowed alcoves hung with drapes.

People are climbing into the rows of stone seats, swarming up from the city below. Their skins are the color of sunrise at high summer.

Aristocrats in fine clothes are followed by servants lugging cushions, wine, and baskets of cold supper. Prosperous middle-class families carry their own cushions and hampers. The poor, in throngs, clutch thin, flat cushions and perhaps a bread roll and a small bag of olives each. The beggars carry nothing at all, but work the crowd pleading for alms.

They are, all, happy and looking forward to an evening's entertainment.

When the seats are full, when the vendors of cushions and telescopes and nuts have done passing through the tiers shouting their wares, a waiting silence falls. A man emerges from the back and walks up on the platform, to general applause.

He is only an actor, but he wears a mask bearing the idealized features of the great poet Wiregold. He hits his mark, bows ceremonially, and addresses the audience. His voice booms with authority, easily reaches the poor spectators up in the last rows.

Not of the gods I sing, their stern justice, their passions and just wrath;
Not of the heroes of Deliantiba, nor of their long wars.
No comedy I present to earn your laughter or thrown coins.
No story of young love here, to make your daughters weep.
No. See now instead a tale to chill your blood,
A monster's history, filled with darkest deeds!

He extends his arms sidelong in a formal gesture of presentation and takes five measured steps stage right. The musicians play a discordance, all shrill flutes and kettle drums. From both sides the actors come capering and sprinting onstage. They are acrobats as well, costumed in flowing shades of night, slate blue, purple, deep-dyed red. Their masks are skulls, beasts, outlandish and horrific. They bound together to form a tumblers' pyramid.

From the darkness at the back a figure strides forth, cloaked all in black. He wears shoulder-padding armor to give him the bulk of a god; his mask is of a bearded and frightful countenance, with circles of painted tin set loose over the eyeholes to give the impression of smoldering flames.

He vaults upward and stands atop the mound of bodies. The flutes fall silent; resonant pounding from the drums and then the deep ship horns thunder out a theme most dramatic, a villain's leitmotif. He thrusts up his black-gauntleted hands and draws, with deliberate slowness, twin swords from the scabbard on his back.

In a technician's box midway up the tiers a shuttered lamp of tremendous brightness is lit and trained on the figure, so that his black shadow is thrown large and sharp behind him, towering on the draped wall.

The audience shudders pleasurably, in the hot night, and leans forward. The narrator in the mask of Wiregold says, with a certain satisfaction:

Regard him now, the Master of the Mountain!
Of him will I sing tonight, and how he came among us!

Gard had been walking for months when he found the sea, and was so enchanted by its light and sound and scent that he followed the beach after that.

He felt a kind of quiet wonder, that he was capable of being happy. He walked on, along the tide line, now and then turning over seashells with the tip of his spear or stooping to pick up a pretty one. Before long his pockets were full of them.

He lay in the dunes at night, sprawled in the long blowing grass, and stared up at the stars for hours before he slept. He didn't think he would ever be able to get his fill of starlight, or sunlight.

Occasionally he saw graceful things out on the silver horizon, white-winged, gliding along. Gard had been mystified by them at first, until he thought back to the travel essays of Copperlimb and realized they must be *ships*.

Four days after he had seen the first one, he spotted something far up the beach to the north. As he approached cautiously, he saw that it was squarish in shape; rather like what a room might look like, if you could see its walls from the outside. A little nearer, and he saw that in fact it had been made from cut stones tidily fitted together. The effect pleased him, for a moment.

Then he thought of the Riders' stone halls and stopped and scowled. The stone thing, in its neat geometry, bore little resemblance to the piled hovels of the Riders. All the same, Gard took a tighter grip on his spear, as he walked forward.

The wind shifted, and he caught the scent of frying food. His mouth watered. Something was painted on the front of the stone room. He peered at it and made out a word, in the language of the Children of the Sun. The word was *Refreshments*.

Gard leaned on his spear a moment, considering. Drawing the necessary spell from his memory, he gave himself the skin color of a Child of the Sun. When he felt the illusion was good enough, he walked up to the stone room.

The front wall had no door, but an opening at chest height. Gard looked in at a little kitchen, where a man was cutting up a fish. The man was a great deal like Triphammer, but as he might have appeared when young. He looked up, noticed Gard, and came immediately to the opening, wiping his hands on a cloth.

"Good morning, traveler. What will you have? Some fried fish?"

"Yes," said Gard.

"And what to drink?" The man waved a hand at the framed slate over the stove, whereupon were chalked many words. Gard studied them a moment.

"A jar of Gabekrian Best Vintage Third Year Lord Spellmetal," he read aloud. "And . . . bread. And olives. And cheese. And apples. And honeyed apricots."

"Certainly, my lord," said the man, suddenly a great deal more defer-ential. "The Gabekrian white, you mean, sir?"

"Yes."

"Quite an appetite, sir, if you don't mind my observation. You must have been hunting, yes?"

"Yes."

"Down from your estates for a bit of camping by the seaside, I gather?"

"Yes."

"First time visiting Gabekria?"

"Yes."

"You'll enjoy it, sir. The air's very good here."

"It is, yes."

Gard watched as the man bustled in the kitchen, dipping pieces of fish in batter and frying them. He thought through his question carefully be-fore speaking. "Do you know the river, many miles to the south?"

"That'd be the Rethestlin, sir? Heard of it."

"Someone has made a garden there, where it runs into the sea, and put up three stones with"—Gard hesitated a moment—"strange carvings on them. Do you know who made them?"

"Sorry, my lord, wouldn't know that. Never been there. Too green and wet and dim for my tastes!" The man shivered as he set red dishes on a tray and piled food on them. "You want to be careful, hunting in places like that, sir. Lot of demons down that way. And those forest ones, what d'you call 'ems, those *yendri*."

"Yendri," Gard repeated, thinking how strange the word sounded here in the blazing sunlight. It was an Earthborn word and it meant, simply, "people." He had wept when he had found the stones, seen the familiar images that covered them.

"If you'll just step over to the side, sir, I'll bring this out in a moment."

Gard looked around the corner and saw a dining area with a tiled roof, open to the air, tables and benches set in the sand. He went in and sat down, and opening his bag, he dug through until he found the money he'd brought with him. He selected a gold coin minted by the Children of the Sun. It bore the profile of a man and the words FRESKIN, DICTATOR, HIS 6TH YEAR.

The man brought out the high-piled tray and set it before Gard. "I'll just go back and get your wine—," he was saying, when Gard held out the coin. The man took it, staring. "Nine Hells! Hope I can make change for this one, my lord, I'll have to see—" He held it up and peered at it. "This is *old*. Mount Flame City, eh? Now, what with your accent and all, I took you for one of the lords from the islands, sir."

"I am," said Gard with his mouth full.

"Ah!" The man looked knowing. "Couple of fast warships in the family fleet? Say no more, my lord." Gard saw the man biting surreptitiously on the coin as he walked away. When he brought Gard's wine a moment later, he bowed deeply and set out scrupulously exact change.

The food was good. The wine was good. Gard ate and drank slowly, looking out at the sea, thinking hard. He heard a noise to his right and turned his head.

Wooden steps came down from the dunes there. A little boy and girl were running down them, followed by a man carrying a bundle of poles and cloth, followed by a woman carrying an infant and a basket. The children ran to the water's edge and halted, waiting until the waves rolled up the beach; then they danced back, squealing. The man set up a little pavilion and a pair of folding chairs. They sat down together, the woman and the man. She drew a veil over her upper body and put the infant to her breast. The man reached out and took her free hand.

A pair of young men came down the steps, stripped down, and plunged into the sea. A solitary man came with a rolled mat and a book under his arm; he spread out the mat, lay down on it, and read. A group of young girls with long, bare legs came down the steps, and tossed a ball around and danced on the sand awhile. Gard watched them keenly. They came up to the refreshment stand and ordered something that turned out to be rainbow-bright syrups, vaguely poisonous-looking, in little glass cups.

Other Children of the Sun came, singly or in groups. They set up sunshades and sat or ran along the wet sand or splashed in the surf. By the time Gard had finished his jar of wine, more people were here than he had ever seen in one place in his life, moving up and down the beach in both directions.

No one knows me here, thought Gard. *The Earthborn won't welcome me, but I could just live among these people, as one of them, and no one would know what I've done.*

It was a gift to be seized with both hands. He rose, handed the tray back in through the opening in the wall, and strode away up the beach. He climbed the steps over the dune and saw there Gabekria, her shops and lodging houses, her wide sunlit streets full of blowing sand.

Gard took a room in a lodging house, though the landlord seemed surprised that he had no servant traveling with him. He walked along the streets and observed what people wore. He found a shop that sold ready-made clothing and bought himself light and comfortable garments, and packed his furs away in the bottom of his bag.

At a bookseller's stall the proprietor stared when he asked for a copy of Copperlimb's *Travel Essays*, but after much searching found one for him. The proprietor spoke persuasively, and at length, on why Gard needed also an up-to-date map book and a modern travel guide. Gard let himself be persuaded. He asked for a book of general history, too, and a child's book of stories about the gods.

Having all these, he retired to his room and remained there, studying.

For some months, as long as his money lasted, he wandered along the route of Copperlimb's travels and treated himself to sightseeing. He walked up the Great Stairs at Mount Flame and bathed in the hot waters at Salesh, and watched barges of goods laboring up the Baranyi River. He took a ride in one of the caravan carts that shuttled along in their grooves down the red roads, though their speed alarmed him and he was certain the cart's mechanism would burst through the floor any minute and kill someone. He took a ferry out to the islands, at harvesttime, and watched the vintners bringing their boatloads of grapes across the water.

It was easy to find work when the money ran out, as Gard was bigger and broader than most Children of the Sun. He called himself Triphammer. He was perfectly content to be a stevedore, hoisting crates and bales in and out of warehouses all day long. When the workday ended, he'd go to the public baths and steam himself and afterward eat dinner in the same waterfront tavern each night. He used no magecraft beyond the spell that disguised him. He spoke mildly and avoided giving offense to anyone.

Afterward he might go to one of the pleasure clubs, where for a modest fee lusts were consensually soothed, and occasionally the conversation was rather pleasant as well. He never slept there, for his disguise took conscious will. Inevitably he returned to his single room, up five flights of stairs, but its one window opened on a view of the sea. He would lie in bed watching the stars drift down into the water, and sleep at last.

He needed nothing. He wanted nothing. Occasionally he would see a family out for a day's excursion, mother and father and little children, and only then he felt a vague sadness.

Gard wondered whether it might be granted him to forget his past, in time, in the serene repetition of labor and pleasure.

One moonless night, coming home late, a pair of thieves assaulted him. He killed them both, but was obliged to struggle. After that he bought himself weapons. From a bookseller Gard ordered all of Prince Firebow's work, intrigued to discover the prince had written a volume on military campaigns. He read it with interest. He spent three nights in every week at the public gymnasium, bringing back his body's memory of the arena. Resolutely he kept the memory out of his mind, as much as he was able.

It was unwise of him.

He was sitting at his dinner in a tavern one night when three men came through the door abreast, leaning on one another as they were. They were staggering, croaking out the "Hymn of Thanks to Fire." One of them waved an empty wine jar.

"Lovely tavern!" said the shortest of the three, pulling his head out of his companion's armpit to look around. "Tables and benches and things. Let's just sit. And have drinks out of wine cups. Like shivi-civilized men, eh?"

"Right!" said his friend in the opposite armpit. "Come on, old Tecker, bear to starboard. That way, that way! Easy does it! Whoof!"

Tecker, who was the midmost drunk and very large, settled on the bench next to Gard's with a resounding crash. He put his head down on the table and giggled. The shortest drunk navigated his way to a seat beside the big one with some difficulty, while the third went off to the bar.

"You won't mind old Tecker, will you?" the short one inquired of Gard. "It's only that we're celebrating. Geeman's wife gave him a baby boy s'afternoon."

"Congratulations," said Gard.

"Gods bless you! Geeman! Four cups! Nice stranger here's going to drink your boy's health! You'll celebrate with us, won't you, nice stranger?"

"Well, gods bless him!" Geeman bawled from the counter. "Barkeep! Make that four cups!"

"Four cups!" echoed the short one. "So Tecker 'n' Geeman 'n' Parlik 'n'—what's your name, eh?"

"Dennik Triphammer," said Gard.

"Dennik, right, well, us four can drink little Bexi's health. 'N' Mrs. Geeman's too, course." The short one beamed hazily at Gard. His friend came weaving back with a tray with four cups of wine. He set one down before Gard and almost dropped the tray; the short one caught it and set it down without slopping too much. "Here we go! Drinks for everybody. To li'l Bexi!"

They both drank. Tecker had begun to snore. Gard drank quickly, not wanting to seem rude. "Shouldn't you go home to your wife and son?" he asked Geeman.

Parlik roared with laughter. "His mother-in-law threw us out!"

"Her and the midwife," said Geeman.

"Pair of old . . . old . . . she-creatures," said Parlik. "Oi, Tecker, drink up or I'll do it for you. Tecker? Gods below, has he passed out?"

"Tecker?" Geeman prodded him. His head lolled. "Bloody hell. We'd better get him home, or we'll have another woman sulking at us."

"How? He weighs twice as much as me," said Parlik. Both of them turned glassy stares on Gard. "Er . . . friend Dennik, you look like a big strong lad. How about you help us get this big oaf home? You'll be doing a lady a service."

"Though not in the *usual* way, har har!" said Geeman, and fell off the bench backward.

"Oh, not you too!" said Parlik. He looked at Gard. "I beseech you. Can't get them both home myself, can I, a little shrimp like me? I'll break in half. Here, if you'll take old Tecker, I can probably manage Geeman. Eh?"

"All right," said Gard, more amused than annoyed. He hauled Tecker upright and staggered out with him, and a moment later heard Parlik cajoling Geeman up off the floor. They emerged into the night. Gard grimaced, trying to see around Tecker, who was as heavy as though his bones were made of iron. "Where are we taking him?"

"Down to Rakut's Wharf," he heard Parlik reply. "Straight down there, see? Rakuty-Rakuty-Rakut's Wharf . . ."

They had gone about five streets down toward the wharf when Gard felt his knees buckling. He was drenched with sweat, suddenly sick and weak. The footsteps behind him were echoing oddly. Tecker's dead weight became unbearable.

"I don't think—," Gard said, and stumbled. Beside him, Tecker fell only to his knees before scrambling upright, leaving Gard on the pavement.

"He's down," Gard heard him saying.

"Strong bastard." Parlik's voice was clear and thoughtful. "You take his arms. Geeman, take his feet. Come on, hurry."

Gard felt himself hoisted up and was only grateful, glad to be allowed to sink into soft oblivion. Down he went, and then he was propelled upward into consciousness on a tide of painful nausea, twisting to vomit. "Oh, bloody hell," someone muttered, and Gard felt acute embarrassment as he retched up his dinner.

"Keep going!"

"Nine Hells, look at him!" someone else exclaimed, and Gard felt himself abruptly dropped. He struck the bricks sharply and the pain cleared his senses even more.

"What *is* he?"

"He isn't—"

"Shut up, both of you! Pick him up and come on!"

Gard was seized roughly and dragged over brick, over stone, over splintery planks, then he was dropped again, to land with a hollow thud on a wooden floor. Floor? It was tilting slightly. A deck. He had been brought aboard a boat. He struggled to his hands and knees and someone kicked him, aiming at his head perhaps but hitting his shoulder instead. It hurt. He was angry. Someone was growling.

"He's waking up!" Someone sounded scared, with an edge of disgust to his fear. "Throw a net over him before he—"

"Hold on! We don't need the net. Where's that thing her ladyship sent? Here! It's a whatchacallit, a spancel. It'll bind him."

"That little thing? You're mad!"

"No, see, it's magical, and she said—"

Gard groped for his boot and found his knife. He lunged upward and killed Geeman and Tecker—one stab through the kidneys, one stab through the ribs, one-two. Parlik scuttled toward him sidelong, holding up something that flickered with witchlight. His face was pale and terrified. Snarling, Gard grabbed up a pail and hurled it at him. Parlik fell and Gard dove at him and drove the knife into his throat.

Then Gard fell again, and vomited again. He crawled away from the bodies and sat awhile, gulping in the night air. At last he knelt upright and looked around.

He was on a small craft, a fishing vessel by the look of it, with one cabin forward. A dim light was burning within. Parlik must have come from the cabin. Watching the light steadily, Gard advanced on the cabin with his knife in his hand.

No one was in the cabin. An open pouch of papers was on a table, its contents strewn about by Parlik as he had dug in it for the spancel. Gard had to blink his eyes two or three times before he could focus on the fore-most written document.

> . . . lodging house in Buckle Street. He is employed as a stevedore on Cresset's Wharf, using the name Dennik Triphammer. His habits are most regular: his shift ends in the afternoon and he goes directly to the Sand Point Baths. Invariably he emerges forty-five minutes later and proceeds uphill to the Flowing Bowl, where he dines and drinks, though never more than two cups. He will generally depart after one hour . . .

Gard grimaced. The report had been written by an Amrick Stone. He sorted through the other papers: maps, safe-conduct passes, letters of marque, and . . . here was a letter bearing the seal of House Porlilon.

And here was a purse containing coin. A lot of it. He spilled it out on the table. Fabulously old coins, of varying denominations. Here was one from the reign of Freskin the Dictator.

Someone was growling again. When he realized he himself was making the noise, he stopped.

Gard swept the coins back into the pouch and put them inside his shirt. He grabbed up the papers, holding them into the flame of the oil lamp until they caught. He dropped them on the table and broke the lamp with the hilt of his knife, so the oil ran out and spread flame in a sheet over the table, dripping flame into a heap of bedding on the floor. Gard backed out of the cabin. He stumbled over Parlik's corpse and, seeing the spancel clutched in Parlik's hands, hoisted the body and pitched it over the side. It sank at once, trailing the glowing spancel after it as it descended into black water.

There was a fountain on the wharf. Gard could hear the trickling water. He scrambled ashore awkwardly, found his way by the sound, and drank deeply. It cleared his head. He washed the blood from his hands and the knife and leaned gasping against the fountain's bowl a moment, waiting to see if he could hold the water down. Someone shouted from Cresset's Wharf, pointing across at the fire, which had just shot up through the roof of the cabin.

Breathing raggedly, Gard focused and pulled an illusion over himself. He shaped it to resemble Tecker, to whom he had been closest in size, with Tecker's striped tunic and Tecker's red beard. Then he set off, as fast as he could, hoping to get to his room without trouble. Behind him, the shouts and commotion were increasing.

As he came around the corner into Buckle Street, a man stepped out of an alley. "Tecker? What are you doing here? You should have had him by now!"

Gard stopped. "Stone?" he said after a moment's hesitation. "There's something her ladyship wants, and he doesn't have it on him. I'm to go look in his room."

"But you have *him*?"

"Yes, we have him," said Gard, feeling the cold calm descend. "Come with me. You can help me search his room."

Two months later, Gard stood in a long line without the gate of Deliantiba, waiting stolidly. His bag was heavy, and so he had set it on the ground between his feet and stood with arms folded. In front of him, a woman jogged a ceaselessly complaining baby in her arms; behind him, a pair of salesmen muttered together about taxes.

When his turn came at last, Gard stepped up to the table. "Your name?" inquired a city clerk, opening a tablet.

"Wolkin Smith."

"Occupation?"

"General laborer, sir."

"Place of birth?"

"Chadravac."

"An island man, are you? I thought so, by your accent. What's your business, Smith?"

"Seeking employment, sir."

"Empty his bag, gentlemen." Gard handed over his bag without complaint and watched as two members of the city guard upturned it on the table. They sorted through his spare suit of clothes and dozen books without comment, but the clerk noted down the book titles. "Amateur scholar, are we?"

"I hope to improve my mind, sir."

"Weapons on the table, please." Gard drew two knives from his boots and laid them out, following them with the short sword he wore at his belt. The clerk noted these also and filled out the tablet. "Open your hands to the gods and repeat after me, please."

Gard opened his hands and blandly swore by gods in whom he did not believe that he intended no harm to the city of Deliantiba, nor any to her citizens in general and particular, nor would he poison her wells nor commit arson. He further swore to abide by her laws and, should it become necessary, help defend the city against attack in time of war.

The tablet was signed, stamped, closed, and handed to Gard with a copy of the civic statutes. Gard thanked the clerk and put his weapons away. He thrust his belongings back into his bag, shouldered it, and walked in through the city gate.

"General laborer, indeed," the clerk muttered to the guard captain. "With those books, and that accent? That's some nobleman's bastard."

"Fallen on hard times, then."

"Haven't we all? Next, please."

Gard found another bare room in a boardinghouse. Its window's view was only of the dry stony hills on which the city was built, but he didn't mind. He didn't plan to stay long.

A notice board in the atrium of his building advertised employers in need of workmen. Inspecting it, Gard saw one requiring the services of a gardener. He had seen gardens; the thought of green lawns and shade lured him, in this dry hot place. He noted the address and within the hour found himself standing in front of an open yard full of cut stone: plinths, urns, obelisks, polished spheres, statuary, flagstones. He was staring around, wondering if he'd got the address wrong, when a thickset man emerged from behind a pair of wrestling gods and looked at him inquiringly.

"Where is 17 Sand Street?" asked Gard.

"That's here." The man gave him an appraising stare. "Looking for work?"

"The notice said you wanted a gardener."

"So I do." The man jerked a thumb at the sign on the back wall. VERKIS WIRECUTTER, LANDSCAPING SERVICES. "You look fit. All right with heavy lifting?"

"Yes, but—"

"I pay as I have jobs. Got one today. Lady up on Leadbeater Terrace with a new town house, and one of my boys went and joined the army yesterday. Interested in taking his place? We load up the cart, we deliver and arrange the merchandise as madam sees fit, we bring the cart back. There's five crowns in it for you."

It was good money for a day's work. An hour later Gard was toiling up a narrow street, pushing a cart loaded with urns and statues, as Mr. Wirecutter and another day laborer hauled on the traces. They drew up before an eminence of rock with a mansion on it, so recent the mortar looked still damp. Mr. Wirecutter went around to the trade entrance, straw hat in hand, and presently returned with a lady apparently high-born.

". . . and madam may of course return any pieces she chooses, if on continued acquaintance they do not please, but I've brought my very finest stock, and I think it'll suit nicely. My staff, madam. Gentlemen, I have the honor of presenting Lady Springsteel."

"Charmed," said Lady Springsteel, with a sniff. She glanced from the other laborer to Gard and fixed her gaze on him, her eyes widening slightly. "How kind of you men to come all this way in the heat. Perhaps you'd like a cold drink, before you unload my goods?"

"Madam is gracious indeed," said Mr. Wirecutter, observing that her interest had settled on Gard. She clapped her hands, and after an interval a sullen servant girl appeared and was given orders. She returned, after yet a longer interval in which madam tapped her foot, bearing a tray of drinks each topped with a little mound of snow.

"Lemon water," said Lady Springsteel with a brilliant smile, handing a glass to Gard. He took it with a bow. She gave the servant girl an impatient look.

"The snow's brought all the way from the mountains. It cost an awful lot," the girl intoned dutifully.

"Hush, girl, it's vulgar to tell people such things," said Lady Springsteel. "I do apologize. She's from Mount Flame; I'm doing my best to refine her." Gard, who didn't care if he never saw snow again, suppressed a shudder, but drank.

Lady Springsteel's garden was on a terrace behind the house, to which she led the way when they had finished their drinks. Gard stared. It was an expanse of flagged walk and raked gravel, in subtly contrasting colors, and bright-painted tiles ornamented the walls. There were benches, and a pond in which sad-looking fish drifted, and a small shrine to Lady Springsteel's particular gods. Not one blade of grass, not one tree, not one flower or shrub of any description disturbed the geometric perfection of Lady Springsteel's garden.

Its geometry was further enhanced by the addition of Mr. Wirecutter's urns and statuary. When they were placed and Gard and his fellow worker stood sweating, Lady Springsteel inspected it thoughtfully. Mr. Wirecutter followed her closely, twisting his hat in his hands.

"Splendid effect, I think," said Mr. Wirecutter.

"Oh, I don't know," said Lady Springsteel. "Perhaps it needs an obelisk or two."

"The very thing! I have them in black marble, white marble, and a very smart red sandstone, which is, I understand, popular in the villas at Salesh-by-the-Sea just now—"

"What do you think, good man?" Lady Springsteel rounded on Gard.

"Er—shouldn't there be some plants?" said Gard.

"Plants?" said Lady Springsteel and Mr. Wirecutter together, and Mr. Wirecutter hastened to add, "He's from the islands, see."

"Oh, I can tell from his voice," said Lady Springsteel, advancing on Gard. "What a charming accent! Is that an island custom, plants in gardens?"

"Yes," said Gard, hoping it was.

"Let's have some, then," said Lady Springsteel.

Gard, seeing Mr. Wirecutter glaring at him, said, "And obelisks. Red sandstone obelisks. Very popular, your ladyship."

"I'll send him up with them tomorrow, madam," said Mr. Wirecutter.

———

As they were trundling the cart downhill, Mr. Wirecutter said, "You're so bloody clever, you can just find a way to get her some plants."

"Don't you have any for sale?"

"What do I look like, a greengrocer? But I'll tell you what: you'll take four of my best stone basins, the glazed ones with grapevine patterns on, I think, and you'll stick something in 'em that looks nice, and you'll take 'em up tomorrow. Along with four obelisks."

"He'll need help with the cart, then," said the other laborer hopefully.

"No, he won't," said Mr. Wirecutter, with a meaningful look.

———

Gard sought through the city, but found no shops at all where he might buy anything green and alive. At last he went out to the rocky hills outside the city wall, and there with effort dug a few scrubby bushes from the bricklike soil and potted them in basins, and arranged them as best he could.

They were the coarsest weeds, but Lady Springsteel professed delight with them and with the obelisks, when he delivered them next day. She had difficulty deciding exactly where they ought to be placed, and followed close at Gard's elbow as he shifted them from one corner of her terrace to another. When he made to depart at last, after all possible arrangements of obelisks and bushes had been tried, she laid her hand on his arm. "I'm thinking of having the lot below terraced for a garden as well," she said, gazing deep into his eyes.

When Gard brought the cart back, Mr. Wirecutter handed him a bag of coin. "That's your five and a retainer. You come back tomorrow. I'll have work for you."

For the next two weeks Gard earned gold for such minor tasks as sweeping the shop floor, rotating stock (which admittedly took strength), and hawking Mr. Wirecutter's wares in the street. This involved standing outside the yard with a small obelisk in one hand and a small statue of a leering demon in the other, while shouting, "Timeless elegance for the home and garden! Sculptural art! Reverent memorials in the finest materials! Step into our showroom for a private consultation!"

At least once or twice a day he would be stared at by a passing citizen, a small man who wore sandals with raised soles. The gentleman's head was egg-shaped and quite hairless, save for a thin mustache on his upper lip. Wary of spies, Gard noted him well. He did not seem as though he would be difficult to kill.

"Lady Springsteel would like to see you," said Mr. Wirecutter, looking gleeful. "Ordered a statue of Rakkha for her fishpond. Said she wants to show you how nice her plants turned out. See can you talk her into a couple of stone balls!"

Twenty minutes later Gard stood at Lady Springsteel's trade entrance, awkwardly shifting a big-bosomed stone goddess to his free arm as he reached for the bell.

"Oh, it's you," said the servant girl, before she was elbowed aside by Lady Springsteel.

"Oh! How charming. Exactly what I wanted. Do come through to the garden, won't you? I am particularly pleased with the plantings."

Gard set the goddess down on her plinth above the fishpond and straightened up. His heart sank as he saw the bushes. They had died. But:

"They've turned this beautiful golden color," said Lady Springsteel. "Much nicer than that dull green, and much more in keeping with my color scheme out here, don't you think?"

"Very attractive, your ladyship," said Gard.

"Do you think they'll stay that shade?"

"Undoubtedly, your ladyship."

As he went slinking back to the stoneyard, Gard spotted the little man with the mustache approaching him from the opposite direction. To his surprise, the stranger stopped and bowed gracefully, if a bit unsteadily on his high shoes.

"Sir! A moment of your time, if you please. Attan Tinwick, at your service. Owner and manager of Tinwick's Theater. You may have heard of me?"

"Sorry, no."

"Ah. Well, you will have undoubtedly *seen* me, hither and yon."

"Often," said Gard, glancing up and down the street to check whether there would be any witnesses to Mr. Tinwick's murder.

"And I have certainly heard *you*. You have a magnificent instrument, if I may say so." Gard scowled at him, but he went on, oblivious, "May I ask, sir, whether you have ever considered a life in the theater?"

"No, I haven't."

"Perhaps I could persuade you to consider it now." Mr. Tinwick beamed at him. "It would be only proper for you to audition, of course, but I feel confident I could offer you three percent of each performance's profits. Our leading Kendon was obliged to leave the company, you see— rather sudden—family obligations in Troon, I believe—"

"Your leading what?"

"Kendon." The little man looked surprised. "As in Epic Theater? The Hero Born in Obscurity? Ye gods, you don't mean to tell me you've never attended a performance of Epic Theater?"

"I'm from the islands."

"Yes, but . . ." Tinwick seemed at a loss for words. "It is such a universal art form . . . I would have thought, surely . . . well, no matter. I'm offering you a job on the *stage*, my friend."

Gard thought about that. He had attended a performance in Konen Feyy once, because Copperlimb had mentioned watching plays there. Gard had found it beautiful, that amphitheater of white stone with its backdrop of draperies, though he hadn't been able to understand much of what had been happening onstage. He had been surprised that the actors all wore masks. Masks . . .

He looked sidelong down the street, at Wirecutter's yard. "Perhaps I'm interested. What does the job entail?"

———

Tinwick told him a great deal about what the job entailed, as they walked along, and most of it made no sense. There was a lot of talk about *projection* and *blocking* and *interpretation*, and a sort of mimed language of stylized gestures that conveyed certain meanings.

"But you'll pick it up quickly, I know," said Tinwick airily, waving his hand. "Some of us are born with the gift, and you, sir, are, I think, included in that number. I saw you waving those bits of statuary about and I said to myself, 'There's a man who knows how to hold an audience's attention.'"

"Did you really?" said Gard, remembering the arena.

"Oh, indeed. And here we are!" Tinwick pointed. Gard looked, expecting the grand sweep of white stone fanning up a majestic hillside. He saw instead a low building of crumbling brick, and beyond it the gape of an old quarry, walls scored and gashed with pick marks. Tall weeds grew in its upper reaches, thistledown seeds drifting.

Tinwick, glancing up at Gard's face, coughed and added, "A rustic venue, you see, is perfectly suited for Epic Theater. You will find that it is actually an ideal performance space. The acoustics are superb! But don't take my word for it. Step inside and hear for yourself."

He opened a gate and bowed Gard in. Gard stepped through, wary of ambush, and saw only a couple of disconsolate-looking youths chipping away at stone slabs. They were evidently making new theater seats. Other seats, roughly hewn, stretched in irregular rows to the back wall of the quarry.

"Pulkas broke the chisel, Tinny," one of the youths announced. "You're going to have to cough up the funds for a new—hello! Who's this?"

"Our new Kendon, I believe," said Tinwick.

"Oh, my," said the one, his face lighting as he surveyed Gard, but the other one pouted and said, "I had rather thought you might promote from within our ranks, Mr. Tinwick."

"Pulkas, my good fellow, it has never been my custom to mar perfection; it occurs so rarely among mortals," said Tinwick soothingly. "Your Elti is perfection. The mere thought of any other actor in the role gives me the horrors. Screaming horrors. Now, this is—" He waved a hand at Gard.

"Wolkin Smith," said Gard.

"And, Mr. Smith, may I introduce our Jibbi and Elti? Clarn Rivet and Pulkas Smith. Perhaps a relation?"

"I doubt it," said Pulkas.

"What are Jibbi and Elti?" asked Gard. They blinked, and Pulkas threw an angry look at Mr. Tinwick, who held up his hands in a placating gesture.

"He's from the islands! Apparently they are unfamiliar with our particular art form. But he'll learn. Have you ever seen a more likely Kendon? As Kendon is the Hero Born in Obscurity, dear Wolkin, Jibbi and Elti are his Happy Companions."

"Otherwise known as his Idiot Friends," said Clarn. "The comic relief."

"Shouldn't he audition?" said Pulkas.

"The very reason I brought him here," said Mr. Tinwick. "Fetch the masks, Clarn, would you? And now, Wolkin, let's see, you'll need a scene—and I happen to have one that will do nicely, here." Mr. Tinwick rummaged in a chest and pulled out a grimy sheaf of paper bound along its spine with string. "The very thing! *The Enchantment of Bregon*. Very popular piece, played for weeks."

He thumbed through it and opened to a particular page. "Here. Just study this speech, here, a moment. Clarn! *Enchantment of Bregon*, act two, scene five. Just after the business with the basin of water."

"Right." Clarn emerged wearing a wooden mask, clearly comic: the nose was snub and uptilted, the eyeholes uptilted too, and the mouth was wide and grinning. He handed a mask to Gard. It depicted the smooth and rather somber face of a youth, with an open downturned mouth. Gard, who had read through the scene once, set the book down and fastened on the mask.

Clarn leaped straight up in the air and came down crouching as though poised to run, his hands spread out in a gesture of astonishment.

Why, who is this? Can this be Kendon, my old friend?
Oh, no! What magic has been worked here
With soap and water? Speak with Kendon's voice,
I beg you, or I'll never believe it's you!

Clarn pivoted his whole upper body toward Gard, one hand extended toward him stiffly, the other cupped behind his ear.

"Ahem—the book," prompted Mr. Tinwick, but Gard recited from memory:

Jibbi, it is truly I, Kendon. Oh, heavy is my heart
To see these features revealed!
Shall I believe the Wizard spoke the truth,
And I am son to a most hated tyrant?
Must I now see, when I look in the glass,
His despised visage, until the hour of my death?
No, no; I will not wear this crown,
Nor govern here. Let the Wizard rage!
I will fare forth to dear Valutia,

Once again I'll live simply, a fisherman,
Poor in gold, rich in virtue.
Rather than live a monster on a throne.

A stunned silence fell.

Pulkas's shoulders sagged. "That wasn't acting, you know," he said at last. "That was just reading it off. But it won't matter, will it? He's got the Voice."

"He certainly does," said Mr. Tinwick, smirking.

"Built like a damned god, perfect memory, and a voice that makes you listen to him. I'm stuck with playing Elti the rest of my life, aren't I?"

"Oh, don't be such a Clemona," said Clarn briskly, slipping his mask off. "One of these days you'll graduate to playing Batto's Old Father, I'm sure. Welcome to the company," Clarn added to Gard, advancing to clap him on the shoulder. "I don't suppose you know how to stage sword fights too?"

"Yes," said Gard.

Epic Theater did not pay particularly well, as it turned out; in fact it barely paid at all. But there were compensations, as Mr. Tinwick hastened to assure Gard. Any actor unable to pay his or her rent was welcome to bed down in the properties shed. When the company had a particularly successful production, Mr. Tinwick had the prudent habit of stocking the back of the shed with sacks of dried chickpeas, flour, bacon, and onions, so communal meals were possible during the leaner times.

"We're in rather a lean period just now, in fact," said Mr. Tinwick. "All this talk of war, you know. Things will improve, however. Epics never go out of style!"

He was standing on the stage as he spoke, waving his latest script. Gard looked around at his fellow actors, assembled with him on the half-circle of stone seats. The meeting was for his benefit, as Mr. Tinwick liked to have what he called a *workshop* every time a new member joined the company. Gard's fellow actors all looked restive and bored.

"Now, the reason that Epics never go out of style," Mr. Tinwick explained, "is that Epics never *change*. Which is to say, the plot details may vary, but the stock characters remain the same firm favorites. Let's review them, shall we?"

Someone groaned. Mr. Tinwick glared and cleared his throat. "The Hero Born in Obscurity. Who would like to describe his character, for Mr. Smith's benefit?"

Satra raised her hand. She was the ingénue assigned to play Clemona, the Girl Disguised as a Boy.

"Kendon is a handsome youth," she explained. "He has been raised in poor circumstances and is therefore honest and brave. He has been touched by Destiny. He is the lost heir to the throne. Usually. And the possessor of the Cursed Item. Sometimes."

"Very good. And the character of Clemona?"

"Clemona is the unrequited lover of Kendon," said Satra, with a limpid stare unwaveringly fixed on Mr. Tinwick. "She has known him since childhood and she alone loves him for himself. No one understands her or appreciates her. She is too brave and clever to stay at home cooking and sewing. She has secretly taught herself to fight with a sword, and when Kendon leaves on his Quest, she disguises herself as a boy and follows him."

"*Very* good. And Batto, the Faithful Servant? Mr. Bracket?"

"Batto is humble yet valiant," drawled Mr. Bracket, who had his feet up on the seat in front of him and his head in the lap of the ingénue playing the Princess. "He is the perfect devoted retainer. He can find no greater purpose in life than carrying the Hero's luggage, washing his clothes, cooking for him, and finishing the Hero's Quest if Kendon happens to faint at the last moment."

"Or is wounded or under a spell," said Mr. Tinwick reprovingly.

"To be sure. Batto will occasionally have a Peasant Sweetheart or an Old Father, who furnish comic relief. They will not, however, deter him from joining Kendon on his Quest."

"And the Princess?" Mr. Tinwick frowned at Mr. Bracket's lady friend, Miss Ironbolt.

She coughed apologetically. "Princess Andiel is beautiful, virtuous, and nobly born. She is the destined bride of Kendon."

"Which means that poor Clemona always has to die heroically by sacrificing herself to save Kendon's life, or something," said Satra bitterly.

"Or discover at the last possible minute that she has always secretly been in love with one of the Idiot Friends," said Pulkas.

"Happy Companions, Mr. Smith."

"Right, Happy Companions." Pulkas jumped up on his seat and Clarn jumped up beside him. They put their arms around each other's shoulders and did a comic dance, singing in falsetto:

We're Elti! We're Jibbi! We are a funny pair!
One of us has a funny nose, the other funny hair!

We do routines, and comic scenes, and sometimes talk in rhyme!
Without our help the Quest would finish up in half the time!

"Comedians," said Mr. Tinwick, shaking his head. "Mr. Carbon?"

An older man, who sat at the back of the house, blew his nose. "Sorry," he said. "There's always this Wizard, see? Wizards are these very spiritual types who go around arranging things so the Quest comes out all right. Like, rescuing Kendon as a baby and hiding him with poor but honest folk. Or if there's a Cursed Object, the Wizard is the one who recognizes what it is and warns everybody. And he casts spells and things to help the Hero on his journey. It's a very self-sacrificing sort of a character."

And utterly unlike any real mages Gard had ever known. He nodded thoughtfully and looked up as Mr. Tinwick cleared his throat.

"And at last," he said, "*my* character. The Dark Lord. Traditionally played by the theater manager, you see. A figure of awe and dreadful power. Master over demonic hordes. His armies of darkness overrun the earth. The wings of his dragons darken the sky. His sorcerous power exceeds the Wizard's by far, and in any contest the Dark Lord inevitably defeats the Wizard."

"Sometimes the Wizard does come back from the dead, though," murmured Mr. Carbon.

"Only at the very end. The only true nemesis of the Dark Lord is Kendon, who generally defeats him by some magical means or other—either he uses an enchanted weapon or he finds and destroys the Cursed Object. In *The Enchantment of Bregon* Kendon was the Dark Lord's long-lost son, and invoked familial sentiment to induce his dread sire to remorse and self-destruction. It must be admitted, however, that we don't resort to that particular plot device often. I find it diminishes the Dark Lord's image to show him with any weaknesses whatsoever." Mr. Tinwick flicked a bit of lint from his shoulder.

"And you play the Dark Lord?" said Gard, trying to picture it. Someone behind him snickered.

Mr. Tinwick smiled self-depreciatingly. "I have that honor. It's no role for a young and inexperienced performer, trust me. You'll see for yourself. I find a certain amount of life wisdom is called for in giving the role its necessary . . . shadows.

"And there we have it! There are subsidiary roles, which may be doubled using appropriate masks or mechanical properties. Occasionally, the

Girl Disguised as a Boy and the Princess are one and the same, and now and again some daring troupe substitutes a Wise Woman for the Wizard. These variations, however, are frowned upon by purists. And with good reason! The Epic, as a dramatic form, has been handed down over centuries and deserves respect. It contains universal truths, which ought not to be obscured by unhallowed alteration."

"Mind you, the audiences do get bored now and again, hearing the same story over and over and over," said Mr. Bracket.

"Not those with a true appreciation of the art form," said Mr. Tinwick, looking at him severely. "Now, if we might turn our attention to the new improvisation outline? The title of the new piece is *Shadow of the Dark Lord.*"

"Didn't we do that one year before last?" said Miss Ironbolt.

"No. You're thinking of *Curse of the Dark Lord,*" said Mr. Tinwick. "Now, the opening scene: you enter at left, Mr. Carbon, carrying the dummy infant. At the rear of the stage we'll have some light effects behind a skyline cutout to signify the burning city. And you'll say . . . ?"

Mr. Carbon scratched his head and thought.

"Er . . . *Oh, horror! If only the queen had heeded my wise counsel and not listened to the Dark Lord's secret emissaries, all had been well! Where now shall I conceal thee, young prince?*"

Rehearsals went badly, until Gard understood the manner in which the Epic was played. It was all improvisation, up to a point; a general outline of each story and some specific text was written by Mr. Tinwick. The actors stepped out onstage and brandished their characters like swords, occasionally scoring points at one another's expense.

Gard found that if he sat down with the immense and untidy heap of thumbed promptbooks, he could memorize the appropriate speeches for any plot twist that might occur. There were only so many situations, so many responses, so many characters. The more he thought of it as arena fighting, the easier it became for him.

> *Vile tyrant! Now thy reign is done*
> *For I have tracked thee over trackless plains*
> *That I might drive this blade, my murdered father's blade,*
> *Through thy black heart!*

Gard brandished the wooden sword and struck an attitude of attack. Mr. Tinwick, teetering on absurdly high patens that were nevertheless not high enough to keep his black cloak from trailing along the floor behind him, lifted his fearsome black mask.

"Cheat out," he reminded Gard. "Again, please."

With a prickle of irritation, Gard faced the empty seats, rather than Mr. Tinwick, and delivered his lines again. Then he turned for the attack.

"Cheat *out*," said Mr. Tinwick.

"But I'm going to attack you."

"Hold on," said Mr. Bracket, lifting Batto's mask and rising from where he had been cowering at the back of the stage. "I see what it is. You've been a soldier, haven't you?"

". . . Yes," said Gard.

"And I'll bet you were a damned good one, old man, but this is a two-dimensional venue. Think of yourself as a paper cutout, eh? We have no depth up here. Take your sword moves and sort of flatten them out."

"Oh," said Gard. "Thank you."

"My pleasure." Mr. Bracket donned his mask once more and resumed his crouch, hands held wide in alarm. "*Oh, my master, have a care lest he smite thee! Oh, that I were back in the meadow stealing apples! Oh, gods have mercy on us!*"

Gard faced front and executed a maneuver that would have gotten him slain in the arena, but Mr. Tinwick said, "Oh, very nice," and then, in the sepulchral boom that was his Dark Lord voice, added:

I know that blade of old. It is
A puny blade, child; it did not save thy father,
Nor will it save thee. Dost thou not know
Whom it is thou facest? I was powerful then;
Ten times more great is my dark power now.

"*For, see, I have but to wave my hand*—and then I bring up my sorcerer's staff like *this* and you come in and attack like *so*—and, oh, wait, that's not the right sword! Where's the break sword?"

"Here! Sorry, it was in the wrong basket," said Clarn, handing it to Gard. "This is the one you want. You just pull this pin down with your thumb, see, when he drops the flash charge."

"Thank you." Gard took it and resumed his pose of histrionic attack.

"*For, see, I have but to wave my hand*—me, staff, you, attack, I drop the flash pellet, and," said Mr. Tinwick encouragingly, "boom! Yes, perfect, and the sword breaks and you fall *and . . .*"

Oh, Batto, bitter is the taste of despair!
I cannot move my arm! The blade is broke
That was my vengeance! His dread might
Overpowers me at last!

Gard, reciting, writhed in what he hoped was a convincing show of agony.

"*Very* nice, and now the twist ending . . ."

"*Oh, master mine, I cannot see you slain!*" Mr. Bracket scrambled to his feet, ran downstage, and grabbed up one piece of the broken sword.

Oh, foul sorcerer, now you'll see
How humble devotion makes a man brave!

"And I stab *you* and of course I'll be wearing the prop hand, and it goes bang and papier-mâché fingers and red syrup go flying everywhere— horrified gasp from the audience—"

"Then I think I'll just wear the explosion vest with the blue and green charges," said Mr. Tinwick primly. "Because, of course, one doesn't want to upstage the Dark Lord's death scene."

"No, of course not," muttered Mr. Bracket.

"And I'll stagger back, all flaring lights and bleeding green and yellow syrup—I'll need a Number Seven Flash charge, Clarn, please have a few made up."

"Right, some Number Sevens," said Clarn, making a note on a tablet.

Now is fulfilled that prophecy
That Kendon should not slay me,
That an insect in the dust at his heel
Should do me more harm.
Triumph while thou wilt, O fool;
For I will rise again!

"And then I drop the Number Seven and roll off the back of the platform and—a word for your wounded manservant might be appropriate here, Wolkin."

Gard scrambled to his hands and knees and grabbed Mr. Bracket's wrist.

"What are you doing?" asked Mr. Bracket, opening his eyes.

"Putting a tourniquet on your wrist with my sandal lace."
"Oh, good touch!"

Er, Oh, Batto, do not say that thou art slain!
Oh faithful friend, stay yet awhile with me
Or I shall die with thee, for shame that my strength failed
While thine was steady as the humble earth!

"Good, good, and, er, I'll say:

Oh, dear master, however shall I cook your breakfast now
And me with one hand gone?

"And I suppose at this point we can either have me die pathetically brave—"

"Not *right* after the Dark Lord's death scene, I think," said Mr. Tinwick, from the floor.

"Hm. All right; I could maunder on about how I think I'm going to die, and do that speech where I ask Dear Master to comfort my Old Father and tell my Sweetheart how I'd been going to set up in business with her and run a clam stand. Shall I?"

"That one runs on a bit, I think. We want to go fairly quickly to the Wedding/Coronation scene, don't we?" said Mr. Tinwick, getting up.

"Do we?" Mr. Bracket glared at him.

"What about this?" Gard got up on his knees.

Fear not, Batto, dearest friend,
Though my strength failed me, still I have enough
To carry thee hence, though thou weighedst twice
What thou dost. Let us go; stopping only
To free good Elti and Jibbi from the Black Dungeon of F'narb.

Without effort, Gard lifted Mr. Bracket in his arms. Mr. Bracket looked up at him, startled.

"Good gods, man, what did you use to do for a living besides soldiery? Load barges?"

Gard sagged, pretending to buckle at the knees. "Whew! No. You're heavier than you look."

"I'll just lean on you, then, and we'll stagger offstage together," said Mr. Bracket, regaining his feet. *"Elti! Jibbi! We're coming for you, brave lads!"*

"A fine house," said Mr. Tinwick, rubbing his hands together as he leaned back from peering through the screen. "All the usuals plus some new faces. Word must have got round that we have a talented new performer!"

"Either that or they want something to take their minds off the war rumors," said Pulkas. He fitted on his mask. "Hi ho, out we go. Death and destruction, all."

Gard stepped up on the platform when his cue came and looked out at the audience. All things being equal, he had expected the same sensation-greedy faces that had watched him fighting for his life in the arena. He was unnerved, then, to see a different look entirely, in their reflecting eyes. There was a grim intensity, a solemn attention, a *humorlessness* that made him wish—briefly—that he were about to face Trathegost or Pocktuun.

He found his mouth was dry when he spoke his lines.

Welcome, Wizard! Often have I thought
Of how thou tutoredst me, in happy days gone by.
What now brings thee to my humble home?

"Well done, well done, all!" said Mr. Tinwick, when the applause died at last and they were backstage, changing out of costume. "Notes tomorrow morning; we don't want to keep our public waiting, do we? I will just say, however, that Satra brought particular pathos to Clemona's death scene."

"Oh, thank you, Mr. Tinwick!" Satra looked at him with adoration.

"And plaudits to Wolkin as well. Though I do think, Mr. Smith, that you made the sword fights look a little too easy. Kendon must struggle, remember. Kendon must suffer. That is what the audience wishes to see in a Hero."

"I'll remember that, sir," said Gard.

"Big crowd outside!" said Mr. Carbon gleefully, coming back in. He had already gotten out of costume, the Wizard having died in the first act, and had in fact had time to go down to the nearest tavern for his dinner. "Patrons galore! Lady Pickrock was asking when you'd be out, Bracket. And there was a Lord Garnet asking after you, Miss Ironbolt."

Mr. Bracket and Miss Ironbolt, who had been kissing quietly in a corner, looked around at that. Miss Ironbolt sighed. Mr. Bracket shrugged. "Duty calls," he said. "See you at breakfast?"

"Mine usually sleeps late," said Miss Ironbolt, pulling on her scarf.

"Mine's been waking with the damned market carts." Mr. Bracket threw his cloak around his shoulders. "Oh, well; luncheon, then. Good night, one and all."

"Many ladies outside?" asked Mr. Tinwick.

"Five that I counted, Tinny, and they're all asking for the Dark Lord," said Mr. Carbon, nudging him. Mr. Tinwick looked as smug as it is possible for a man to look. Satra looked pale and stricken. She watched without a word as he swaggered out and was greeted by eager women.

Gard stared after him. Clarn, observing his bewilderment, chuckled. "I know what you're thinking. But it's astonishing, the effect black armor has on some ladies. Cheer up! He can only go off with one or two; we usually get the leavings."

"What?"

"Patrons!" said Pulkas, hurriedly fastening his sandals. "They'll pay us to entertain them. A drink, at the least. Dinner, probably. Sweet dalliance if you're *very* lucky and they're *very* stagestruck. Other little presents, if you sing them a song or two. Though all my last one wanted to do was ask me about what Tinny's really like." Pulkas threw on his cloak and rushed out the door, followed closely by Clarn.

"You'd better catch up to them," said Satra in a woeful voice. "The wealthy ones will be all gone if you wait."

"I thought I'd go home to bed," said Gard. "I'm tired. Aren't you?"

"Oh, I always stay late." Satra blinked back tears. "I need to tidy up Mr. Tinwick's armor."

"Don't mind me," said Mr. Carbon, who was spreading out a sleeping mat in the corner. "I do hope you won't take too long, though, eh? A man my age needs his rest." He raised his head, and over Satra's shoulder he mouthed at Gard, *Take her out to dinner!*

"May I take you to dinner?"

"Screwbite's down the lane is still open," said Mr. Carbon helpfully, shaking out his blanket.

"Please," said Gard. "The costume won't go anywhere before morning."

Satra hesitated, biting her lip.

Gard took her hand. "Please? It would be nice to have company."

"All right. I can always come back early tomorrow." Satra took her scarf from its hook. Drawing it over her head, she followed Gard out.

They walked down the steep lane, between the flaring lamps, through the shadows and the light. Gard thought, *I am walking out with a girl I have invited to dinner. Not servicing my owner, not paying for love in a club. How strange.* He looked up at the stars and tried to imagine them shining above a dancing green, instead of these stone streets. He tried to imagine the scent of white blossoms. He couldn't, and gave it up with a sigh.

The tavern was a small place, quiet. They sat outside in a tiled courtyard, by a brick oven. The waiter brought them wine and grilled sausages and onions. Satra was beautiful by firelight, melancholy in a poetic sort of way. Hesitant, Gard asked her to tell him about herself.

She didn't tell him much—not about herself, in any case. She was twenty-two, had been born in a little town near Troon, and at the age of sixteen had visited a friend here in Deliantiba. They'd gone to the theater. Mr. Tinwick's performance had left her spellbound. She had known, then, with blinding clarity of revelation, that nothing was more important than a life in the theater. She'd quarreled with her parents, she'd been disinherited, she'd come back to Deliantiba with nothing, but bravely; she'd gone to the theater and begged to audition, and Mr. Tinwick had admitted her into the company.

So much Gard learned from Satra before she got on the subject of what a genius Mr. Tinwick was, after which she talked for two hours straight. Gard nodded and listened and refilled her wine cup until she began weeping into it, after which he finished the jar himself. When the waiter came out and banked the coals in the oven against the morning, Gard suggested gently that he ought to take her home.

Satra thanked him profusely, tearfully. He escorted her downhill to the wretched quarter where she had a room in a lodging house, even barer than his room, with no window at all. When he took her hand and bent down to whisper good night, she put her arms around his neck and kissed him passionately. Her tears were hot on his face. She pulled him into the room and they ended up coupling on her narrow bed, desperate with longing, though Gard knew well she did not long for him.

He left her, courteously, before he could fall asleep and betray himself. Walking back up the hill, he was rushed by a thief with a club and merely broke the man's wrist before driving him off. No dancing green under these stars, no white blossoms.

Next morning at the theater Satra smiled at him, but distantly, as she polished the Dark Lord's mask with its crested helmet. When Mr. Carbon went out to find some breakfast, they had a moment of privacy; she thanked Gard for a lovely evening, but said it was probably best they didn't do it again.

————

Gard was mulling that over when Mr. Bracket wandered in, yawning, still in the clothes he had worn the previous night.

"Morning, Smith. May I just say I thought you did well, for a novice?"

"Thank you."

Bracket sat down beside Gard and eyed him critically. "Found a patroness last night, did you?"

"No."

"Ah." Bracket looked over at the properties shed, where there was a faint clatter as Satra hung up the Dark Lord's armor. "I see. Well, better luck tonight. A word of advice, my friend?"

"If you like."

"Drama's delightful on a stage, but a damnable thing in a bedroom."

"I'll remember that. Thank you."

Mr. Carbon wandered in from the street, clutching a paper sack. "Look at these!" He hefted the sack. "Yesterday's rolls from the bakery. One copper piece for the lot, can you imagine? Have some. I've lots."

"*Ooh, Master Wizard, can't you magic up some food for us?*" quoted Bracket absently, helping himself to a roll and handing one to Gard. They were sitting there chewing laboriously when a bright trumpet-call came from the street.

"That'll be a runner with the broadsheets," said Bracket, and leaping up, he sprinted to the gate that opened on the street. The runner in her red uniform was just passing, a roll of the fresh-printed stuff under her arm.

"Here!" Bracket tossed her a coin. She peeled off a sheet and handed it to him, as Clarn and Pulkas edged past her and came into the yard.

"Reviews, is it?" said Pulkas. "Don't expect them to be good. Plater was in the front row last night, you know."

"Who?" Gard looked curiously at the wide sheet of cheap paper, as Bracket returned with it.

"One of Deliantiba's literary lights," said Carbon.

"He wishes," said Clarn, delving into the bag of rolls. "He's a bastard."

"Is that the broadsheet?" Satra emerged from the properties shed.

"The fellow in the purple tunic, Wolkin," said Bracket, scanning the rows of print. "Perhaps you noticed? Stared without blinking or smiling the whole time."

"At least he pays attention," said Satra.

"Bloody hell, here's more war rumors. I don't care whether Parrackas or Skalkin gets the throne, but I wish they'd just fight a duel like plain men and get it over with. Here we are: 'Shadow of the Dark Lord, at Tinwick's Theater. A review by Enokas Plater. Attan Tinwick continues his worthwhile effort to present the classical Epic in its purest form. Last night's entertainment, while solid overall, nevertheless put us in mind of the manifest truth that a chain is only as strong as its weakest link.'"

"Oh, here it comes," said Clarn, groaning.

"'The story was yet another of Mr. Tinwick's brilliant and moving variations on the Great Theme. Kendon (played with splendid gravity and sincerity by newcomer Wolkin Smith; we hope to see more of him, as he seems to have an innate understanding of heroic solemnity) is, unbeknownst to himself, the last heir of the nearly extinguished line of Northern Kings. He is living in poverty and obscurity when his old tutor, the Wizard, brings him an unexpected gift: the Lost Sword of Farnglast, misplaced by Kendon's father twenty years earlier. The Wizard also brings him fearful news: the Dark Lord has once again risen and is gathering his forces at the Crater of Dread, and only the Sword of Farnglast can kill the Dark Lord.' And blah blah blah."

"Be amazed, Wolkin; he liked you!" said Pulkas.

"'. . . tragic death of Clemona,' blah blah, '. . . dragon fight particularly good . . .'"

"He liked you too." Pulkas addressed the dragon, lurking at the side of the stage: a barrel painted with scales and wings, a wooden head on the front end with staring glass eyes and gaping jaws, a bellows in the other end to blow red ribbons out of its mouth for flames, and the whole mounted on a pair of wheels.

"'. . . carried by the power and majesty of Mr. Tinwick's performance as usual. His Dark Lord is a masterpiece of suppressed inner turmoil and remorse, the whole driven by steely and unswerving purpose. Having said that, we could only wish his supporting players'—ouch, now falls the blow—'supporting players were as dedicated. The necessary jesting of Elti and Jibbi is fitting in its place, but to our eyes Mr. Smith and Mr. Rivet veer perilously close to self-parody. These young gentlemen would do well to learn from the generations of comedians who have proceeded them.'"

"What a command of language," said Clarn. "Learned it at his mother's knee, no doubt, while she was performing favors for sailors."

"Ahem. Oh, dear, Mr. Carbon: 'Moreover the actor portraying the

Wizard brought an unwelcome note of levity to the scene wherein he informs Kendon of his Destiny. Conjuring tricks may delight the lower element in the audience, but we could wish Mr. Carbon had chosen a more dignified interpretation of this crucial role.'"

"He didn't like the colored scarves?" Mr. Carbon sagged. "I spent *hours* learning to do that one."

"'Miss Ironbolt was exquisite as Princess Andiel, and Miss Joist brought a suitable pathos to the role of Clemona.'"

"That's all he ever says about us," said Satra, sighing.

"Be grateful," said Bracket distractedly, reading on. He winced.

"What's he say?" asked Pulkas.

"The pompous bastard. 'If Mr. Bracket has, with Mr. Carbon, taken it upon himself to add vulgar interest and amusement to Mr. Tinwick's script, he would be well advised to leave off. While Batto's bravery in the fourth act was adequately portrayed, his previous tendency to clown and steal scenes from Kendon sharply undercut the essential heroism of the role.

"'All in all, I expected more from this company. It is to be hoped these flaws will be corrected as the season progresses.'"

"Sod him," said Mr. Carbon, feeling about for his smoking tube. He drew it out, packed it with an aromatic weed, and lit up.

"Good morning, one and all," said Mr. Tinwick grandly, entering through the street door. "Seen the review? Congratulations, Wolkin! A triumph!"

"We *have* seen the review, thank you, and it's nothing to celebrate," said Pulkas. "What makes you so damned cheerful?"

"We have a new patroness," said Mr. Tinwick. "An extraordinarily generous one. Fancy a new Wizard's costume, Mr. Carbon? And what about getting that broken corner of the stage fixed?" From his belt pouch Mr. Tinwick pulled a bag of something that clinked suggestively.

———

The new patroness was Lady Filigree. She was tall and slender and exquisitely bred, if a little past her prime; she came and sat in the back of the house, smiling in an ethereal sort of way, and watched rehearsals. When she was formally introduced to the cast, she shook each one by the hand and murmured "How do you do?" or "Delightful to meet you" or "I am so happy to make your acquaintance, sir."

"That's how the old blood do it," said Clarn out of the side of his mouth to Gard. "Ever so polite."

When she took Gard's hand, she said, "And how long have you studied under Mr. Tinwick?"

"Only a month and four days, madam," said Gard.

She cocked her head slightly. "May I ask, sir, where you were born?"

"The islands."

"Whereabouts?"

"Chadravac," said Gard warily.

"Now, that's interesting. I would have taken you for a Patrayka man.
You have the accent. Not one of the farming folk, though. Tell me, were
you raised in one of the great houses there? You speak just like one of the
Silverpoints."

"My father worked for the Silverpoints."

"I see." Lady Filigree looked at Gard thoughtfully. "Lovely family. I
knew them, when I was a girl. Of course, they're all gone now. Pity."

"Indeed, madam." Gard was aware of his fellow cast members eyeing
him in a speculative sort of way.

———

Lady Filigree's money paid for a gorgeous robe of blue shot silk for the
Wizard, trimmed with silver thread. Mr. Carbon was forbidden to smoke
anywhere near it. She also provided the company with five new masks—
an Old Nurse, three Gods, and a Demon—as well as a prop tree with a
bird puppet mounted in its branches, useful for prophecies and warnings.
Mr. Tinwick wrote a grand new piece incorporating all these new elements, to be titled *The Doom of the Northern Kings*.

On a humbler note, Lady Filigree also paid for a mason to come in and
repoint the mortar in the stage platform. It turned out to need one entire
corner relaid, however, and—sensing the depth of the purse—the mason
suggested that a new retaining wall at the back of the house would not only
be safer but improve the overall acoustics of the place. He pocketed the coin
and left his apprentice to do the work. The apprentice, a badly stagestruck
youth, spent a lot of time watching rehearsals with his trowel in his hand.

———

"Right," said Bracket. "We can at least begin blocking the scene, until he
gets here."

"It's not like him to be so late," said Satra fretfully. "Should we report it
to the city guard?"

"No," said Mr. Carbon. "They'd only arrest us all, the bastards. He's
probably still dallying with the patroness, that's all. Breakfast in bed or
some such."

Satra turned away, her eyes welling with tears. Gard looked at her, wondering if he ought to say something consoling, but Clarn caught his eye and shook his head.

"So, here we are, scene at the Outskirts of the Forest—which means we'll have the two little trees out here and the Prophesying Bird tree there. Kendon and Batto are beset by forest bandits—that'll be you two in the Brigand masks," added Bracket, nodding at Pulkas and Clarn.

"Oh, that'll look realistic, won't it?" said Pulkas. "Two little shrimps like us defeating the two of you?"

"It could happen," said Bracket. "For one thing, Batto can be clumsy and trip or something. Suppose I leap up crying, 'Oh, dear master, have a care,' or some such, and—I know! I can drop my string of cooking pans and fall over it. And one of the Brigands can club me."

"Even so, how do we take down Kendon?"

"I'll show you." Gard handed out wooden swords and coached them through the choreography of the fight. They finished up with Gard disarmed and their blades at his throat. The mason's apprentice applauded. "You see?" said Gard.

"Nice!" said Pulkas. "Had a private arms tutor, your lordship?"

"No," said Gard, scowling. Lately it had been assumed he was some bastard of the Silverpoint house, living incognito. "I was a soldier."

"If you say so. Well, and so then your line is . . ."

Quoted Gard,

Alas, good Batto, art thou slain?
Varlets, what wantest thou
With two poor travelers? We have no gold,
Nothing except our honesty and firm purpose.

"Of course you know your lines by heart," said Pulkas. "And we'll do a lot of har-har, nudge-nudge, and then the line is usually something like:

His Dark Lordship cares not for your gold,
It is your life he'd have us rip away!

"And then there's a long torture scene, before Clemona comes to rescue you."

"There is?" Gard was disconcerted. "What for?"

"It's just one of the Epic conventions," said Bracket, from where he sprawled on the stage. "The Hero gets tortured. Repeatedly. So we'll need the prop brazier and the pokers, and the knives with syrup packets in the blades, Carbon."

"Right." Mr. Carbon tapped out his smoking tube and wandered off in the direction of the properties shed. "Been using the brazier as a wash-stand. It's under my shaving mirror."

"And whatever you do, *don't* laugh while you're being tortured," said Clarn. "That gets Plater especially pissy."

"Just keep telling yourself, 'I'm a serious artist,'" said Bracket.

The street door opened and Mr. Tinwick walked in arm in arm with Lady Filigree. She fairly glowed with happiness. He looked giddy. The mason's apprentice rose and bowed low.

"My apologies, all," Tinwick said, waving his hand. "Ah! You're hard at work. What good children. Act two, scene one, I see. They seem to have everything well in hand, my dear. What about a bottle of wine at the Marsh Goose?"

"I should like that very much," said Lady Filigree, smiling. "But your art must come first, dear Mr. Tinwick. May I watch the rest of the re-hearsal?"

"I should be desolated if you didn't," said Mr. Tinwick, kissing her. She found a seat as he swaggered forward and mounted the stage. Satra, who was just emerging from the properties shed with her wooden sword, saw the kiss. She turned pale and rushed back inside.

"Now! The Brigands capture Kendon," said Mr. Tinwick. "Which brings us, of course, to the torture scene."

"I was just bringing out the brazier, Tinny," said Mr. Carbon, holding it up. "We might want to repaint the coals. They're a bit dusty."

"We should, yes. But . . ." Mr. Tinwick stroked his mustache. "You know . . . let's try something new. I think we'll have him tortured offstage, in this one."

"Plater won't like that," said Pulkas.

"A fig for Plater. This sort of scene is far more horrible if left to the au-dience's imaginations, you see? And so you'll drag Kendon off, leaving faithful Batto for dead. And Clemona finds him, when she comes search-ing. Yes!" Mr. Tinwick looked immensely pleased with himself.

"All right," said Clarn, and mimed tying Gard's wrists.

His Dark Lordship cares not for your gold,
It is your life he'd have us rip away!

Come away now to, er, the Castle of Doom!
There in its dungeons we'll teach you
The true meaning of pain!

"Har-har, nudge nudge. And we exit."

"Very good," said Mr. Tinwick. Gard stepped down from the platform and seated himself in the audience.

"I thought you were great," said the mason's apprentice sotto voce. "I'd give anything to be able to be up there."

"It doesn't pay very well," said Gard.

"I wouldn't care."

"Good morning, Mr. Smith," said Lady Filigree, rising to approach him. He and the mason's apprentice rose awkwardly, and she gestured to indicate they should sit again before seating herself beside Gard.

"Now," said Mr. Tinwick, "let's see . . . Batto has been left for dead. Miss Joist, I think Clemona enters from the left, falls to her knees beside him, and . . ."

Oh, faithful Batto! Art thou truly slain?
And where is my love, princely Kendon?
Let me but find his noble corpse
And three shall lie dead in this accursed forest!

"Wouldn't she scream first?" said Mr. Tinwick.

"I'm sorry, Mr. Tinwick," said Satra. "I'll do it again."

"Too right," said the mason's apprentice. "Of course she'd scream. He's a bloody genius."

"He is that," said Lady Filigree quietly.

"I mean, you'd never think to look at a little fellow like him that he's that Dark Lord. He comes out in that mask and all, and you just can't take your eyes off him," said the mason's apprentice. Gard glanced over his shoulder at the unfinished retaining wall.

"He understands how to appear more than what he is," said Lady Filigree.

"And that Dark Lord! He's so . . . like . . . *powerful*," said the mason's apprentice. "Really, even with him being evil and all, I like him better than the hero. No offense, sir," he added hastily, nodding to Gard.

"That's all right," said Gard.

"He does haunt the imagination," said Lady Filigree. "He is a looming mystery. People love that."

In that moment, clear as though she sat behind him, Gard heard Balnshik's voice:

But those who are weak love the appearance of power. How they worship it in others! . . . You be the unspoken threat, the never-raised voice, untouched, unmoved and implacable. . . . They will fear you, without quite being aware they are afraid. Then they will admire you. Then they will desperately love you.

Gard shook his head, wondering.

"No, dear," Mr. Tinwick was saying. "Let's try it again with just those little changes, shall we? One more time." And Satra, clenching her fists until the knuckles stood out, took a deep breath.

Faithful Batto, lean on me; together we'll go forth
The Castle of F'narh to seek, and there
We'll rescue valiant Kendon—

"Castle of Doom," Mr. Tinwick corrected her.

"I'm sorry, Mr. Tinwick."

"Don't apologize, dear, just go on with the line."

"Yes, Mr. Tinwick."

"It's a grand and a noble thing you're doing, being a patroness here, mistress," said the mason's apprentice. "That Wizard's new robe is just a treat to look at. If I was rich, I'd do the same with my money, so I would."

"It's as good a way to spend one's fortune as any other," murmured Lady Filigree. "Service to the arts. With the world spinning into madness, why not? A little entertainment takes one's mind off the troubles."

"Oh. You mean the war?" The mason's apprentice remembered his trowel and stirred his basin of mortar with it. "I can't understand what it's all about, myself."

"The same old story." Lady Filigree looked sidelong at Gard. "Two clans hate each other and find a reason to quarrel. They fight and innocents die on both sides. Sometimes everyone dies. The Silverpoints went that way. Any survivors must flee and take new names, or they'll be followed for blood debt."

"I have heard that is true, madam," said Gard cautiously.

"Well, what I say is, Duke Parrackas is our man, and that other fellow can go stick his head in a bucket," said the mason's apprentice.

"At *last*," Mr. Tinwick was saying, "let's move on to the Castle of Doom, shall we? Kendon is unconscious in chains."

"Pardon me, madam," said Gard, rising to bow to Lady Filigree. He stepped onstage and hit his mark, huddling himself into something approximating the posture of the beaten and unconscious slaves he'd seen.

"And let's have one of the Brigands about to commence torturing him again," said Mr. Tinwick. "Clarn?"

"Right. *Har-har, sleeping, are you? I'll rudely awaken—*"

"So, are you going to want the brazier of coals or not, then?" Mr. Carbon inquired.

"No. Just bring out the daggers, will you?" said Mr. Tinwick. "Are they all charged? The audience will want a little blood."

"Oh, I know!" said Clarn. "What about the flaying scene?

Your skin is smooth, bold hero,
I'll make a present of it to my dark master,
Scraped parchment on which he'll write
The doom of all your house.

Clarn rummaged hastily in the basket of daggers as Mr. Carbon brought them out and drew the blade of one down Gard's raised arm, depressing the catch with his thumb. The wooden blade was pressed back into the hollow hilt, breaking the little bladder of red syrup inside. It made a quite painful-looking red line along Gard's arm. Gard pretended to struggle, baring his teeth.

"And while the Brigand's so engaged, Clemona enters and stabs him," said Mr. Tinwick. "Miss Joist? Where has she got to?"

"Here!" said Satra, emerging from the properties shed. She wiped her eyes with her sleeve. "Sorry."

"Your beloved is about to be flayed alive, Miss Joist; I'm sure he would appreciate a little punctuality on your part," said Mr. Tinwick pleasantly enough, but Satra went pale with mortification. She pulled a dagger from the basket.

"*Die, vile wretch! That skin is dear to me—,*" she began, advancing on the Brigand.

"Wait! Clarn, for whom are we playing this scene? I'm sure Wolkin finds your menacing leer profoundly upsetting, but wouldn't it be nice if the audience could see it as well?" said Mr. Tinwick. "Cheat out!"

"I *am* cheating out," said Clarn.

"Oh, gods below," said Mr. Tinwick, advancing on him. "Here, give me the dagger. Go sit in the audience. Watch." He crouched over Gard, dagger upraised.

"*I'll make a present of it to my dark master,* la la la, and Clemona comes in with *her* line—"

"*Die, vile wretch! That skin is dear to me!*" cried Satra, and stabbed Mr. Tinwick.

Gard saw Mr. Tinwick's eyes open wide. He lurched upright, staggering back. "Gods!" screamed Satra, and fainted. Mr. Tinwick reached around and tried to pull the wooden blade from his back.

"Oh. It's really gone in, hasn't it?" he said, gasping.

"Nine Hells!" shouted Clarn. Gard scrambled to his feet and grabbed Mr. Tinwick, whose knees were starting to fold, as Clarn vaulted onstage and reached for the dagger.

"Don't pull it out!" Lady Filigree's voice carried steely authority. "Hold him up and still. Girl!" She addressed Miss Ironbolt, who had just come in through the street door. "Run to my house. Number Three, Street of the Pines. Have them bring my personal physician and a sedan chair, immediately."

Miss Ironbolt, eyes wide, turned and fled.

"I'm sure it was an accident," murmured Mr. Tinwick.

"Course it was," said Clarn, attempting to sound hearty. "It's the stupid dagger's fault. The catch sticks. I nearly stabbed Pulkas last week with it. Not to worry. Didn't go in all that deep. I don't think."

Gard looked down over Mr. Tinwick's shoulder at the projecting hilt. He was fairly sure the blade must have punctured Mr. Tinwick's lung. "We need to bind him to a ladder. Something that'll hold him still without putting any pressure on the knife."

"Yes," said Lady Filigree, striding onstage. She was followed by the mason's apprentice, who was weeping and wringing his hands. "You've seen such wounds before, then."

"Our Wolkin was a soldier," said Bracket, hauling a ladder from the rafters of the properties shed.

"I thought as much," said Lady Filigree.

"Is there anything I can do?" said the mason's apprentice.

"Yes. Help me fasten him to the ladder," said Lady Filigree, and began tearing her veil into wide strips.

"I had rather die than that the sun should spoil such beauty," said Mr.

Tinwick with a feeble giggle. A pink froth dribbled from the corner of his mouth.

"Don't talk nonsense, my dear," she replied briskly. In less than a minute Mr. Tinwick was immobilized and propped against the wall.

"I expect I'll go out and take down the posters for *Doom of the Northern Kings,* then," said Mr. Carbon. Mr. Tinwick's back—he was facing the wall—twitched.

"You can't!" they heard him say, with a gasp. "We've sold out the first three nights!"

"Look, Tinny, you'll never be able to go on," said Bracket. "It's only two nights from now. You can't go onstage and faint in your damned mask."

"Temporary," said Mr. Tinwick. "Understudy."

"Understudy *you?* None of us can do the Dark Lord," said Clarn.

"I rather think young Wolkin is equal to the task," said Lady Filigree. "He has the presence."

There was a silence, punctuated only by Mr. Tinwick's wheezes. "Yes," he said at last. "He'll do. Bracket, you're Kendon. Been onstage with him long enough, you know his lines."

Bracket opened his mouth in amazement but said nothing. "Who's Batto, then?" said Mr. Carbon.

"Please!" The mason's apprentice dropped to his knees against the wall, peering up sideways at Mr. Tinwick. "Oh, sir, I know all his lines! I've been listening to the play for three days now! I could do it, I know I could! It'd be an honor!"

"Who the hell are you?" said Mr. Tinwick, trying to turn his head to see.

"Jort Flywheel, sir! I been doing your retaining wall. Please! I've wanted to be a player half my life!"

"Er . . . you can audition," said Mr. Tinwick. "How would that be?"

"Oh, sir!" Jort burst into tears again, and caught Mr. Tinwick's hand and kissed it. At this moment Miss Ironbolt returned, followed closely by a battle-scarred surgeon and a pair of servants with a sedan chair.

The next few minutes were busy for Gard, as he found himself conscripted into the role of the surgeon's assistant. Sometime during the repair and bandaging of Mr. Tinwick's wound, Satra was revived by Clarn and led to the back of the house. There she wept on his shoulder and he made sympathetic and reassuring noises. Mr. Carbon packed his smoking tube with pinkweed and brought it back to share with them, and the three of them grew glassy-eyed and calm.

Mr. Tinwick was bound into the sedan chair at last and borne off, with Lady Filigree marching along behind. Gard was just collapsing into a seat when Pulkas came in by the street door.

"Sorry I'm late," he said. "I had to go the long way around. There's an army recruiter team working Oilpress Street. Have I missed anything?"

After two days of sleeping upright and taking clear broth, Mr. Tinwick was pronounced out of immediate danger, though strictly forbidden to speak in anything louder than a conversational voice.

His actors had little time to worry about him, preparing for the opening of *The Doom of the Northern Kings*. Jort Flywheel passed his audition handily, to Pulkas's irritation, and won the role of Batto for his own. He was not especially bright, but he could memorize lines.

"Gods below, look at them out there," said Bracket, watching through the screen. "It's packed. There are people sitting up above the quarry cut. Free seats! Go out and make them buy tickets, Mr. Carbon."

"Sod off," said Mr. Carbon, who was being dressed in his shot silk robe and desperately wanted a smoke to calm his nerves.

"There's Tinwick!" said Clarn. "Milady's got him trussed up to a frame beside her. He looks like a ship's figurehead."

"Let's make him proud, everyone," said Miss Ironbolt.

"Bloody right!" said Mr. Flywheel, tearing up. "Come on, three cheers for Mr. Tinwick!"

"Not back here, you ninny," said Pulkas. He prodded the front of Gard's papier-mâché breastplate. "You all right in there? His armor's a little tight on you, isn't it?"

"I feel like a cockroach," said Gard.

"Well, you don't look like one," said Bracket. "You look frighteningly effective. Masks, all. Elti and Jibbi? Let's go, boys. Death and destruction."

"Death and destruction," they all echoed.

When he went back to his bare little room that night and took up his pen, Enokas Plater would stare at the blank page for a full five minutes before carefully inscribing the characters for *Perfection*.

The Doom of the Northern Kings went off with an eerie smoothness. Kendon the Hero was gallant and brave, but no fool. His faithful servant Batto fairly trembled with honest devotion, and tragic Clemona was red-eyed and miserable. Gard made his entrance at last as the Dark Lord and heard the audience draw breath, just as they had in the arena when he had been about to deliver the killing cut to an opponent.

He thought his performance was wooden, compared to Mr. Tinwick's. He drew on everything he could remember of Balnshik's advice, keeping his reactions muted, his speeches to a minimum. But he had never spoken in the arena, and so he had to fall back on Mr. Tinwick's delivery, the same pauses, the same inflections. So focused was he on getting it right that he was halfway through his duel with the Wizard before he thought to look out at the audience.

They might have been made of stone. Intent, spellbound, leaning forward every one except for Mr. Tinwick, and in his eyes Gard saw agony and was startled.

"I don't think Mr. Tinwick likes it," he said to Mr. Carbon, when they stood together in the properties shed after the Wizard's death.

"Bloody hell, of course he doesn't like it," said Mr. Carbon, as he shrugged out of his Wizard's robe. "You're better than he is! Congratulations, boy. It's your theater now. Shouldn't be surprised if Lady Filigree pulls some more strings on your behalf."

"But I don't want a theater."

"Oh, yes, you do. With all the posh ladies you can tumble? And there's nice food and a nice villa of your own and maybe even a title in it for you. Take it, son. We don't get chances like this every day. Some of us never get them. Your cue's coming up, by the way."

Stepping back out onstage, Gard delivered his lines with thunder in his voice and saw the audience respond. Involuntary shivers, moist lips, gleaming eyes, utter fascination. Gleaming eyes.

Two pairs of silver eyes were in the audience.

They belonged to a pair of men, identical twins apparently, somewhat lumpish and misshapen-looking but with a general resemblance to Triphammer. Their gazes were fixed on Gard, tracking him upstage and down.

The Doom of the Northern Kings had been intended as a trilogy, and so the Dark Lord did not die at the end but merely escaped with his minions in a chariot drawn by dragons. Gard's breastplate was therefore still smooth, shiny and black when he took his bows at the end, as the audience stamped and screamed and applauded. Because it was too tight for him to remove without help, he was still wearing the breastplate when the others trooped in after the lamps had been extinguished onstage.

"Oh, we *nailed* it tonight!" shouted Clarn.

"They're packing up five deep at the back gate," said Mr. Carbon in awe. "Ye gods, Wolkin, you can have any one of them. Any *dozen* of them."

"Will you help me out of this?" said Gard, but before Mr. Carbon could oblige, Bracket leaned over and said in a low urgent voice, "Wolkin, Tinny's here to see you. Be tactful, eh?"

Gard edged his way through the other actors crabwise and came face-to-face with Mr. Tinwick, rigidly upright in his brace. He was pale, but smiling as he looked up at Gard. "Here's the man of the hour. My boy, you've made me very proud." He reached out awkwardly—one of his arms was bandaged to his side—and clasped Gard's hand.

"I thought I was awful," said Gard.

"But the audience didn't," said Mr. Tinwick. "And that is all that matters. You gave them exactly what they wanted."

"Speaking of wanted," said Clarn, "they're asking for you at the gate, Wolkin."

"I need to change out of costume," said Gard, feeling his heart racing.

"No, no!" said Mr. Tinwick. "Go out in the armor and the black cloak. They love it. You'll be treated to the best dinner of your life. Go out and enjoy your fame, my friend."

"Thank you," said Gard wretchedly, thinking of the silver-eyed men. He managed to grab a pair of knives from his street clothing as he sidled back to the gate, and hid them away on his person. Clarn helpfully threw the gate open, and Gard looked out on a crowd of eager-eyed citizens. There was applause.

"The Dark Lord!"

"Oh, Mr. Smith, you were magnificent!"

"Mr. Smith, I wonder if I might have a moment of your time?"

"Mr. Smith, I have a son who wants to become an actor, and I wonder if you might talk to him—"

"Mr. Smith, I wonder if you'd be interested—"

"I, er, was going to go for dinner at Screwbite's," said Gard. "If any of you would like—"

"Screwbite's? No, no! Mr. Smith, I have a room reserved at the Chalice," said one woman, reaching through the sea of faces to clasp his hand. "Aleka Tourmaline, drama critic for the *Sun Viper*. Please join our party. I'd like to talk to you about doing an exclusive interview."

The men with silver eyes were standing back from the crowd, across the street.

"Why don't we all go?" said Gard, sweating.

"But I—," said Miss Tourmaline, and was drowned out by a gleeful chorus of acceptance from all the other women present. She looked around sulkily. "All right, then."

Gard moved off down the street in the center of a milling mass of admirers both male and female. The men with the silver eyes kept their distance, but kept pace.

The Chalice was on the Street of Golden Lamps, in the nicest part of Deliantiba. Glittering shops lined either side of the street; Gard found it perilously similar to the Upper Tunnels under the mountain, and only the clear stars overhead—as opposed to cunningly worked lanterns—assured him that he wasn't back there now.

His party was ushered into a private banquet room. He was seated at an immense table draped in fine cloth. Obsequious waiters recited a list of dishes and asked him to choose; when he stammered, Miss Tourmaline chose for him. Wine was brought to the table, not the plain red stuff served at Screwbite's, but something bright, fragrant of almonds and flowers, sparkling in crystal.

The dishes, when they were carried in, were exquisite. Gard had never tasted anything so wonderful in his life. He ate ravenously, asking for more when he had cleaned one plate, and his smiling hostess had more set before him. He paid particular attention to her questions, answering as best he could with his mouth full. Bluff soldierly candor seemed the safest mask.

He had lived some while in Patrayka as a child, had a good education, knocked around a bit before going on the stage. Where? Oh, here and there. No, he was not married. When had he known he was a genius? Oh, he wasn't anything of the kind; just an ordinary working actor. Mr. Tinwick was the genius. What did he think of Epic Theater? He thought it was all right. Didn't he plan to move on to *real* theater soon, instead of this quaint genre stuff? He hadn't thought about it. Compliments and inane questions from the others in the party fell about him like flower petals.

All during the meal, the other women in the party (and some few of the men) kept passing small objects up and setting them beside his wineglass. Quite a mound of them was there by the time he had a moment to look at them, and he blinked in astonishment. Each was a clay disk soaked in a differing floral scent, stamped with a name, an address, and the hours when a visitor would be welcomed. Mr. Tinwick had accumulated bags full of them, and they were coveted by the other cast members. Now

Gard had his own pile of tokens, any one of which would admit him to a perfumed boudoir.

There he sat, in the finest society, in the midst of cultured people who adored him, answering their chatter with calculated phrases as ably as a courtier. And on the other side of the restaurant's window Gard's old life waited in the street, watching him with unblinking silver eyes.

He excused himself at last, to everyone's dismay. Smiling, he told them about the tight breastplate and his need to remove it, to appreciative giggles. Several people offered to remove it for him there and then, but he declined courteously, citing a desire to get some sleep after the rigors of the evening's performance. He swept the black cloak around himself for a showy exit and left to cheers and applause.

It was quiet in the dark streets; the stars had dropped far down to the horizon. Gard stared across at the silver-eyed pair and walked away rapidly, heading for the edge of town. They followed him, keeping to their own side of the street. He led them off into the maze of alleys near the apartment block where he lived. When he had found a place that seemed suitable, he stopped. They came a little closer and stopped too.

"We liked the play," said Grattur.

"You were good. You made us proud," said Engrattur.

"By the Blue Pit, that's what a demon lord ought to look like!"

"It makes me feel terrible about what we were sent to do."

"What have you been sent to do?" said Gard, bringing out the two knives he had concealed in his cloak.

"Oh, we're forbidden to tell you that," said Grattur.

"Her ladyship laid strong spells on us to prevent us telling you," said Engrattur.

"So, of course, we *won't* tell you we're supposed to kidnap you."

"No, indeed. That would be disobeying."

"And you know what she's like when she's disobeyed."

"So we won't disobey. For example, we won't tell you what happened after you broke the mountain."

"We won't tell you how her ladyship survived, and Lord Vergoin, and enough of the others to dig out some of the tunnels."

"Nor how they figured out what you'd done—oh, you were so clever!—and swore to have you dragged back and sacrificed."

"No, we can't tell you that. Or why they don't just send an assassin to kill you here, because you twisted up old Magister Porlilon's spell, so that now it can only be untwisted by your blood, before they can escape."

"If you told me such news, I might feel like kicking myself," said Gard. "Because that would mean they'll never rest until they get me back. But, of course, you haven't told me."

"So we haven't," agreed Grattur.

"We'd never warn you like that," said Engrattur.

"You're wearing new bodies," said Gard.

"Yes. Our old ones were crushed when the mountain fell," said Grattur.

"I'm sorry," said Gard.

"Oh, we didn't feel a thing," said Engrattur. "We'd drunk all that wine you so kindly left us, by then."

"Too bad her ladyship knew our real names, *which are Grattur and Engrattur,* and was able to summon us back to serve her."

"You should have seen her, clawing through the debris in her fine clothes, cursing and pitching rocks out of the way."

"She's at her best when things are going badly for her."

"Never loses heart, that one. You should have heard the way she ordered everyone around."

"You should have heard the things she threatened to do to us if we didn't bring you back bound and drugged to the mountain."

"I can imagine them, though," said Gard. They laughed.

"Well, no help for it; we're going to have to kidnap you now," said Grattur.

"Yes. Here we come, little brother," said Engrattur.

They came at him slowly, arms raised ineffectually, and he was easily able to cut both their throats. They dropped gurgling into the street and died.

On impulse, Gard searched their bodies. He retrieved a pair of purses full of the same miscellany of old coins, and two packets bearing letters of mark. These he tucked away in his cloak. He went up to his room, stuffed a bag with his books and a few other necessary items, and hurried on to the theater.

When he walked into the properties shed, he nearly stumbled over Mr. Carbon and Pulkas, who were grappling together on the floor. He staggered back, on his guard until he realized they weren't fighting. "Sorry," said Mr. Carbon.

"Don't mind me," said Gard, shrugging out of his cloak. "I'll only be a minute. Just, er, getting my clothes."

"That's right; you've still got the damn black armor on," said Pulkas, rolling over. He was drunk and had been crying. "Wh—what are you do-ing back here with us peasants? I thought you'd be bouncing some duchess by now."

"The life doesn't suit me," said Gard, struggling with the catches of the breastplate.

"You know, it never suited me either," said Mr. Carbon, getting up and helping him with the catches. "But you ought to make a show of it, any-way. It keeps them happy."

"Actually, I'm leaving," said Gard.

"What?" said Pulkas, struggling to his feet.

"I'm going to enlist. It's my duty."

"You what?" said Mr. Carbon. "Who's going to be the Dark Lord, then?"

"What about him?" Gard tossed the breastplate at Pulkas.

"Me!" Pulkas sobered up immediately.

"Why not?" said Mr. Carbon. "You've always said you'd be good at it."

"But—but—" Pulkas turned the breastplate in his hands. "But, don't you see? He's the greatest Dark Lord the city's ever seen. How am I sup-posed to follow an act like that? You're setting me up for failure, you bas-tard!" He threw the breastplate at Gard and burst into tears.

"You know, some people are never happy," said Mr. Carbon, pursing his lips. "Good-bye and good luck, Wolkin."

"Thank you," said Gard, and walked out into the night.

———

He found a way through a drainage channel that cut under the city wall, and went down to the shallow muddy river that crawled away on the plain below. There he cast about until he found a good deposit of clay and clawed it out with his hands in great lumps. Gard worked steadily, taking no shortcuts, so it was nearly dawn when he finished. He was grateful; the flare of white light as he completed the spell was less obvious, against the brightening sky.

First one and then the other figure sat up, slowly, gleaming with wet-ness under the dawn, and the mire of the riverbank squelched as they got to their feet. They opened silver eyes. "Oh, we'd hoped you'd think of this," said Grattur.

"Now you can bind us to *your* service," said Engrattur, gleeful.

"I won't bind you at all," said Gard. "We're brothers. You ought to be free."

"That won't work," said Grattur.

"If we're not bound, we're fair game for her ladyship," said Engrattur. "She knows our names, see."

"She can pull us back to her service anytime."

"Unless someone else has snapped us up first."

"Which would be you."

"All right," said Gard. "Grattur and Engrattur, thou art bound to my service. Thou shalt perform all that I require of thee."

"We shall!" they chorused, grinning.

"And now we're going to go see if we can hire ourselves out as soldiers."

He threw them his spare garments and coached them in putting them on. Then they walked away together as the sun rose, toward the armed camp out on the plain.

———————

"What's your business here?" the watchman demanded.

"I'm here to offer my services to Duke Parrackas Chrysantine," said Gard. "These men are my servants."

"And what are you?"

"Aden Bullion, of Patrayka," said Gard in a quiet voice, as nearly like Duke Silverpoint's as he could manage.

The watchman shivered, as all the class-consciousness in his nerve endings jumped, and he was much more deferential when he said, "Please wait here, sir."

"This doesn't seem very safe," said Grattur, when the man had gone.

"All these red men with weapons," said Engrattur a little plaintively.

"This is the safest place we could be," said Gard. "If her ladyship sends anyone else after us, we'll be surrounded by comrades with weapons."

"Oh, that's clever!"

"What are those things on their banners?"

Gard glanced up. "I think they're fish."

The watchman returned with a harried-looking man in a tunic bearing the fish emblem. "I am the duke's steward. You wish to speak to Parrackas Chrysantine?"

"Oh, by no means, sir," said Gard. "I wish merely to enlist, with my servants."

The man frowned, listening to him. "Aden Bullion, you said your name was?"

"I did, sir."

"And you are?"

"A plain man wishing to serve as a common soldier."

"Yes, very likely; a plain man, with that Silverhaven accent, and travel-ing with servants? Sir, you're welcome here, whoever you are, but you should be aware we have all the generals we need. Unless you're inter-ested in an arms master position," the steward added as an afterthought.

"I am," said Gard.

"You can always—really?" The steward looked at him closely.

"My tutor studied under Prince Firebow," said Gard.

'Really," said the steward, his face brightening steadily. "What did you say your name was?"

"Aden Bullion."

"Of course it is," said the steward conspiratorially. "Please come with me, sir. I believe his lordship would like to speak with you."

He led them into the camp, past the rows of plain field tents and into the zone of the pavilions. They were bowed into a particularly fancy one—it had a carpeted floor and folding chairs, as well as a sort of side-board bearing wine and food—and asked to wait.

As soon as they were alone, Gard upended his bag of books and rum-maged through, looking for his volumes on history and tactics.

"There's food in here," said Grattur.

"There's *wine*," said Engrattur.

"Help yourselves," said Gard distractedly, thumbing through one vol-ume. The brothers ate and drank eagerly while he read enough to dis-cover that Silverhaven was the port formerly ruled by the Silverpoint family. It had been claimed by Duke Chrysantine since that line's extinc-tion. Silverhaven was also the site of a famous academy for the arts of war.

Gard grinned and stuffed the books back in his bag. He was sitting calmly, sipping from a cup of fairly good wine, when the steward looked into the pavilion.

"The duke will see you now," said the steward.

"He is too kind," said Gard. He followed the steward out. Grattur, stuffing a last roll in his mouth, grabbed up the bag of books and together with Engrattur followed him.

They were shown into the grand pavilion at the center of the camp. Gard looked around him in wonder. The walls were blue silk, embroidered in gold with little fishes; there was fine furniture, at least what he could see of it for the books and masses of paper strewn about. A thick-necked man in fine clothes sat at a table, poring over a map. He looked up as Gard entered. Gard bowed, putting into it all the rigid formality of Duke Silverpoint.

"Now, who do you claim to be?" said Duke Chrysantine.

"Aden Bullion, sir. I was given to understand you had an opening for an arms master."

"I do. Bullion, is it? I don't know any Bullions."

"I am the last of my family, sir."

"That's likely enough," said Chrysantine, giving him a keen look. "And you claim to have been at school in Silverhaven, do you?"

"No, sir, I never made any such claim. My father was a poor man in Patrayka. What I said was that my tutor studied under Prince Firebow."

"If your father was poor, how'd he get you such a tutor?"

"Good birth and good fortune do not always travel together, sir."

"That's true," said Chrysantine, continuing to study Gard. "Certainly it was true for the Silverpoints. Did you ever hear of them?"

Gard looked him in the eye. "I understand the last of that family died some years ago, in a blood feud. I imagine that if there were any bastards of that line still living, they would scarcely wish to make their existence known to anyone."

"No, they wouldn't," said Chrysantine, sounding pleased. "I'm putting together a campaign against Skalkin Salting, you know. He wants Deliantiba. Deliantiba is mine." The duke paused, smiled at Gard. "His father was hunted down by the last Silverpoint. Killed too, it's been assumed; neither of their bodies were ever found. That was a long time ago, but I don't imagine he's forgotten."

"I daresay not. None of my affair, of course."

"Of course. I can't pay you much. Booty's contingent on victory, as usual. I have a platoon's worth of untrained men to offer you; most of them don't know one end of a pike from the other. Shopkeepers' sons and half-breed trash. And one monster. Train them, and you'll be their officer."

"I am equal to the challenge, I hope," said Gard, making a mental note never to sleep without either Grattur or Engrattur on guard at his door.

"Very good. Filecutter! Requisition a tent and gear for Mr., er, Bullion. And servants. What are you boys, twins?"

"Yes. They're mutes," said Gard quickly. "Their name is Grating."

"Mute identical twins," said Chrysantine, amused. "Damn, that must be useful at times. Not sure how exactly, though. Can they fight?"

"Like demons," said Gard, and Grattur and Engrattur grinned.

"This is your lot," said Filecutter, the steward.

Gard looked out on the row of ill-assorted tents. They had been pitched at the edge of camp, and ragged-looking men wandered between them or crouched beside cooking fires. "They have no banner."

"That's because they aren't soldiers yet," said Filecutter. "Aren't anything to speak of. Lumps of earth. I don't envy you your work, but the better units got assigned early. Best of luck!" He leaned forward and cupped his hands around his mouth. "Enlistees! Stand to attention! We've got you an arms master." Then he turned and walked away, as the men formed a line.

Gard walked down the slope toward them. Several of them were tradesmen's apprentices who had volunteered in patriotic fervor and clearly regretted it now. Some, he could see, were old mercenaries, a little the worse for wear: one or two were missing a hand, though their prosthetic claws looked efficient, and one was missing an eye. Nor was this all. . . .

"Little brother," hissed Grattur. "Some of them are *demons*."

Yes; some two or three of them were projecting spells over themselves to conceal their true appearances, even as Gard was doing. Several more were undisguised half-breeds, shaped like Children of the Sun but with thundercloud skin, or striped markings, or strange eyes, or crests of hair. One stood upright like a man but had the head of a wolf, somewhat gray in the muzzle.

As Gard came to the line, one of the apprentices stepped forward.

"Sir, please, you must help us! We volunteered to serve out of loyalty to the duke, and this is just too insulting!"

"What is insulting?"

The apprentice stared at Gard as though he were mad. "That we're expected to serve with—with *those*!" The apprentice flung out his arm at the half-breeds. "I mean, look at the werewolf, for gods' sake!"

Gard looked. The werewolf looked back at him, through slitted yellow eyes.

"Do you know how to fight?" Gard asked the apprentice.

"No."

"I think the werewolf knows how to fight."

"Look, we want you to see that we're put into a proper regiment!"

"That's not my job. My job is to train you to fight. You won't belong in any regiment until you're a soldier. Do you understand?"

"Yes, sir," said the apprentice, drooping.

"Good," said Gard, and walked slowly down the line. Those in disguise themselves had seen through his own disguise and watched him with guarded amusement. He studied them, in turn.

"Right," he said. "All veterans with axes, raise your hands."

Five hands went up.

"Good. Go cut some poles at the thicket over there. I want five practice dummies set up. Who's been a soldier the longest?"

"That would be me, sir," said one of the demons, stepping forward. His disguise masked eyes like red coals; tusks jutted from his jaw, though the glamour made it seem like a particularly bad underbite.

"How many years have you served?"

"Twenty, sir," said the demon with a wink.

"Then I think you know where to find paint in a military camp. Go requisition some for us. Red, green, and yellow. And requisition ten practice blades, while you're at it."

"Sir!" The demon saluted and hastened to obey.

Gard had come full circle. Now he stood, intoning the postures of attack or defense, while some awkward boy lunged with a wooden practice blade. It was just as monotonous and dispiriting from the master's point of view as from the student's. Even the werewolf was slow and awkward, no lithe killer.

Nonetheless, Gard made progress with them. Redeye, the old veteran, was an expert at scrounging broken and discarded gear and somehow found enough to equip the whole platoon with mended stuff. Gard made him his sergeant. One afternoon as they stood watching the apprentices and half-breeds at pike drill, Gard felt the faint questioning tug at his consciousness.

He settled himself firmly on his feet and went out of himself a little. A slow-flaring red light was at the edge of his vision, like a fireworks show. It was Redeye.

. . . Do you know how to talk to us?

I do.

Where'd you come from? You're young, to have such control over yourself.

I was a lost child.

You found your way home quickly, then. Not like some of these poor lads. They've had it hard. Wandered around for years, never knowing where they fit in.

I too. But you are no half-breed.

No. I was slave to an old mage. Me, and Arkholoth there, and Stedrakh. The mage died at last, and we still had these nice bodies he gave us to wear, so we ran free and enjoyed them. At least, they were fun until they got so cut up.

How is it you can disguise yourselves?

He had little amulets we could carry with us when he sent us to do his marketing.
They make us look like Children of the Sun. Hard to get the shopkeepers to wait on you
otherwise, isn't it? We took them with us when we left his house for good.

Amulets. Gard was astounded at the simplicity of it, and the brilliance;
an external spell that did not require a constant exertion of will to run. For
the first time it occurred to him that he did not, perhaps, know all that
might be known about sorcery. Perhaps the mages under the mountain
had not been so very learned after all.

What about the werewolf?

Poor old Thrang? His master bodied him like that. Wanted something fearful-looking
to guard his treasure. Then the master died and left him to his children, and they didn't
want him. The duke heard they had a werewolf and offered to buy him. A werewolf in
your army, you know—ooooh, how frightening. But it turned out what the old master
collected was porcelain, you see.

Is that why Thrang carries around that painted cup?

It's all he has left. He curated his master's collection for fifty years, and then the sons
took it all away from him and sold it, except for the cup. Sometimes he goes out to the edge
of camp at night and howls over it.

I wondered why he didn't seem to know how to kill.

Ah! Just you knock over that cup sometime. You'll see he's still got teeth.

They had no banner, but they had a name: the Disgraces. Men from all
the other parts of camp, even the women of the artillery division, would
come and stare, and laugh, when Gard marched his platoon along the
edge of the river. Their laughter fell silent, though, when he would set the
Disgraces to mock combat with spear or sword and buckler.

One afternoon Gard looked up from a pike drill to see that Duke
Chrysantine himself had come to the edge of the bluff to watch. His son
Pentire stood beside him, chuckling, but the duke looked thoughtful. He
nodded as Gard approached.

"Congratulations, Mr. Bullion," said Pentire. "Your Disgraces very
nearly look like men."

"Some of them are men," said the duke. "Look there, that one's pure-
blooded. So are those two. What are they doing in with this lot of crip-
ples and mongrels?"

"I believe they were put in my platoon because they didn't know one
end of a pike from another," said Gard, "sir."

"Well, they damn well seem to know now," said the duke. "Look at that! That was a Firebow's Counter. Pure Silverhaven style. Gods below, Bullion, you know your business too. Those boys don't belong here. They ought to be in one of the regular platoons."

"I have implied to them, sir, that they might be transferred out if they made an honest effort to learn," said Gard. "I hope you'll excuse the liberty."

"Oh, quite all right; good motivation. Call them up here!" said the duke.

"Wrenching! Smith! Gearlock! Fall out!" shouted Gard, and waved them up the hill. They came, streaming sweat, and formed a line before the duke.

"His lordship is pleased with your progress, gentlemen," said Gard.

"I think you lads have earned places in Sunrise Company," said the duke.

"Thank you, sir!" they chorused, saluting.

"But that's *my* platoon," said Pentire, looking at his father.

"You'll thank me," said the duke. "These men could teach your elite guard a trick or two, I think. Go pack your kit, you three. You're the archduke's men now."

"Sir!" Another sharp salute, beaming, and they were gone to their tents so fast a dust cloud followed them.

"You've earned the right to better society yourself," said the duke to Gard. "You're wasted on those boys down there."

"With respect, sir, I'm enjoying the challenge," said Gard. "I believe I'm making progress with your werewolf, in particular."

"You think so? Moth-eaten old thing, isn't he? I was sadly disappointed in him. If you can give him a bit of, you know, horrific *presence* or something, I'd be much obliged."

"I shall do my best, sir."

———

They were sitting around their fire that night, Redeye and Arkholoth and Stedrakh, when Gard emerged from his tent and approached them. "Good evening, Sergeant. Gentlemen," he said, and settled into a comfortable crouch.

"Good evening, sir," said Redeye. "Just our lot now, isn't it?"

"Yes. Just us."

They considered Gard warily. He looked back at them, seeing through the illusions that made them seem a trio of grizzled Children of the Sun.

Arkholoth had had green-faceted eyes, until a bit of shrapnel had put one out; Stedrakh was a red-scaled thing with one shapely right hand and one set of iron claws bound to the stump of his left arm.

"What do you want in all this, sir?" Stedrakh waved his claw in the direction of the main camp. "If you don't mind the question."

"What do you want?" Gard replied.

"Us?" The demons looked at one another. Stedrakh said, "Well, it's something to do, isn't it? We get to eat, we get to drink. We get to fight and kill. When we win, we get to fuck somebody. The hotheads aren't so bad, even if they do fancy themselves. It's better than being a damn slave again."

"Ah," said Gard. "That's true."

"Were you a slave?"

"I was, yes. May I see one of your amulets?"

Redeye shrugged and, with a glance up at the main camp, pulled the amulet off over his head and handed it to Gard. The illusion went with it, like a discarded robe, and he laughed quietly and flexed his heavy arms. "Don't look down, little hotheads. You'll run home crying to your mothers."

"This is a simple spell," said Gard, studying the amulet. "This is nothing more than a formula inscribed on silver."

"That's right. What's it to you?"

"I intend to make one for myself."

They raised their heads to stare at him. "*Make* one?" said Arkholoth. "You'd have to be a mage to make one."

"Yes."

"But you're one of—" Stedrakh fell silent. Gard raised his eyes and met his stare.

After a long moment, Redeye whistled softly. "By the Blue Pit and the Little Red Dog. Someone was a fucking idiot."

"They were," said Gard. "But not for long."

Redeye began to laugh, and the others laughed too, raucous unbelieving laughter. Gard only smiled and handed the amulet back to Redeye.

"But there's never been one of *us* trained up as a mage!" said Arkholoth. "Didn't they know what you were?"

"They knew. They needed to sacrifice someone with a mage's powers. They thought they could substitute a slave, if they taught him a little magecraft."

"Where was this?" said Stedrakh, leaning forward. Gard pointed in the general direction of the mountain. They turned to look and shuddered.

"That place," said Arkholoth. "The Ice Trap, we call it. You got out of *there*? Then you're a better man than I am, brother, and if we were in a city, I'd buy you a drink."

"Thank you," said Gard. "I bought a jar of wine at the commissary this afternoon. It should be arriving shortly—"

"Here we are, little brother," said Grattur, hurrying forward into the firelight. He hefted a wine jar, grinning. "Drinks for everybody!"

"And we brought the two boys, just as you asked," said Engrattur. Two of the half-breeds followed him, blinking in the light, hanging back a little.

"Evening, Sergeant. Evening, sir," they muttered more or less together. Dalbeck was the taller, young but terribly scarred: knives had gashed his chest, the lash had striped his back. He looked like a Child of the Sun, but for the fact that his eyes were those of a cat. Cheller, the shorter of the two, had thundercloud skin and a crest of hair that rose like a helmet's decoration.

"Evening, lads," said Redeye not unkindly. He looked at Gard. "What's this about, then?"

"More training," said Gard.

"Sit down, little brothers," said Grattur, prizing the stopper out of the wine jar. He peered in. "Not enough in here to get good and drunk, if we all share it," he said, sounding somewhat reproachful.

"We'll share it, all the same," said Gard.

"These are good boys to train, sir," said Redeye. "Dalbeck's been fighting since he was a baby. Haven't you?"

Dalbeck kept his eyes down when he spoke. "My mother was blind. People would try to steal from her bowl. I fought off people who tried to, to hurt her. After she died I still had to fight all the time."

"And you're a fine stone killer too," said Redeye. "The other one knows some fancy tricks, don't you, Cheller? He was a foundling raised up in a runners' mother house, would you believe it? Learned all their acrobatics. He does worse damage with his boots and elbows than most men can do with a warhammer. Got thrown out on his ear when he got too interested in the girls, though!"

Cheller squirmed in embarrassment. He looked sidelong at Gard as he accepted the wine jar, which was being passed around.

"Somebody told me you're, er, like us. Sir," he said, and drank.

Gard nodded. He let his spell of disguise drop away. The youths stared.

"Handsome, isn't he?" said Engrattur proudly.

"You look a little like—," Cheller began. "There are these people that live way back in the southern woods. They hide in the forest. I saw a couple. *Yendri,* they're called."

The word rang like a bell for Gard, but he did not let it show in his face. How strange to hear it here. . . .

"Yes, I look like them. A little. Not enough to pass for one, any more than you could pass for a Child of the Sun. Gentlemen? Reveal yourselves, if you please."

One by one, the old veterans slipped off their amulets and showed their true forms, blinking a little sheepishly at the boys. Dalbeck clenched his fists, but after a moment began to smile. Cheller grinned wide. "Don't tell me we're *all* demons here!" he said.

"We are," said Gard.

"These bodies are just disguises," said Grattur.

"He's clever too," said Engrattur.

"How do you hide your real self like that, sir?" Dalbeck asked. "Can you teach us how to do that?"

"Probably," said Gard. "You're learning well. It's time you learned something more advanced. Do you know what meditation is?"

Dalbeck shook his head.

"I know," said Cheller. "It's games you play with your mind, to make you able to do hard things. The runners teach it. The long-distance couriers can run a hundred miles without stopping, because they can sort of go out of themselves and rest someplace else."

"It's useful for a fighter too," said Gard. "Would you like to know what it's like, walking without flesh?"

"Yes," said Cheller, and Dalbeck nodded.

"Then look at me," said Gard.

He went out of himself and pulled them after him like two kites, into the sea of stars. Dalbeck was a sputtering golden light, a phrase of yearning music; Cheller was a bright and rippling blueness, with a smell of baking bread. There were Redeye and Arkholoth and Stedrakh, stolid mountains of light, and here the twin purple gleaming that was Grattur and Engrattur.

The boys squealed like babies in their excitement. They shot away from Gard, they soared, they spun.

There are others here!

Others like us! We're stars!

No, we're music!

No, we're . . . everything!

This is what you really are. The low rumble was Redeye. *The bodies we wear aren't real. Fun to have, sometimes, but really only temporary.*

Tell them about the danger. That was Grattur.

Right. That was Arkholoth. *You have to be careful, children.*

One day you'll be going along here minding your own business, and you'll hear somebody calling you. It'll be some mage in a casting chamber. If he's a decent sort—not that there are many of them—he'll offer you a body in exchange for work. Redeye's voice darkened to a growl. *But there are some sly bastards who'll set out a feast for you, wine and meat and all good things. They'll show you a body they've made for you and they'll say, "Come wear this a little while, come enjoy yourself!"*

And if you go down and put that body on—Grattur sounded woeful, he became melancholy music.

And if you eat of the good things and drink all the wine—Engrattur was a doleful counterpoint.

Why, then, just when you're full and stupid, they'll trick you into telling your name, said Redeye, and there was a blast of sound like an avalanche in many colors, as the old demons chorused, *NEVER TELL THEM YOUR NAME!*

If they know your name, they can make you a slave.

It's like a noose around your neck.

A wire pulled tight around your testicles.

They'll make you serve.

They'll make you fetch.

They'll write your name in their books, so they can catch you again, even if you get free.

You'll never really be free, even if they die. Some busybody will go poking through the old books and find your name, and you'll be pulled back.

Unless . . . Grattur whirled to consider Gard. *Unless you meet someone like him.*

What's that? Redeye's attention was like a spotlight.

We were slaves to the Narcissus of the Void, in the Ice Trap.

He stole us away from her, hid us in these bodies he made.

She can't get us back now!

He set us free!

Now Gard was fixed in the beam of Arkholoth's and Stedrakh's attention.

Because you're a mage . . . and yet one of us. A good master?

I am no master, Gard replied. *I am your brother.*

We'd serve you! cried Dalbeck and Cheller, orbiting Gard in streams of bright fire. *We'd be your sworn men!*

Shut up, you little fools, thundered Redeye. *You don't know what it is to be a slave, or you'd never talk that way.*

Let us be a company of brothers, said Gard.

At that moment there was a disturbance in the camp; Gard pulled them back, and they sat gasping in the firelight, turning their heads from side to side as they tried to adjust to seeing with two eyes. Gard resumed his disguise; the older demons had discreetly slipped their amulets back on.

One of the sergeants from Forgefire Company came stalking up to their fire. "Hai, Disgraces! There was a spy reported on the other side of the camp, lurking in the woods. Keep an eye out for anyone trying to swim across the river."

"We will, sir. Thank you, sir," said Redeye.

When the sergeant had gone, Dalbeck and Cheller whooped with held breath and fell over. "Brothers!" crowed Cheller. "That's what we are, we're brothers! I never had any family in my life before. I never belonged anywhere before. Now I know who I am!"

"Just you take care nobody else knows," said Redeye.

Hallock had skin irregularly patterned with stripes; Nyren's legs were disproportionately large for his body, and he had moreover a tail. Both had been foundlings, raised by an entrepreneur who exhibited them, until one night Nyren had kicked out the bars of their cell and they had gone free. They had learned to fight for survival in the wild, and there Arkholoth had met them, on his way to enlist. He had persuaded them that a soldier's life was better than starving in the forest, so they had come along and enlisted too.

They came now privately to Gard, asking shyly whether a darkness full of lights and glorious music, where ungainly flesh was left behind, truly existed. That night, by the fire, Gard brought them there. They were as thrilled as Dalbeck and Cheller had been, though perhaps more inclined to listen to Redeye's stern warnings; for they had worn chains, in their brief time.

When Toktar and Bettimer came to the fire on the following night, the whole business had begun to assume an air of ritual.

Toktar was a hermaphrodite, ugly but extravagantly endowed and bo-somed. In the sea of stars, he was a brilliant point of silver, a high trumpet call at dawn, a shout of joy to find himself free of his ridiculous prison.

Only Bettimer, who had been raised in Salesh by his mother and step-father and who hated his ice-white skin, drew back from the bright gulf. He was a mere point of flame there, flickering wildly in his disorientation and terror. Where the others had seen freedom, he saw only chaos. He wept afterward at his failure.

"Don't feel badly, son," said Redeye. "Maybe your father wasn't a de-mon."

"Maybe he was a god," said Dalbeck helpfully.

Gard, watching the boy where he sat staring miserably downward, said, "What did you hope to find, when you came to this fire?"

"I wanted to be something besides *me*," said Bettimer. "Something be-sides my mother's shame. I disappointed my stepfather. Now I'm a disap-pointment here. I hope I die in battle."

"No," said Gard. "If you could begin your life again, if you could choose, what would it be like?"

Bettimer raised his tear-streaked face. "Nobody would stare at me any-more. I could get a job in a forge. My stepfather was a blacksmith. I loved the red iron, I loved blowing the coals to bright fire. I loved the way the water foamed white when steel was tempered in it. When the coals glowed, when the place was full of red light, nobody could see my skin was the wrong color. If I could just live in a forge and never come out . . ."

Redeye shook his head. "You're a Child of the Sun, inside."

"You needn't be ashamed," said Gard. "Not one man here is where he ought to be, if the world were right. It isn't. We aren't. We make the best of things."

Gard circled Thrang with both wooden swords drawn. The old werewolf turned warily, keeping his buckler up.

Are you silent because it's difficult to speak? Gard inquired, going out of him-self enough to address the dull amber light opposite him.

What do you think, with a mouth made like mine? Below, Thrang showed his stained teeth. *No lips, two-inch fangs, and a tongue fit only for lapping water. A head made to frighten burglars, and the rest of me no use for anything now. What should I say, even if I could speak?*

I'm sorry. You had a cruel master.

Light flared in the yellow eyes, and Thrang growled as he advanced on Gard. *My master was a gentleman! He knew beauty, he appreciated fine things. His collection was the finest in the world. It took us years to gather it! Four hundred and seventeen cups of perfect celadon from the kilns at Ward'b, ranging in shades from apple green to virgin's milk. A complete set of the comic figurines of Paltas Stoneward, each one hand-painted and gilded. Four matched vases of Rose Garden pattern, the last made by Thraxas of Salesh before his studio was burned. A portrait bust of Marlans the Dictator, one of only three made, in ivory white kaolin clay. A redware krater depicting Book Three of Andib the Axeman—we had found a dealer who had the ones for Books One and Two, he didn't know the worth of what he had, if my master had lived only another week we'd have had them—but—oh—*

Overcome by grief, the old creature dropped his shield, threw back his head, and howled.

Forgive me, said Gard, lowering his swords.

Lost, lost, scattered to the four winds. Fools! They won't value them, they won't care for them properly. They damaged the bust of Marlans when they were carrying it out to the cart. I saw the white chip fall. My heart wept blood. All my books, all my careful records torn apart and used to wrap what was sold. It was the finest collection in the world and it is gone. Everything goes. Nothing remains.

But you kept something, said Gard encouragingly. Thrang, panting, swung around to peer at him. Tears had run down through the matted fur on his face.

I did. Yes, I had to. Master sought so long for it—he dreamed about it every night for ten years, and I dreamed of it too. The rarest of the celadons, the only one known to exist in that shade of robin's-egg green. The potter was experimenting with a new glaze and died before he could write down the formula. I hid it away from his damned sons, I brought it with me into bondage.

May I see it?

Thrang blinked at Gard. He lowered his head suspiciously, but signed that Gard should follow him and limped away to his solitary tent. There he brought out a sack and from that drew a wooden box, and opened it, and dug through fistfuls of dried leaves to produce an object swathed in furs as against the cold. He unwrapped it—his hands were fine, smooth, though the knuckles were knobbed with age and labor—and held forth at last a tiny cup of white clay, glazed with transparent blue-green, pale as seawater.

What an extraordinary color, said Gard. *When I was a slave, my mistress had a set of such cups, but only in the green. And of course she had no appreciation of what she had.*

They never do, said Thrang, shaking his head. *I'm glad to know you are a gentleman of perception.*

He was a little more at ease with Gard from that day, though no less silent, and even consented to join the others around the fire of an evening.

———————

The arms lessons went well. Gard brought out his Firebow volumes and read aloud some nights, and the boys listened intently, and even the old veterans leaned close to hear. By day, training on the trampled strip of earth beside the river, they were increasingly watched by the other platoons, who mocked them less and less.

In the privacy of his tent, Gard took a silver piece and filed away the duke's profile and, using the tip of his knife, scribed in the disguising spell he had seen on Redeye's amulet. It worked admirably. He punched a string-hole through and wore it around his neck thereafter.

Cheller made a banner for them. It was a black field on which were scattered stars, red and green and golden.

———————

The news came while they were at practice; Thrang heard the trumpet before anyone else, so that Gard, mounting the rise of land, was the first to see the runner coming across the plain. He went down into the main camp and joined Duke Chrysantine and his officers, as the girl in her scarlet uniform entered the camp.

"Written or spoken?" said the duke.

"Both," said the runner, drawing a sealed tablet from the pouch she carried. "Coalbrick said: you are to know, sir, that Skalkin Salting left the coast two weeks ago and was at Kottile last night with his army. Particulars are enclosed." She presented the duke with the tablet.

"Give her wine and gold," said the duke to his aides, as he opened the tablet. He glanced up from it at the runner. "I'll have messages for you to carry on to Deliantiba."

The runner bowed her head and followed an aide into the guest pavilion. The duke read closely what was in the tablet, silent a moment or two. At last he lifted his head and looked around him for his aides.

"Send me my officers. Give the order to break camp. We'll march this afternoon."

Half an hour later Gard stood with the other captains around the table in the blue pavilion, and the little golden fish seemed to float as the wind gusted against the walls.

"Here," said the Duke, pointing at the map. "It's an easy march; six miles downriver. I want to be there by nightfall, setting up camp. The mountains come close in here, and Penterkar Ridge reaches out to the river to block his way. We'll come up the ridge from behind and make camp on the height. I mean to engage him here, below, with our backs to the ridge."

Gard studied the map. The enemy must come up the plain, following the river, to get to Deliantiba; he must follow the road up over the Penterkar Ridge, and so he must march into a box, closed in on one side by the river and on the other by the descending hills, with an army blocking his path over the ridge.

"My troops here, forming the center," said Duke Chrysantine, pushing the counters into place. "Mr. Firechain, your men to my left; Mr. Goldsmith, your men to my right. Sunrise Company form the left flank, here where the hill curves around. We'll station the artillery on the hillside above you, son."

"And the plan is to close the pincer once they've been softened up with rocket fire?" said the archduke.

"If it please the gods. Mr. Bullion, your company form the right flank here, on the riverbank. You've done remarkably well with them, but they're untried and unknown in combat. They need simply stand fast and kill when Sunrise Company drives the enemy toward them."

Gard nodded, without comment.

"Then we mop up the field, walk back up the hill, and eat dinner whilst enjoying the lovely view," said Pentire in satisfaction.

"If it please the gods," said the duke.

———

The top of Penterkar Ridge offered a fine view indeed, of the long plain to the west and the battlefield and wide river below. Gard looked out on it all as the Disgraces made their camp, some distance down from the main body of the army.

"Stuck by the river again," said Redeye. "They want to make sure we don't run, eh?"

"Can you swim?"

"Not in my bloody armor." Redeye peered out into the twilight. "I don't see any campfires out there, nor any dust clouds. So if they arrive tomorrow, they'll have been marching a long, hot time across that plain. That's something, anyway."

"Are you worried?"

Redeye spat. "No. That's a death trap, down there. They can't outflank us, can they? All they can do is crowd forward into the meat grinder, with the ladies over there raining down bombs on them." He nodded across at where the artillery division was setting up positions on the hill to the south. "Plus they'll have the sun in their eyes, if they attack in the morning."

"Let's hope they do, then."

"Going to pull out any mage tricks?"

"I shouldn't have to, if it's as easy as all that," said Gard. "And I'd rather not draw attention to myself. You never know who might be watching."

Redeye scowled over his shoulder, in the general direction of the mountain, and made a rude gesture.

On the morning of the second day they had been at Penterkar, the dust cloud was spotted, and shortly thereafter the glint of the sun on shields and lances. Salting's army came on up the road.

The morning mist had burned off the river before they were in clear sight, dissipated into a hot bright haze that no wind freshened. Duke Chrysantine's army took their positions, sweating, swatting away little flies, and their banners hung limp.

"Good," said the duke, pacing before his lines. "They're marching into the sun. Tell your men, hold position until they come within range. A nice wheezing, panting, limping army they'll be by then." He turned to address Gard. "You make certain your boys understand that, eh? No half-breed berserkers running out ahead of time. Unless you can get the werewolf to do some howling and slavering," the duke added, as an afterthought. "That would be a nice touch."

"I'll see what I can do," said Gard.

"Good man," said the duke, and walked away.

Gard paced back to where the Disgraces were, with their backs to the hill and the river to their right. "We hold position until they're in range."

"Right," said Redeye, leaning on his spear. "You hear that, Disgraces? Let them wear themselves out coming to us."

"I always like that maneuver where some of us go running out and fire off a few spears and then run back," argued Stedrakh. "There's always some string of fools who'll bite on that one. Chase us back into range and get chopped to bits by our side. I've never seen it not work."

"Orders are, hold position," said Redeye. "And we'll obey orders."

Gard surveyed the boys. They were pale, watching the enemy advance.

Redeye glanced back at them. "Look at them, sweating buckets out there. I'm looking forward to helping myself to some of that fancy gear, though, I can tell you that. Cheller and Dalbeck know what I'm talking about, don't you, lads?"

"Yes, sir, Sergeant," said Dalbeck, trying to sound bold and confident. "Looting's the best part. We strip the bodies and sack the baggage train. Everybody gets rich!"

"Or at least better off," said Arkholoth. "Hallock, Nyren, you make sure to grab yourself a good helmet each. Never know what you'll find on a dead man. It's a right treasure hunt."

"And remember!" Cheller held up the tail of the banner and spread it out. "Remember *this* place. Remember what we really are. Don't be afraid of anything. We're brothers!"

Bettimer glanced at the banner and looked away, trembling. Gard watched him. The boy settled his gear about him, took a tight grip on his spear, and fixed his gaze on the advancing enemy.

The banners of Skalkin Salting were red, bearing on them the image of a golden ship. The armies of Salting were well armed, bearing a front line of identical shields and lance tips that glittered in the sunlight. Gard, following Bettimer's gaze, looked on them and felt uneasy. The shields were like an advancing wall, no random collection of mismatched bucklers.

He went out of himself, soared up, saw the whole of the advancing army, and was relieved. The enemy forces were smaller, only perhaps two-thirds of the troops Chrysantine had assembled. Over on the hill above Sunrise Company, the women were readying their charges, and as Gard watched one girl set the butt of her mortar's lance into the earth, braced it there, and loaded in the rocket. He saw the spark—

Fhut, and with a hiss the rocket soared up, trailing its plume of smoke, and dropped toward the advancing line of men. It burst, scattering its load of shot and hot shards just short of the line; the shields went up and fended off the shrapnel, and an officer screamed for the men to stop.

The line stopped. Someone in Sunrise Company fired an arrow. It arched and fell by the smoldering debris of the rocket. The enemy remained where they were, just out of range.

"Was that supposed to be a warning shot?" Redeye squinted up at the artillery positions.

"What are they going to do now?" said Bettimer in a shaky voice. No one answered him, but in a moment it became plain what the enemy intended. One of their officers shouted a command. In perfect unison the ranks sat down behind their shields, each in the rectangle of shade narrowly provided. They pulled out their canteens and drank, put the canteens away, and relaxed.

Redeye guffawed in disbelief. "That's balls for you!" All across the duke's lines, the same thing was being said, in greater or lesser degrees of obscenity, with some shouts of protest too. Gard squinted up at the sun, his uneasiness returning. The enemy was resting now, contented in the shade, while his men stood sweating under the sun.

"I could run out there and nail a couple of them," said Stedrakh. "They're sitting down!"

"We hold our position," said Gard. Thrang held up his little round buckler, making a tiny circle of shade for himself, and glared at Gard.

Sunrise Company began to jeer, and the taunting swept across and the other divisions took it up, a roar of insults, invective like a wave boiling out into the pitiless sunlight. The enemy sat placidly, ignoring them. After a half hour or so Chrysantine's men had shouted their throats raw. The sun rose higher. Flies swarmed and bit.

As the shadows grew shorter, Salting's troops merely tilted their shields.

"The sun's not going to be in their eyes when they charge now, is it?" said Bettimer sadly.

"They can't keep this up all day," said Cheller.

"If they do, the sun'll be in *our* eyes by the time they move their asses," said Toktar.

"We have to do something!" said Dalbeck.

"We will hold our position," said Gard.

"We will hold because *you* ordered it," said Grattur.

"Not because some red fool orders it," said Engrattur.

The wind shifted. It blew cool across the river; the white line of haze on the horizon deepened and perhaps rolled a little closer. The sun passed its zenith and began its descent.

In the end, Sunrise Company broke first, with a screaming charge leading the left flank out, and Gard groaned and could hear the groans coming from the older fighters. "Flaming little hotheaded idiot," muttered Redeye, but the majority of Chrysantine's men cheered, desperate to join battle at last.

The cheering did not last long. Salting's men were on their feet in an instant, big shields up, and they deflected the flight of spears and cast their own. Men dropped in Sunrise Company, and then the armies were locked together, swords out, fighting hand to hand but still mostly out of range of the artillery. Gard heard the duke roaring orders, and a detachment of archers ran forward and sent flight after flight off at Salting's troops. The rear guard weathered the rain of arrows with their shields up, taking little damage.

"Messenger!" cried Dalbeck, for a runner in Chrysantine's livery was struggling along behind Goldsmith's company lines, screaming, "Hold! Hold! Duke says hold! Pincer!"

"Too fucking late for that," said Redeye, but across the field they could see Firechain's platoons racing forward to fill the position Sunrise Company had vacated.

Before ever they got there, the shield wall parted. From the midst of Salting's forces a surge broke through, armored men running with their shields up, across and around the remnants of Sunrise Company, only the outer edges engaging with swords to cut a way through, as the main body struck straight uphill for the artillery. The women let off a barrage of rockets into their faces, causing a horrendous moment of carnage in the front line of the oncoming men; but those behind them kept coming up, over the bodies of the slain.

Firechain's men started uphill after them, but, again, too late. The enemy took the artillery positions. Gard winced at the screaming as the women died up there.

There was no holding now. The duke's forces came forward in a mass, and Goldsmith's company came too, and they collided in their haste to get to where the remnants of Sunrise Company were being hacked into yet bloodier shreds. Peering through the dust, Gard saw the red banner raised on the hill above the artillery, and saw the rockets being trained on the duke's center.

"That's done it," said Redeye, drawing his sword. "Well, this was a good body."

"Little brother will get us out of this," said Grattur.

"He's clever that way," said Engrattur.

"Remember!" Cheller waved his banner desperately. "Remember where we're going! We'll all meet there!"

Gard glanced over his shoulder at Bettimer, who had drawn his sword. He was weeping, praying to the gods of the Children of the Sun. "Can you swim?" Gard demanded of him.

"What?"

"Can you swim?"

"Yes—"

"Throw off your coat and helmet," said Gard, pulling his silver amulet up through his breastplate. "Get across the river. Run to Deliantiba and tell them what's happening here."

The boy skinned out of his armor. Gard took off the amulet and stood in his true form, and a moan of approval went up from the Disgraces. He handed the amulet to Bettimer, who put it on wonderingly and stood as like any Child of the Sun in appearance as might be.

"You have your life. Go and live it, if you can," said Gard. He turned, hearing behind him the splash as Bettimer slipped away into the river. Redeye tore off his amulet too, and Arkholoth and Stedrakh followed his example.

"Let them fear us now!" said Grattur.

"Hotheads, we are coming to eat your livers!" said Engrattur.

"Kill as many as you can," said Gard, drawing his sword. And then the duke's trumpets sounded a retreat.

Gard peered through the smoke and flame, unbelieving, and saw men in the duke's livery scrambling back, up toward Penterkar Ridge. Goldsmith's men were following them. The Disgraces were about to be cut off.

"Fuck. Retreat!" said Redeye, and Gard led them sidelong, running back down the right side of the field toward the ridge. The oncoming tide of the enemy caught them two-thirds of the way there.

They turned as one man and stood. Gard snarled, Grattur and Engrattur on either side of him bared their teeth and roared, and the enemy who faced them drew back in astonishment. Gard went out of himself and began to kill. It was an ecstasy.

At some point he found himself on the hill in the ruin of the camps, with an arrow in his breastplate. It hadn't penetrated far enough to wound much, but it was scratching him and it hurt. He pulled it out and looked around. There was no sign of the starry banner; the young boys had died like mayflies in the climb up the hill, all but Dalbeck, who was streaming blood but still fighting. Grattur had lost a hand and was clutching at the stump, as Engrattur stood over him, holding a swordsman at bay with a spear.

Hearing growling and a wet screaming to his left, Gard turned and saw Thrang with his teeth in a soldier's throat. Gard ran forward, engaged and beheaded Engrattur's man, and shouted, "Run. Get away up the ridge. Enough of us have died for these fools."

"We'll stay with you," said Grattur, weeping.

"I said run!"

"Good thinking," said Redeye, appearing out of nowhere and crouching to throw a twist of cord around Grattur's stump of a wrist. "Come on, lads."

"Run!" Gard shouted to Dalbeck, and the boy turned to obey, just as a rocket came sailing out of the smoke and burst in front of him. It blew away much of his face and he dropped on his back, trying to scream, but what was left of his mouth filled with blood and he only made choking noises. Gard ended it quickly for him and looked around. Thrang had killed his man but two more were advancing on him, and he was crouched low, growling, defending—his tent, where he kept the celadon cup.

Gard bounded toward Thrang and killed the two men, overhand and backhand, and sliced open the roof of the tent. He reached in, grabbed the sack with the cup, and threw it to the old demon. "Get out of here!" he shouted, and felt something strike his helmet. It dropped him to his knees. Everything went green.

Someone had grabbed him, he was being pulled along stumbling, a claw was raking his arm. He was between Stedrakh and Engrattur. They ran straight into a knot of the enemy trying to cut off their escape, and Gard roused himself enough to grab an enemy's sword and cut him down with it. He heard Engrattur cry out in pain to one side of him. Stedrakh was on the other side, raking a way through with his claw. Arkholoth sprinted past them, ramming a spear through someone else who popped up to block their retreat, but he took three arrows in his back, all at once. He staggered but kept running.

Another moment of clearheadedness: their feet were tangling in something blue. Blue, with little golden fish. Duke Chrysantine's tent fabric. Gard fell and heard the arrow before he felt it go through his hand. He found his feet and wrenched the hand free, with the arrow still protruding from it. Redeye was beside him, snapping the shaft and pulling it out. Redeye grunted as an arrow creased his cheek, but pulled Gard after him into the roiling smoke.

It must have been a long while later. They were in the bottom of a valley, crouched in a thicket of willows along a streambed. Someone was whimpering. The sky was gray, it was getting cold. Fog sat right down on the mountaintops, erasing the upper half of the world. Someone was holding a split helmet in front of him.

". . . lucky to be alive," Stedrakh was saying. "Your skull must be made of stone."

Gard put up his hand in wonder—he had a bandage tied around it, a blue one with gold fish—and felt the back of his head. A long, stinging line ran down his scalp.

". . . like fucking Andib the Axeman. How's Arkholoth?"

"How are you, Arkholoth?"

Arkholoth was murmuring to himself. He looked up at them in surprise. "My boys went away," he said indistinctly.

"So they did," Redeye told him.

"Where's Thrang?"

"Haven't seen him."

Gard pulled himself upright and attempted to speak, but his mouth seemed glued shut. He leaned over to the creek and cupped his palm in the water, and managed to get enough to swill out his mouth. Someone dipped up a helmet and held it for him. He looked up at Engrattur, who was holding a wad of banner to his left eye.

"Thank you," Gard said, and drank. He leaned back against a willow trunk and watched idly as Redeye and Stedrakh moved back and forth, tearing up more bits of banner to bind wounds.

". . . need to move on soon, because we're not far enough away."

"What I say is, we'd be better off going back and surrendering. We might spend a few weeks in a prison, but all we have to do is swear to serve this Salting bastard. That's how it works. They never like to waste mercenaries, if they can use them," said Stedrakh. "And we'd be fed and get our wounds seen to."

Arkholoth slumped where he sat. Gard watched the green light spiraling forth, floating up against the pale sky.

". . . wouldn't trust those bastards any farther than I could spit," Redeye was saying.

"We should ask him." That was Grattur.

Redeye came close and leaned down to look into Gard's eyes. He raised his voice a little when he spoke. "What do you think, sir? Should we go back and surrender?"

"No," said Gard. "They killed the women."

"He's got a good point," said Redeye, looking over his shoulder at the others. "They butchered the artillery girls. What d'you suppose they'd do to the lot of us? I don't have my amulet anymore, either."

"Well, I've got mine," said Stedrakh. "I'm for taking my chances. Anyone else want to come?"

"We're staying with him," said Engrattur, pointing at Gard.

"You go if you like," said Redeye. "And good luck, brother."

Stedrakh said nothing more, but got to his feet and pushed out through the underbrush. They heard pebbles clattering as he climbed the hill behind them. Redeye sat crouched a moment, rubbing his chin thoughtfully.

"We'd better get going again," he said, when they could no longer hear Stedrakh's footsteps. "Not safe to stop here long. We'll go downstream, eh? It'll be dark soon. Ready to move on, Arkholoth?

"Arkholoth?"

"He's gone," said Gard.

"Ah. Just us, then."

Gard was helped to his feet. He staggered along between Grattur and Engrattur, as Redeye went ahead. They went a long way. It got dark. It got cold. They had to stop once, when Gard vomited. A fire was burning in his head, and a flare of light before his eyes every time he stumbled on the uneven ground.

At some point they stood beside a roaring whiteness, and Redeye was saying, "Fuck. It's a river."

Grattur said, "What do we do now?"

"Look for a place to get across," said Redeye.

"There are some stones here," said Engrattur.

"I wouldn't trust his balance. No offense, sir. That's a long drop and I for one can't swim. You lads stay here with him. I'll follow the bank a ways and see if there's a narrow place or a fallen log, eh?"

"Yes, Sergeant," said Grattur.

Gard nodded between them, wondering if he could sleep standing up. Minutes passed.

"What was that?" said Grattur and Engrattur together.

Gard lifted his head. "Hush," he said, listening hard. Fire crackling? Men pushing through bushes? Voices. Yes, voices, and then a firebird traveling upward that burst into a second sun and lit the river gorge bright as lurid red day.

"Little brother, they're coming, and we don't know how to swim," said Grattur.

"But we have to get you across. Please don't fall," said Engrattur.

They scrambled down the bank and splashed in, trying to wade, but the current ran swift and deep. The water was like ice. It tumbled them all three against the rocks they had thought to use as stepping-stones and effortlessly swept them over. The cataract dropped them a long way. There was nothing but noise, and cold, and darkness.

Gard opened his eyes in the gray light of dawn to find himself lying half in and half out of the water, sprawled on wet stones, his fingers clenched so tightly around a willow root he could not open them. The whining in his ears was as though midges circled his head.

He pulled himself out of the water and was at last able to release his grip. His hand fell like a dead weight. He turned himself over and sat up.

There was mist in the river gorge, with the sky above it brightening for a white dawn. Mountains were on all sides. A little way downriver he could see Grattur floating, caught in wet branches and foaming mud. His eyes were open and sightless. There was no sign of Engrattur's body.

The whine in his ears resolved into pleading voices. *She'll catch us again, little brother, she'll have us back, we don't want to go to her! Help us!*

Blue clay was in the bank where the willow grew. Gard massaged life back into his unwounded hand and flexed the fingers, and dug a fistful of clay. He sculpted a little bird, awkwardly, giving it sticks for legs and tiny pebbles for eyes. He paid particular care to the wings, hoping they would work. The blood of his body oozed into the clay, for he had had to give up and use his wounded hand too.

When he had finished it, he dug more blue clay and made another. "They aren't very good," he said aloud. "I'm sorry. I don't have the strength for anything bigger."

He set them side by side and spoke the words to summon them into flesh. The white flash knocked him backward, and he passed out again.

Two lumpy-looking, little blue birds were sitting on his chest, watching him sadly with silver eyes. Gard sat up in stages, and they fluttered awkwardly to the gravel beside him. He stood, swaying, clutching a low branch of the willow, groping in his boot tops to see if any of his knives were still there. He found one. "Better than nothing."

The little birds hopped and flopped, attempting to fly. He picked them up and they scrambled onto his shoulders and clung there.

"Hold on. We have to keep moving. Can't let you die again."

It was too bad about his books, he told the little birds. He really regretted losing Copperlimb's travel essays again, because it was his favorite and it seemed to be out of print now, whereas Prince Firebow's work was available all the time. He had seen a really nice omnibus edition in a shop window in Deliantiba. Had they had time to look in the shop windows in Deliantiba?

The little birds could only cheep disconsolately in reply.

"That's too bad. It had some lovely shops," said Gard, and fell on his face. The bird were thrown clear. They hopped back and peeped at him until he got up again and staggered on with them.

———

He was lying on his back. It seemed to be twilight; he could see one star in an orchid-colored sky. The little birds were huddled under his chin, shivering.

Something big and pale was moving nearby. A white stag, glimmering against the green mountainside. He watched as it walked close. It looked at him calmly. It stepped over him and walked on.

He sat up, catching the little birds as they fell, and held them against his chest as he struggled to his feet. The stag had stopped a little distance on, not looking back, but he thought it might be waiting for him.

"We have to follow," he told the little birds. "Oh, doesn't it shine? Just like a star. Ranwyr, look, it's beautiful!"

Gard hurried, not wanting to lose sight of the stag. It went down into a hollow under some trees. He could see it shining down there. He stumbled, caught his balance, kept going. He saw it clearly for a moment and then it winked out—

Something rose up in front of him, something with skin that gleamed softly, like a thundercloud brooding lightnings. "My dear, whatever have you done to yourself?" said Balnshik, and caught him as he fell.

———

He was warm. He was looking up at stars, through a latticework of firelit branches. Someone was talking. Something smelled good.

". . . glad you weren't with us, lady, or you'd have been cut to pieces too."

"I might have surprised you." That was Balnshik. Her laughter smelled like night-blooming flowers. Gard turned his head.

Above a campfire, meat sizzled on a spit. Balnshik sat beside it, with the little birds nestling in her bosom. Across the fire sat Redeye, and beside him—still clutching the sack in which he kept the celadon cup—was Thrang.

Thrang looked over sharply as Gard turned his head. He set down the bag and came and knelt beside Gard, then prostrated himself further, whining softly.

You saved the cup. You are a gentleman. I will be your servant and your children's and all theirs to the ending of the world, I swear by the Blue Pit of Hazrakhin and the Void of Stars.

Gard, with no idea what he ought to say, said, "I'm glad you didn't die."

"How are you feeling, darling?" Balnshik inquired, rising. "I have some broth here for you, and you really ought to drink it."

"Can I have some of the meat?" Gard tried to rise on his elbows. Thrang drew back for Balnshik, who stepped close. The little birds lost their footing when she moved, but clung batlike to her shirt and pulled themselves up to her shoulders.

"No," she said. "I'd rather see how you keep the broth down first. Don't argue with nursie; you have a cracked skull. You're really rather lucky to be alive." She knelt beside him and set down what she had been carrying, which was Redeye's helmet full of rabbit broth cooked with wild onions. Dipping in a wooden spoon, she fed him a little at a time.

"Are we safe here?" he asked, between one spoonful and the next.

"Safe enough," said Redeye grimly. "Skalkin Salting's called his men together and marched off to Deliantiba. Those bastards with the flares saw me; I led them away and we ended up circling back toward Penterkar Ridge. I got up in a tree and spent the night there. Come morning I had a good view of the whole damn army marching off up the road." He spat. "His honor guard, I guess that's who they were, marched in front of the whole lot, right behind his trumpeters. They carried poles with heads stuck on them. Most were too bashed up to tell whose they were, but one was the archduke's, I'm pretty certain. And one head was Stedrakh's."

"Oh," said Gard. "Oh, I'm sorry."

Redeye shrugged. "He oughtn't to have trusted them to do the sensible thing, that's all. There's nobody as spiteful as a hothead, when he's got a feud going."

"Almost nobody," said Balnshik. "We need to discuss your future, darling."

"Mine?"

"Yours?" She widened her eyes at him. "Yes, yours. You were a hunted man long before you fell foul of petty warlords, you know. Grattur and Engrattur told me about the Bitch Princess. And, by the way, darling, you need to make new bodies for them as soon as you're able. They're adorable like this but absolutely helpless, and you'll want every able-bodied ally you can summon against the mountain."

"How did you get out of there?"

"Well, you did kill my master with your clever spell," said Balnshik, tilting Redeye's helmet to get the last of the broth. "As well as cave in half the black halls. I was with Duke Silverpoint when the Training Hall began to collapse. A wall fell out and sunlight poured in, and I ran for my life with an avalanche of rock and snow after me."

"The duke . . . ?"

"Died," said Balnshik matter-of-factly. "When the first tremor came, he began to laugh. The last I saw of him he was looking up at the roof as it fell in on him, and he was still laughing. I never saw such a look of triumph on any man's face, as he had in that hour."

"Hotheads," said Redeye, nodding. "They're crazy, all of them."

"But ultimately rather trivial, as enemies go," said Balnshik. "Compared with the Narcissus of the Void. Now, listen to me, my dear: it sounds as though you've had a jolly time masquerading as a Child of the Sun, and I wish I'd seen you at the height of your acting career, I really do, but all this nonsense must stop.

"You are a mage. You can't pretend you aren't one, especially not when you have the likes of Pirihine hunting for you. She wants your heart's blood on her face and hands, and the little viper has a way of getting what she wants. You have the power to deny her that particular treat, but only if you *use* the power."

"What can I do?"

"With respect, sir, you could do a lot worse than set up shop in your own fortress," said Redeye.

"Exactly. You need some sort of lair and you need an army. Might I respectfully suggest summoning up demon servitors?"

"I don't want slaves," said Gard, scowling.

"You wouldn't need 'em," said Redeye. "Every man in your platoon would come back and work for you, if you offered them bodies. Those boys adored you, sir. There's never been anybody like you, see? You're one of *us*, only you're not . . ."

"A drunkard, a glutton, or a fool," said Balnshik crisply. "As so many of our people are."

"Right, you're, er, *organized*, you see, sir? And a mage and all too. It's perfect. It's like in those stories other people have, about a prophecy that somebody special will be sent by the gods to be their savior, or their long-lost king or whatever."

"Though we have no such prophecies," said Balnshik.

"No. Nobody ever makes any prophecies about the likes of us," said Redeye, with a bitter chuckle. "We're always the hordes getting slaughtered by the hero, or the monsters in the mountain passes the hero has to defeat. Or at best we get to be the minions and henchmen of some sort of, I don't know, some sorcerer or other."

"A Dark Lord," said Gard meditatively.

"Right! That," said Redeye.

Gard stood on the top of the mountain, looking down.

He had come a long way to find this place. It rose out of great dense oak forests, and it was as formidable as the mountain of his captivity. That lay far behind him, over the edge of the world, lost in its glaciers and mists. Before him here he saw the curve of the earth in the blue sea, and, nearer in, the river-crossed plains where the Children of the Sun lived and quarreled, and nearer in still the green lands that were henceforth his own.

Nearer in still—but far down all the same, just barely visible—he made out the tents of his camp. Many tents were there, and he knew a crowd stood looking up, watching hopefully.

He closed his eyes, breathed deeply, and went out of himself.

Power was flowing in the rock. Latent thunder was in the sky. It was thunder weather and the sky was leaden, no breath of air in the silent tree halls, and he had come into being in this weather, on just such a mountain. This time was his. This place was his. He claimed the power in the rock for his own. He drew it upward into himself. He drew it down from the gathering storm clouds.

It surged. It crackled. He reached out and sculpted the mountain with it and called up his desire. Rooms, corridors, windows, doors, high balconies viewing the sea, open places that might be gardens later, or might not. Deep pools and twisting stairs. Chamber upon chamber, storerooms, dungeons, halls, a palace to make the mountain of the mages look like the delvings of blind moles. Hypocausts and baths warmed by subterranean fires artfully directed, no labor of grinding slaves, and ventilation through apertures in rock that pulled in the west wind.

Now, the theatrical elements: the frowning battlements of black stone, carefully calculated to daunt, by their very appearance, any would-be hero hoping to scale them. Gutters and drain spouts in grotesque shapes. Cupolas whose arrangements of windows suggested skulls. A dozen needlelike spires of no architectural function whatsoever, unless as lightning rods. A weather vane featuring another bat-winged grotesque. Black stone, black slate, black-enameled steel everywhere. A quarter mile down the slope, a death zone of bare rock, scattered and tumbled black boulders ringing the mountaintop.

It was finished in a flare of light, white radiating into indigo, and with a thunderclap the Children of the Sun heard as far away as Silverhaven.

Gard came to himself as the first big hot drops fell. He inhaled the fragrances of stone and rain, and smiled to see what he had made.

He found his way out through one of the lower postern doors. He was picking his way down the slope below when he saw the death zone before him, and was momentarily disconcerted to discover that he had left no pathway through. Luckily, he was able to summon a little residual power and, with a wave of his fist, opened a mazy trackway there, impossible to find by uninvited travelers. As an afterthought, he added a few spikes surmounted by silver skulls, just for decoration.

They were coming up the mountain already when he emerged at the front gate, Grattur and Engrattur, Balnshik and Thrang, Redeye and all those bodied demons he had called to his service over the past three months. They were cheering. He grinned and waved his hand at his great house. "Welcome home," he told them.

"It's magnificent!" cried Grattur.

"Stupendous!" cried Engrattur.

Balnshik craned her head back to study it. "*Skulls?* Oh, really, darling, isn't that a little much?"

"Well, it's supposed to be frightening," said Gard.

"I hope you remembered the plumbing?"

"There's some plumbing," he said carelessly. "Of course."

"I see."

"There won't be an army on earth that can touch us," said Redeye, grinning. "We could hold off a siege up here until Grell cracks the Moon-Egg at the end of the world. Well done, my lord."

"And I'll thank you to observe that red road down there." Gard pointed down the mountain. "That's the main route used by the freight caravans. Duke Salting owns the freight company. They go through once a week. Won't that be convenient?"

"Very, my lord," said Stedrakh, glaring down at the road.

"We're going to be demon bandits!" cried Cheller happily.

"But we're only going to prey on the rich," said Gard.

"Well, of course we are, sir," said Redeye. "The poor haven't got any money!"

They all laughed heartily at that.

The masked figure stands atop his black mountain, and carefully directed lights make his eyes seem to blaze with triumph. The audience shivers, and applauds, though some wrooch about on their stone seats and look around to see if a cushion vendor is anywhere near. Some use this pause as an opportunity to refill their wine cups.

But the poet Wiregold, or at least his masked representation, is walking out once more to center stage. He clears his throat, and waits until cushions are tucked into place and wine jugs are tucked back in baskets before speaking.

> *Now what offense walks boldly under heaven!*
> *The Master of the Mountain here begins*
> *His reign of infamy. No caravan's safe*
> *Between Troon and Salesh, no virgin travels*
> *Unravished, no righteous man*
> *His path may take along our roads without challenge.*
> *The Dark One, the Black-a-vised, fearless walks*
> *Even in our cities, where he will.*
> *Monstrous his lusts: six women, terrified,*
> *Our own pure girls, he keeps as mistresses,*
> *Visiting when he will. They dare not protest.*
> *In his black halls he holds carousal,*
> *Feasting and drinking on our stolen store*
> *While orphans starve in Deliantiba!*

The audience leans forward, fascinated. Quite a show is going on behind Wiregold to illustrate his words, and not a few parents are relieved their smaller children have dozed off.

"But!" Wiregold raises his hand.

Such wickedness offends the very gods!
Now they take counsel in their cloudy home
How best to punish such impiety!

At the back of the performance area the gods appear—which is to say the accepted theatrical convention for The Gods, six or seven high poles draped with white fabrics, each bearing at its top an immense mask representing one of the better-known deities. One teeters out from their midst and is turned as though to address the others.

"Hear me, immortal ones! I, the Smith Father,
Can take no rest, while my lamenting children
Hourly beg for rescue and release!
How will you smite this thief and sorcerer?
Do not delay in council; until I know
That he is doomed indeed, no more I'll raise
My hammer, no more my forge shall glow
To make your crowns of gold, your silver spears,
Nor even the hinges of your palace doors!"

The masks turn to and fro.

The gods confer. Now speaks the mighty goddess,
She without whom all life would perish,
She who maddens the young, and of the old makes fools.
"Long-suffering smith, your wrath is just.
I will send forth a daughter of mine own
And she will break this demon in her hands.
Behold her now, the Green Witch of the wood!"

Wiregold extends his hands and exits sidelong stage left, as from stage right comes an actress painted green. She is somewhat provocatively clad, but what little of her is covered, is covered in purest white. Her mask is of serene beauty.

She proceeds, in the sidelong dancing steps prescribed for a heroine of this type, toward the actor in the Dark Lord's mask. He turns to regard her and leaps down from his mountain, landing in a theatrical demon-crouch, and whirls both his swords at her.

She thrusts out her arm, palm extended toward him, and he freezes. With her other hand she reaches into his black robe and draws forth a black heart. She holds it up in triumph as he falls to his knees before her, broken.

The audience applauds. They like love stories.

4

the Letters

The good brothers are robed in white, speak in hushed voices. Yes, you are welcome to study in their library. Will you be staying? They point out the grottoes in the rock that are their guest quarters, each with its woven mat and water jug. Simple meals are served twice a day, signaled by a rhythm beaten on a wooden drum. If you miss the signal because you are deep in your research, they will understand. One of the brothers will be happy to prepare a late repast for you. You are welcome to join their prayers, even though your gods are not theirs. They feel your gods wouldn't mind.

You are grateful for the coolness of the cavern, as they lead you in; the air is dry here. The breath of the desert exhales its sullen heat into this miraculously green valley. You are shown the rows of books. They resemble packages wrapped in silk. The brother librarian pulls down the volumes you have requested and shows you to a reading stand, mounted under a skylight in the rock.

You open the silk wrappings. This is not a book, as you understand books. It is a neat stack of leaves, though very large leaves, pressed flat and dried. They are a delicate ivory color. They are covered in writing, clear characters in black and distinct brushstrokes. You lean close to read. What is that fragrance, rising sweet from the pages as they warm in the light?

She never accepted that he had gone away. She missed him. She remembered him, a little, she thought; but she was never really certain whether the voice in her dreams, the kind face, were memories or things imagined.

Her earliest clear memory was of watching with interest as her people tried out the first boat ever made. Someone had woven a round thing like a basket, and covered it all over with something sticky that she wasn't allowed to touch. It had dried in the sun. Then one of her people set it in the water and climbed in, and it floated and went round and round in the river's eddy. Everyone else stood on the riverbank and raised up their hands and exclaimed.

A few days later the boatman worked out that he needed a paddle for his little boat, and made one. Then the boat went where he wanted it to go, and once again people raised their hands and exclaimed. She looked out across the gray sea and understood what a boat was for.

She found a big leaf to be her paddle, and a basket she thought would fit her nicely, and dragged them down to the river's edge. She was getting into her boat when the people came running up, shouting in alarm.

It took a wearying long time to make them understand that she was going to go look for him. But when they understood her at last, they made crying mouths and said, *Oh, Child, you mustn't go away and leave us! Oh, boohoo, boohoo, we'd miss you so! Please stay with us, little Saint! Everyone will cry if you go away! Boohoo!* And they pretended to wipe away tears.

She looked up into their eyes and into their minds and saw the truth there, just under their amusement. They were afraid to be alone. They wanted her to take care of them. They wanted someone to tell them what to do.

It made her sad, and a little angry.

But she let them pick her up and carry her away from the river's edge, and Lendreth came striding up with his face like a thunderstorm. He shouted at them, *How could you have been so careless? She might have drowned!*

Drowned? How should she have drowned? She is the Saint! Didn't she float in the pool, at the waterfall?

We cannot always hope for miracles, Lendreth had said, and after that she was never allowed to be alone with her nurses, but that one of the trevanion had to be there too, watching her. And so she never got the chance to run away from them.

When she was a little older, when she had listened to them speaking over her head often enough and looked into their minds a little more, she understood why her people were the way they were. She felt sorry for them.

The green meadows by the sea were becoming crowded, because her people were having lots of babies now. She looked across the river and knew that there were other places her people could live, and so one day she told them they needed to go there.

Some people wept because they didn't want to leave the place where he had left them. She understood that; it made her sad to leave there too. She would have told them it was all right for some of them to stay, but Lendreth raised her in his arms and said, *She has spoken!* And so they all went, wading across the river where it spread out on the beach at low tide. Big Kdwyr carried her.

That night they stopped in a green forest, warm and pleasant, where there was plenty of room. Her people sang under the stars. And yet, when morning came, it was discovered that some of her people had crept away in the darkness. The man who had made the boat was one of them. It was plain by their tracks they had gone back to the meadows by the river.

Lendreth was angry and wanted to have them brought back. She raised her voice, the first time she had ever done so, and told him to let them go.

Blessed Child, you do not understand, he had said. *We must keep together as a people. It is safer that way.* She looked at him and saw how frightened he was, had always been, how little he trusted anything.

She saw that though her people wanted someone to tell them what to do, none of them could ever be made to do something they didn't really *want* to do.

She told Lendreth that the ones who had gone back would be safe by the river. He bowed his head grudgingly. He and she were to have the same argument many more times, as the years went by, as her people wandered and some settled down in places they liked.

———

"Look at this!"

Prass extended a taloned hand and pointed down into the valley. Prass was a tawny color, with wings that hung in folds under his arms, though he seldom flew because he was rather fat. Kolosht, his companion, was less settled in his shape, but had lately been appearing in the form of a drowned youth because he liked frightening people. He now pulled his sagging head up by its hair, so he could direct its white eyes where the other demon pointed.

"What are they?" he said in a clear and rather eerie voice that did not emanate from his corpse mouth.

"They're the Earthborn! Remember them?"

"No," said Kolosht, but he had difficulty remembering things longer than a week or so. He was young, as demons went, not much more than an adolescent.

"They used to live up in a valley near the Ice Trap."

"What's the Ice Trap?"

"Someplace we don't want to go. I heard they were trapped up there too. They must have found a way to get out."

"Can we eat them?"

Prass scowled, revealing a mouthful of razor-edged teeth. "They weren't supposed to make good eating. The older ones always told us not to bother with them."

Kolosht giggled slyly. "Can we do anything *else* with them?"

"Now, there's a thought."

"I want to hurt one. I want to kill one."

"I want to do something else to one. No reason why we can't share, is there?"

"Not if you go first."

"There's a little one, look! And it's a she! Oh, look at the little sweet-meat. Come up here, little beauty, come just a little closer, oh, please!"

"The Lord of Fear will tear your flesh and drink your blood!"

"Shut up, you idiot. That's no way to lure a child!"

The little girl in question had, meanwhile, noticed them and now wandered up the hill in their direction. She appeared to be about six years of age and was naked but for a white flower tucked in her hair.

"Hello, little girl, won't you come play with us?" said Prass, simpering. He shoved back Kolosht, who was trying to drool blood at her to scare her.

The little girl raised her eyes and looked at them. She did not seem frightened, only interested. Her gaze met Prass's and he had the sensation of twin beams of light stabbing in through his eyes, lighting his mind clear to the back wall of his skull. He had never felt such discomfort in his life.

Kolosht, for his part, was so startled by the merciless clarity of the child's eyes that he lost his concentration, and the corpse body melted down into a mass of confused body parts. He gurgled in a heap on the ground, trying to move any part that was capable of visual perception away from her cold-eyed inspection.

"Why do you like to scare people?" she asked Kolosht. "Is it because you're afraid?"

Kolosht tried to tell her that he wasn't afraid, that he was a Lord of the

Abyss and a Death Spawn and a Soul Crusher, but he couldn't form enough of a mouth to say it. In any case, the child's calm contemplation was *doing something to him*. It was erasing his image of himself, all the dark, violent pictures he'd formed for his comfort, and showing him something horribly different and entirely true: a dim and pathetic little cloud, not very bright, circling slowly in a universe of brilliant stars.

What her gaze was revealing to Prass is best left undescribed, but the experience horrified him. It stripped away his self-illusions like a flensing knife. He had never thought he was a *good* creature, but had carefully avoided noticing that he was a contemptible one. No lies now hid his trembling stinking heart. And the worst part of it all was that the little girl saw what he was being forced to see, she saw everything calmly, she *knew* and there was no escape because she was—she was—

"Why do you like to hurt little girls?" she asked him. "Is it because you can't—"

"Please! Let me go!" Prass's skin was fading, his fat running off him in streams of grease. "I'll never come near you again—I'll never touch your people—"

"But I want to know why," she said. "Why did you make yourself look like that? Your wings don't even work."

"I'll make myself look like anything you want, if you'll only let me go!" Prass shrieked. Kolosht had already disbodied himself to escape her, leaving a puddle of slime in the dust as he fled back into the void.

She stared at Prass. He began screaming uncontrollably, flinging himself from side to side, and his scales fell out in handfuls. Below, the adult Earthborn had noticed and now came running up the hill. "But I'm not trying to hurt you," she said, dismayed at his agony. "What's hurting you?"

Prass, strangling on himself, was unable to reply.

"I know what it must be," she said helpfully. "It must hurt to be you. Why don't you be something else?"

He was rolling on the ground now, for his legs had fallen off, but he managed to nod frantically and imply that he'd appreciate any suggestions.

"You should be a mouse," she said. "They're little and they don't hurt anything."

He collapsed inward on himself, like a rotten melon dissolving into mold, and from the squashy mess a small thing scrambled, slipping and panting. It ran at once into the long grass and was gone.

"What is this?" shouted Lendreth. "What has happened, Child?"

"They were demons and they wanted to be bad," she said, pointing at the twin smears of nastiness in the dust. "I just looked at them, but it hurt them. They stopped wearing those bodies."

Lendreth recoiled at the sight, and one of the ladies caught the Child up and hugged her tight, beginning to cry. "I'm all right," she told them. Lendreth pulled her from the woman's arms and held her up for everyone to see.

"A miracle!" he cried. "She has slain demons for our sake!"

"But I didn't—," she said, and was drowned out by everyone chanting, "A miracle! A miracle!" They all raised up their hands and she was carried down the hill in triumph.

––––––––

They settled in that place for a long while. A lake was nearby, full of clean water. Someone else was able to make a boat, then made more boats. They found mussels in the water and were astonished to discover pearls inside their shells. They gave her all the pearls. She didn't know what on earth to do with them, but thanked everyone.

Lendreth told her they needed to live in a safe place, pointing out to an island in the lake. He gathered the men who had brought tools away from the fields where they had been slaves, and they cut palings sharp and set them to ring the shores of the island. More palings were cut to make the frames of little houses, like boats or baskets turned upside down.

Her people waded and swam across to the island. They were happy to spend the night there, and even a week; but once they were settled in, Lendreth organized the men with tools into patrols. They called themselves the Mowers, and they walked the shores on the island keeping watch. He was astonished when people protested this, and many gathered up their belongings and made to leave again.

But we will be safe here! Lendreth told them.

One gaunt man, who had outlived all his children in the slave pens, glared at Lendreth. *A prison is a prison, no matter who builds it. I see the walls, I see the guards. I will take my chances under the open sky. We were not made to live this way.*

How dare you call them guards? said Lendreth. *These men are heroes, these men bought your freedom in blood!*

That isn't how I remember it, said another man. *We were freed by the Child.*

She was the sign and omen of your deliverance, Lendreth argued, *but who stood in our defense when the Riders came across the field? They had cut us down like summer corn, if not for these brave men. Even the Beloved Imperfect was powerless to stop them.*

Imperfect, was he?

He said so himself, Lendreth replied.

But we never lived like this when we were free, said a woman. *There were no closed-up places, no armed guards before the Riders came.*

But we no longer live in that world, and it's foolish to pretend we can live that way again without endangering ourselves, said Lendreth. *Did the Beloved Imperfect himself not say, "Your old ways are lost. I can never sing back the child into the womb, the leaf into the bud"?*

There was a grudging silence to admit that much. Then the woman said, *He also said the little Saint was perfect. He said she'd lead us. What does she say now, about making us stay where we don't want to stay?*

And everyone turned to look down at her, where she sat playing with bright fallen leaves, but listening to them all.

She looked up at them. "You don't have to stay here if you don't want to. You can live in the woods, if you'd like that better."

They lifted their hands and praised her, though Lendreth pressed his lips tight shut and at last said, *Then it is decided. We will live here and on the forest shore as well.*

Lendreth spoke to her afterward, explaining that the people were like children, who must be watched over to see that they did not wander foolishly into harm's way. He told her about her duty and her responsibility to them. He told her how heavy the burden of their safety was and said that even so he had carried it without complaint, while she was a little child; and that he would carry it for her many years yet, until she was grown. He suggested that she lend her voice to his, when he spoke for their own good.

"But they're not children," she said. "They're grown people."

"But they—" Lendreth tried to compose his thoughts. "They are only freed slaves. They never had the chance, as I did, to learn the Songs."

"Then we should teach them."

"But not everyone can learn the Songs. It's not easy. Even the Blessed Ranwyr tried hard and couldn't learn them well enough."

"And he was a very good man. So, you see? It doesn't matter if people don't know the Songs. All they want to do is live in the woods and be happy. That's not hard."

"But—but people can only live in the woods happily if someone else is protecting their right to do that. We learned that, in terrible sorrow. Even the Beloved Imperfect accepted it at last, on that great day in the wheat field."

"No, he didn't. He told you what you did was wrong."

Lendreth was silent a moment. "Who told you that?" he said at last. "Was it Sister Seni?"

"No. No one told me. I knew."

"Then tell me what we are to do, Child," said Lendreth, with bitterness. "Seven years I have waited for your great counsel. Let me receive it now."

She got to her feet and looked into his eyes. He blinked and drew back a little, and at last dropped his gaze. "We will leave people alone," she said. "They will be happy and free in the woods. If people want to learn the Songs, they can come to me and I'll teach them."

"But I haven't taught you the Songs yet."

"I know them." To prove it, she sang the Song for Easing Pain.

He listened and wept, for she sang it perfectly, and when she stopped, he raised his hands and praised her. "Now there is nothing left for me to do."

"Yes, there is," she said. "We should plant a garden on this island, instead of putting houses all over it. We can grow medicine plants in the garden. That way if people get sick, they can come here and get anything they need."

"You are most wise," said Lendreth, bowing his head. "It shall be done."

But, looking at him and seeing into his mind, she saw how unhappy he was. "What do you want to do most, Lendreth?"

"To go from here. To be alone awhile."

"Then you should take your stick and go exploring. Look for medicine plants to bring back. Visit my people who went to live other places. See if they need anything. Come back and tell me how they are."

"I will do your will." Taking his staff, he bowed and left her.

———

The first thing she did, when he had gone, was ask the Mowers to pull up all the sharp stakes they had put around the island. The empty houses were dismantled and neatly stacked. She had the Mowers use their tools as tools again, digging up the ground to make planting beds, though some of them grumbled at that a little, being proud of the sharp edges they had put on their spades and mattocks.

She called all the other disciples to her, then, and set them to making the garden she wanted. It pleased her to be spoken to instead of over, and to have adults listen to her without smiling and winking at one another.

People from the forest on the shore came willingly to help, when they saw they weren't going to be forced to stay there. They brought young fruit trees and planted them on the island.

One little house was saved out for her, and there she kept the pearls and the toys people brought her. By night she slept on the island, with the disciples.

The years passed happily then.

One by one the other trevanion came to her, those disciples who grew restless and wanted to be out in the world, accomplishing things, gathering knowledge. They asked for permission to roam like Lendreth, and she sent them off gladly.

The Mowers came to her too and humbly asked whether they might be her special guards. As gently as she could, she explained that she didn't need guards, though she was always grateful for their labor in the gardens.

The Mowers withdrew, a little sullen, and she saw that they thought themselves unappreciated, because they had greatly enjoyed marching along the perimeter of the island watching out for dangers. They had liked being called heroes. It let them forget the truth of what had happened that day in the wheat field, when they had given way to rage and clubbed dying men and animals to bloody pulp.

Some of them went away into the woods and formed a guard anyway and patrolled the forests on their own. She knew that anyone who sought for trouble must, sooner or later, find it, and she sent them word to that effect; they returned word that they were not afraid to face danger for the sake of their people.

But the sun streamed down by day, and stars lit the night. Her people lived in peace, as they had lived in the old times. Children were born. Dances were held in the open meadows, under the moon, and then more children were born.

She grew older. Suddenly men who had used to speak readily and pleasantly to her stammered when answering any question she put to them. No man could meet her eyes, now. Those men among her disciples found reason to go on journeys, like the wandering trevanion. She was bewildered and a little hurt, until she looked into their minds.

"If they want to lie down with me, why are they so unhappy about it?" she asked Seni.

Seni made a face. "Because they're ashamed. This started with

Lendreth and his disciples, and I always said it was a bad idea. Coupling's wrong, they said; too much distraction for a disciple, they said. Pleasure's a trap, they said, and lust betrays you into loving one person when you ought to love them all, but chastely."

"But how can coupling be wrong? There wouldn't be any more children if everyone stopped. And people always look so happy together."

"And so they are," said Seni. "Look at the world, Child. The stag and the doe find each other, the little birds make their nests together. The butterflies join in midair. It's the comfort and glory of the world, and all life comes from it. When the Beloved was with us, oh, he was all our delight! Many's the time I lay in his arms." Tears began to well in Seni's eyes, as always happened when she spoke of the Beloved.

"Should I take lovers?"

The question stopped Seni's descent into weepy memory. "You? Well—perhaps you're a little young yet. And it's not a question of *should*, Child. It isn't a duty. You find some pretty boy and . . . it's a good idea to go to the dances, you know, because the boys gather there waiting for the girls, and you find someone nice and you talk a little and, er, perhaps you dance together and then you . . . just . . . go off into the bowers with him. And drink of the cup of delight."

"I think I'd like that," said the Saint.

Seni laughed a little uneasily. "I'm sure you would, Child. I would only hope the boys wouldn't fight each other for you."

"Why should they fight?"

"Dearest Child, haven't you seen your reflection in the water? You're the most beautiful girl in the world."

———

She waited half a year, and then one night she went across the lake, with Seni and Kdwyr, to the people who lived in the forest there. The drumming had already begun when she arrived, the little white flowers perfumed the night air. The stars were like the flowers across the sky.

The drumming stopped at once when she came to the dancing green, and after a frozen moment all the people rushed to her with glad cries and welcomed her, and found a seat of honor for her. They brought her gifts of pearls and spilled them into her lap. It seemed like a good omen.

The trevani who lived among them came and bowed to her, sat beside her, and spoke long and sonorously to her about how little fever there had been that year, how well the community was doing, and how well he had heard all the other communities were doing.

Eventually she was able to intimate that she would like to dance. It took her three iterations before she was able to make herself understood to the trevani, after which he stammered and coughed and finally announced to the world that the Blessed Saint would dance. Instantly, a throng of boys was before her, every one of them eager to lead her out on the green.

But none led her aside to the bowers afterward. She looked into their minds, each one, as she danced with them and saw their simple and straightforward lust wilting, unable to stand under the weight of awe. Not one of them dared so much as kiss her.

———

"It's all that trevani's fault," said Seni angrily, as Kdwyr rowed them back across the lake. "He's made them think it's shameful. As though there were anything wrong with a little tumble in the flowers! But you should have seen the way his sort used to look at Meli and me, when we'd been with the Star. Lendreth took me aside once, asked whether I didn't think I was distracting our Beloved from his holy work. Do you know what I said to him?"

"It doesn't matter," said the Saint, gazing over the side of the coracle and watching the stars slip by on the black water. She felt a numbness around her heart and wondered if she'd cry later, when she was alone.

"You are their daughter," said Kdwyr, as he worked the oars. Both women lifted their heads, for he seldom spoke. "Or you are their mother. No man lies down with his mother or his child."

"Hm." Seni looked down, pursed her lips, and was silent a long moment. Finally she muttered that the right boy would soon come along, then said nothing more the rest of the evening.

———

The Saint felt ashamed of her self-pity, angry at herself, and scoured it away with work. Seeing how widely the communities of her people were scattered, it seemed good to her that she should establish another garden of medicinal herbs.

The preparations took most of a year, cutting slips for transplant, collecting roots and rhizomes and seed. She gathered her disciples together and set out through the forest, traveling far.

Little communities were everywhere now, and she enjoyed visiting them as she traveled, hearing news, seeing the ways in which they had begun to grow. In one place, they had learned to build airy platforms in the branches of trees and lived in them; in another, they wove walls of rushes and lived under trees; and in another place they lived in caves along the bank of a river.

Now and again the Saint and her disciples encountered demons stumbling along on the forest trails, some of them violent and mad from chewing a certain root, laughing wildly to themselves. She would signal her followers, and all together they would step off the trail. They sang the Song of Concealment and the demon passing noticed only a grove of slender trees to one side, if he noticed anything at all. When he was well past, the Saint would dispel the illusion and they would journey on.

Far to the west she found a green sheltered valley with a spring, and planned her garden here. One great tree stood in a wide meadow. Working with her disciples—and many new ones had come to her, as she traveled—she made rooms under the tree's low branches, the walls woven of willow, to be a place for the care of the sick. They made a garden in the meadow all around, neat beds of herbs and woven frames for vines.

It was a place of exquisite peace.

————————

The Saint was sitting at the loom under the tree, weaving cloth, when she heard the cries of alarm. She rose and through the lattice saw a blur of scarlet, racing down the hill and through the garden, across the carefully tended beds. Something was running, seeming not to see the fences broken through or trampled as it came on, until at last it crashed into a stand of palings and toppled.

Even then it arms and legs thrashed, in a curious automatic way, for its body thought it was still running. Its stare was blank and set.

The disciples gathered around it, fearful, mattocks raised. The Saint pushed her way forward. "What is it?"

"Is it a demon?"

"It's a girl!" She knelt beside the body, looking on horrified as the flailing limbs grew still. Only a girl, younger perhaps than she was herself, but belonging to no people she had ever seen; for the girl's skin and hair were both the color of the setting sun, and her open eyes were like black stones. She wore a scarlet tunic. Clutched in one hand was a flared thing of some golden metal, like a curved tube ending in a bell shape. The arrow in her back was golden too, with scarlet fletching.

"Is it dead?"

"No," said the Saint, seeing that the runner now closed her eyes and lay trembling. "Together with me, lift her! Let's bring her into the house. Bring water. Bring bandages and salves. We'll save her."

They had to cut the red tunic, for it was glued to the girl with dried blood. She was emaciated, the edges of the wound were torn and blood-less, she had run a long while and a long way with the arrow in her back. Little blood welled up when the Saint drew the barbed head of the arrow forth, singing the Song to Ease Pain.

"Why would someone shoot a girl? Have the Riders come back?"

"Is she one of the Riders?"

"No!" said Seni. "They were nothing like this."

"The Riders have not come back," said the Saint firmly. "I would know. When she's well, she'll tell us herself what she is."

"There's a man among my people who might know," said Lut, who was one of the new disciples. "Uncle Gharon. He knows about things like this."

Washed and bandaged, the runner was put to bed. They eased her head down on the pillow. She sighed, opened her eyes and perhaps saw the Saint, there beside her. A pleading look came into her eyes, the first human expression she had shown; then she died, without ever having said a word.

The Saint reached out and caught the slack hand, as if she could pull the girl back from the shadow. "No!"

"Aht, aht." Seni shook her head. "I thought we might lose her. Poor thing, she'd bled out too much."

"But we'd saved her." The Saint burst into tears.

"Sometimes they still die, Child." Seni put an arm around her.

"But I never—this never happened before!"

"It won't happen to your people. This was someone else's child."

The Saint sat alone by the body a long while, miserable with guilt, exam-ining the things they had found with the girl. A small, flat wooden case contained a written message of some kind; it was in no language the Saint had ever seen, nor could she guess at its meaning. The curved thing of golden metal was beautifully made, its function a mystery until one of the disciples put his lips to what seemed to be a mouthpiece. He blew, and a high hard bright note sounded.

The arrow that had killed the girl was beautifully made too, no chipped stone head but golden stuff cruelly sharp, and so were the matched and curved blades she had worn strapped to her forearms. Yet there was nothing to tell whose daughter she had been, who might mourn her, or why she had run so far before her fall.

———————

They buried the girl in the garden, keeping back her possessions to give to any who might come searching for her. The Saint summoned to her Lut, the young disciple who had been born in that country, and he went to the place his people lived and brought back Uncle Gharon.

Uncle Gharon came slowly, for he walked on one leg and one wooden stick fitted to the stump where his other leg had been, and this was not the greatest surprise: he was a demon, with skin like greened copper and eyes like rubies. He was able to meet the Saint's gaze for a moment before wincing and looking away. He bowed his head in greeting politely enough.

"So you're the Holy Child," he said, in a voice like river gravel crunching. "Grown-up now, though, aren't you? My wife always speaks of you as a baby."

"You married one of my people?"

"I did, Lady. A pretty thing, and she keeps a pear orchard. I get all the pears I can eat." His eyes blazed crimson with the intensity of his emotion. "Big buttery yellow ones, and the red ones that taste like smoke, and the sweet green ones, and the late ones you have to pick out of the red leaves in autumn, brown and soft but, oh, what nectar!"

What a strange lust, thought the Saint, but she merely bowed her head and said, "I am glad you live in peace among us. And you may tell my people I am sixteen now."

"I will, Lady. I'm two thousand, myself. Well, and you wanted to see me about a dead girl? Wasn't me killed her, though it might have been one of the young ones. They're all fools, the young demons."

"No; she died here." The Saint beckoned, and Seni brought the runner's effects, with the arrow that had killed her. She set them before Uncle Gharon, opening out the cloth in which they had been kept. He looked down at them and grimaced.

"Ah. No, not my people at all." He picked up the arrow and turned it in his hand. "She was Fireborn. Her own people killed her."

"Why would they do such a thing?"

Uncle Gharon shrugged. He pointed westward with the arrow. "A day's journey that way, Lady, you'll find a strip of red stone, running in either direction to the horizon, wide enough for five men to walk abreast. Sit and watch it long enough and you'll see boxes come down that track, propelled on round feet, and in the boxes sit red men working a kind of land oar that makes the boxes go, and other red folk riding along in the boxes, with all their goods and gear.

"Before them you'll see a red girl running, and every now and then she'll blow on one of these." He tapped the golden horn. "And, now and again, you'll see just a girl, running alone. But, Lady, take my word for it, and don't go look yourself, nor send your people. You don't want a flight of these nasties coming your way." He set the arrow down. "Nor their axes, nor their spears, nor their fire-flowers neither."

"But why would they hurt us?"

"Ah, I'm not saying they'd hurt *you*, not on purpose. But they war amongst themselves. They live out on the plains in hives of stone, and the different hives quarrel, and the red folk die in tens and hundreds in their wars. They're all mad as stoats." He pointed to his temple with one finger. "Sometimes you can go down to the red road with boxes of fruit and they'll stop and trade things for it, axes and beads and whatnot, nice and friendly as you please. Isn't that right, Lut?"

"It's true, Mother," Lut said to her, a little sheepishly.

"Other times they'll scream at you and shoot. I've dodged a few of their arrows in my day, by the Blue Pit. You just never know, with them."

***

She came back sadly to the island garden. Her people were well and happy. The sun still shone, the gentle rains fell. But when she lay down at night and closed her eyes, she saw the dying girl.

***

In the next spring, Lendreth returned. He was lean with his travels, the sun had darkened his skin, but his face shone with eagerness as he strode along, swinging his staff. He bore on his back a heavy bag, stuffed full and bound shut.

"I have gifts for you, Child," he announced. "And wonders to tell you. Call our people together!"

"That would take awhile," said Seni. "There are more new children than white flowers on the dancing green these days, Lendreth."

That astonished him, and so did the Saint's being now a woman grown, when he noticed it. He had to settle for all the disciples that could be called in from the garden, and two visiting trevanion. When they sat together before the Saint's little house, he leaned forward and spoke.

"Brothers and sisters, when I left you, I thought the world was two green valleys and a river—this place, and the other from which we came.

I never thought the world was so big, but I have come back to tell you that our long prison was an eggshell, a tiny world, and we walking forth were only little birds that had never flown.

"Believe me when I say that I walked for long weeks across fields of corn, wild yellow meadows no slave ever labored in, and in the midst of them there was no limit, no edge to the horizon. Beyond them rise more forests, like these but bigger, great high trees such as I have not seen since my childhood before the Riders came.

"Beyond these forests is a black mountain that rises against the moon, and a place where rivers are born and drop in rainbows down its sides, fives times taller than any we saw when we walked free at last. They come down to the yellow plain and roll away to the sea, rivers so wide you could not sling a stone across, great waters that make the river of our birth seem nothing.

"I traveled for years in the wild, seeing only demons there. And then, one night, I came upon a made fire in a clearing, low coals and low flames. About it lay men and women, far gone in fever. Their skins were red as fire. Two or three tried to rise and spoke to me in threatening voices. But I sang them the Song to Ease Fear; I drew water and eased their thirst, I brewed medicines for them. Three days and three nights I stayed there, and by the third day they were well again.

"They piled little pieces of gold before me, and knelt, and said by gestures that I should go with them. So we went a day's walk, and we came to a hall made of stone, with smoke going up from it."

"Oh, fool! These were Riders!" cried one of the trevanion, scandalized.

"They were not," said Lendreth. "Do you think I wouldn't know them if I saw them again? A bat flies, and a bird flies, but they are not the same creature. The red people lived in a beautiful hall. There were no slave pits stinking under their feet, no stables where beasts were kept. But their dying lay everywhere in that place. Some had already died and lay still where they had fallen, for the others were too sick to bury them.

"There were wonders there I wouldn't know how to describe to you, but the strangest of all was that medicine grew all around their fine hall, on the waste ground where they had cut down trees, and yet they didn't know it would have saved them—"

"They cut down trees," said the trevani who had spoken before. "So did the Riders, Lendreth."

"They were not Riders," said the Saint. "Go on, please, Lendreth. Did you save them?"

"Child, I did," said Lendreth, looking gratefully at her. "It would take seven nights to tell you everything I saw and everything I did there, but I lived among them a year, and I learned to speak their words. They call themselves the Children of the Sun. They are reasoning people like we are, nothing like the Riders, certainly nothing like demons!"

"I know of them," said the Saint. "A little. I'm glad you saved them, Lendreth." The trevanion turned to stare at her.

"I knew it would have been your will," said Lendreth in triumph. He reached for the sack he had carried and opened the top. He brought out things wrapped in fine red cloth, opening them one after another.

"They took me to one of their communities. Smooth straight ways to walk in, beautiful high houses, glorious bright lamps by night and by day, light coming in through windows set with crystal like sheets of clear ice! Look, look here, this is only a toy for children, but there are big ones made, and people travel in them, they roll along from a *mechanism* under them that men work with levers. And, see this? This is a book with their writing in it, but it's all stamped like cloth patterns, every page. And here are more of their pieces of gold—they used them to trade—and here is a little model of one of their famous buildings, there was a man selling these outside the real one, and I brought one back so you could see how beautiful their houses are."

"It is all very brightly colored," said one of the trevanion rather grudgingly.

"This is nothing to what you would see if you were there," said Lendreth. "There are walls and houses painted every color. You can walk a mile down one of their ways and see no white thing but the seabirds overhead. Here's a wonder, though, look at this! Child, this is for you. A paradox: no color, and yet all colors."

Lendreth drew forth something that sparkled. It was a pitcher. It seemed to be made of clear ice, cut and faceted in patterns, perilous beauty, throwing out brilliant lights edged with rainbows.

The Saint caught her breath. Slowly, she put out her hand and touched it.

———

Later, when the other trevanion had gone, she went into her house and brought out the flat wooden case the runner had been carrying. "This has their writing on it." She held it out to Lendreth. "Can you tell me what it says?"

He took it and frowned over the scrawled characters.

"This is a salutation. 'To—' Hmmm, hmmm, the next word means a kind of leader. 'Duke Strake of, the house of, Firechain.' Then the message, I think. 'Worthy' or perhaps that would be 'Honored Firechain, your—' I think the next word is 'son' or 'daughter.' Hmmmm, no, no, it's 'son.' 'Your son is dead.' Oh. Er, 'We have withdrawn to the—' Hmmm, 'house with walls'? 'Strong house'? Something like that. 'Duke . . . Duke Salting—' The next word is, er, either 'assails' or 'attacks' or . . . let's say 'attacks us, with the sunrise. Please come with . . . with all your . . .' I don't know what this word means, it's like a plural for 'men.' 'Many men'? 'Come very quickly. We will all'—oh, dear—'all die here soon.'" Lendreth lowered his eyes and closed the case.

"They are not entirely reasoning people, are they?" said the Saint.

"They can be quarrelsome. I meant to tell you about that later."

When she looked into his eyes and bid him speak frankly, he had to admit that in fact the Children of the Sun were given to vicious wars among their great families. Moreover, despite their brilliant inventions, they were ignorant of any medicine but the repair of battlefield injuries.

"There are other peculiarities," said Lendreth. "They love beautiful things—I saw no surface that was not decorated, in some way—and yet I saw no single tree nor blade of grass in their cities. But this ignorance, Child, is to our advantage!"

She frowned at him. He turned his head hastily. "Why should we take advantage of them?" she asked.

"I meant rather, that it will be to our advantage to help them. We can trade with them, knowledge for knowledge. They make wonderful tools of good metal—not the brown kind the Riders made, but hard and bright, in colors like the sun and the moon! A mattock or a hoe made of it would keep its edge for days of use. They make vessels of it too, unbreakable, unleaking.

"They might be persuaded to make them for us, in return for medicines. They suffer from fevers. They have nothing to ease pain except a drink that intoxicates them. They eat things which would kill us, and frequently kill them. The filth of their cities drains into the water they drink."

"Have they no one to teach them better?" the Saint said, dismayed.

"None. No trevanion walk among them. They have many spirits they believe in, whom they call *the gods*, but so far as I was able to learn they believe *the gods* to be people like themselves, given to quarrels and lusts. There is no wisdom, no perception of the Infinite. There are no Songs."

"Then we must give them the Songs!"

"With respect, Child," said Lendreth, keeping his eyes lowered from her face, "I think there are none among them able to learn the Songs. Not yet. Perhaps, if we give them the benefit of our wisdom a little at a time—and ask them for bright metal in return, and other things perhaps—then we will come to know whether it is safe to teach the Songs to them."

The Saint set her hand on Lendreth's chin, lifting his face so he must look into her eyes, and saw the truth. "They sent you back, asking you to bring them more healers."

"Yes," he said, squinting, not daring to look away.

"Then we will send them healers, out of compassion. And we will ask for nothing in return. Go among the trevanion and find the younger ones, the ones who are still learning new things. Take them back with you. Let them walk among the Children of the Sun and teach them how to make gardens for medicine, if nothing else."

"It will be done," said Lendreth, drawing back the moment she released him. He shook himself, looked aside. "You are a woman now," he said at last. "I had not understood."

"You do now."

He bowed and walked quickly away from her. She stood, looking after him, reflecting on what she had seen in his thoughts: the pride, the restlessness, the eager ambition. She saw what he had not spoken aloud: that he saw her people now as a small nation, woefully poor and backward. She saw his dream of raising a great city in the forest, like the ones in which the red folk lived, but cleaner, and loftier, making a civilization to surpass that of the Children of the Sun.

Most clearly, she saw that he had made this bright illusion to fill the hole in his heart where faith had never grown. The darkness of chaos frightened him. Orderly plans kept him from having to contemplate it.

"Child, the trevanion are here to speak with you," Seni told her. The Saint smiled a little; she was twenty now, and only Seni and Kdwyr addressed her as Child anymore.

"Which ones?"

"Shafwyr and Jish and Vendyll," Seni replied, with just the suggestion of a disdainful sniff. "They're waiting for you in the apple bower. They've come a long way, it seems."

"They will be thirsty, then. Would you bring out the green pitcher, and the cups that go with it?" The Saint rose from her loom.

"The dragonfly pattern? If you wish, Child."

The three were sitting in silence under the great apple tree, looking about them with dissatisfaction, but they rose and bowed to the Saint when she came to them.

"Unwearied Mother, we rejoice to see you well," said Jish. The Saint felt a pang of unhappiness; no lover had ever come to her, and at times the honorific seemed bitter mockery.

"I am glad to see you safe," she said. "You were away a long time. Where have you walked?"

"We have been among your children who settled upriver, in the warm country," said Jish. "They thrive, I am pleased to say, though they greatly desire to see you again."

"Perhaps I could visit them," said the Saint, taking the tray with the pitcher and cups from Seni. The Saint poured water and offered it. "I'd like to see that country; I only passed through there once, as a baby, and I don't remember it."

"It would delight your children inexpressibly to behold you once more," said Shafwyr, holding up his cup and regarding it suspiciously. It was celadon, deep green glaze over white clay figured in a pattern of dragonflies. He drank from it and set it down. "Thank you."

For a while they spoke politely of the weather, and of the growth of the far settlements, and what new gardens had been planted there. She was aware they were waiting for an opening, however. When all the news seemed to have been told, she gave them one.

"You are concerned about something," she prompted. Jish and Vendyll set down their cups at once.

"Mother, we are," said Jish. "We have seen strange things as we traveled to you. Everywhere our people make gardens, which is fair and good, but they cut the soil with strange tools and raise more food than they can eat. We asked them, 'For whom do you grow all this?' And everywhere they smiled and said, 'For the Children of the Sun!' And then they would take out things to show us, made things, pots and pans of metal, cloth stained in bright colors and woven with gold. Their little ones played with strange, bright-painted toys. We saw this, and sorrowed."

"Why did you sorrow?" asked the Saint, though she could see the answer coming.

"Because it seemed to us our people are in a second bondage," said Vendyll. "Slaved to new strangers, and made to labor not with whips and overseers but with a vain love of painted things."

"And everywhere we asked whose doing this was, our people said, 'Lendreth!'" said Jish, putting remarkable venom into the word. "And he was praised!"

The Saint looked into her eyes, wondering at her anger, and saw there an old story. They had been lovers once, Jish and Lendreth, until he had decided that flesh was incompatible with holiness. The Saint leaned back, regretting that she had seen this.

"He is praised, Sister, because he has done my will and rendered a service to my people," she said. "Did you see anywhere my people lamenting these new things?"

"No," said Jish. Shafwyr and Vendyll had been shocked into silence.

"They like the bright toys. They like having cooking pots of steel," said the Saint. "They take up the spade and mattock because they wish to. They sell the Children of the Sun vegetables and also pearls. I see no harm in this. It's certainly not slavery. You know that perfectly well, you who walked in the pits when the Beloved was with us and saw true misery."

"Then I suppose we have grown old and foolish," said Jish tartly.

"By no means; though you are nursing anger like coals in a pot, feeding it with these things as with tinder, and that's foolish," said the Saint, looking at Jish with a steady gaze. "The Riders are gone forever. Now my people are free to grow; growing things change. That is their nature. It is enough that they are at peace, and well, and happy.

"The Children of the Sun, however, are ignorant and suffer greatly. If they go on as they have done, they will all die of war and famine and disease, and that would be a pity."

"They are not our concern," said Shafwyr.

"I have made them my concern," said the Saint. "And they ought to be yours. What did the Beloved teach, about compassion for others?"

"But—but—by *others*, he meant the others of our people," said Vendyll.

"No," said the Saint. "He did not. And you know this."

They sat staring downward, unwilling now to meet her gaze. "He never ministered to the Riders," muttered Jish.

"They did not require his help. But he had compassion for them in the hour of their downfall," said the Saint. "You know the truth about what happened that day."

Shafwyr and Vendyll shifted uncomfortably, but Jish looked up sidelong. "Indeed, young Mother, I remember," she said. "It was Lendreth who struck the first blow and set the example for the Mowers. And are *they* also doing your will, strutting about with their new weapons? They go to the settlements and call on young boys to join them. They might be Cursed Gard, every one."

The Saint stared at Jish, until she was compelled to raise her eyes to avoid rudeness. The Saint saw there all that Jish had seen: that the Mowers had bought themselves swords of bright steel and gone about recruiting an army. The Saint saw too the spiteful glee with which Jish related this. The Saint's heart sank.

"Ah. I didn't think you knew about that," said Jish.

"I didn't. This is madness. Where are they?"

———

The Saint went to the Mowers, at the camp they had made near the river, and was appalled to see how their numbers had grown. The older men who had worn chains in the wheat field were a minority now: most were boys, born in freedom, wearing all alike a green cloak, eager to find and defeat an enemy.

She spoke plain words to them. The older men threw themselves down and begged her pardon, unable to meet her gaze. She made them bring her the swords they had bought, one by one, and when they had finished, the piled blades rose as high as her waist. With white fire in her eyes, the Saint forbade them ever to handle edged weapons again.

She had the swords wrapped up and brought away with her when she left that place. Two of the older men went with her, apologizing profusely. She was aware, however, that behind them the boys were already muttering among themselves and planning ways to disobey without disobedience; for hadn't they learned to fight with quarterstaves and slingstones and clubs?

The Saint came back to her island weary, knowing that she could not stop what had been set in motion. That night she prayed to the Star.

This was what you meant, that day in the wheat field. You saw this, didn't you? I can't stop it, and I don't know where it will end, but it will end badly. Please, help me! Come back from the flood tide, come back and make them see reason. And if you can't, then grant me greater strength than I have; for I will soon need it.

———

She was writing a letter to the community by the river when Kdwyr came to her in haste. "Child, there are red men on the shore."

She rose to her feet, laying aside her brush. "Are they armed? Is one of the trevanion with them?"

"I didn't see any," said Kdwyr, and by now the other disciples had come running to her, crying that the Children of the Sun had taken one of the boats and were rowing over. She calmed them. By the time the boat had come across, she was waiting at the landing, with the disciples gathered about her.

Only two came in the boat, though perhaps a dozen more were on the shore, and they were busily setting up tents and unloading wheeled carts. They were armed, each man with a scabbard at his side, but none of them had drawn their blades.

The two in the boat clambered out awkwardly and stood. One bore a chest in his arms, inlaid wood bound with silver; the other wore fine robes and a golden collar, and some badge of office on his chest. He looked up, smiling hopefully.

"Greet you, green men," he said. "We come see for Green Witch Lady, got big present for him. You say us where he is?"

One or two of the disciples giggled, if nervously. The Saint looked into the man's eyes, read his language there, and in his own tongue replied, "I am the Mother of my people. Am I the one you seek?"

The man's eyes widened. He dropped to his knees, as did the other. "Oh, Goddess, forgive my presumption. I meant no disrespect."

"I am not a goddess," said the Saint, smiling at him.

"You look like one," he said fervently. "You really do. You have the most beautiful breasts I've ever seen in my life!" He stopped, appalled at what he'd just said. "I mean—I meant to say—great lady, I am Trenk Brickmold and I have been sent from the Trades Guild of Karkateen with a token of our goodwill and earnest desire to establish a bond of friendship. Behold."

Nothing happened. He nudged his companion, who held the chest. The companion blurted, "Lady, I'll give you anything, I'll sell everything I own and give you a house and—and be your servant for life, if you'll only lie down with me once!" He began to weep.

"Idiot!" Mr. Brickmold turned and boxed his ear. He tried to grab the chest away to open it, but the companion pulled it back and opened it himself.

"There," he said, sobbing. "It's nothing as lovely as you are. Oh, Lady, have pity on me."

It was a bottle of cut crystal, nested in green silk, and full of some golden fluid.

"Oil of pressed flowers, imported from the islands, so concentrated the perfume lasts a week on the skin," explained Mr. Brickmold. "You could buy a town house with what this cost. And the crystal's from Salesh, Cutgarnet's studio. Finest made. Hai! Hinge, for gods' sake, get a grip on yourself, you're making us look fools!"

"What are they saying?" Seni asked.

"They have brought us a present," the Saint replied.

"That's nice," said Seni doubtfully.

"I thank you for your gift," said the Saint to the red men. She took the chest from Mr. Hinge, who stared into her eyes. She looked into them, seeing straightforward and desperate lust and an honest soul. She drew back a little at the novelty. "Please come and sit in the shade and have a cup of water."

"Thank you, Lady." Mr. Brickmold grabbed Mr. Hinge's arm. "My friend here will stay with the boat."

Mr. Brickmold was seated in the apple bower and presented with a cup of water, and a cup was sent out to Mr. Hinge. Mr. Brickmold drained his cup in one long swallow and, effortfully keeping his eyes raised above the Saint's breasts, said, "Thank you. The Trade Guilds of Karkateen hope you enjoy your gift and assure you we wish to continue as trading partners for the foreseeable future. Your medicines have saved uncounted lives in the fever season."

"That pleases me," said the Saint, smiling.

He caught his breath at her smile and leaned forward involuntarily; then pulled back, coughed, and stammered on, "We are happy to please you, Lady. Now, first matter: I speak again on behalf of the Trade Guild of Karkateen when I implore your aid against the Dark Lord."

"Who is the Dark Lord?"

"Oh, you must have heard of him! The Master of the Mountain? Keeps a fortress up on Black Mountain, with his demon army? Comes down and preys on the trade caravans. Fights with two swords. He's a sorcerer too, the most powerful one there is. Disguises himself as one of us and comes down bold as brass to ravish our women, once or twice a week, they say.

"We thought, with your people being the next thing to demons and all, and you having mystic powers as well, there might be something you can do about him for us."

"I don't know what I can do, but I will look into the matter," said the Saint. "In the meantime I should stay away from the places he inhabits."

"Bless you, Lady," said Mr. Brickmold. "He's ruining our insurance firms, driving the rates up something terrible.

"Now. Second matter. I speak on behalf of Brickmold Physic, which is to say my family firm. We have been compounding cures for all ills for seven generations now, with the best intentions you may be sure, but until you graciously sent us your miracle herbs, we hadn't really found any that actually worked. Now what we were thinking was, we'd like to take your likeness and put it on our bottles, so as to make it plain that ours is the real, authentic Yendri Potion."

"My likeness?"

"Yes, Lady. By way of an endorsement, see?" Mr. Brickmold opened a pouch at his belt and drew out a small tablet and a stylus. "So if I could just make a picture of you here and now, we'd consider it a done deal, eh? And of course we'd pay you a percentage on each bottle sold."

"Sold?" The Saint knit her brows. "Do you *sell* the fever cure?"

"Why, Lady, it sells like water in the desert," said Mr. Brickmold jovially.

"But I meant for the medicines to be *given* to your people, asking nothing in return."

Mr. Brickmold shrank somewhat at her expression. "Well—that is to say—your Mr. Lenderett, he always wants trade in steel and glass and what have you—and then it costs us to make the bottles, you know, and we have to pay our workers—so, yes, we make it available to the public for a modest fee."

She looked into his eyes. He gulped, as the secrets of his soul appeared, blazoned large in his sight and hers too. The Saint was so diverted by them she nearly lost the edge of her wrath, but hawklike seized the essential statement and sprang away with it. "So Lendreth is selling you the herbs?"

"More like trading for them, Lady, but, well, yes."

"If I sent you seeds and roots at no cost, and some of my disciples to show you how to grow your own herbs, would you give the medicines freely to your people?"

Mr. Brickmold was dazzled. "Lady, you are generous as well as exquisite—only—well, we still have to stay in business, you see? The staff won't work for no wages."

The Saint knew this was true, having looked into his soul. She thought quickly. "I will have the fever cure given away free, for lives depend on it, and life is not a commodity to be bought and sold. But herbs have other uses. Inessential ones. Flavorings in food and drink. Scents. Soaps."

"Soaps as in, what you wash your face and hair with?" said Mr. Brickmold, attentive.

"Yes."

"What *you* wash your face and hair with? Personally?"

"Yes."

"Haiiiii," exclaimed Mr. Brickmold, but quietly. A faraway look had come into his eyes. "Your personal beauty-care product. And *your* likeness on the bottle. Oh, yes. Oh, we won't be able to make it fast enough."

"And this you may sell to your people, since it is only a vanity. In return for which I require you to make the fever cure available freely to all."

"We'll give it away on street corners," said Mr. Brickmold with tears standing in his eyes. "I swear by all the gods."

"Then we have an agreement."

The Saint consented to sit for her portrait. When the red men had gone back across the lake, she went to her bower and wrote a stiff epistle to Lendreth.

A month later he presented himself at the island, to explain.

"What will you explain, Lendreth?" asked the Saint, and he had to look away from the light in her eyes.

"That I have lived among these people, and I understand them," he said. "They are mercenary. What is offered at no price, they view with suspicion. A thing must cost money to have value, in their world. If I had not demanded goods in trade, they would have thrown away your gifts as worthless."

"And why did you never speak of this before, even if it were true?"

"I thought to make it plain to you in a gradual way. In any case, what I did, I did for our people."

"That they might have vanities? Pleasant things they had easily lived without, before you brought them? That your Mowers might buy themselves swords and magnify their offense? My dragonfly pitcher and cups are pretty, but what did they cost some mother whose children were sick?"

"And what should we do, then?" said Lendreth, raising his voice. "Give away all we have, and all we know, to help strangers?"

"Yes! Though they are not strangers now. For better or for worse, we are neighbors. Look at me, Lendreth, and dare to tell me the Beloved would not have said the same."

Lendreth would not meet her eyes, but said with some heat, "The Beloved was only a man. I saw his imperfections. You never really knew him, or you'd know."

"I knew him better than you did."

"Child!" Seni was shouting from the boat landing. "Child, come quickly! Here are wounded men!"

———

They were not wounded, as it turned out. They were paralyzed.

Eight or nine of the Mowers were borne on litters by their grim-faced brethren. They were frozen in postures of attack, though their faces were mobile enough; tears streamed from their eyes and they lamented constantly, as they were rowed to the island one by one.

"What happened?" The Saint knelt by the first to be brought ashore. He was one of their senior officers.

"Oh, oh, don't drop me—don't drop me! I'm frozen, I'll break! Child, Mother, help me—please, the ice burns—"

"There is no ice," she said, examining him. "Tell me what happened."

"Cursed Gard is alive!" he told her, rolling his eyes wildly. "He did this to us!"

Seni cried out in horror, putting her hands to her face. The Saint, having tugged experimentally at the man's upthrust arm and found its sinews rigid, leaned down and looked into his eyes. She saw the spell there clearly enough, the illusion that fed into his fear and expectations and held him captive.

"I'm going to heal you now," she said, and broke the illusion. He collapsed at once, screaming in pain as his muscles released. "Bring the others across!" she ordered, and the boat put out immediately. "What do you mean, Cursed Gard?"

"You never knew him," said the Mower, writhing on his litter. "But I remember him, I was a child, I saw what happened that day when he killed Blessed Ranwyr and the Beloved cursed him! I saw him!"

"You must have been mistaken," said the Saint patiently. "Cursed Gard went into the snows and was lost."

"I tell you it was he! He told us so, himself!" The man went into spasms, biting his tongue. She placed her hand on his brow and willed him to relax, and he sagged back weeping.

"Carry him into the bowers for the sick," she told his bearers, and rose to watch the next man being rowed across.

Beside her, Lendreth spoke with barely concealed triumph. "If they had had swords with which to defend themselves, they had not come to harm."

"They have come to no real harm," she said, turning to regard him. "And you ought to be ashamed of yourself for gloating like this."

"I told you we had enemies," he insisted. "You did not foresee this, it would seem."

————

When the last of the Mowers had been unensorcelled, when they had been given water and calmatives, the Saint got the following story out of them:

They had gone far in their patrols, even to the red road that ran near the edge of the northern wood, faithfully seeking any harm that might come near their people. As they watched from the shadows, a big and black-a-vised man came walking along the road. He was dressed in garments such as the Children of the Sun wore, carrying a jar of wine under one arm.

He did not appear to be armed, and they had let him pass without challenge; but he turned his head and saw them, though they were artfully concealed and would certainly have been invisible to the Children of the Sun. He stared at them a long moment, and then, in their own tongue, addressed them.

"Why, Earthborn, it has been a long time since I saw the like of you!"

They had stepped forth then, asking how he had seen them and known them. He had replied that he used to live among them, but long ago. "Tell me," he said, "how it was the Star made such a hole in the mountain wall? For I never thought he had power to do such things."

And that had been when Falway, the senior officer, recognized him and cried out that it was Cursed Gard. At which the man had scowled at them in a terrifying manner. "Cursed indeed, and banished too," he had said. "And unforgiven still, I see."

Whereupon one young Mower had cried out that Blessed Ranwyr's blood still cried from the earth for revenge. "Fool," said Cursed Gard, "I never shed his blood, though certainly I killed my brother. Learn the truth before you threaten me."

The Mowers had said then that they would do more than threaten. They circled him, meaning to fight him in the way they had learned, kicking and striking with the hands. Some loaded stones into their slings, and others drew out blowpipes with which to shoot darts at him.

Before they could assail him in any way, however, Cursed Gard had raised his hand and said a Word, and they had frozen where they stood. Nor was this all: from up and down the road demons in black armor came, horrible to see, and they ran at once and threatened the Mowers with spears.

The demons rudely searched them then, taking from them everything of value.

When Cursed Gard saw the gold cloak-brooches they had worn, which bore the emblem for the Mowers, he taunted them. "So you are a wealthy people now. So you are a fierce people, with slings and poisoned darts for your enemies. You are not the Earthborn I knew."

And a horrible demon had asked Cursed Gard whether he would like all the prisoners' throats slit. Cursed Gard had laughed scornfully and said it would be punishment enough to leave them there, in their shame.

"Besides," he had said, "they may carry my message back to their people. Listen well, fools: I am honored that you kept my name alive, in your curses. I am called the Master of the Mountain now, when I am being cursed.

"While I thought you still meek and poor, I did not trouble you; but now that I find you so proud and so rich, you may expect to see me again."

So saying, he had gone his way and left them, and his demons had vanished. There the Mowers had remained, until their brothers-in-arms had come out to see what had become of them.

If they had expected sympathy from their Saint, they were to be disappointed. She called them together, when they were recovered, and reproached them in sorrow. She pointed out that this had come of their eagerness to do violence; that Cursed Gard, who had heretofore ignored her people, would now fix his baleful attention on them; that the Star himself had seen fit only to banish Cursed Gard, so there had been no excuse for confronting him when he had, after all, been doing no harm to anyone.

One of the Mowers was unwise enough to murmur, where she could hear him, that if they had been permitted to carry swords, the affair might have turned out differently.

"Indeed it would have," she said, looking him in the eye with white wrath. "You would have all died. If he could freeze you with a Word, what would blades have done but made him angrier than he was?"

The Saint was to learn, within the month, that Cursed Gard was a man of his word. She was at her writing platform when the messenger came.

"Mother." The man knelt and bowed his head. "I have come from the apple orchards in the north, and my name is Deluvwyr. Your weeping children implore you for aid."

Sighing, she blessed him, and he rose. "Tell me everything," she said.

"Cursed Gard came down and raided us. We were working in the orchard when he came out of the woods and strode between the trees, with an army of demons, hideous to behold. We attacked him with our pruning hooks. He waved his hand and we were blown back like leaves. Our pruning hooks were broken. His demons laughed at us. We could not stop them coming into our village."

"Village?"

"We live in houses in a meadow, Mother, with a fence of palings around. The Trevani Lendreth suggested it, when he visited us, and we have found it more convenient for our work. The animals are kept out of the apple storehouse."

"And did your fence of palings keep out Cursed Gard?"

"No, Mother." Deluvwyr lowered his eyes. "He extended his hand again, and the palings flew apart like straws. He marched into the center and stood by the fire, and asked what cheer we had to welcome a tired traveler. Those of the men who had not been in the orchard took quarterstaves and went to attack Cursed Gard, and the quarterstaves might have been straws too, for all the harm they did him. When our men lay groaning on the earth, Cursed Gard rubbed his hands together and said, 'My lads, these folk don't know how to answer politely. Just look about and see what entertainment there is in this fine village.'"

"What happened then?" said the Saint.

"Our trevani came forth to stop him and struck him with her staff. I saw the power flowing off it like water, but Cursed Gard spoke a Word and the staff broke, and the trevani fell down unconscious. Demons ringed us round with their spears.

"Other demons he sent into the houses, to see what was there. They found the storehouse we had filled to trade with the Children of the Sun and brought out the bags of pearls we had collected, and the lacquerware, and the honey, and the jars of cider. They broke the jars open and drank. They took all the cider we had stored and became drunk. Cursed Gard laughed and said, 'Where are your boys in green cloaks? They must be sick; I know they are not afraid to come out and fight me for your sakes.'

"We thought he would go then, but worse was to come; for some of his men had found our drums and our flutes and lyres, and they cried, 'Let's have music!' And then he had his demons take the mothers and children and the old people and shut them in the storehouse. The young women he then made to dance, as the demons played. And there were de-monesses among his people, and they made the young men to dance also. And then they made them drink of the cider too, and then . . . there was ravishment."

"Were any killed or wounded?" said the Saint. Deluvwyr looked at the ground and in a small voice said that none had been killed or wounded.

"But at last a demoness spoke to Cursed Gard, telling him he had drunk too much. And so he got up and roared out that all were to leave. They filled their arms with our goods and marched away, but before he left, Cursed Gard drew forth a black knife and drove it into the doorpost of our storehouse.

"'Give this to your boys in green, when next you see them,' he said. 'Tell them any one of them who dares is welcome to bury it in my heart, if he can.' And so he left."

The Saint herself came to the village, though by the time she got there grass had grown again in the place where the demons had celebrated, and two of the village girls were near to term with children begotten on that night. She took down the black knife and felt power crackling in it; inspected the ruin of the storeroom, the smashed jars. Most of the houses had been abandoned.

"Where are the people who lived there?" she asked.

"They are afraid to stay here now," said the trevani, Paltyll. "They have gone back to live in the woods, as we did in the old days."

"I think they are wise. If we have no villages, Cursed Gard will not know where to find us. If we have no stored wealth, he will have nothing to take from us. We lived happily enough for many years without houses or riches. Let us live so again, until his anger fades."

"The Mowers will not like it, Mother."

"They must endure it," said the Saint sharply. "Their pride and wrath started this. Let them remember what the Beloved said: 'The snare you make for another will catch your own feet.'"

"Well, but the Beloved," said the trevani with a shrug, "he was imperfect. And the Mowers say among themselves that his teachings were for slaves, and we are no slaves now."

"What else do they say?" The Saint looked full into her eyes, and she winced.

"They boast that if they had lived in the old time, we had never been slaves."

"No," said the Saint. "If they had lived in the old time, they would have been Cursed Gard."

―――――――

The Saint stayed in that place to midwife the two girls, when their time came. The births were easy, but when the children were laid in their arms, the mothers shuddered and pushed them away: for the little girl had silver eyes, and the little boy had skin blue-black as a damson plum. The Saint took them away with her, when she left, and gave them into the care of her disciples, on her own island.

―――――――

The Saint opened her eyes. She lay still awhile, listening for what had awakened her. Not the cries of the children; she could hear little Bero snuffling contentedly as he nursed, and a tiny snore was drifting from Bisha's cot. Her disciples were asleep, all but the drowsy nurse. She reached out with her mind and perceived the knot of agitation moving through the gloom. Someone was running along a trail, heart pounding, ducking to avoid branches as they came.

She sighed and rose, wondering if Cursed Gard had attacked another village. There had been five now, and the last one had been set afire. No one had been hurt, but the fire had burned for two days and laid waste a great swath of the northern woods. Three more half-breed babies were expected. She had given stern orders that they were under her protection, and written again to exhort her people to leave the villages and seek safety in the deep woods. Some few had done as she asked, but not enough.

By the time the messenger had scrambled into one of the coracles and dipped his paddle in the water, she was dressed and waiting at the landing.

With some surprise she recognized Feldash, whom she had sent to minister to the Children of the Sun. He was still trying to catch his breath as he stepped from the boat and knelt before her for her blessing. She raised him and looked into his eyes.

"What's the matter?"

"Sickness, in Karkateen," he said. "Not the fever. They've poisoned themselves—vomiting and sweating, and a dozen people have died. Something has been spilled into the lake from which they drink. I went down to the shore and saw blackness in the water, and the reeds dying, and dead waterbirds. There is a man living on the edge of the lake who makes ink, and there was an accident—one of his vats cracked, and the ink ran down through the drains into the water."

"Ink isn't poisonous," said the Saint, wondering if she had enough purgatives for a town.

"Not ours, but theirs is made to smear on their printing blocks. They put cerelath gum in it."

"And only a dozen have died? Their gods must be protecting them." The Saint turned to run for her stillroom.

Feldash ran beside her. "It will take more than I can carry. Can you spare five people?"

"I will come myself and bring a dozen others," she said. "We'll need to treat the immediate symptoms—and I'll have to bring water-lily bulbs, to purify the lake—and purges—"

"We'll need to make a steam house for them, they have no idea how to bathe properly."

"Haven't you been teaching them?"

"It's hard to make them understand, Mother. They don't believe in dirt they cannot see."

"And yet they believe in gods," said the Saint in exasperation.

———

Two hours after sunrise they set out, a dozen figures robed in white, making their way along the forest trail. Feldash led them, followed by the Saint, and the others bore between them great jars of water-lily bulbs nested in wet fern, or carried on their shoulders bundles of herbs and roots.

———

At midday they had gone less than a third of the distance, for the trail was overgrown and winding. "Is there a quicker way?" the Saint asked Feldash.

He looked over his shoulder at her. "We cross a red road not far ahead. It curves a little out of our way, but we can make better time if we take it."

"Then we'll take the red road."

———

They went much more swiftly now, as the sun crossed the open sky above them, though some of the disciples were fearful at being so far from cover. The sun had begun to dip down toward the west, the shadows were lengthening, when Feldash halted and stared ahead. He put up his hand to signal that the others should stop.

"What is it?" asked the Saint.

"Spears," said Feldash distractedly. "Oh, no, no, there are spears— there's an army marching this way. We must hide!"

"Step off the road," said the Saint. "Set your burdens down in the ditch and step into the meadow. Don't be afraid."

They obeyed her, trembling. Plain now they heard the tramping of marching boots, and a rough song. They stood in the meadow in the semblance of a grove of blossoming trees and saw the column of demons come along the road.

The demons bristled with weapons, immense and dreadful in their black and silver armor. Though the armor all alike bore the image of a white stag, none but two of the demons were alike at all. Some were furred, some were scaled, some bore tusks, and some had talons. Some were demonesses, lithe and beautiful as a quick death. They sang as they came along, and the earth shook with their deep voices:

> *If I ever get out of here*
> *I will drink their blood*
> *It will be my wine . . .*

They strode on without even noticing the grove of blossoming trees hard by the road, though the Saint watched them keenly. And then—

Beside them, walking from the back to the front of the column, was a great black-a-vised man, with a calm and mild gaze under black brows. He alone turned his head to regard the grove of trees. His gaze intensified. He stopped, stepped across the ditch in one stride, and walked in among the slender trees where petals were falling.

The strong and confident script breaks off abruptly. You see that, a few lines below, the account is continued in a different hand.

And Cursed Gard reached in among the flowering branches, and when he stepped back, he drew forth by the wrist a woman, the fairest lady that had ever been seen.

With a shout of laughter he threw his cloak about her. They vanished together, in a white flash and a clap of thunder.

You turn the leaf and see you have come to the end of the bundle. You shuffle back through the leaves, thinking you must have missed one, but no pages are out of sequence.

You rise and take the bundle to the brother librarian, asking for the second volume. He shakes his head sadly. He tells you there is no more.

5

THE BOOK

In a wineshop in Mount Flame City, just around the corner from Copper-plate & Sons' Press, a lady sits alone at a table, waiting. She is a Child of the Sun and also a beauty, in a hard professional sort of way. On the ground beside her chair is a large woven bag, sagging as though it contains something heavy.

She taps her foot as she waits. Presently a man enters the shop. He looks intelligent, in a hard professional sort of way, and perhaps a little impatient. She waves to him. He sees her, glances out the window at the water clock in the city square, and comes to her table with reluctance.

"Let's make this quick," he says. "I have about fifteen minutes before I'm supposed to be at a meeting."

"Then I'll be brief." The woman reaches down, hauls the bag up into her lap, and dumps a manuscript out on the table. It is bound with twine.

The man stares at it, unimpressed. "And this would be?"

"A tell-all unauthorized biography."

"Really." The man is still unimpressed. "A biography of whom?"

"The Master of the Mountain."

The man's eyebrows jump straight up his forehead in disbelief. "And you're qualified to write his biography because . . . ?"

"I was his mistress. One of his mistresses, anyway. He visited me once a month at least for four years, before he took up with that greenie woman. Trust me, I've seen a side of him the caravan masters don't see. And I learned a lot about him, when I could get him to talk about himself. You may think you've published scandals before, but you've never read anything like this."

Against his inclination, the man pulls the manuscript across the table and opens it at random. He reads in silence for a moment. He turns the page and reads more. "Gods below," he mutters. "Did this really happen?"

"Most of it," she says with aplomb. "Where it's faked, it's a plausible fake. I thought of calling it *I Was the Dark Lord's Passion Slave*."

"That's certainly a possibility," says the man, unable to lift his eyes from the page. "Yes. Indeed." The minutes tick by. He looks up at last and makes an attempt to pull himself together. "So, er, you're taking revenge on him for abandoning you?"

She shrugs. "He did leave me with a town house. But one has to buy groceries, hasn't one?"

"Well," says the man, gathering the pages together with slightly trembling hands and retying the twine. "I'll have to show it to my other editors, of course. Can't promise anything. Think I can talk them into a reasonable advance."

"Do let me know what you decide, won't you?" she says with a charming smile. "Mr. Pulley over at Pulley and Joist was interested in seeing it as well."

As rooms went, it was luxuriously furnished. A carpet was on the floor; the bed was covered in pillows, in furs and silks. A little table of beaten brass was in one corner, bearing a wine carafe and goblets. In another corner was a table with compartments, and above it a mirror of silvered glass.

None of this made up for the bars on the windows, for the air being thin and cold, for the fine layer of grit on every surface, for the silk sheets being musky with more than stale perfume.

Once she had regained consciousness, the Saint had searched the room three times, before finding the hidden compartment in the table. It contained nothing useful: the tawdry finery of a dancing girl and two half-empty jars of cosmetics, in garish and cheap colors. The discovery added an element of injured pride to the commotion in the Saint's heart.

To calm herself, she sat and sorted through her emotions. Injured pride, why should she feel that? Fury, certainly, like a river in spring flood. Dismay, that she was in this place where she could help no one, and had no idea what had happened to her disciples or what her people would do now.

Fear? . . . No, she was not afraid. Grief?

. . . Some part of her was remembering the dancing green the night she had gone there, the way the stars had glittered and the white flowers had shone in the grass. There had been laughter in the night, as the young people discovered love. She had put the memory away from herself as selfish, but it had been there all along, buried deep. Love had shown her a different face.

And to think about that was to tremble with self-pity and unshed tears. She was not injured; she could effect her own release, if she could once look in the man's eyes, and then she had only to walk from this place and go home. It would be months yet before the consequences must be dealt with.

She paced the room, making a circuit of it three times, collecting her strength. She began to sing.

She had been aware of peripheral sound far below, echoing footsteps, conversation, clinking tableware, the clash of armor. At her song, it stopped dead. The Saint held them helpless and the thought gave her strength, lent volume to her voice. She went up an octave and the room trembled, the bars in the windows vibrated and began to work loose, the door started and shook on its hinges.

She knew that if she held a certain note, she could blow off the roof, force the walls outward like flower petals opening. She might do anything then: summon the wild swans to bear her forth or the north wind to carry her like thistledown. She had never drawn on certain powers because they had seemed absurd and theatrical and useless in the business of daily life. Now, however, she could use them.

But she would look in his eyes first.

She heard his footstep. His hand was at the door. She let her song drop to a throb on the air, palpable but barely audible.

Gard opened the door and stood there swaying slightly, looking pale and sick. He breathed out fumes of wine; the smoke of weed was in his hair. He squinted in pain at the vibration of her held note. She ended her song, and when he opened his eyes in relief, she looked full into them.

She saw regret in his soul, but no self-deception. He hid behind no illusions.

He returned her gaze steadily. "Lady, I have done you an evil."

"You have. Where are Feldash and the others?"

"Who?"

"My disciples! The others who were with me!"

"We left them there. We didn't bother them. I suppose they ran away. In any case, Lady, I apologize."

"Then you will let me go at once."

"There is the matter of the child."

"Indeed there is. How do you know about the child?"

"I am a mage, lady. To my eyes, he shines through your flesh like a star. He will not be welcome among your people."

"Then I will send him to you."

"Let me make compensation. Marry me, Lady. Be my wife, and the mother of my child."

"I will be the mother of your child regardless."

"And I will honor you as my true wife and never lie with any other woman," Gard continued hopefully, for she had not screamed or wept or tried to kill him yet, and he had been standing before her a full thirty seconds.

"Even the one whose rags and paint were left here?" she said, and instantly felt self-contempt for stooping so low. He looked blank and puzzled at that, for a moment.

". . . Oh. I'm sorry. That was . . ." He tried to remember the girl's name.

"A crass and insensitive oversight?"

"Yes. And if you will be my true wife, I will never raid your people again."

She was silent at that, astonished.

Encouraged, he added, "And I will give you all I have, and I'll make you a garden on this mountain."

"A garden?"

"Of surpassing loveliness. I'm not asking you to love me. I know what I am, and what I've done. Only marry me, lady."

"*Why did you do it?*"

"Because you were beautiful, and I had the opportunity. I was angry with your people. It seemed like the best possible revenge. By the time I knew what you were, I couldn't have stopped myself if I'd wanted to. But I didn't want to.

"Marry me. Please. Marry me, and my revenge ends here, now. I will never hurt you again. I will never hurt your people again."

As an afterthought he went down on his knees. He did it awkwardly, and even kneeling, he still filled the doorway, he was so big, and his broad shoulders pushed against the frame. He lifted his face and met her eyes again. What man had ever been able to do that?

He looked nothing like the monster of the old stories, the frightful image sketched in sand or charcoal to frighten children. His face was square, but his features were even and handsome, if a little rough. His mouth was fine, firm. His eyes were wide and dark and somber, under black brows curved like scythe blades.

Scythe blades, she said to herself. *I'm making a poem of his face, like a girl in love.* And he had not smirked about what he'd done, nor denied it, nor tried to make light of it. *I'm making excuses for him. Why can't I stop thinking about those big square hands?*

She looked down at him in consternation, realizing that a selfless act could be a selfish one too.

"I will marry you," she said.

He strode out across the parapet, grinning like a fool. Balnshik and Thrang watched him approach.

"She must have said yes," said Balnshik.

"She did," said Gard.

"You're a lucky man," said Balnshik. "In her place, I'd have been bowling your head across the floor by this time."

"I know," he said happily. "She doesn't love me, but it's all right. She'll stay with me. She's beautiful and good and I'd die for her. Maybe she'll forgive me someday. Do we have any flowers?"

I will send one of the guard down the mountain to see what can be found below the death zone, sir, Thrang told him, as Balnshik shook her head. *And I will have a chamber prepared with clean linens and proper furniture. That room is no fit place for your lady wife and the mother of your heir. You should have let me clean it first.*

"I know."

"And you need to send a messenger to pay off your mistresses, because there'll be no more of that, ever," said Balnshik sternly. "And I hope you know you can't just climb into my bed whenever she's indisposed. I won't have that."

"I know."

"Oh, gods, you didn't even wash the smoke out of your hair before you went to her, did you? What on earth were you thinking? Listen to me. Go bathe. Now. Put on clean clothes."

"I don't know where any are."

In your wardrobe, sir! Thrang bared his teeth and snarled, with his ears laid back. *Where I hung them up after I had them ironed!*

"Oh." Momentarily chastened, Gard looked around at the sky, the sunlight, the distant sea. His grin came back and widened. "Have the black wine served out, in the mess hall." It seemed like the sort of thing a Dark Lord would command.

———————

They took their vows in a high courtyard with a dizzying view of the world. The Saint could just see the green forests she had lost, far to the south and east, in brief glimpses between the spears and garlanded flowers on the honor guard. The waving pennants bore white stars and a white stag on a black field.

She had refused to wear the elaborate (though inexpensive, being stolen) gown that had been offered her, preferring to wear her plain white robe instead. He wore black armor, with a great deal of barbaric jewelry in the worst of taste.

She watched Gard as he spoke his vows to her. She looked into his heart and saw his desires, and they seemed pitifully simple: remaining alive. Having a wife and child. Nothing so complicated as Lendreth's need for power and order, or Seni's aching desire for a lost golden age.

He is innocent as a beast is innocent, she thought. *And with a beast's innocence, he must have killed Blessed Ranwyr. I must not be unkind to him.*

She spoke her vows then. They did not ask for love; they asked for fidelity, honesty, duty to spouse and children. She resolved to keep them.

The cup was filled. They drank together. The hideous old creature with the wolf's head stepped forward and carefully bound their wrists together with the silk cord. She was surprised; he had fine hands, though they were gnarled with age. The knot was tied. The demons beat their spears upon the ground and roared and howled their congratulations.

High on the wind above, a cloud drifted. It had the shape of a face. The eyes watched what was going on below. They were unfriendly.

———————

Gard and the Saint were escorted through his black halls by a cheering crowd, already half-drunk. She looked about her in wonder as she walked along on her husband's arm. The place had a massive splendor, but also a curiously unfinished quality. The doors and windows had all manner of ornamentation, grimacing demon heads, skulls; yet in places rubble still lay in heaps, and in one spot what appeared to be a hot spring trickled down the wall and flowed across the floor, running along the hall for several yards until it seeped under a doorway.

The bedroom, when they arrived at last, was in a similar style. Black, hung with black draperies, rich worked carpets the color of blood on the living rock of the floor, and an immense gloomy bed hung all in black.

The bedposts had silver skull finials. Someone had hastily cleaned, for a few cobwebs had been missed, and the top of the bedside table bore several sticky ring-marks from someone's having been drinking in bed. The upper reaches of the canopy were furred with dust.

The door closed, leaving them alone together as the tide of revelers drew away down the hall.

"Would you prefer to undress by yourself?" said Gard, stammering a little.

"Thank you, but no," she said. "We are husband and wife now."

"Would you like me to undress you?"

"If you wish."

Hands shaking, he lifted her robe, slipped it off over her head, and let it drop. She stood naked before him in the light of the torches, looking at him with defiance. He stared at her, rapt. When he did not pick up her robe, she bent and retrieved it, folded it, and laid it on a chest.

"I'm sorry," he said, fumbling with the catches of his cuirass. They stuck. She helped him, and a moment later the armor came clattering off. The jewelry followed. Now he couldn't move fast enough; he spilled his mail shirt on the floor and hopped on one foot as he yanked off first one boot and then the other, peeling off the arming clothes he had worn underneath, and then the breechclout. He stood before her, breathing hard, heavily male.

She looked in wonder at his body. "So many scars."

He looked down at himself. "Yes. I'm sorry, I know they're ugly. I used to have to fight for my masters' amusement. Would you like me to put the lights out?"

"You needn't. What masters?"

"I was a slave. For a long time. May we get into bed now?"

"If you like."

He lifted her into the bed and, climbing up beside her, knelt.

"I know this is strange," he said. "The skulls and things, and everything black. You mustn't mind it. It's just a costume. If I'd known it was you . . . If I'd known what I was doing . . . it would have been different. Would you like to see what it would have been like? I can make it what it should have been. Watch."

He lowered his head. His eyes burned with a green light like the air before a thunderstorm. She felt the surge of power, felt her hair rising with the electricity in the room. There came the music of drums, from out in the hall, she supposed; but when she glanced that way, she saw a forest under starlight, and the wide green starred with little white flowers. They had a perfume like mown hay. She looked up, glimpsing white stars through interlaced branches and blossoms.

He began to sing to her. His bass voice seemed to rumble up out of the earth. He was singing the song for virgins.

The stars blurred, and the Saint realized she was seeing them through tears. She meant to tell him how well he sang, when it ended; but she hadn't time. His mouth was on hers and her arms went around him, and she felt the scars of an old beating under her fingertips.

The stag and the doe find each other, the little birds make their nests together. There were no words spoken, no tortured consideration of whether it was right or wrong, indeed no thought at all. There was only sensation, exhilarating as though she soared on wings.

She woke smiling, before memory and guilt descended on her. She looked up into his eyes. He was leaning down, speaking gravely: ". . . duties to perform. My steward will come to you and show you the house. He will see to anything you require."

"I must write to my disciples," she said, clutching his arm. "I must let them know what has become of me."

He scowled, but said, "If you must. Thrang will fetch you something to write with."

He turned away and dressed himself by lamplight. She watched. "What time is it?"

"The second hour after sunrise."

"I wish we had a window in this room."

He turned to her. "Would you promise not to try to climb out, if we had one?"

"I'm your wife," she said reproachfully. "I will not leave you now."

"I'll put in a window, then." He turned away to hide his smile. "I meant to anyway; I hadn't had time to get around to it."

He pulled on his boots and was halfway to the door before he turned back, leaned down, and kissed her again, roughly.

She put on what she had worn the previous day, for lack of anything else, and was looking in vain for a basin and water when a discreet knock came at the door. It took her a moment to realize what a knock signified, and another moment to work out how the door's latch worked.

She opened it and managed not to scream at the werewolf standing on the other side, waiting patiently between the two armed guards. He bent down, in something between a bow and a submissive crouch. *Madam,* said a voice in her inner ear, *will it please you to see your house?*

"Yes, thank you," she said. "Are you Thrang?"

Yes, Madam. He rose and walked a little way down the corridor, turning back to see whether she was following. The guards remained behind, for which she was grateful. She hurried after him.

I must apologize to Madam for the state of the halls. We had very little warning of your arrival.

"I, too."

The Master has been preoccupied with his business. It has been a little difficult to get things done properly.

"Has it?"

Yes, Madam. The werewolf looked at her sidelong and made a noise that sounded like an impatient sigh. *Madam will forgive me for asking, but has Madam any other garments?*

"I'm afraid I haven't. Not of my own."

White linen, I believe, Madam? There are several bolts of linen in the storeroom. I will have a seamstress take Madam's measurements and make up a wardrobe for daily wear. And if Madam will leave the present robe by her chamber door tonight, I will see that it is laundered and pressed for tomorrow morning.

"I would be very grateful."

I will show Madam the household service now.

She followed him, wondering what "household service" might be. Thrang turned off down a narrow corridor, somewhat better swept and lit than the main one, and paused outside an immense ironbound door. Taking a ring of keys from his belt, he opened the door and bowed her inside. He lifted a torch from its sconce by the lintel, that she might see. She looked around in wonder.

This room was paneled, carpeted, and spotlessly clean. Ranged in cabinets along the walls were dishes and vessels of every size, of gold, of silver, of porcelain and crystal. Covered tureens and ewers had armorial bearings on them, though they did not feature a stag or stars. There were massive silver candlesticks. Some things were clearly meant to go on a table, but their function she could only guess.

Madam will observe the particularly fine collection of celadon ware. The voiceless voice sounded proud.

"It's beautiful," said the Saint. "I have—I had a pitcher and a set of cups like that, in a dragonfly pattern."

Ah! Thrang's eyes burned with a yellow light. *The Dragonfly by Ironbrace!*

In Spring Mist, Jade, Moss, Emerald, and Melon. First fired in Mount Flame City in the twelfth year of Drence the Dictator. Still being produced. He went to a particular shelf, hunted among the cups stacked there, and took down a cup in the Dragonfly pattern, which he brought to her eagerly. *Would Madam like a drink of water? Or perhaps some tea? We have a matching teapot.*

"Thank you, I would like that very much," she said, a little bewildered, "but I had hoped to bathe first. And I wanted to write letters—"

Of course. Madam will excuse me, I hope; this will all go more smoothly when we have established a daily routine. I will lead Madam to the baths and take a breakfast tray into the Master's study. What is Madam's customary preference?

"Preference? . . . I used to boil straj meal. And make a pot of tea."

Very good, Madam. Thrang set the cup back on its shelf and took up the torch again. As he bowed her out of the room, she glimpsed a low bed in one corner, tidily made up, and realized that he slept here.

Back in the main corridor, they proceeded to the door under which water was still running. Growling to himself, Thrang opened it and splashed over the threshold.

The baths, Madam. He halted a few paces in, with his ears laid back, and she nearly collided with him as she stepped cautiously into the room.

It was an immense vaulted chamber, as unfinished-looking as the corridors outside, dim with steam; not so dim as to hide the pool in the rock, into which the stream ran and in which lolled some dozen of the household guard, uniform only in their nudity. They looked up, aghast.

Thrang's growl became a threat as he bared his teeth at them. They grabbed frantically for towels as they scrambled from the water, and one creature with a tentacled head wept inky tears of embarrassment as he sidled toward the door, webbed hands spread modestly over his groin.

How dare you? This is the Master's private bath! You belong in the officers' bathhouse on the second level! howled Thrang.

"The drains are plugged up there again," said a slate-blue demon with silver eyes.

"We've been using this one for a month and nobody complained," said a demon who seemed to be his twin brother.

"Please," said the Saint, "it's not necessary—tell them they can stay—"

This did not have its intended effect. They looked at her in horror and stampeded from the room, not even bothering to retrieve their discarded armor from the heap where it lay. One alone remained in the pool, lounging back against its far edge, a demoness, watching the drama with a lazy amused look.

This is inexcusable. Thrang was snapping the air in his wrath, tossing pieces of armor out the door. *Madam ought to have privacy—Madam ought to have proper attendants—we ought to have a proper tiled bath. I've served in houses where people had proper tiled baths, I've begged and begged to have some decent plumbing put in—*

"Please, it's all right—"

"Thrang," said the demoness, "fetch her a clean towel and soap."

The werewolf turned, distracted. *Yes! Madam must have clean towels and soap. One moment, please, Madam.* He hurried out the door.

"If you can give him tasks to fulfill, he's much happier," the demoness explained.

"Thank you." The Saint slipped out of her robe, lay it over a boulder—there being no furniture in the room—and waded into the pool. The warmth of the water took her by surprise, but it was fresh-circulating, and after a moment she was able to enjoy it. The demoness slid down from the edge and swam toward her, cutting through the water like a snake.

"You mustn't mind our little peculiarities, Lady," she said. "We're a diverse lot, up here, and some of us haven't the most polished manners."

"Are you one of my husband's mistresses?" said the Saint, slightly narrowing her eyes.

"He has no mistresses. Not now. And never again, Lady, be sure."

"Those weren't your things left behind in the . . ."

"The Jewel Box, we call it. Gracious, no! I'd never wear rouge that color. No, those were relics of a brief infatuation. She's long gone back to her people. You have no rivals, now. You are the mother of his child, after all."

The werewolf entered the cavern again, bearing towels and soap. "Good, Thrang," said the demoness, raising her voice. "Now, take her robe and have it laundered and pressed. Bring one of the Master's dressing gowns for her."

Dressing gown, yes, of course, Captain Balnshik! Madam shall have her gown back after breakfast.

"You see?" said the demoness, when he had gone. "He's an obsessive. Even more so than is usual in a demon. If you know how to keep him busy, you can get a great deal accomplished."

The Saint looked at her thoughtfully. "Is he a slave?"

"No, Lady, he is not. We are all freed slaves here. Even Gard himself was a slave. We serve him, willingly, because to us he is the Good Master. He has made it impossible for anyone to force us into slavery again. This is our refuge. Unfortunately, it must be a fortified stronghold."

"Captain Balnshik, he called you."

"I am, Lady. Those were my men taking the liberty of bathing here, after we'd come off the night watch. We're hoping you can prevail on your husband to have something done about the drains."

"Is that why there's a stream running down the hall?"

"Oh, no, that was always there. You must excuse Gard; he summoned the whole fortress up by sorcery, all of a piece, and unfortunately his knowledge of plumbing was rudimentary. We have lived with the inconvenience. Of course, that must change now, with the Heir to the Black Halls on the way. They needn't be *literally* black, but I'm afraid some places have gotten rather filthy. You have the chance to be a civilizing influence on your lord."

"Is he likely to do what I ask?"

Balnshik laughed. "You have power over him, Lady. The other women were pleasant diversions, but I have never seen such a look on his face as when he came to tell me what he'd done to you. 'What shall I do now?' he cried. 'I have pulled the fairest rose in the world, and my heart is run through with the thorns.'"

The Saint looked into her eyes. Balnshik endured it a long moment before turning her head, smiling ruefully. "Oh, yes, you have power. I hope you love him in return."

"You love him too."

"Of course I love him. I have known him since he was very young, and he is a good man. But you are his wife and bear his son."

"Has he no other children?"

"None."

———

Later, wrapped in an immense black robe, the Saint sat at an immense black desk in an immense black room, staring around her. A skylight above her admitted one shaft of brilliant light, by which she saw that the walls were lined with bookshelves. Books were everywhere, the bound volumes printed in their thousands by the Children of the Sun.

To one side was a tray containing the empty celadon vessels in which her breakfast had been served. Before her was a stack of writing paper and a bottle that had proven, on examination, to contain ink. She was turning a pen in her hands, uncertain how to use it. At last she dipped the pen point in the ink, on general principles, and drew a few hesitant lines on the paper by way of experiment. When she thought she had had enough practice, she took a fresh sheet and wrote:

To my most beloved disciples, greetings.

I write to console and assure you I am alive and well, nor am I in any danger. It is my earnest wish that you continue as though I were there among you. I hope Feldash was able to continue on to Karkateen and minister to the sick there among the Children of the Sun. Seni, please care for the little ones. I may have located their fathers.

Do not fear for me. It is true that I was abducted by he who has been known among us as Cursed Gard. However, I have bound him to an agreement and he will no longer raid our villages nor harm our people in any way. The price of this is that I have become his honorably wedded wife and will bear his child.

In this way, what was broken will be made whole; what was evil will be turned to the purpose of compassion.

I continue in my duty to you as I have always done, and will write again at my earliest opportunity for your further instruction.

I am your mother and daughter.

She spent the balance of the day in Gard's library, examining his books. When the illumination from the skylight waned, she sat quietly, praying, until Thrang opened the door and peered in. *Dinner is served, Madam. Master awaits in the dining hall.*

"Thank you," she said. He waited until she came to the door, then started down the hall, looking over his shoulder every few dozen paces to be certain she followed. He led her through another doorway into another high cavern, lit by torches. Its floor had been leveled and swept, a carpet set down, a rough trestle table placed in the middle. Gold and silver plate decked the cloth. Two massive chairs, nearly the size of thrones, faced each other across the table. For all the splendor there was little food: a joint of meat of some kind, a bowl of fruit, a loaf of bread. Four decanters of wine, and two golden goblets.

Gard was pacing back and forth, looking ill at ease. He came to her at once and kissed her. "Good evening, wife."

"Good evening, husband."

"I, er, I suppose we'll eat now." Gard went to pull back her chair, but it seemed wedged under the trestle, and at last he simply picked her up and set her in it, before going around to his side. Thrang came to stand at her elbow, looking from one face to the other, wringing his hands. "Well. Yes. I—"

Shall I carve for Master?

"All right," said Gard, and sat patiently as Thrang carved off slices of meat and set them on his plate.

"Do you always eat in here?" inquired the Saint.

"No. Usually I eat in the guardroom—"

And for Madam?

"I would rather not eat meat," said the Saint.

Thrang stiffened somewhat. *I shall carve bread for Madam, then.*

"I'll eat her portion of the roast," Gard volunteered, looking at the paper-thin slices on his plate.

Thrang did not reply, sawing away at the bread loaf. He set out four slices of bread on the Saint's plate. Gard reached for the nearest wine decanter and Thrang grabbed it up, whisking it away to remove the stopper and fill the pair of goblets, which he then set before Gard and the Saint.

"Thank you, Thrang," said the Saint.

Will Madam require anything else?

"I don't think so."

Gard rolled the slices of meat into a cylinder, stuffed it in his mouth, and reached for the knife to cut more. Thrang seized it first and again set about carving from the roast. Cautiously, the Saint took a slice of bread and nibbled it. Gard, scowling, took up his goblet and drained half its contents in one gulp.

"The bread is very good," said the Saint.

I shall relay Madam's compliment to Rakshagthreena in the kitchens.

"Is he the baker?"

She is, Madam.

Gard emptied his goblet and reached for the decanter to refill it. Thrang dropped the carving knife and fork with a clatter and got to the decanter first. He refilled Gard's goblet and presented it to him. "Thank you," said Gard in a voice like distant thunder.

"May I make a request, Thrang?"

Thrang turned instantly, ears pointing straight up. *Madam wishes the melon?*

"Not just yet. I wonder if you would make the arrangements for certain dishes, in the days to come? I have the baby's health to consider."

Of course, Madam!

"I realize there hasn't been time to plant a garden yet, but if you have any lentils or olives—"

We have!

"And then later we might plant kale or some fresh peas."

I will see to it at once. Thrang ran from the room.

Gard took the carving knife and hacked off a substantial slab of the roast. "Were you all right, on your own, today?" he asked, through a full mouth. She nodded. "Good."

She cleared her throat. "Thrang showed me his collection of celadon."

"Mm."

"It's in a beautiful room. Very clean. I think it might be easier to keep the other rooms clean if they were like his room."

"Mm."

"So I would like to have our rooms paneled and plastered. And perhaps something might be done about the plumbing. The drain in the officers' bathhouse on the second level is blocked."

"It is?"

"Yes."

"I'd need the Children of the Sun for that," said Gard. "They understand pipes and things. Plastering and tiles too. I'd have to get a whole army of workmen up here."

The Saint took up another slice of bread. "I will live with you in a cave, my lord, if that is your desire, but do you really propose to raise your child in one?"

Gard frowned. He drank more wine. "I lived in a hole under some tree roots until I was fifteen," he said at last. "Didn't do me any harm. But you'll have your wish."

"Thank you," said the Saint. "I wrote a letter today. Will you send it down to my people?"

Gard's frown grew deeper. "What'd you say to them?"

"I told them I am all right and stay with you of my own free will. It's on your desk."

"Good." Gard's expression lightened. "I'll have it sent."

Thrang ran back into the room, clutching a jar of olives. He set them at the Saint's right hand and looked at her hopefully. *Will Madam require the lid opened?*

———

There was another mountain, far away. Whereas Gard's mountain had been wilderness and was slowly having comfort and cleanliness forced on it, the other mountain had once been all elegance, all refinement, and was now a cracked and broken ruin. Yet not an empty one; some fitful life moved through it still.

The man watched his cup filling, drop by drop, from the snowmelt trickling through the crack in the ceiling. His jaws moved ceaselessly, munching away at the last of the tallow candles.

On the day the mountain had been broken, he had survived because a great block of stone had fallen from the ceiling and jammed in place on a plinth, a hand's breadth above him. The other prisoners in the pen of sacrifice had been crushed; so had the chain coupling that bound him to them. When he had felt brave enough to move, he had crawled as far as he could and emerged into the outer passageway. Faint gray gleams of sunlight were filtering down through tons of rubble, enough to see his way.

He had lived for a little while on the bodies of the dead, until they were beyond what even a starving man could face, and on the melted snow that dripped in here and there. Then he had found a storeroom and lived on its contents for a long while, as he explored what remained of the lower galleries.

He lived in hope. Sooner or later he would find a corpse with boots, or a coat. Sooner or later he could dress himself warmly enough to dig through into the outer world, and then he would be free.

It had been a bad hour for him when he had discovered that the upper halls were still inhabited. Fleering torchlight, shouted orders, a woman's high voice raised in anger; sometimes a distant *boom*, perhaps something being opened, or more of the mountain falling in. Gradually, however, he had dared to venture upward and found the upper storerooms. He had crept in, cleverly working his way to the back for the crates farthest from the light, and carried out as many boxes as he was able, pushing them down his access tunnel. Most of their contents were edible, one way or another.

He had survived on them for months, but now he would have to go up again.

The cup was full at last. He drank the water, replaced the cup, and wiped his hands on his long beard before venturing out.

Poking his head up through the hole in the floor, he sniffed the air. It was warmer, these days; they must have found a way to get the central fires burning again. The dead still feeling was gone from the place, the tomblike atmosphere of the early days after the mountain had fallen. He wondered who else had survived.

They had been clearing debris from this passageway, at any rate. He squeezed through and hurried up the black corridor by memory, thirty paces, sixty paces, and the storeroom ought to be *here*—

He collided with something soft. It felt like a blanket hung across the passageway, but as he fought with it, it became viscous, adhered to his limbs. He struggled frantically, flinging himself backward, but it only sent him farther into the obstruction on the recoil. The obstruction began to glow too, with a pink light.

He floated now in a solid cloud, keeping his nose and mouth clear with difficulty. Gasping for breath, he hung there. The grip on his limbs tightened. He couldn't draw in enough air to scream.

Not long afterward, torches flared, high up the passage; there were voices and laughter. With infinite effort, he turned his head to see who was coming for him.

Demons in livery, trooping along sullenly. A smaller figure in the midst of them, swathed in furs.

"I *told* you!" The voice was a woman's, triumphant. "I told you we'd catch our rat, and there he is. You've fattened on our stores, rat; shall we fatten on you, now?"

"It's a Child of the Sun," said one of the demons.

"Is it?" The woman drew close and looked at him, though she kept well clear of the pink cloud. "Why, it is. He was so filthy I couldn't tell, at first."

He hung there staring back at her. Her long skirt was of the costliest brocade, though it trailed in the dirt and the hem was ragged and soiled. Her rich furs were rank with the smell of beasts. She glittered with jewels, rings on each finger, rings that were too large for her little hands threaded on chains around her neck, bracelets, necklaces, earrings, a coronet set with red stones. Her eyes flashed at him, her smile of contempt revealed missing teeth.

And then all at once her expression changed utterly.

"Why, it's *Quickfire!*" she said, and in a changed voice too. "Quickfire the champion! Oh, I remember you. Poor, poor Quickfire, what are you doing here?"

He couldn't answer her. She waved her hand and the cloud dispersed, let him sag to the ground. He collapsed, unable to feel his limbs.

She squatted beside him. "You were always a brave fighter in the arena," she crooned, stroking back his hair to look into his eyes. "They sent you down after Gard defeated you, I heard. I thought you were dead long ago, or I'd have had you rescued. You were a favorite of mine, did you know? So handsome. Why, I used to keep your likeness in my chamber, when I was quite a little girl."

"Please—"

"Oh, don't be afraid! I wouldn't have *you* harmed, not now I've found you again. Traq! Have your men fetch a litter. Poor Quickfire's too weak to walk. Don't worry, dear Quickfire, the effect will wear off in a few hours. By then you'll be bathed, and shaved, and dressed in some really nice garments, Lord Vergoin's own in fact. Much nicer than anything you could ever have owned. And then you'll have lovely hot food and drink. And *then* I'll have a proposition for you." She stroked his cheek.

The litter was brought. He was loaded into it and carried to the upper levels. Lady Pirihine walked beside him, holding his hand the whole way.

———

Quickfire was borne through halls so ruined he would not have known them, had he not here and there recognized a bit of wall frieze or a surviving section of mosaic floor. The great central cavern around which the Grand Concourse had run was still standing, though it too had changed almost beyond recognition. The shops full of costly wares had been gutted; folk were living in them now, to all appearances, and a great fire burned in the center area where flowers had once bloomed with the aid of sorcery.

Some few of the gentry sat near the fire, in gilt-iron chairs, attended by demons. They turned listless faces to watch as the Narcissus of the Void came up the side tunnel. She progressed with her servants into what had been a jeweler's shop and was now, apparently, private apartments.

All Lady Pirihine had promised was indeed done. She undressed Quickfire and bathed him with her own hands, smiling to see the effect her intimate caress had on him. She shaved him and combed out his hair. She helped him into fine garments. He recognized Lord Vergoin's colors and wondered what had become of Vergoin until he glimpsed the figure lying in an alcove, in a humming fog of spells.

"Vergoin, dear," said Lady Pirihine, going to the alcove and looking down. "Look what I've found, in the cellars! It's the great champion Quickfire. We prayed for a hero and, poof! One appears. Isn't it extraordinary?"

Vergoin made a sound.

Quickfire looked closely at him, then looked away. "What happened to him?" he asked, and that was the longest sentence he'd spoken in seven years.

"The rock fell on him," said Lady Pirihine. "I suppose I ought to have let him die, but there are so few of us left, nowadays. And he has his uses. He's a great listener, for one thing. Sometimes a girl needs someone to listen to her troubles. Don't I, Vergoin dear? Oh, don't look like that; you're really too ungrateful, looking at me like that, and just when our luck has taken the most extraordinary turn!

"Come along, Quickfire. The slaves have prepared us a little feast. We have much to discuss."

The Saint sat alone in Gard's study, working at a loom he had brought in for her, singing as she worked.

She was happy in her marriage. It was as though she had managed to push her little boat out into the river at last and been carried away all alone, into a new world of discovery. The sense of freedom was intoxicating.

It was true that she was constantly watched; it was true that the Black Halls were cold and barbarous. She had walked out with Gard to survey the site of the promised garden and found it acres of rock-strewn mountaintop, with scarcely a blade of grass growing there. Her attendants were fearful-looking creatures, some of them.

But she was learning the way their minds worked: some were all simple emotions in bright primary colors, nearly untouched by any sense of good or evil. A few older ones, such as Balnshik, were serene and wise, though she found their sense of humor bewildering at times. Some, such as Thrang, were obsessives with minds like maze patterns, fabulously spiraled and knotted. She had learned that Gard was like none of them.

He had begun to tell her a little about himself, as they undressed for bed, as she lay in his arms before or after the act of love. She watched his face as he spoke, hesitantly, of grinding slave labor, or of fighting for his life in the arena, or on the battlefield. One night he astonished her by declaiming poetry, in the style of the Children of the Sun.

He was not innocent as a beast is innocent, she saw now; he had an outer layer of simplicity like leaves in sunlight, but shadows were beneath, and a somber, thoughtful soul watched her from them.

She was aware she was infatuated with him. She was aware his body acted on hers like a drug, in the long hours of the night, in his high black bed. She was aware she felt a selfish happiness at being a wife at last, at being a mother soon.

But who could reproach her? Had she not sacrificed herself for the good of her people?

――――――――

"Lady."

She looked up from her loom. The sergeant of the guard, the one with red eyes, bowed to her. "Sergeant?"

"Lady, we have the workmen for you. The Children of the Sun you wanted. With all their tools and gear. Himself says come and see."

"Thank you, Sergeant." She rose, smiling. "Where are they?"

"Got 'em in the lower courtyard."

He escorted her down through the corridors. Hideous monsters saluted shyly as she passed them. She stepped out into the courtyard and beheld red men, kneeling in a long row. They were blindfolded, their hands bound before them, and some wept and prayed to their gods. Piled in a heap to one side of them were chests and trays of tools. Gard stood to the other side of them, in his full black armor. When he spoke, it was not to her but to the prisoners, in a voice full of rolling thunder.

"Now, Children of the Sun, if you die tomorrow, you will still have seen the fairest sight of your lives, and you'd not see anything fairer if you lived on a thousand years. Free their eyes!"

His guards stepped forward and pulled off the blindfolds, one by one. One by one the red men blinked, stared around, then gasped as they saw the Saint. Some of them fell prostrate before her, bound hands outstretched. "Oh, Lady, save us!"

"Have mercy on us!"

"Don't let him kill us!"

She looked on them in horror and looked white rage at Gard. "What have you done?"

"Brought you workmen, as I promised," he said in that same theatrical tone, meeting her eyes without flinching. She saw amusement there, and a covert purpose. "Why, madam, are you displeased? Shall I have them hanged?"

"No!" she cried. "You will have them released at once!" The red men crowded forward on their knees, weeping, thanking her, imploring her, praising her.

"Then I will spare your lives," said Gard to the Children of the Sun. "But you will slave for me nonetheless, to make fair the rooms in which my lady lives."

"They will *not* slave!" said the Saint. "*If* they choose to work, you will pay them in gold, and then you'll let them go!"

"Lady, is it fine work you want?" said one of the prisoners. "By all the gods, I swear you'll have rooms finer than a duchess's!"

"Wife, I will defer to your wishes," said Gard. "For I am your slave in all things. Should one of them displease you, however, his head shall look down sadly from a pike."

"May I speak with you alone a moment?" said the Saint to Gard.

He bowed her to the door, and she pulled him within the hall after her. "Now they will do anything you ask them," said Gard smugly.

"How dare you!" The Saint looked him full in the eyes with all the force of her anger, and he rocked back a little on his heels but did not look away.

"Wife, this is the way a Dark Lord accomplishes his affairs. And I had to bring them up here blindfolded, you know, that's elementary security. They haven't been hurt. They haven't been robbed. If they do a good job for you, by all means pay them what you will. They'll have to be taken down the mountain blindfolded too, but you have my word they'll be released alive and unharmed. That's fair, isn't it?"

"That isn't the point! Why couldn't you have asked them to come?"

"Because they wouldn't have. What with me being a Dark Lord and all, as they'd say. But look now: we'll get your rooms redecorated. They'll go back home and spread tales about the terrible Master of the Mountain and his beautiful and saintly Lady who saved their lives. It'll do both our reputations a world of good."

"But this is all absurd!"

"Isn't it? I lie to survive, because people fear and respect a black mask more than an honest face. Life became much simpler once I understood that."

"We have not done with this conversation," she said. He bowed to her. She turned and went out to the Children of the Sun.

———

To her irritation it was as he had said: the red men were pathetically eager to please her. A plumber among them immediately unblocked the drain in the officers' bathhouse on the second level, though he fainted when he saw what had been blocking it and had to be revived with distilled spirits.

A pair of masons assured her the rock walls throughout the house could be cut clean and finished, and either polished to the gloss of black marble or plastered fine, with molded decorations. A tile setter promised her floors of exquisite inlay work, anywhere she should care to walk. There was a cabinetmaker, and a glazier, and a blacksmith.

She didn't understand half of what they said to her and at last called for Thrang. His ears went up when he saw them, his eyes gleamed. Once they understood he would not attack them and could moreover communicate in sign language, they allowed themselves to be led away by him to the places he felt were most in need of work.

The Saint sat once more at her loom. Thrang returned to her twice during the day, for her approval on certain questions of design and, after having it, her authorization to go into the storerooms below for quantities of building materials. Near the hour of the evening meal he brought her a sheet of paper, containing the estimates for all projected work and materials that needed to be ordered.

She presented the estimate to Gard that evening, as he sat down across the table from her. He picked it up and read it through. She watched his black brows knit. "This is robbery!"

"You would know," she said, calmly dipping a slice of bread in olive oil.

With respect, sir, this is no more than what the workmen charged my old master to build his treasure house, said Thrang, pouring the wine. *And it must be done, sir.*

"Oh, must it?" Gard scowled and reached for his goblet.

With respect, sir, if Madam is to be expected to raise healthy children in a clean and civilized house, then, yes, it must.

"I used to live in a cave under some roots," Gard muttered. He looked at the Saint. "And you used to live in a withy hut under a tree."

"That is true, my husband. But I was not then the Lady of a great and fearsome Dark Lord with a reputation to keep."

"Fair enough," said Gard with a sigh.

He complained again that night, when they retired to the great black bedroom and he found a gaping hole in the wall, over which planking had been set while the glazier and cabinetmaker framed a proper window to go there; but after that he kept his temper and paid the bills.

The Children of the Sun, for their part, quickly understood his chosen decorative motifs and got to work with enthusiasm, producing crown molding in a pattern of skulls, quaint skeletal grotesques in latches and drawer pulls and other ironmongery, and a splendid frieze of white stags in the dining room. Any rooms chiefly for the Saint's use, however, were done in white and gold, with floral and bird patterns.

She was effusive in her thanks to the plasterer, at least until he threw himself at her feet and begged to be allowed five minutes in bed with her. "I'm a quick workman," he insisted.

After than Gard forbid her to be alone with the workmen unless Balnshik attended her, and that put an end to importunings of any kind.

All the while the Saint knew, in her heart, that the improbable idyll could not roll on without consequence.

She was sitting at her loom, in the bright new well-lit chamber appointed for that purpose, when a pair of the demons came to her and saluted, looking nervous. She looked up at them. They were the big twins with silver eyes.

"Lady, there is a man coming up the mountain," said Grattur.

"He is one of your people," said Engrattur.

"He will not be able to get through the death zone unless we lead him."

"So Madam Balnshik sends to you to know, should we let him through?"

"Where is my lord husband?" The Saint stood.

They exchanged glances. "He is working on something," said Grattur.

"It's a surprise," said Engrattur.

"Take me to Balnshik," said the Saint.

They led her down through the house, down staircases and ramps, past innumerable pairs of guards who saluted. At last they emerged by a small door onto an open area below the battlements. Balnshik stood there with a platoon of demons, looking out on the field of black and jagged boulders.

"Is it one of the trevanion?" asked the Saint.

"I'm afraid I wouldn't know, lady," said Balnshik.

"He would be robed in white and carrying a staff."

"No. He carries nothing. He went into the maze five minutes ago; he ought to be well and truly lost by now."

"Please," said the Saint. "Bring him through."

Yet even as Balnshik went to the first of the skull markers, a lone man came walking out between the gates: Kdwyr.

"Oh," said the Saint, and ran to him.

He stopped, staring at her, and went down on his knees. "Child, I have found you again."

She took his hands and raised him, tears in her eyes. He looked old and gaunt. "Is Seni with you?"

"No," he replied, lowering his eyes. "She went back to the river at Hlinjerith, where the Beloved went away."

"How did you get through the maze, may I ask?" said Balnshik.

"The shadow of the raven led me. I prayed to Blessed Ranwyr, and he went before me like smoke. Now I will bring you back with me, or I will die."

"Kdwyr, I can't go back," said the Saint. "I'm married to Gard now. I bear his child. I have bargained to stay here. Didn't you get the letter I sent?"

"We got your letter, yes. But we got his letter too, his wedding announcement, bidding us celebrate his conquest. It was a very rude letter. Your people are afraid, Child."

"Oh, dear," said Balnshik.

"Many young men have gone to the Mowers. They talk about coming up here to die for you. Lendreth has called the trevanion together and they want to make a Song to bring you back."

"I don't want this!" said the Saint.

"I didn't think you would," said Kdwyr. "But they didn't listen to me. So I came here. How are you, Child?"

When Gard came storming into his house, the Saint was pouring a cup of water for Kdwyr. Gard threw open the door to the weaving room. The Saint spoke first.

"And this is my lord husband," she said composedly. "Gard, this is Kdwyr, who found me in the place where I came into the world. I have just been telling him how you are a kind and loving husband and not at all the monster my people have taken you to be."

Gard looked black lightnings at Kdwyr, but said only, "Is that so?"

"Yes. This despite the wedding announcement you sent, without my knowledge."

"Oh."

"And I have explained to him that I am happy to live with you here and bear your child, and am not returning to the world below. Haven't I, Kdwyr?"

"You have, Child."

"And it might interest you to know, my lord husband, that some of my people interpreted your wedding announcement to mean that I was in fact a prisoner here, and now there is talk of mounting a rescue party."

"Which would fail," said Gard.

"Of course it would. How are we best to prevent such a misunder-standing, my lord husband?"

"I could write them another letter, I suppose."

"I don't think so," said the Saint, allowing a slight edge to come into her voice. "I think rather it would be best if I were to send Kdwyr back to my people with the news that henceforth my disciples must be free to come and go on this mountain as they wish, so they may see I am truly no prisoner here."

"May I speak with you alone a moment?" said Gard.

"Certainly." The Saint rose and left the room with him. Kdwyr sat alone, looking around him in wonder at the fine-painted walls. After a while he heard raised voices, but, being a polite man, thought it would be rude to try to make out what they were saying. In any case, he was not curious. He had expected to die today. Since that possibility now seemed remote, and he had seen the Child with his own eyes, he was ready to accept with a calm heart whatever else fate had in store for him.

After a long while, the Saint reentered the room, with Gard following close behind her.

"It shall be as I have said," the Saint told Kdwyr. "Would you be will-ing to carry a letter down to my people?"

"I would, Child."

"Then I will write one." The Saint went to a cabinet and took out pa-per and ink, and a pen.

Gard cleared his throat. "Come and walk with me, disciple."

Kdwyr looked hesitantly at the Saint, who was kneeling to write. "You will come to no harm whatsoever. Will he, my Lord Husband?"

"No, Wife, he will not."

Whereat Kdwyr followed Gard from the room, and out through long corridors where fearful-looking creatures stood to attention, leering at him as he passed.

"So you are the one who found her, when she was a baby?" said Gard.

"I am," said Kdwyr.

"And I suppose you were one of the Star's disciples?"

"No. I was only a slave. One day my chains fell away and I escaped. I went up the mountain and I found her, newborn, lying in a big flower."

"Was she crying?"

"No. Sound asleep."

"Was she alone? Was anyone nearby?"

"We were alone. I didn't know what to do. I picked her up and carried her, looking for a woman to take care of her. We came up out of the fog into the sunlight and there was the Star, with all his people."

"Convenient." Gard eyed Kdwyr, as they came out on the wall that circled the mountaintop. In the bright harsh light Gard saw clearly Kdwyr's stooped shoulders, old scars of shackles. "How long were you a slave?"

Kdwyr shrugged. "Always. I remember the night the Riders came. I was a boy. We were on the dancing green."

"So was I. I remember that night."

"I think I ran. I think they caught me. I don't remember. I was a slave a long time. They worked me hard, but I didn't die."

Kdwyr said it without pride or anger. Gard, watching him, wondered whether Ranwyr would have looked like this now, so worn and old.

Kdwyr looked back at Gard. "You seem young, to have seen that night."

"I am a demon, and Changeless. What do you want, Kdwyr who found my wife?"

"Only to know she is safe and happy. Only to do her will, as long as she has something for me to do."

"You don't want to rescue her from Cursed Gard?"

"How can you be cursed?" Kdwyr looked at him in surprise. "She has taken you for her own. Green vines grow over white bones."

Gard gave a brief laugh. "Do they? I'll show you something." He led Kdwyr to the edge of the wall and pointed out at a wide empty area, sunblasted, full of shattered rock. Someone had been digging there, sculpting the bare earth, clearing the stones and piling them. A few yellowed bushes had died where they had been planted.

"I promised her a garden, to make her happy. I can shape the mountain, but I can't make a garden grow. If I let you go back to her people, if I let you bring them here, would you plant this place and make it beautiful for her?"

"Yes."

The Saint's epistle was long, full of reproaches and exhortations, and by the time she finished it night had fallen; so a bed was made up for Kdwyr in the weaving room, and the Saint bid him come sit at the table and dine with her, at the evening meal. The dinner was lavish, served on gold plates. Kdwyr gave polite thanks and ate in silence, watching Gard and the Saint as Thrang waited on them. Gard drank rather more than had been his habit and was scowling by the time he went to bed.

The Saint did not refuse his touch when Gard put his arms around her, but neither did she respond with her full attention. His arms tightened. "Stop thinking about them," he told her, with the suggestion of a growl.

She looked up at him, startled; then anger shone in her eyes, like white suns. "What did you say?"

"I said, stop thinking about them. You've done enough for your people. I will let them come into my house for your sake, but I'm damned if I'll let them in my bed."

"I will think as I please. You're in a foul mood tonight. Are you that jealous of poor Kdwyr?"

"No! He's all right. I don't mind him. It's all those damned . . . *yendri*. They'll pull you back, if they can. All those bully boys in their green cloaks."

"Do you really think I'd break my wedding vows to go back to them? You don't know me, then. Not at all. But I have duties, all the same. I am their mother and their daughter."

"No," said Gard thickly. "You're my son's mother. And as for whose daughter you are . . ."

The pause went on too long, with too much implied. Her eyes widened, their expression was painful, and yet he had never wanted to kiss her more than in that moment. "I don't know what you mean," she said.

"Don't you? You must have suspected. Didn't your *children* gossip? They did when I knew them. For a people who spent all their time cowering under rocks, they did an amazing amount of gossiping."

She was silent, staring at him, and he blundered on angrily, "There was a man once. He was a fraud. Maybe he didn't know he was a fraud, but he presented himself as a miracle man when he was only a second-rate mage. And the poor stupid people thought he was a god, even when he slept with their daughters. Comforter of Widows, they called him! I'll leave it to you to imagine how he comforted them.

"I saw through him. Nobody else did. Not my brother, not my sister, not my mother. I lost them to him, one by one. All of them believed him when he said, 'Bow your neck to the Riders! Don't fight them! Be patient,' he told them. 'A Holy Child is coming to save you all!'

"And the people must have begun to get impatient for her, and he must have wondered what he was going to do. And then, surprise! A miracle baby was produced from somewhere. Lucky for him. Funny, isn't it, that her eyes looked so much like his? . . .

"So I ask you, now: why shouldn't I take his daughter for my wife? Don't you think that man owes me a family?"

She spoke with white ice. "You are drunk, and you are being deliberately insulting to your wife."

"I'm not insulting you! What's insulting about the truth? You never speak anything but the truth, so why should your life have been founded on a lie? You aren't theirs, you're *mine*. You led them out of slavery. Good for you! But that was twenty years ago and they don't need you anymore. *I* need you! Where are you going?"

"To sleep on the floor. I had rather sleep there than beside you, to-night."

"No!" Gard caught her wrist. "You think I'm a monster? You think I'm going to let the mother of my child sleep on the floor? Stay in the damned bed! I'll go somewhere else." He rolled out of bed and fell to the floor with a crash. Cursing, he staggered upright, grabbing a blanket and throwing it around himself. He went stumbling out into the hall, slamming the door.

Alone, the Saint closed her eyes. The temptation to cry was too great to resist. She buried her face in her pillow and stifled the sobs, and a part of herself watched in amazement. *I am alone in bed, weeping after a quarrel with my husband.* It seemed such a pathetic thing to be doing.

She thought of the women who had come to her, weeping, complaining, begging for counsel. *Nothing I do pleases him. . . . He has been jealous and cold to me ever since the baby came. . . . He cries and says I am cruel to him, and I was only teasing. . . . I didn't mean to laugh at him, but he won't forgive me. . . . He said I did it on purpose, but I didn't. . . . He comes in from the fields tired, and if his meal isn't ready, he speaks harshly to me. . . .*

And she would look into their eyes and see the truth, whatever it might be, and find a tactful way to tell them what they must do, or must not do, and speak words of general comfort.

Stop crying. Wash your face. Turn the pillow over. Get some rest. Don't think about this again until morning.

———————

Gard strode down the corridor, ignoring the pairs of guards who saluted and inquired, cautiously, if they might be of assistance. On through his great dark house he went, slower at last, shivering, for the night was cold and he had got into the parts where the hypocaust wasn't working very well.

He went down into the guardroom, looking for company, but no one was there with whom to drink; the shift that had gone off duty were all in their beds. He turned his steps at last to the handsomely appointed chamber in which Balnshik slept, and knocked.

There was no answer. He tried the doorknob.

"The door's locked, darling," a sleepy voice called from within.

"Let me in." There was a thump, and a bright steel blade-point poked through the door.

"The door is locked."

"I just wanted to talk."

"Very well; you've been an idiot. Go back to your bedroom, make up a bed on the floor, and go to sleep. In the morning, apologize. Don't go to bed drunk again."

"Thank you." Muttering to himself, Gard walked back to his room and did as he had been advised.

His wife was asleep. He listened to the sound of her breathing and ached to hold her.

———

Quickfire was pleased with himself. He was trudging along on a red road, free under the open air, pulling a cart.

Three weeks past he had left the mountain with a trading caravan; Lady Pirihine had paid his passage along their mazed and hidden routes, with ice axes and ropes, across snowfields and down glaciers.

Two weeks past he had escaped the caravaners, stealing a two-wheeled cart from their camp and loading in the two trunks Lady Pirihine had sent with him. He had ensured a long head start by offering them drugged wine beforehand. He had never seen any signs of pursuit. Perhaps he had given them enough of the drug to kill them. Perhaps they didn't know the Narcissus of the Void well enough to dread failing her.

Quickfire knew her well enough, but then again he had no intention of ever returning to her embrace. His plans, in brief, were to make his way to Mount Flame City, sell whatever was in the trunks to any mage willing to offer the right price, and live like a prince the rest of his days.

To this end he walked on patiently. A structure was far ahead, the first he had seen in this desolate backland. Something about it tugged at his memory. By the time he was within a mile of it, he recognized the place.

It was a Red House, the last on the caravan line . . . or the first, depending on the direction from which one had traveled. Within the high fortifications, he could just make out the peaked roof of the Common Hall. He fancied he saw smoke rising from the chimneys.

Quickfire came to the gate. He smiled up at the statues of the two heroes Andib the Axeman and Prashkon the Wrestler, on the gateposts. "Hello, old friends," he said.

A head in a pot helmet poked over the parapet. "Hai! Who's down there?"

"Only a happy traveler. Are you going to let me in?"

The guard looked past Quickfire and to either side. "There's just you?"

"Only me. I'd open the gate, if I were you. My family avenges insults."

"I was just hoping for a few more in your party, is all. Times are hard."

The guard vanished behind the wall, and a moment later the gate swung open. Quickfire walked into the courtyard, pulling the cart after him. He saw that he had been wrong about the smoke: it rose not from the Common Hall but from a forge to one side, where a man was repairing a broken cartwheel. The Common Hall looked silent and deserted.

Quickfire delved into his pouch and brought out a coin. "Carry my trunks within, won't you?"

The guard muttered something about how that was a porter's job, but pocketed the coin anyway and took the two trunks inside, staggering under their stacked weight. Quickfire followed, looking around gleefully.

"Paver! You've got a guest," the guard said, wheezing as he set the trunks down by the fire pit. A man walked out of the kitchen, rubbing his hands dry on an apron. Quickfire threw the guard another coin, a gold one this time, and the Housekeeper saw its glint and hurried to greet Quickfire.

"Welcome to Red House, traveler. You catch us at an awkward time; half the staff's away, foraging. We can feed you, though. I was just fixing myself a meal. Care to share it with me?"

"Yes, indeed," said Quickfire, looking at the Housekeeper attentively. "Did he say your name was Paver?"

"Paver it is, sir. And what's your house, may I ask?"

"Beatbrass. I'm Vergoin Beatbrass. I'll just warm myself here, shall I, while you bring out the food?"

"You know, it's a curious thing," said Quickfire, helping himself to a handful of figs, "but I'd heard the Housekeeper here was missing an eye."

It had grown late; the sun was long since set, the gates barred for the night, and the fire had burned low in the pit. "Ah! That was my father, Bexas Paver," said the Housekeeper. "He kept the place for years, before I took over."

"Dead now, I suppose?"

"Five years since. Bunch of drunken demons tried to break into the cellars. He died defending his kegs," said the Housekeeper with a chuckle.

"What a pity. Well, what's the news? I've been out of touch."

The Housekeeper sopped up oil with a piece of bread and stuffed it in his mouth. "What's the news . . . had you heard the Master of the Mountain's gone and taken himself a wife? And she's keeping him home nights? In a manner of speaking?" he said indistinctly as he chewed.

"The Master of the Mountain? Now, who would that be?"

The Housekeeper stared at Quickfire in surprise and swallowed. "The Dark Lord? Him that's built a fortress up on the Black Mountain in the Greenlands? You must have heard of him!"

"Sorry, no."

"Gods below, where have you been these five years past?"

"Overseeing one of my family's mines, back here. I never heard any news from home, except complaints over the cost of shipping ingots. So tell me, Mr. Paver, what have I been missing?"

"Bloody hell." The Housekeeper rubbed his chin. "Where to start? Well, the Chrysantines are all dead; they got in a war with Skalkin Salting, and he wiped them out. He's duke in Deliantiba now, and Silverhaven, and lately there's been talk he's going after Port Blackrock. I don't think he'll dare try, though, as long as the Steelhands are running the place.

"And he's got this other problem, see, which is that this Master of the Mountain has been raiding his caravans and even his warehouses. Don't know why he's got it in for Duke Salting, but he's made it hard for the duke to keep sticking his little flags on the big map. Got a demon army and that big fortress, and he's a mage, too."

"Is he, now? Where'd he come from?"

"Nobody knows." The Housekeeper refilled their wine cups. "Though I've heard the greenies know something about him. They hate his guts; he raids them too, see. Doesn't raid our cities, though he comes down bold as you please to visit his ladies."

"Ladies? Is he handsome?"

"Gods, no. Big dark bastard. Even when he disguises himself as one of us. But you know how women are. Decent red men like us, they treat like garbage; but they'll lie down for demons and half-breed trash every time. Six mistresses, he has!"

"And he started raiding five years ago?" Quickfire said thoughtfully.

"Just about. And now he's raped some priestess or goddess or something that belonged to the greenies and got a baby on her."

"A child? Really."

"Mr. Paver, I've finished cleaning," said the scullery boy, emerging from the kitchen. "May I go to bed?"

"Go," said the Housekeeper, with a wave of his hand. The boy went out, and the Housekeeper got up to bar the doors behind him. "There," he said, returning to his seat by the fire. "Shut up for the night. You've got the place to yourself; plenty of room to stretch out, eh?"

"The staff don't sleep in here?"

"Just me. The rest of them have the sheds under the wall."

"Ah. Well, what other news? What do you hear about Mount Flame City?"

"Mount Flame? Nothing much . . . the street wars are still just as bad. The Knives were having a big funeral for one of their own, with a parade and a Cursing Priest and everything. The Broadaxes showed up and called them down. There was a riot in the stoneyard. Three hundred dead. The smoke of the pyres covered the sky."

"What do you hear of the Quickfires?"

"Quickfires?" The Housekeeper frowned, shook his head. "Sorry, don't know them. Are they a gang?"

"No! They're one of the first families of Mount Flame! There was a Quickfire commanding one of Duke Rakut's fleet. There've been Quickfires on the Council since the city was founded."

"Haven't heard much of them lately, then," said the Housekeeper apologetically, avoiding Quickfire's gaze, for a disturbing glitter had come into his eyes.

"Why then, I'll tell you a story about them," said Quickfire. "Their bitter enemies, in Council and in trade, were the Smaragdines. The Smaragdines were an old house, and there was no heir. The old Lord Quickfire had no heir either; all his sons had been killed. But he took a young wife and got himself a new boy, so the line would go on. Old Lord Smaragdine couldn't even get it up, no matter how many wives he'd had, and it must have been sand in his bread and bitter wine for him to think of the Quickfires living on when his house died.

"So he got a man into the Quickfires' house, and one day when the child was about five, this man told him there were plum trees full of fruit in the forest, and if the boy would come with him, he'd take him there, so he could eat all he wanted. The boy agreed to go with him at once, he was so young and trusting. What d'you think happened then?"

"No idea," said the Housekeeper, throwing another log on the fire.

"The man showed the boy a set of clothes, poor beggar-child clothes, and told him he'd have to disguise himself, or the city guard would never let them go out to the forest where the plum trees grew. So the boy took off his fine little tunic and his golden chain and put on the dirty old clothes. Then the man took him out of the garden and out through the streets of Mount Flame City, and through the Brass Gate. The city guard never so much as looked twice at him. Care to guess what happened then?"

"I expect he killed the boy," said the Housekeeper, shifting in his seat.

"No, no; he wasn't that kindly. He led the little fellow by the hand into the deepest part of the forest, with the boy asking all the time where the plum trees were, and they came to a camp in the woods where there was a sort of a dirty trading-caravan, all half-breeds and low races, with their carts full of loot. The man sold them the boy. The boy screamed and fought, but they locked him in a cage in the back on one of the carts. They took him away with them, on dirty little forest tracks. What do you think of that?"

"Sorry to hear about it," muttered the Housekeeper.

"Now, here's the really interesting part of the story. After weeks and weeks of traveling, the boy had managed to work a couple of the bars of his cage loose. He was scared to run away, though; he was a long way from cities or anyone he knew.

"But then, one night, the stinking bastards stopped at a Red House. You can't imagine how glad the boy was to hear real people speaking at last! And that was when he pushed out the bars and crawled from under the sacking that hid his cage, and ran limping to the Housekeeper and told him everything, with the half-breed caravan master standing right there to be accused. Shall I tell you what the Housekeeper did then?"

"What'd he do—," the Housekeeper began. Quickfire produced a knife from his boot and moved too fast to be seen; suddenly he was staring full into the Housekeeper's face, with bright hard eyes. The Housekeeper, gasping, looked down at the knife protruding from his sternum.

"Have I mentioned that the Housekeeper had only one eye? He had," said Quickfire pleasantly, driving the knife in a little deeper. "And he laughed at the boy and pocketed the bribe the caravan master gave him. The boy was beaten and bound and thrown in a new cage. They took him away in the morning and he ended up in a place you can't even imagine. That was the last the little boy ever saw of the cities of the Children of the Sun.

"Wasn't that vile of the Housekeeper, betraying one of his own race like that? The more so as he must have had a son of his own, just about the boy's age." Quickfire gave the knife a twist and pulled it out, and the blood ran out fast.

"Nothing personal, son of Bexas Paver, but you know the proverb: 'If the father can't pay, the son must.'"

The Housekeeper sighed, slumped in his seat, and died. He looked as though he had fallen asleep.

Quickfire smiled. His smile faded as he considered what it would take to get out of the Red House alive. He went to the kitchen and washed the blood from his hands, and cleaned and oiled his knife. Then he came back and looked thoughtfully at the little sea of blood under the Housekeeper's chair, which was seeping down into the fire pit and hissing in the embers. His smile returned.

He went back into the kitchen and emerged with an apron, tying it on. Blood no longer dripped from the chair. Effortfully he lifted the housekeeper's body and carried it off to a small curtained alcove at the rear of the room. The curtain, shoved back, proved to have been concealing the Housekeeper's bed. Chuckling, Quickfire laid the corpse in the bed, arranged it on its side, and drew the blanket up.

After pulling the curtain to, he went back and tossed the apron in the fire pit, following it with the Housekeeper's chair. The fire blazed up agreeably. "That just leaves you," he said to the bloodstain on the floor. "What'll I do about you?"

As he stood there, his gaze fell on the trunks Lady Pirihine had sent with him. He knew they contained thaumaturgic apparatus of some kind; he wondered whether something in them might remove or hide the blood. He went to the larger of the two and opened it.

Something lay under a shroud of silk. He pulled the silk away and exclaimed softly. Then he shouted in horror and leaped back. The thing had moved.

It shook itself and rose slowly from the trunk, until at last it hung in the air like a puppet on invisible strings, like a marionette the size of a living woman. It seemed made of burnished gold, and though there were no strings, the individual limbs and joints dangled loosely, apparently unattached to one another. He could see firelight through the doll's elbows and knees. The head was like a masked helmet floating above the neck.

It shook itself again and its floating parts came a little more into alignment. The head turned toward Quickfire. The eyes opened with a tiny *clink*. Two white spheres bobbed behind the empty sockets and rotated until a pair of irises centered themselves. The eyes seemed to focus on him.

The mouth dropped open with another *clink*. He could see straight through to the back of the head. The lips clattered open and shut a few times, before a high sweet voice sounded. "Oh, Quickfire, for shame. You weren't thinking of deserting me, were you?"

"No—" He took a step backward. To his dismay the thing floated toward him, its golden toes dragging just above the floor.

"You wouldn't do such a dreadful thing, would you? After all I've done for you? I'm depending on you now. I've no one else left. Not even poor old Vergoin."

"Wh-what happened to Vergoin?"

"He died." The golden shoulders rose and fell in a shrug, chiming slightly. "Probably a mercy, don't you think? But I'd be sorry to see *you* die too. I hope you won't make me angry, Quickfire."

"I didn't trust the caravaners. I heard them plotting to cheat you. That was why I left them."

A trill of scornful laughter was the response. "Hardly likely. We've used that firm for years. They'll always come back. Shall I tell you why?

"Each one carries in his soft flesh a little sealed vial of glass. Each vial contains a host of tiny creatures. They have all they need to live in there; and live they do, and breed, and multiply. They're quite harmless . . . as long as they remain in the vial. Any attempt on the part of the bearer to cut it out will make the vial shatter, and then the little monsters swarm out and consume flesh with a ravenous appetite. It's a nasty way to die.

"And suppose the prudent bearer leaves the vial alone, but fails to obey my orders and return to the mountain? Why, then the creatures in the vial go on breeding, and breeding, and one fine day there will be so many they'll burst out of the vial from mere pressure. And then, as he's rolling on the floor screaming in his agony, don't you think that bearer will regret his disobedience? Because if he'd come back as he was bid, I would have safely removed the vial before it was too late.

"Have you noticed a soreness in the small of your back, dear Quickfire? Just in a place you can't reach? That's where I put your own little vial."

Involuntarily, Quickfire clutched at his back. "But I don't remember—"

"Oh, you were sound asleep in my arms at the time. Aren't you glad I found a way to come along and watch over you? Still, no harm done. Here we are!" The head turned, as though looking around. "So this is the outside world! Rather sordid. I always thought your people lived in splendid palaces."

"This is only a way station. We're still out in the wilderness."

"Really." The simulacrum made a few experimental walking motions, to and fro. The limbs rose and dropped with little bell-notes. The head turned from side to side. "What's this on the floor?"

"Blood. I had to kill someone."

The simulacrum bent at the waist, arms dropping forward loosely. A moment of practice and it was able to coordinate one arm and hand enough to dip one of its golden fingers in the blood. It straightened up, in little jerks, and opened its mouth; slid the fingertip in. Though Quickfire, watching in appalled fascination, could see no tongue there, the blood had been licked clean away when the fingertip was withdrawn.

"Oh! That's good. Oh, I can't wait to taste Outside food. This is going to be distracting, I can see. So many new experiences."

"How are you doing this?"

"How do you think, silly? Aren't I Pirihine Porlilon, Narcissus of the Void? My grandfather was the greatest mage who ever lived, and all his power is distilled in *me*. The rest of them were a lot of old dullards! They might have walked free of the mountain ages ago, if they'd discovered how to animate a simulacrum. Only *I* have ever worked out how to do it. Don't you think I'm clever?"

"Very clever."

"I hope you're clever too. Have you found out anything useful for me?"

For the first time since the simulacrum had emerged from the trunk, Quickfire smiled. "Yes. It would appear that Gard now has a wife. And a child."

———

The Saint sat bolt upright in bed, gasping. Gard, instantly awake beside her, put out his hand and caught her shoulder. "What is it?"

She had to draw two deep breaths before she could answer. "Nothing.

Only a dream." But she clutched at her belly as she sank back on the pillow. She gazed up at the black hangings, the black depths of the midnight room.

"Were you frightened for the baby? Don't be," said Gard. "He's alive and strong."

"I know." The Saint could not tell him about the reasonless terror, the conviction that some shapeless thing flailed within her womb. *Women have such fears. They're groundless, always. I am like other women, therefore my fear is groundless.*

But was the baby's father like other men?

Gard watched her trying to calm herself. He put his hand on her belly, spreading out his fingers. "Shame on you, Son, dancing in the middle of the night. Here, Wife, put your hand here. That's a little foot. Can you feel?"

"Yes . . ."

"And here's the other little foot, and here's his head. No wings. No hooves. No tentacles. His mother is the most beautiful woman in the world, and he'll inherit his looks from her."

"Not from the Dark Lord?" The Saint smiled a little.

"How can a baby inherit a mask?" Gard smiled too.

He left her sleeping the next morning, nodded brusquely to the pair of disciples waiting in the corridor without, and returned the salute of his two guards who waited there also. "Let her sleep late," he told the disciples. "Her rest was disturbed."

He went down to the baths and was mildly annoyed to discover Mr. Ironweld still hadn't finished the grand mosaic-tile floor. The Child of the Sun, on hands and knees fitting tiny tiles in place, nodded to him. "Morning, Dark Lord, sir."

Gard paused to study the image forming, which seemed to be of an immense man bearing a trident and doing something improbable with a leviathan. "What's that?"

"That's Lord Brimo of the Blue Water, sir. Riding his sea serpent to the place of the sea nymphs. Other end of the room, that'll be the panel where he's *found* the sea nymphs. You'll like that part."

"This is going to cost more than you estimated, isn't it?"

"Ah." Mr. Ironweld wiped grout from his fingers. "Well, that's the great thing about doing a marine motif, you see, sir? Lots of blue. Blue's a very cheap color. I can get blue mosaic tile for practically nothing. Red, now, red's expensive. But you've got to have it for the sea horses and some of the fish."

"Make them blue, then."

"Couldn't do that, sir. Wouldn't be enough contrast. Foul up my color scheme." Mr. Ironweld looked at him reproachfully.

Gard growled but let the matter drop and walked down into the bath. There he splashed around awhile, looking up at the ceiling mural of blue sky and white clouds, the whole of it lit by a circular skylight. "How much did that cost me?" he inquired, pointing at it.

"Wouldn't know, sir. That's Gritpolish's work. Your werewolf, sir, he's got each of us under separate contracts. Best way, really."

"Is it?" Gard reached for a towel and waded out.

"Yes, sir. Careful stepping on that bit, sir, the grout hasn't set."

Muttering to himself, Gard made his way to his dressing room, where Thrang waited with Gard's valets.

"Good morning, little brother," said Grattur, holding up three yards of linen. Gard took it and wrapped it around himself. "Guess what my girl did this morning!"

"Good morning. What did she do?"

"Took her first walk!"

"And my boy said his first word!" said Engrattur.

"What was it?"

"'No,'" said Engrattur proudly.

"Congratulations."

Madam Balnshik wishes to confer with Master concerning the duty roster at his earliest convenience, Thrang advised him. *And the spoils from the last raid have been brought into the lower courtyard for Master's inspection. I have an itemized list here; I thought Master might be particularly interested in the crates of ceramic plumbing pipes.*

"Pipes? That was a lucky score," said Gard, pulling his tunic on over his head. "Hardcoal can finish the nursery plumbing."

I thought so, sir. I took the liberty of opening one of the crates and sending it down to the job site.

"Thank you."

Will Master be dining in the officers' mess?

"Yes."

Straj, sausages, toast, figs, and tea are available this morning.

"Oh, good."

Dressed and groomed, Gard dined with Balnshik while going over duty rosters, discussing household security and intelligence reports, and planning the next raid. It took most of an hour before he emerged from a side gate in the inner wall and walked out into the garden.

And clearly it was a garden now, with an orchard and reflecting pool and rows of herbs, though the trees were small and shielded from the wind by woven screens. A few white-robed figures moved along the rows, with urns of water. Gard grunted in satisfaction. He picked up a shovel and strode out to join them.

"Where do you need the next hole dug?" he inquired of Kdwyr.

———————

The Saint, having risen late, sat frowning at her writing table. She reread the letter.

> . . . *and while we of course rejoice in your triumph over evil, it falls to me to tell you that there are those among our people who do not accept your letter as authentic. There are some too who accept that you wrote it, but under duress, or under ensorcellment. This of course has caused tremendous disputation among the trevanion, with the final agreement that you, being the Promised, cannot by your very nature be subject to enchantments or force, though some reserved judgment on the second point until you can yourself explain more clearly the circumstances of your departure from us.*
>
> *I regret to inform you that the Mowers in no wise accept that you wrote the letter of your own free will, nor that you would willingly submit to bearing Cursed Gard's offspring. This will distress you, without doubt, but it is the natural consequence of what has befallen us.*
>
> *I am doing as much as I can to see that your intentions go forward with respect to ministering to the Children of the Sun, though of course my success must be limited, for I have neither your skill nor perfect knowledge. And while we rejoice to hear that Kdwyr and the others who have joined you there are not lost as we feared, uncounted others long for the blessing of your regard once more.*
>
> *I urge you, Mother and Daughter, to return to us, that you may yourself satisfy us as to the truth of your condition and intentions. The Mowers stand ready at any time to escort you in honor to the meeting place you shall appoint.*
>
> *I strongly recommend you give my words serious consideration.*
>
> *With all respect,*
Lendreth

She set the letter aside and had reached for her pen before noticing the young disciple Dnuill standing, hesitant, in the doorway.

"Mother? There is another letter here for you, from the trevani Jish."

"Where is the bearer? Is it Seni?"

"No, Mother. It's Nelume. She's Jish's student."

The Saint rose, a little wearily, and received Nelume.

"Mother." Nelume knelt down for blessing, staring up at her. "It's true, then! You are to bear another Child!"

"I am to bear my husband's child. A little boy. There's nothing extraordinary about him, so far as I know."

"They are saying, Mother, that now that you have gone, the Star will come back to us. Do you think it's true?"

I wish it were, thought the Saint. Aloud she said, "But I haven't gone. I have simply married and live here now. Nothing else has changed."

"But people say you're under a spell!"

"Do I look as though I'm under a spell?"

"No—but—then, perhaps it wouldn't show," said Nelume breathlessly. "And people say this is all a plot of Cursed Gard's to destroy us."

"People are wrong," said the Saint, as mildly as she might. "And his name is only Gard. Have you brought me a letter?"

"Oh! Yes, Mother, it's here." The girl presented the leaf roll.

The Saint took it. "I'll read this at once. Dnuill will bring you water and show you a place to rest."

To the young Mother, greetings.

We scarcely know what to believe, following your departure. If you are indeed happy and well, then we must accept the truth of your letter and wish you may be blessed of a fair child. And if we can believe that you have subdued he who was Cursed Gard to your will, then we must praise your power and wisdom. I can myself well believe it; for I remember you slew demons when you were but a child.

But you should know, young Mother, that there are those among us whose faith is imperfect and who do not believe.

Lendreth has taken it upon himself to usurp your place, in your absence. He resides on your garden island and has sent your disciples away, and called the Mowers to attend him. He has sent out orders that all our people are to organize themselves into villages once more. He requests that boys from all families be sent to swell the Mowers' ranks. I need hardly tell you that our people murmur at this and do not obey, though many have joined the Mowers, out of a desire to avenge your abduction.

I cannot think this is good. The Star himself would have protested it.

And this is another thing you should know, that after years of diminishing our Star's light by referring to him as the Beloved Imperfect, Lendreth now speaks of him as having possessed wisdom and strength beyond your own and encourages those who say that the Star will come back to us again, to lead us in new and better ways.

Which only shows that Lendreth never understood him. I myself did not understand him, then, to my regret. The eyes of the young are often blinded by distractions.

You will wish to amend this lamentable state of affairs, I know. I urge you to speak out and condemn Lendreth's behavior. A firm letter would be useful but not as effective as your own presence condemning him out of your own mouth. He would wither in the sight of your eyes.

Why could you not return to us, if only to deal with this matter? Your presence would deprive him of his authority. I assure you that we, by whom I mean all we trevanion of the eastern forests, would fully support any measures you took to resolve the situation.

With love and duty,
Jish

The Saint leaned her head on her hand. She thought of the disciples as they had once been, as Seni was forever describing them, young and innocent and united in love. How had it come to this backbiting, rancorous mess?

She felt the hard throb in her lower back and sat upright, easing it, breathing deep. She reached once more for the pen and dipped it in the inkwell.

To my disciples, to all trevanion and students, to any who claim to accept my authority, this general epistle is directed.

I am grieved to see such dissension among you in my absence. Must I believe that

The pain came again, urgent. She dropped the pen and looked down at herself, in surprise.

————

"Sir!" Redeye emerged from the gate in the wall and looked around. "Sir! Your lady wife's gone to her bed!"

Heads rose all over the garden, from where they had been bent over their labor. Gard threw down his shovel and ran. "Is she all right?"

"Likely; it's just the baby coming," said Redeye, and jogged along after, but Gard soon outdistanced him. So did the disciples, coming swiftly from behind and passing him in the corridor. Redeye gave it up at last and went down to the officers' mess for an early celebratory drink, but was bowled over at the door by Balnshik, emerging at a dead run.

"I don't care for the skulls," said the Saint.

"What?" Gard stared at her. She drew a deep breath, waiting for the contraction to pass, controlling the pain.

"The skulls. I don't want my child born in a bed watched by emblems of death."

Gard drew a sword from the weapons rack on the wall and hacked the silver finials from the bedposts, one after another. He gathered them up and handed them to Thrang, who hovered at the door. "Have them melted down and recast as stars," Gard said, then returned to his seat by the bed.

"Thank you," said the Saint. "It was a silly request. Oh—"

"They're only decoration," said Gard.

"The nursery isn't ready—"

It will be, Thrang assured her. *Captain Balnshik herself has gone through the house and collected the Children of the Sun, and given them personal assurances of reward if they will finish the nursery before the sun sets on this fortunate day.*

"See? It'll be all right," said Gard. "And anyway, I lived in a hole under some roots when I was young, and it didn't do me any harm."

"I know," said the Saint. "Oh—Husband, I received two letters today, and they trouble me greatly—"

"Letters? Who from?"

"The trevanion—"

"They're a bunch of idiots. I don't want you thinking about them now."

"I don't *want* to think about them now," she said, glaring at him, "but they demand my attention. I need to meet with them."

Gard scowled. "You can't travel. Not with the—"

"Oh!"

"Oh! Again, again, I can see the head!"

"Oh!"

"At least—" Gard stared down, looking dubious. His face cleared. "Yes! It's a head!"

"Is he all right?" Frantic, the Saint rose on her elbows. But Gard was laughing, bending down with hands wide, and the boy slid into his hands and was deftly caught and hoisted up into the light shrieking.

"It's my son! Look at my son! Look at this boy!" roared Gard. Laughing, he leaned down to kiss the Saint and put the child in her outstretched hands. "He's the most beautiful baby in the world!"

She cradled him and studied him closely. The little boy was perfect, tiny and fair, no tail, no scales, no claws. "We need to cut the cord—"

"I can do that," said Gard proudly. "It's just like putting on a tourniquet." He tied off the cord and grabbed up a dagger, sliced it through. "There!"

There was so much noise she thought the roof might come down: crying and song out in the hall, and Thrang's deep-throated baying as he ran down through the house with the news, and the cheering that rose now from all quarters. Gard let in her disciples, who instantly clustered around the bed with cries of adoration.

The baby was taken from her arms, washed in sweet water, wrapped in fine silk trimmed with pearls, and returned to her. She scarcely noticed their ministrations to herself, as she peered into the little face. The baby had clamped firmly onto her breast and nuzzled there greedily, with his eyes crossing.

She looked into his eyes. Try as she might, she could not see his soul.

———————

Duke Skalkin Salting was displeased with his spoils.

He sat in the front row at Tinwick's Theater, surrounded by bodyguards, and watched the sweating actors perform *Mage's Gambit, or The Black Dungeon of F'narb*. He'd never cared for this kind of thing, himself; the declamatory style seemed stilted and old-fashioned. He much preferred the witty urban comedies of Tourmaline.

Not only was the theater small and a bit grubby, there was only one really wealthy street in the whole of Deliantiba, and one really nice district of mansions. Its quarries were all right, in their way; he thought he might get them turning a profit again, in another year or so. The pottery industry, likewise. And it was useful to have a river down which to ship stone and pots to more civilized places.

If he'd known how little return he'd get on the expense of taking the place, however, he'd have let old Chrysantine keep his miserable little city.

Provincial miserable little city. There, two rows over to the side, sat a veiled woman without the slightest idea of how to behave at a play, even a stinker like this one. She chatted constantly with her gentleman companion about the plot, ignoring the dirty looks she was getting from her fellow theatergoers. She munched from a paper sack of sweetmeats, rustling the paper, smacking her lips when she bit into a good one, or exclaiming in annoyance when she got one she disliked and tossing it at the actors.

She watched attentively when Kendon the Hero was being tortured and applauded afterward; but during the comic business between Elti and Jibbi, she announced she was bored. She got up and left, seeming to sway a little drunkenly as she made her way out, with her companion hurrying after her.

The play ended at last. The Dark Lord died in a blaze of blue and green flames; that was pleasant to watch, at least. The duke had had enough of Dark Lords, these days. He arose and applauded dutifully, and had one of his men toss a bag of coins to the actors. One of them caught the bag and they bowed, without as much enthusiasm as he felt they might have shown him.

"Now, for gods' sake let's get out of here," he muttered to his sergeant. "I want a drink."

Not soon enough, he was at the ducal table in the Chalice, sipping his wine alone, but in peace; for a frozen silence had descended on the other diners as soon as he had entered with his men. One by one they rose and left the restaurant, some of them leaving their meals unfinished.

"Should have burned the whole place to the ground," said the duke, quite loud enough to be heard. "See what I get for being a merciful conqueror?"

A waiter rushed to refill his wine. He was just raising it to his lips when a couple entered the Chalice. It was the absurd veiled woman from the theater, with her companion. To Salting's astonishment, she walked straight up to his table.

"Greetings, Duke Salting. I wish to discuss something with you. You will find it to your advantage."

Her voice was sweet, but the foreign accent made him suspicious. His bodyguards turned and stood regarding her, knives drawn.

Her companion, a harried-looking man in early middle age, smiled at them. "No, she's not one of us. I'd suggest you let her speak, all the same."

The duke raised his eyebrows and had another sip of wine. "You wish to sell me information?"

"Sell? Oh, no, dear sir. I want nothing from you. I wish to make you a present of something. We have an enemy in common, you see."

"Is that so?" The duke set down his wine. "Be seated, then, madam.

Sir." When they had taken seats across from him, the duke's guards moved unobtrusively to stand one behind each, knives in hand.

The veiled woman rested gloved hands on the table. "My understanding is that you're a man of vision. You seek a great state under one banner, rather than little scattered cities who won't cooperate with one another. You know it will take a great deal of money, and patience, and cunning, to bring this about.

"But, alas! There is a certain thief who steals your money, and tries your patience, and exceeds your cunning. Is there not?"

"There is," said the duke.

"The Master of the Mountain, I've heard him called," said the woman's companion, with a sneer. "But *we* knew him when this Master was no more than a slave. A greenie freak, trained up as an arena fighter."

"Really," said the duke, sitting up straight.

"He belonged to my family," said the woman. "Most unwisely, we gave him certain liberties. He used them against us. I will not trouble you with the sad details, but many of my kinsmen died. He has since come forth to this land, as I hear, and has set himself up as a brigand chieftain and preys upon your caravans. Now, wouldn't you like to eat his liver?"

The duke looked askance at her. "I'd like to cut it out, at any rate. I'm bleeding money to the bastard. I can see looting a gold shipment now and then, or wine, or silks, but he takes *everything*. Pig iron. Olives. Lumber. Paint and sewer pipes! What's a damned bandit going to do with fifteen crates of sewer pipes?"

"It's an outrage," said the woman. "I'm sure there's a good reason why you haven't taken your army and dealt with him."

The duke laughed sourly. "I'm sure you haven't seen where he's set himself up. He's fortified a mountaintop. He has a demon army up there. Horrible black castle with skulls all over it and armed demons leering down from every guard post. Even when he ventures out of it, we can't catch him—the lower slopes of that mountain are a maze of trees, and higher up there's a maze of obsidian, boulders with edges sharp as knives."

"Then it would take magecraft to get inside," said the woman. "And an army to destroy him, once you'd broken his walls down. Now, sir, I have deep magic that will melt his high wall like so much sugar, and I have the just and holy hatred of blood debt against him. I require only an army.

"You have an army. Were I to make you a present of my craft, would you lead your army to his mountain and take his head for my sake?"

"I might, if I had any proof you weren't a charlatan."

The woman laughed merrily. She drew off her gloves and raised her veil.

The duke spilled his wine. "Gods!"

"You see? I am, in truth, at the far end of the world. Dear Quickfire is merely escorting this simulacrum of me." The thing batted its eyelashes, with a noise like a tin butterfly opening and shutting its wings.

"She's telling you the truth," said Quickfire grimly. "She is Lady Pirihine Porlilon, the Narcissus of the Void. All her family were mages of deadly puissance, and she is deadlier still."

"Oh, what a flatterer you are," said Lady Pirihine. "Poor dear Duke Salting, your wine is all gone. Let's have another jar! And what is there to eat here? Quickfire, order me something nice."

For the next hour the duke watched, horrified and fascinated, as Lady Pirihine devoured a trayful of little meatballs in sweet sauce and drank most of a jar of wine. He kept expecting the wine to splatter forth from the bottom of the mask, or the meatballs to roll down on the cloth; he could *see* that there was no tongue, no mouth beyond the golden lips, and yet the food vanished somewhere. He went so far as to lift a corner of the cloth surreptitiously, expecting to find a puddle of chewed supper under her chair. He saw nothing but a trim pair of ankles, with a half inch of lamplight between them and the legs to which they should have been attached.

None of which kept him from hearing her story, for she chattered as she ate and drank. By the time she came to outline her plan for Gard's downfall, the duke had gotten over his shock at her appearance and was listening intently.

I did not enter this world to provide an object of reverence for you, as though I were one of the goddesses of the Children of the Sun. I came, as the Star came, solely for the good of our people.

The duty of the Beloved was to sustain them through the long time of their sorrow, and to educate them that they might be able to live in the greater world once they were free. To this end he taught you the Songs, that you might help him.

My duty was to free our people from their prison and guide them to this land where they now reside in peace. This I did; and, when a new danger arose to threaten them, I gave over my own peace and all that I knew to reside with a stranger, that they might be spared. This I did not merely for duty's sake but in obedience to the rule of Compassion for others, which ought to govern us all above any other motive.

Having noted with sorrow the dissension among you now, I know it is my
further duty to resolve these matters—insofar as you will still accept my authority.
I will list the errors I have observed.
Some among you have exulted in your wisdom and so proven yourselves
fools. The object of learning the Songs was not to make you more powerful, or
more spiritually advanced, or even wiser. The purpose of the Songs was, and is,
only to help those in need.
Some among you have taken up arms

The Saint set her pen down, hearing the clash and salute out in the hall. The door burst open and Gard entered the room, carrying little Eyrdway. Gard was dressed in his most barbaric splendor. The baby was wrapped in embroidered silk.

"Look, Eyrdway, here's Mama! Tell Mama how you were presented to the army, and how they cheered, and cheered, and cheered. Tell Mama how they made you a general." Gard tossed the baby into the air. Eyrdway crowed and gurgled.

"Oh, they didn't," said the Saint, holding out her arms. Gard plucked the baby out of midair and gave him to her.

"They did. And then Eyrdway sat down in the officers' mess and got drunk, just like a big man!"

"He didn't." Then the Saint smelled the wine and saw it dribbled on the front of the baby's nightgown. She turned to Gard, outraged. "You gave the child wine?"

"Just a little," said Gard, sobering quickly. "He liked it. We rubbed it on his poor little gums and he smacked his lips."

"And—is this *blood?*"

"The lads hunted down and sacrificed a ram in his honor. It's traditional. For demons. Then we broiled it over coals and everyone had some. I just gave him a little blood in a spoon. It didn't hurt him."

Appalled, the Saint held up Eyrdway and examined him. He hung there kicking, apparently happily, drooling and regarding her with bright blank eyes. Wondering again whether he was an imbecile, the Saint felt the sting of tears. She held them back. Then—

"What's he got in his mouth?"

"Nothing," said Gard, but leaned down to stare. Instantly he pulled off his gauntlet and thrust a finger into Eyrdway's mouth. "Spit that out! Spit it out right away!"

"How did he get—" She was drowned out by Eyrdway's muffled screams of rage.

"Here it is," said Gard, fishing out a small object. "Oh!"

The object in his palm was a black pearl, glistening with baby spit. Gard lowered his head, trying to see the place where it had been on his fancy breastplate. He looked so big and handsome and stupid, the Saint's heart broke.

"How'd he get it off? I wasn't holding him up there more than a minute or two—"

"You've been drinking. And smoking that intoxicant again. You wouldn't have noticed. He might have choked on it. Please, in future, *don't* play with our child when you're in that condition."

"Demons get drunk. It's what they do!" said Gard. "And anyway it was a party in his honor. And anyway, how the hell could he have gotten it off? It must have been loose in the setting."

"If you hadn't been drunk, perhaps you'd have noticed that."

"Maybe. Look, he didn't come to any harm after all! But I'll leave him with you, now, since you don't trust me with him."

He strode out, slamming the door behind him. She managed to put Eyrdway in his basket and give him his teething toy—a wooden wolf-puppy, painstakingly carved for him by Thrang—before turning away and bursting into tears. She out her head down on her writing table and sobbed.

Let it all drain out with the tears. When you've wept your heart empty, get up and wash your face and go on with your work. After following her own advice, she sat down and picked up her pen once more.

Some among you have taken up arms and gloried in your power to harm others. I see here nothing to distinguish you from Cursed Gard as he was, and he at least

Something made a noise, at the periphery of her attention. It was not Eyrdway gurgling, or banging his toy against the side of the basket. Something was yipping softly. Something gave a tiny growl.

The Saint turned and put her hands to her face in horror.

Two fat wolf cubs were in the baby's basket. One was made of wood. One was flesh, worrying the nose of the wooden one. No sign of Eyrd-way, other than the tiny pearl-trimmed nightgown lying empty in the bottom of the basket.

"My baby has turned into a wolf," she said aloud, in an attempt to anchor the moment in reality. She picked up the little animal gently. It wriggled and tried to lick her face. She looked into its eyes.

She saw a soul, for the first time, something absurd and bright-colored. A little mad star, spinning in its cosmos with a sound like starlings chattering.

The Saint took her child in her arms and walked, as in a dream, through the black halls. The guards saluted and did double takes as she passed them. She went to Gard's study and found him sitting there, still in his fancy armor, scowling over a volume of travel essays.

He looked up at her, still scowling. Noting the cub, his scowl deepened. "Where'd you get that? You think it's *safe*, raising a wolf around our baby?"

The cub, squirming, thrust its nose inside her robe and found her breast. Gard's scowl faded, he stared in astonishment. She bit her lip at the touch of needly little teeth. Gard jumped to his feet, shouting with laughter like a thunderclap.

The cub started and cowered in fright; its whimper became a scream, as its shape ran and melted in the Saint's arms. Then she was holding a naked screaming baby. Eyrdway roared, he flailed with his fists, and big fat tears of terror rolled down his cheeks.

"That's Daddy's boy!" Gard came from behind his desk so fast he nearly knocked it over, and flung his arms around the Saint and kissed her, hard, and kissed the top of Eyrdway's head. "That's Daddy's *clever* boy! Don't cry, boy, you mustn't cry, this is wonderful!"

"He did it after I gave him his teething toy," said the Saint. "He's a demon, isn't he?"

"He's—er. No, he couldn't be a demon. Not all the way. I'm only half-demon and you're not at all, so . . . at least I assume . . ." Gard gave her an odd look. "Hm. Well, maybe it has something to do with the way we, er—"

"The circumstances of his begetting?"

"Right, because of all the . . . spells and everything." Gard lifted Eyrdway up to look at him. "*Ssh, ssh,* Daddy's sorry he scared you. Daddy was just so happy to know what you are, at last."

"You've been afraid of something too," the Saint said, feeling faint with relief at having it finally said. "Because he isn't at all like little Bero, or Bisha."

Gard was silent a moment. Eyrdway, distracted from his tears by proximity to Gard's breastplate, poked at the remaining black pearls. "I think he takes after my mother," said Gard at last.

"After Teliva—," said the Saint, then bit her tongue. "I'm sorry."

"It's all right. I met my real mother, you see." Gard's voice was steady. "Our boy may take a while to grow up, but he'll be clever enough in his way." He retrieved a pearl, prizing it gently from Eyrdway's fingers. Eyrdway screamed in temper. "Hush, Son. Come here! Daddy and Mama want you to play a game with us." He strode to his desk and set the baby down. Eyrdway immediately reached for the inkwell, but the Saint caught his hands as Gard pulled down a book and opened it. He held it up. It was an engraving of a forest bird, painted in colors.

"See the birdie? Can you be the birdie?"

Eyrdway looked up from trying to pull his hands free. He stared uncertainly, drooling, as Gard pointed at the engraving. Eyrdway leaned forward and reached for the page, but the Saint tugged him back.

"Be the birdie, Eyrdway," said Gard. Suddenly something changed in the little face: interest? Comprehension? He stared hard at the picture, his eyes crossed in his concentration, and then—

It was rather dreadful to watch, as feather quills erupted all over his skin, and his nose and mouth ran together and protruded into a beak. When it was done, though, a living image of the picture stood fluttering its little wings on the desk.

"That's Daddy's good boy," said Gard shakily. "Well, now we know he isn't just a werewolf."

"Come back to Mama," said the Saint, sweeping him into her arms, for she was afraid he would fly. He lifted up his head and crowed defiantly, but when she bared her breast for him, he changed back at once and snuggled into her bosom.

———

. . . And as for the requests that I come down and meet with you, I must ask your forbearance; for I have a young son I cannot leave and, moreover, have discovered I am now to bear another child. I am sad to know that this news would be greeted with congratulation, were I any other woman.

Nonetheless, I see you will not be satisfied until we may meet face-to-face. I cannot travel. Therefore I bid you come to me.

I would have all the trevanion travel to this mountain, with any of their students they choose to bring, that all may see I am well and under no constraint. Having been seen, I will present to you a letter I have prepared, for general circulation among our people. I will explain it to you in person, that there may be no misunderstanding, and you will then carry copies to every community and village, that all may read my will without gloss or misinterpretation.

I appoint the first full moon of summer as the day of our meeting. The disciples bearing these letters will provide you with directions. Do not fail to come as you have been bid.

"No," said Gard, incredulous. "No, no, *no*. I'm not having those people in my house!"

"It's my house too," said the Saint firmly. "I am your wife. Or am I only your prisoner, and the bearer of your sons?" They were on their way to the nursery, for a bedtime visit.

Gard gnashed his teeth. "Of course it's your house too. But there is the little matter of all those daggers I left in the villages, with the invitation that anyone who dared was welcome to stab me with one of them."

"Then that was a stupid thing to do, wasn't it?"

"I used to do a lot of stupid things. How was I to know I'd meet you and we'd get married and have babies? You do see, though, that it presents a certain danger?"

"I have not invited the Mowers. And if I remember correctly, they were the objects of your scorn, and not my disciples."

"Don't you think for a minute your trevanion wouldn't love to see me dead and rotting too," said Gard irritably.

"I know that. But when they have seen me at last, when I send them down with my letter, they will have no choice but to accept my will. Which is to stay with you."

"And when did all this disapproval of coupling happen, anyway? The Star used to roll girls amongst the flowers two and three at a time." Gard blushed as she turned to glare at him. "Well, he did! How did the yendri change to the point where you were expected to stay a virgin your whole life?"

"It's an accretion. The opinions of a few trevanion taking on the force of law. It was no part of the Star's teaching, and I mean to stop it. This is one of the things I address in my letter. This is why it's important."

"I suppose," said Gard. "I still don't want them inside my walls. They're a security risk. I have other enemies, you know. You can have your council down the mountain, maybe. Good evening," he said to Balnshik, for they had come to the nursery door.

"My Lord. My Lady," said Balnshik, saluting. She lowered her blade and stepped aside. "The Heir to the Black Halls has had his bath and eagerly awaits his dinner."

"Thank you," said the Saint. Gard opened the door for her and followed her across the threshold.

Bero and Bisha came toddling to them at once. Bisha, the silver-eyed girl, turned her little face up to them. "Baby ball," she said in urgent tones. "You come see. Baby ball." She caught hold of the Saint's hand and pulled her toward the crib.

"Where's Dnuill?" said Gard, looking around.

A voice floated from the next room. "I'm folding the laundry, sir. He spilled juice all over his—"

What else she said Gard did not hear, for he collided with the Saint, who had frozen in her tracks and was staring, speechless, at two identical painted wooden balls in the crib. An empty nightgown and a pearl anklet lay on the blanket. She put out a distracted hand, found Gard's wrist, and gripped it tight. "Do something," she said.

The balls were yellow, painted with blue and red stars. They were motionless, as unliving things tend to be. Gard felt his heart pounding loud in the silence.

Not knowing what else to do, he pulled down the shoulder of the Saint's gown. He picked up the balls and held them, one after the other, to her bared breast.

He felt the second one shift its center of gravity in his hand; a moment later little arms and legs uncurled, like a crab emerging from its shell, and expanded. The painted stars faded and Eyrdway chortled, settling in for his dinner. The Saint caught him in her arms.

Gard collapsed backward onto a bench, putting his face in his hands. "We have to start his lessons now."

She came and sat beside him. "How does one train a shape-shifter?" she inquired, staring at the nursery mural.

"I have no idea." Gard looked over his fingertips at the mural too. It was done in soft pastels, featuring little rabbits dressed like people. Some of the rabbits, he noted, wore armor and carried spears.

There was a tavern in Konen-Feyy-in-the-Trees, and in it a man sat, celebrating his good luck by getting as drunk as he could. Because he had begun his celebration with an immense meal, the inebriation was proceeding more slowly than it might otherwise have done; so he had had time to tell his story, coherently, to three or four different sets of tavern patrons.

He was momentarily without an audience, but smiled as he tilted the wine jar to refill his cup.

His name was Chelti Stoker. He had been an itinerant painter most of his life. It was not a profession to make a man wealthy, and Stoker was bone thin, with old paint under his nails and engrained in his skin, and a permanently desperate look in his eyes. His quiver of brushes and case of paints lay now at his feet. He was never so drunk as not to keep one foot across the quiver, in case someone tried to steal it.

He prodded it protectively, now, as two men came to his table. "Oh. Hello," he said, looking up at the man he recognized. This was a nondescript fellow who had listened to his story, without comment, the first time he'd told it. The other man was bigger, wore flashy clothes; he looked like someone's hired bully.

"I'd like you to tell your story to my friend here," said the nondescript man, in a nondescript voice.

"Strangest week I ever spent in my life," said Stoker. "I'd offer you fine gentlemen a drink while you listen, but I seem to have emptied the jar." He patted it suggestively.

The bully grinned. "We wouldn't want you to pass out before you finish your tale. Let's hear the story first, eh? Plenty of wine afterward, if it's a good enough story."

"Oh, you won't have heard its like before! Listen well, friend. This time a week gone, my luck was out. I'd spent the day long crying my services up one street and down the next, and had nothing to show for it but the price of a bowl of broth.

"So in here I came, to this very tavern, and ordered my poor mean bowl. And here I sat supping, lamenting that my mother ever bore such an unlucky son, when in through that very door came a lady. And such a lady!

"She was tall, with long hair black as night, and a bosom like two boulders, and a red red mouth, and long gorgeous legs, and leather boots with such heels! Hai, I thought to myself, there's a woman to make a man crawl at her feet, and weep, and plead. Now, you won't believe this, gentlemen—I didn't believe it myself. What should this proud beauty do but seat herself across from me and give me the look of invitation?"

"What happened then?" said the bully, keenly interested.

"Well, like I told you, I didn't believe it. I turned and looked over my shoulder, to see who it was she'd settled her fancy on. Nothing behind me but the blank wall! I smiled, being polite, you know, and presently she ordered a jar of wine and two cups. When they were brought out, she crooked her finger through the jar handle and slung it over to my table, easy as though it weighed nothing.

"She said, with kind of a throaty purr, 'Little painter man, I'll bet you're a master at your craft.' And she poured me a drink. I told her I was good enough for whatever job she had in mind. And I winked, like *this*, you know. She just laughed and told me to drink up. And I did. We chatted pleasantly here at this very table, if you want to know, and she was hot-blooded and amorous, and the end of it all was—well, I don't remember the end of it all so well, but I remember she threw me over her shoulder when it was time to leave and walked out with me.

"Next thing I knew, I was waking up from the loveliest sleep, only I couldn't open my eyes nor move. This is because I was tied up and blindfolded, see, and I was wondering what in the world we'd been getting up to, when I noticed I was lying in something that was pitching and moving.

"I thought for a minute I'd been carried off into service on a ship again, but I couldn't smell nor hear the sea. And then her voice came quite close to my ear, telling me I was going for a ride in her sedan chair, and I'd find out more when we got where we were going.

"It seemed like days we traveled, and she had a special way with her for keeping a man from getting the cramp, I'll tell you. At last we came to some place like a palace, from the way I could hear guards shouting challenge-and-return, and clashing their axes and all. Then indoors and turning this way and that, right and left, upstairs and around, and at last the sedan chair was stopped. I got hoisted out and sat down in a chair. My hands were untied, and my blindfold was taken off, and—you'll never guess where I was."

"Where were you?" demanded the bully.

"In a nursery," said Stoker. "A new one, with plaster still fresh and wet on the walls above the paneling, and cradles and cribs all pushed to the center of the room and covered with tarpaulins, and the carpets rolled up. And there was my beauty, only now her skin was a different shade and she was wearing armor. She smiled at me. I hadn't noticed before how long and white her teeth were. Gods deliver me, I thought, that's a demoness.

"She only put my paint case and brushes in my hands, though, and she said, 'Hello again, little painter man. Here are walls. Paint a mural to please a child.'

"And I stammered a bit as I said I had one I did for kiddies' rooms, with bunnies playing about and such, would that suit? She said that would be fine and asked me was there anything I needed. I asked for food and drink and she said she'd have some sent, and the lads would look after me in the meantime.

"I asked what lads and she pointed behind me and, gods below, you don't want to know what those two fellows standing guard behind me looked like. They carried black spears and hideous big swords. My beauty laughed and said they'd do me no harm, so long as I did my job.

"Well, you can imagine I set to with a will then, eh? It was all freehand, no cartoons, but I'd painted those damned bunnies a hundred times and I could have done them in my sleep. The demons watched me, and after a while one of them asked me, quite civil, whether I couldn't make some of the bunnies purple or green, and maybe paint some of 'em with red eyes and tusks. So I told him, yes, indeed, anything to oblige.

"And then after a while the other one asks whether some of the bunnies couldn't have spears and be marching in an army, in addition to the other ones that were gardening and frying sausages and reading books and sailing little boats on a pond, and I said why not? And some of the bunnies had two heads by the time I was done, and some of 'em had wings, and really I didn't want to think too much about what kind of kiddies was going to be sleeping in those cribs.

"But I finished it; I finished it before it all dried, so I did, even with me stopping for my meal, which was sumptuous, by the way. The beauty came in and congratulated me on how nice the walls looked. Then she gave me a fine big purse of gold and sat me down to another sumptuous meal, with plenty of wine, and I don't recall how that evening ended either.

"I woke up in a field by the side of the road, but I still had the purse with all the money and my gear. And here I am."

"You're right," said the bully. "That was worth a jar of wine. Fetch our friend a drink," he added to the nondescript man, who rose silently and went off to the bar.

"You're most gracious, Mr.—?"

"Quickfire," said the bully. "You know, my friend, I think your amazing streak of luck is going to continue? I know a lady who just might pay you to tell her your story. She likes details, though. For example, have you any idea where in the house this nursery was? What could you see, out of the windows?"

"Oh, I couldn't tell things like that," said Stoker, smiling to see the nondescript man bringing a fresh jar of wine and a fresh cup.

"I think her ladyship could pay you enough to persuade you other-wise," said Quickfire, pouring out a drink for Stoker.

"No, see, I couldn't, much as I'd like to oblige. The beauty said there'd be a spell on me, to freeze my tongue against talking about that part of it." Stoker accepted the cup of wine and spilled out a drop or two for the gods.

"But spells can be broken, you know," said Quickfire smilingly. "Drink up."

And, most unfortunately for him, Mr. Stoker did.

Five minutes later he was being dragged out the door between Quick-fire and the nondescript man, who told the tavern keeper they were tak-ing Mr. Stoker to have his head cleared. The tavern keeper shrugged and went back to frying onions.

Not until he walked out into the common room to clear away the empty cups did he notice Mr. Stoker's paints and brushes were still sitting there, abandoned, under the bench he had occupied. The tavern keeper shivered and said an involuntary prayer, though he could not have said why.

Gard sat at his black desk, studying the reports the spy had brought him. "What do his troops think?"

"That he's going to try to take Port Blackrock," said the spy, one Mr. Bolt. "They're not happy about it, either. They're afraid of the Steelhands. Last time there was an uprising, Duke Steelhand hung men from the yards of every ship in the harbor, and the ones he didn't kill got chained to oars in galleys."

"Do you think that's what it's all about?"

Mr. Bolt shrugged. "Might be. My contact says there's this mysterious veiled lady in the duke's house, some kind of mage queen, and she's sup-posedly given him some sort of secret weapon. If he had something mag-ical, I suppose he might think he had enough of an advantage against the Steelhands to try for the city."

"Who's your contact?"

"Ah! He asked me to remember him to you. An armor smith named Bettimer Prise."

"So he makes armor now?" Gard smiled. "The boy's come up in the world."

"He was in the duke's own chamber, doing a fitting, when he saw the lady. And he's got the contract for all the new helmets for the conscripts. He'll likely be going with the army, when it moves."

"Very good. Tell him I remember him well. Tell him I'll order a fancy helmet, one of these days when things are quieter. He can charge me whatever he likes."

Gard paid Mr. Bolt, who bowed and was escorted down through the Death Zone. Gard remained at his desk awhile, frowning as he reread the reports. At last he set them aside and went out to the garden.

He found the Saint seated under a pergola, thinly shaded with vines. She had had her loom moved outdoors, in the mild weather, and Eyrdway slept in a basket at her feet. Bero and Bisha chased each other round and round a fishpond, watched shyly by a third child, who hung back. "Who's that one?" Gard inquired, nodding toward the boy.

"His name is Fyll," said the Saint. "His father is someone in your army. His mother can no longer care for him. The messenger brought him up."

"What messenger?"

"The one from the trevani Jish. She advises me all the trevanion are coming to my council."

"That's nice," said Gard vaguely. He held out a hand to the new child. "Come here, boy. Are you going to come live with us, now?" The child sidled close, but stood with his eyes downcast, saying nothing. Gard reached out and picked him up, studying him, noting the boy's red eyes.

"Mm. Yes, your daddy's up here. Did you know your daddy was a brave fighter, boy?"

"His name is Fyll."

"Fyll."

The child bit his fist. "My daddy's a bad man," he said at last.

"Yes, he did a bad thing. But he won't do it anymore, and he'll be very pleased to meet you, Fyll. He'll be happy his lost child has been found. So there's nothing to be scared of, you see?"

Fyll slid from Gard's lap, edged away from him, and unobtrusively took hold of the Saint's robe. Gard sighed. The Saint lifted the child to her lap and held him.

"The garden is beautiful," she said to Gard. "If you let me hold the council here, the trevanion might believe I stay with you by choice. We could put up pavilions over there."

Gard shook his head stubbornly. "I'll set up pavilions in any meadow you like, down the mountain. Too many people know the layout of my house as it is, without inviting actual enemies to have a good look at it."

"They aren't your enemies."

"Aren't they, though?" Gard looked regretfully at the child Fyll. He looked at his own child sleeping soundly and thought of the new boy budding under the Saint's heart. He thought about lost children, and the song the yendri had used to sing on starry nights when the world was new. *Where did the boy come from? . . .* Where did any of them come from?

He remembered Teliva's curse. He wondered, uneasily, about mysterious mage queens.

"I want it *now!*" insisted the simulacrum.

Quickfire stared, appalled, at the brassy hemispheres of its hindquarters. They floated adjacent to each other, but the furrow was open air. So was the space lower down. He could see straight through the crack and glimpse the pattern of the blanket beneath.

"But you don't have any—"

"Of course I do! You know I do. It doesn't matter about the simulacrum. Just put it in!" The voice grew more strident.

Quickfire felt a twinge in the small of his back. Gritting his teeth, he lifted his tunic and thrust into what he thought might be the appropriate place. He felt nothing but air, and the cold edges of the metal where he touched the hemispheres to either side. It was quite the least erotic moment of his life.

Yet the simulacrum backed to him and cooed and squealed, and in all ways reacted with pleasure. "Move!" it ordered.

He went through the motions, frantically imagining warm and buxom women, their mouths, their hands, anything to keep himself erect. The act seemed to go on forever. The simulacrum's noises became more and more unnerving, until at last his imagination failed him. The simulacrum was rounding on him with a snarl of disappointment when a loud voice floated through a near window.

"I really do not understand your lack of enthusiasm for this," said Duke Salting, in what he felt were mild tones. The city council of Konen-Feyy, assembled before him on their knees, looked at one another miserably. Not one of them dared speak, however.

In their pavilion, Quickfire sprang away from the simulacrum in relief. "Sssh!" he cautioned it. "Don't want them to hear us, do we?"

"You of all people ought to be grateful for my presence here," said the duke, raising his voice. "I thought I'd be welcomed as a liberator. Here you dwell practically in the shadow of his house; how long do you think it's going to be before this Dark Lord reaches his hand out to raid *your* homes and caravans? How have any of you managed to sleep these seven years, with that monster up there? Do you *enjoy* the prospect of demons raping your wives and children?

"You can't have thought this through very clearly. That's the only possible explanation for why any of you would have the unmitigated gall to complain about quartering and provisioning my army!"

His voice had gotten progressively louder through this speech, and seeing that he was likely enough to be killed anyway, the council head mustered the courage to say, "Please, sir, it isn't that we aren't grateful. We merely fear for your safety. Some of us have ventured up as far as we dared and seen his walls. They are terrifying. His sorcery rings the place round in black fire. Any force attempting to lay siege to the Master of the Mountain must surely die on the slopes! We would not see so brave a man, and such a valiant army, destroyed."

"Oh, is that it?" The duke sneered at them. "It's the sorcery you're afraid of? I'm glad to know that's all it is. If I thought you actually doubted I could burn out a nest of greenie brigands, I'd be monstrously insulted. You needn't worry; that's been planned for. On your feet! Come and see."

"Damn the man," muttered the simulacrum, but it clattered to its feet and found a robe and pulled it on. Quickfire, sick with relief, pulled on his breeches.

The councilmen were, meanwhile, prodded to their feet by the duke's elite guard, who ringed them round with spears. They were escorted after the duke, who strode out to the yard behind the council hall. Here he had had his pavilion and those of his staff set up, after ascertaining that Konen-Feyy had no hotels worth commandeering as temporary headquarters.

"Quickfire! We need to prove ourselves, it seems. Show this esteemed body of nobodies how we plan to break the Dark Lord's house."

Quickfire strode from the pavilion, grinning. "But this courtyard is paved, sir; otherwise I'd find an anthill and trample it underfoot."

"Quickfire, don't boast; it's tiresome. Do as you're told." The simulacrum, veiled, emerged from the pavilion. The councilmen gaped at it. "Fetch out the weapon!"

Quickfire obeyed, vanishing into one of the pavilions to reappear pushing a trunk. He opened it and tilted it outward, displaying the contents. A tube of some black and gleaming metal, ornamented in gold, was mounted on a pair of red-and-gold-painted wheels. Nested in the trunk's lid was what appeared to be a much smaller model, lacking the wheels but mounted on a stock like a crossbow. "Is that an enchanted weapon?" asked the council head, feeling a glimmer of hope in his heart.

"Watch it, and see what you think," said Duke Salting. "I find their council house blocks my view of the lake, Quickfire. Do something about it."

Quickfire made to hoist the wheeled weapon out, but the simulacrum stepped forward and raised its gloved hand. "Dearest Duke, this is so mighty a weapon that its force would destroy their city. Be merciful, and let us demonstrate with the model instead."

"Madam, as you will," said the duke. "Gentlemen, your wretched little walls will remain standing; now, remember how the gods punish ingratitude."

Quickfire took up the model, resting it in the crook of his arm. The simulacrum placed its hand on his shoulder and leaned forward, as though whispering in his ear. He pointed the model at an obelisk, carved with the names of past council heads, that stood in the center of the yard.

There was no sound; there was no flare of light. The obelisk merely sparkled and dissolved into red sand that fell in a heap and smoked where it lay. "Gods below," said the council head.

"Hardly," said the simulacrum with pride.

"Doubt me now?" said Duke Salting, grinning at the council head. "I didn't think you would. What about a little cooperation?"

The council head reached out distractedly and caught the sleeve of one of his subordinates. "Go. Run to the storehouse and have them open it to the duke's men. No paperwork; the army can take what they like."

The subordinate turned and ran as he was bid. Fear lent such wings to his heels that he easily passed the duke's armorer, who was strolling to a certain tavern on the edge of town.

Bettimer found the place easily enough, for it was exactly as it had been described to him. He arrived at its door and paused to examine the bill of fare posted outside, noting the tiny green mark, like a diagonal pen stroke, in the upper right-hand corner of the menu. A moment he stood there, with the package he carried still under his arm; then he went inside.

He ordered bread, wine, and olives and was placidly eating when Mr. Bolt walked in. "Cousin!" said Mr. Bolt with a slight quaver in his voice. "Well, what a surprise. I was coming to visit you in Port Blackrock next month."

"And instead I've come to you," said Bettimer. "Just as well; I've got that present for Cousin Bullion. You're likely to see him before I do." He pushed the package across the table to Mr. Bolt.

"So I am," said Mr. Bolt, unwrapping the package. He withdrew a throwing ax, beautifully ornamented, the polished steel head incised with a pattern of stars that continued down in brass inlay along the wooden handle, terminating in a starred cap of ivory and brass. "Nice!"

"Bread?" Bettimer pushed the loaf toward him too. Mr. Bolt saw spidery words there, punched into the crust with a knife tip: 3 LEFT TURNS OF CAP, THEN PRESS IN THIRD STAR.

"Yes, thank you," said Mr. Bolt. He put his finger on what he took to be the third star and looked at Bettimer with raised eyebrows. Bettimer nodded almost imperceptibly and handed him his knife. Mr. Bolt cut away the message and ate it. He helped himself to olives too. He rewrapped the ax and ordered a cup of wine.

They chatted about the weather until Mr. Bolt finished his wine. Then he excused himself and, tucking the package under his arm, walked out.

When he passed through the northern gate, he began to hurry.

In a high meadow on the mountain, long ago, an oak tree had grown, not tall but immensely wide, stout, gnarled by seasons of howling wind and driving rain. Its low-hung canopy had spread out over most of an acre. Generations of little creatures lived out their histories in its shelter. Its roots broke rock; it dug in under winter's wrath and endured and had seemed as though it would always be there.

Then one summer evening in thunder weather, the fire of heaven had flickered down and touched it with the heat of the sun's face, and it had exploded. Shards of wood hard as flaming iron shot out and buried themselves in the mountainside, or in the trunks of other trees. A whole world died in an instant.

Briefly, there had been fire, before the hot rain came and washed scattered leaves and ash down the mountain. Red coals smoldered on, blinking through the darkness of night like red eyes. Even they died at last. Morning revealed the shattered stump still feebly smoking, hollow. Years of winters bleached it silver, wore its raw edges down. The wide meadow, cleared by wooden shrapnel, remained open to the sky.

Gard stood there now, regarding it somberly. "This will do well enough. Clean it, and set the pavilions up."

His guard moved across the meadow with rakes and shovels. Some leveled and filled as best they could; others grunted with effort, pulling fragments of old wood out from where they had been driven into the earth like teeth.

"What about the stump, sir?" Arkholoth rapped it with his knuckles, and it rang like steel.

Gard eyed it. "Let it alone. Let it remind them that everything changes."

———————

The Saint looked up at the waxing moon, faint as though chalked in on the blue of the afternoon sky. She felt the baby kicking and rested her hands on her waxing belly. On either side of her, guards stood by her chair, ready to carry her back up through the postern gate before nightfall.

Her disciples moved across the meadow, setting up tables and mats in each pavilion, sweeping, decorating with pots of sweet herbs, watering the earth to encourage a quick greening. Already little spear-blades of grass had shot up.

Dnuill looked sadly at the stump of the oak, rising implacable against the sky. "We could tie streamers to it. Or train a creeper over it. There's one in a big planter in the eastern courtyard. That would make it prettier."

"No," said the Saint. "Let it serve as a reminder that some things are final and will not change."

———————

Three days more and the meadow was green, the dozen pavilions shone white in the sun, and the Saint sat under a sunshade by the broken tree, gazing down the mountain. "I don't trust them," said Gard, pacing beside her. He wore a plain green tunic, and no barbaric ornaments at all.

"I do," she replied.

"Wouldn't we look more like a happily married man and wife if I sat beside you?"

"We would. And later on, we will. But today it would only provoke their anger."

"I thought holy folk weren't supposed to get angry."

"I get angry," said the Saint. "If I lose my temper, how can I demand that they keep theirs? They will be unhappy enough with what I have to say to them, without adding more fuel to the fire."

Gard growled, but he knelt before her and kissed her hand. "I'll go, then, and sit out of sight, like a child being punished. Only for love of you."

To his astonishment, she put her arms around his neck and drew him close, leaning awkwardly to kiss him. "I love you more than my duty."

Startled, he drew back a little and looked into her eyes. "You never lie about anything."

"Never. I love you more than a peaceful life, or reason, or hope. I love you selfishly. Greedily," she said sadly, stroking back his hair. "All I want in this world is to live with you, in quiet, here; but nothing comes without consequence.

"I could close my eyes and pretend my people weren't afraid, I could tell myself the trevanion were as good and wise as the Star himself and never act out of pride or spite or prudery. It would be a lie. My duty is to speak the truth to their faces. Do you understand, now, why I must meet them here?"

Gard nodded, not trusting himself to speak. He got to his feet, bending to kiss her again; then he turned and walked off quickly, to the black pavilion pitched at the far edge of the meadow. He went inside and drew the curtain and sat peering out at her through a gap in the fabric.

The trevani Faala was the first to arrive, escorted between Kdwyr and Stedrakh. She ran from between them when she glimpsed the Saint and fell to her knees before her. Smiling, the Saint rose and took her hands.

"Child! Oh, Child, how I've prayed for this hour, to see you alive and well!"

"Please, don't kneel. May I offer you a cup of water?"

"But are you truly all right?"

"You can see that for yourself," said the Saint. "I am a wife and a mother. This is my home, and no prison."

"But it looks like a prison," said Faala, peering distrustfully upward at the black battlements of Gard's house.

"The skull decorations are for show," said the Saint firmly. "It doesn't look like that inside. Sit down, now, and drink."

She had more or less the same conversation a dozen times, over the next several hours. One by one the trevanion came up the mountain. Some came fearfully, some came wrathfully. The fearful she calmed and the wrathful she placated, and each of them she presented with a cup of water. Gard rose inside his pavilion and began to pace again, maddened with impatience; jealous, in a puzzled kind of way, that she should give so much of her attention to something so boring.

"Young Mother," said Jish, embracing the Saint.

"Trevani," said the Saint. "I'm glad you came."

"It's true, then," said Jish, looking down at the Saint's waist. "You bear a second child. He will be the one who balances!"

"I beg your pardon?"

"It is my understanding you bore a demon to your husband. This boy will be your own child, and do *your* work in the world! At which we rejoice."

The Saint thought of Eyrdway. He had wept and held out his arms to her when she had kissed him good-bye that morning, before Balnshik had distracted him with a jeweled bangle. "Both my sons are my children," she said, controlling her temper with effort. "And the children of my husband."

"Of course," agreed Jish quickly. Looking into her eyes, the Saint saw the tide of whispered rumor that could never be stopped now, the fantasies, the half-truths, the willful misinterpretation, the unjustified opinions or outright lies that would become articles of faith. For a moment she felt her strength would fail her.

And all I can do is speak the truth, she thought. She glanced involuntarily at the black pavilion and wished Gard were at her side.

"Lendreth is coming too, you know," said Jish.

"I bid him come."

"Not, I imagine, in the style in which he travels. He goes nowhere, now, without a bodyguard of Mowers. He has trained them in Songs, as though they were trevanion, did you know? But he has made new Songs for them, for fighting, for silent movement, for striking, for concealment. There are no women among them. In fact, they pledge themselves to refrain from love."

"Why?" asked the Saint, shocked.

"Why, the old story: to give them greater powers of concentration." Jish actually bared her teeth. "It's an abomination!"

"It's wrong. And you are too angry about the things Lendreth does, Jish. I must hear what he has to say."

"You won't wait long. I saw him below, starting up the trail as I ascended. Alone, for once; but I saw one of his bullies sneaking along through in the forest behind him."

Yet Lendreth alone was escorted up to the meadow, striding along with his staff.

He was smiling as he greeted the Saint. "Child." Surveying her, he added, "And Mother indeed. You seem well and happy! This is excellent. Now I can speak the truth to any fool who still imagines you are languishing in a prison. I can say, 'I have seen her with my own eyes, and all is well.'"

"I am glad to know you accept my choice," said the Saint warily, for he was avoiding looking her in the eye.

"It must be accepted. It is your will. And, to speak truth, it is the natural progress of your destiny. You were sent to free us from our long sorrow. Now that we are free, how can we deny you your own freedom? You deserve the simple happiness all women desire, in a husband and children. That you have them at last delights my heart, and I wish you well."

"Thank you," said the Saint. "I wanted to ask you if you'd heard anything of Seni."

"Seni?" Lendreth looked surprised. "No."

"I was told she went to Hlinjerith, by the river."

"Did she? Well, she never could bear change; may she be happy there, with her memories. But we are all here!" Lendreth looked around at the pavilions. "All the trevanion, in one place. How many years has it been since we were all together? You have my congratulations; they'd only have done this for you. May I be permitted to make an opening address?"

"If you wish," said the Saint, thinking that he had no heart at all.

The last of the trevanion were brought up. Stedrakh and Arkholoth went to stand at attention before the black pavilion, unobtrusively as they were able. Kdwyr went round the pavilions with a basket of codices, each sturdily bound between wooden covers, and the yellow pages within were closely written in a firm, clear hand. He gave one to each of the trevanion.

The Saint rose from her pavilion and stood by the trunk of the shattered oak.

"Brothers and sisters," she said. "Thank you for making this journey, and coming so bravely to a place so many of you have feared. You can see, now, that it is only a mountain, and that fearful-looking house only my husband's house. What you cannot see, from the world below, are the gardens he has made for me, the fair bright rooms painted with flowers; but I hope that in time you will see them, as you come to accept my choice.

"The Star taught us to use power in the service of Compassion, to ease suffering. He and I together led you from that valley where our people sorrowed. You know that I have sent trevanion among the Children of the Sun, to heal the sick. Now I have come to live with Gard, among demons, and Compassion again guides me: for your sake, that he might leave you in peace, but also for his sake and the sake of our children.

"Yet I know well the dissension this has caused among you. Let this meeting bring us into agreement, and peace. Kdwyr has given you all copies of my letter; when we have discussed it here, I ask that you take them to all communities where our people live and read them aloud, in order that there should be no misunderstanding of my will.

"Brother Lendreth has asked to address you, before we begin. Let us hear him." She returned to her pavilion, and Lendreth stood and walked to the shattered oak.

He turned, regarding them all, smiling. "Brothers and sisters, how my heart rejoices, to see this day.

"I remember well the horror of the past. We were once beaten and terrified children, ignorant, helpless. You remember, you trevanion, what it was like. Those who have come since can never know the unrelieved darkness of those days.

"And then, one night, hope came to us.

"I remember climbing that mountain, to hear that glorious music that promised so much. Do you? I remember my first sight of the Star in his high place. Those remarkable eyes! And I remember the way our poor people moaned and begged him to return us to our past, when we had been as unborn children dreaming in the world's womb.

"What did he say then, our Star? 'Your old ways are lost. I can never sing back the child into the womb, the leaf into the bud.'

"Do you remember? Consider what the Beloved said to us. Consider what it implies: that Life is never unchanging, and one must grow. What else did he say?

"'No more scattered in lurking isolation, no more slaves slaughtered and forsaken. Learn what I have learned! Come and let me teach you, and you will walk, as I walk, unfearing in the light.' What a glorious challenge! I remember how those words went straight into my heart.

"I remember too how an impatient young man rose to dispute him, one of a pair of brothers. You all know what followed. One brother strove to follow the Beloved's teachings, and dared to try to set us all free. All praise to Blessed Ranwyr!

"And yet, brothers and sisters, I must ask you: have we perhaps judged that other young man too harshly? Wasn't his desire, in its essence, the same as Blessed Ranwyr's? He wished to fight for our freedom. That he was demon-born was none of his choosing; that he fought the Riders in the only way of which he was capable, being demon-born, is even praiseworthy. That he quarreled with his brother and brought a tragic fate upon them both is to be lamented, certainly."

An outraged murmur had been growing among the other trevanion, but Lendreth's smile never faded. He held up his hand.

"If you please, brothers and sisters. I was there that day, I remember *exactly* what the Beloved said. Teliva cursed her foster son, in the understandable rage of her heart, but the Beloved admonished her! He said, 'Teliva, for the sake of lost Ranwyr, cry down no death upon your foster son.' And he doomed Gard to nothing worse than exile.

"Yet who can blame our sons, raised upon legends of Cursed Gard, if they attacked him when his path crossed ours again? And who can blame him, demon as he is, for striking back at them? Brothers and sisters, it is time to turn our backs on the sorrows of the past. Our Child, who brought us forth from that valley of lamentation, has in her wisdom chosen to forgive Gard. Must we not do the same?"

Gard sat listening in his black pavilion, scowling in disbelief. From her white pavilion, the Saint watched Lendreth and thought, *I wonder what he will want, in return for this? And he has not won them over, even now.*

"Brothers and sisters!" Lendreth raised his voice. "I call for an end to childhood! Our Child has become a wife and mother. When will we too follow our destiny as a nation?

"We stand today at a crossroads, brothers and sisters. One way leads back into the past, into the darkness of legend, into stagnation in the habits of our infancy, into mindless obedience to tradition, into passivity and death.

"Will we go that way, or will we take the other path and fulfill our potential greatness? Will we strive to change and adapt to this world of limitless possibilities? Consider the Children of the Sun! They are dirty and quarrelsome, they are stupid, but look at the magnificence of their civilization! How might we not surpass them, we who are blessed with knowledge and wisdom?

"Our Star showed us the way, brothers and sisters, in almost the first words he ever spoke to us. 'No more scattered in lurking isolation!' We must call our people together, lest they remain a handful of forest tribes, accomplishing nothing. We must rebuild the villages. We must farm the meadows and learn the skills of the Children of the Sun.

"We must train our young men in the practice of arms, that they might defend us if we are attacked, and so make certain we will never be slaves again. You will tell me, this was once forbidden! But consider that a child is, rightly, forbidden to play with knives; a man must learn to use them.

"Our people will murmur at these changes, and for that reason we must assert our authority. A child knows nothing, until he is compelled to learn and grow. Now our people must be compelled, for their own benefit.

"This is our opportunity. Here and now we must resolve on a new set of laws by which our people will live. Brothers and sisters, the moment has arrived!"

The trevanion had fallen utterly silent.

The Saint rose to her feet. "No," she said. "You have offered them false choices.

"We do not stand at a crossroads; there are multiple ways, as many as there are trails in a forest. One may grow without changing one's nature. One may remain stable without stagnating. You wish to become something new; that's admirable in you and always has been. But you have no right to force others to walk the path you have chosen for yourself."

Lendreth rounded on her. "Nor have you, now. Your authority ended when you left us. Lie with your husband and bear his children; but *we* are no longer your children. A man reverences his mother, and so we will reverence your name, for the Star's sake; but henceforth we will rule ourselves."

"You mean *you* will rule us!" screamed Jish, and the trevanion cried in outrage, and some leaped to their feet.

"No! What he said was just and right!"

"Blasphemer!"

The Saint held up her hand for silence. "I will relinquish authority, if my people wish. But not to you. You would only make them slaves again, to your own ambition."

Lendreth's face was dark with rage. "Woman, be silent!"

"How dare you!" shouted Shafwyr.

"Bloody hell, they're going to have a holy war," said Arkholoth, shocked, then staggered aside as Gard rushed between the curtains of his pavilion and strode across the meadow to the Saint.

"You smooth-lying bastard," Gard shouted at Lendreth.

In a blur of green at the edge of the meadow, suddenly they were there: three armed men, running at such speed their cloaks floated out like wings, straight for Gard. The foremost raised a sickle as he ran.

Lendreth, horrified, stepped before them and threw up his arms. "Fools! I told you to stay—" The thrown sickle caught him in the throat, and he fell. One of the Mowers pulled up short in dismay, staggering, seeing what had happened; one ran around and the other ran over Lendreth's body, still coming for Gard.

"Stop!" the Saint cried, looking into the eyes of the nearest with a wrath that made him clutch his head and stop in his tracks, spinning about in pain. The other one averted his eyes, drawing a machete. Gard stepped back, seizing the Saint and thrusting her behind him. Arkholoth and Stedrakh closed on the Mower from either side and cut him down.

"But we had come to rescue you!" said the Mower who had stopped first, beginning to weep. The Saint ignored him, pushing past Gard to get to where Lendreth lay. She dropped to her knees beside him.

He was staring up at the sky. His eyes swiveled to see her as she knelt beside him; then they rolled back in his head, and the painful rattle of his breath stopped. "You have killed him," she said to the Mowers, feeling the foundation of the world dropping away.

"No! *He* was the cause," said one of the Mowers, pointing at Gard. "This blood is on his hands!"

"And the trevani betrayed us," said the other, looking bleakly at Lendreth's body. "I heard the things he said. He deserved his death."

"You are murderers. Shall I curse you?" said the Saint quietly.

"Kill them," said Gard to his men, but the Mowers took a single step that brought them within arm's reach of each other.

The older one looked at the younger and said, "Follow orders." They drew machetes and buried them, each to the hilt, in the other's breast. They fell, embracing.

The trevanion had been silent; finally a long gasp came from Jish, who was staring at Lendreth's body as though her eyes would start from her head. She drew a few strangled breaths. The Saint took her hand.

At last Jish made a sound, a sob and a laugh mixed. "They cut off his voice," she said, pulling her hand away. "He'd have hated that. How that man loved to talk."

"I'm sorry," said Gard to the Saint. The Saint turned to him and held him, tight, and he bent and kissed her.

Now the trevanion all began to talk at once, but even so they were outshouted by voices from below the meadow. "Sir!" Redeye came running with Cheller, bounding up the twisting path, and between them they bore Mr. Bolt. "Sir, messenger! There's an army coming up the road!"

"What?" Gard turned and stared. They set Mr. Bolt down before them, and he wheezed as he held up the decorated war ax. Gard took it, turning it in his hands in bewilderment.

Mr. Bolt took it back and worked the trick handle. "Hollow," he explained. The end cap slid off the haft and revealed a roll of paper inside. He plucked it out and handed it to Gard. "Contact says, Duke Salting's bringing his troops. They're going to lay siege to you."

"Well, that'll be pointless," said Arkholoth, grinning. "We'll just sit up there and pick his men off with rocks." But Gard's face had gone pale, as he read.

> *Sir,*
>
> The duke advances on you, planning to arrive at the full of the moon. He will avenge himself for that you raid his shipments. His numbers I have listed below. Beware for he has with him a witch, or it is some puppet worked by magic, and her escort who is called Quickfire, but she is called Pyreeheena. She has no proper flesh and is fearful to see. She boasts she will take you alive, with some device that will break your walls.
>
> Gods lend you strength and be merciful to you. I still wear the amulet.

A list of troops followed: so many infantry, so many archers, so many artillerymen . . .

Gard looked up from the paper, looked around him at the pavilions, at the trevanion who still stared at Lendreth's body. The Saint, who had been watching his face closely, said, "What is it?"

"You must send your people away. Send them down the mountain, as quickly as you can. My enemies are coming."

"Nobody's going down the mountain," said Redeye. "They'll run right into the army, sir."

"Then I'll have to bring them into the house," said the Saint.

"All right," said Gard distractedly. "Withdraw! Stedrakh, Cheller, lead these people up through the maze."

"So this is how he does it," said Duke Salting, peering with interest at the trail up the mountainside.

"It's wider than it looks," the scout explained. "Most of the crevices are illusions. You can't see the real surface until you're right on top of it. If they aren't distracted by the illusions, you can get a column ten men wide up there, and quickly."

"The bastard must have studied stage effects," said the duke, grinning. "I wonder how many of his other defenses are a sham? Forward!" he shouted over his shoulder. "Standard-bearers to lead! Let all other men keep their eyes on the standard, and don't look down!"

The army moved forward, ascending the mountain with remarkable ease and speed. At the rear, Quickfire walked beside the sedan-chair bearers carrying the simulacrum. "This may be easier than we thought," said Quickfire.

"Oh, I hope so," said the simulacrum. It stared around, admiring the view. "You know, once we've broken the spell, I think this might make a perfect home. All the enclosure to which one has been accustomed, but a much nicer climate should one care to venture outside." It tilted its face to study the fortress above. Though its golden features were expressionless, the sneer was unmistakable. "Of course, one would wish to redecorate. What ghastly taste! But he was never anything but a jumped-up gladiator, really, was he?"

———

Grattur and Engrattur raced after Gard, attempting to arm him as he made his way to the door in the wall. Behind them, the corridors echoed with shouts as the army mustered. Before them, in the moment Gard threw the door wide, was an eerie peace: the silence of the garden, as remote and untroubled as the clouds that floated above. The trevanion sat or stood around the reflecting pool, in various attitudes: some weeping, some numb with shock, some few possessed of slightly surreal tranquillity.

The Saint rose to her feet and ran to meet Gard. "How long before they arrive?"

His face was expressionless, like an animal's in its blank calm. "They're in sight now. Another hour at most before they get to the Death Zone. Listen to me: there's an escape route. Grattur and Engrattur will lead you through it. Take the children. Take Eyrdway. Go back with your people and live among them, but let no man know my children's names. Say they are foundlings you rescued, like the others. Say I kept my boy and he died with me."

"No!" The Saint looked up at him, horrified. "How can you think you'll lose? You said no army could take this place!"

"And that may be true, and you and I may live to tell this story to our grandchildren. But I'd be a fool to count on it. Lady Pirihine is with them. My two bitterest enemies on my doorstep, and who wouldn't guess they've got sorcery to break the door down?"

"Little brother, hold still," said Grattur, weeping as he tried to fasten a pair of vambraces on Gard's arms.

"Then come with us," cried the Saint.

Gard was vanishing, piece by piece, under his black armor, becoming the Dark Lord. He shook his head. "You have a duty to your people; I have a duty to mine."

"They can't get through the Death Zone. I won't go unless they get through," she said, desperate.

He shook his head again. "If they can get through, it'll be too late."

"No! You're a mage! You're more powerful than she is! You can fight!"

"Little brother, she speaks the truth," said Engrattur.

"Oh, I intend to fight," said Gard. "Maybe I'll even win. But if I lose, I'll die rather than go back in chains. It'll be all right, whatever happens. You see?"

"No," she said, wondering if he had gone mad. "I don't see."

He leaned down and kissed her, then murmured in her ear, "The Dark Lord always comes back. That part of the story never changes. Give me a name."

"What?"

"Name me. You are my wife and my heart. Give me a name, and it will be my true name."

She looked up at him, feeling the tears welling in her eyes. Then she stood on tiptoe and whispered a name in his ear.

He grinned. "There! Keep it safe in your heart. Tell no one. Only call me to you and I'll find you again, if I have to make myself flesh out of leaves and dust."

He kissed her and strode away. The trevani Shafwyr, who had been sitting by the pool staring at them, rose and turned to the Saint. "I see, now," he said. "The Mowers took your garden and made it a fortress. This man has made his fortress into your garden."

"Yes," said Kdwyr, as though that were the most obvious thing in the world. "He did not capture her. She captured him."

"Is this an illusion too?" Duke Salting asked his scout. They stood before the black boulders of the Death Zone.

"Unfortunately it is not, my lord. This was where my associate died. At least, I assume he died; he went into the maze and never came out. The rocks are sharp as broken glass."

"They won't trouble us." The duke turned and strode back through the ranks, to where Quickfire was just helping the simulacrum from its sedan chair. "Madam witch! We've arrived. See the maze, there? I want a path cut across it. Shall I have the device uncrated for you?"

"Not yet." The simulacrum turned its face toward the maze. "We must save power for his walls. The model will burn through this part easily enough. Fetch it, Quickfire."

Quickfire ran to the baggage train and returned a moment later carrying the model. The simulacrum took his arm and they walked to the edge of the Death Zone. The assembled troops watched as the simulacrum bowed its head and seemed, for a moment, to sag, as though the will that held its limbs together had directed its focus elsewhere.

This time there was a jangling sound, like the strings of a harp being cut through with a saw, as the spells of the Death Zone broke. The black stones melted into glittering sand and drifted away on the wind.

Quickfire walked forward with the simulacrum and trained the model on the next rank of stones, burning through them also; and so to the next, and the next, until at last a path had been cut through wide enough for three men to walk abreast. Duke Salting, following them closely, smiled up at the open space before Gard's high wall. "Well done! Now let's bring the whole pile down around his ears."

"I beg your indulgence, sir," said the simulacrum in a faint voice. "Let me retire to my chair first. I am only a woman, and do not wish to see so much blood shed."

"Of course, madam," said the Duke. "But have the device sent up from the carts. I'll fire it myself; my revenge will be the sweeter. I have only to turn the switch, am I right?"

"Yes," said Quickfire. "The big red switch. Pardon me while I help the lady to her chair, won't you?"

Quickfire hurried to the back lines, supporting the drooping simulacrum. Once she had returned to her chair, he shouted, "Some of you, help me with the device!" Uneasy men obeyed, hauling out the trunk. The black tube was hauled forth and proved to be monstrous heavy; it creaked as it settled on its red-and-gold-painted wheels. Quickfire pointed to the great red switch on the back of the mechanism.

"Listen to me! Keep your hands away from that switch! No one must touch it but my lord the duke! If any man is fool enough to meddle with it, I can't be answerable for the consequences, do you understand?"

"We hear you," said the captain among the rear guard, looking sullen. "Not going to explode on my boys as we push, is it?"

"Not if you're careful. Go slowly, and don't jostle it, but go. Now!"

When they had moved away, trundling the device uphill with infinite care, the simulacrum jerked erect and hopped from its chair. "There. Now, let's waste no time."

"You men come with us," Quickfire told the chair-bearers. "We have a secret mission, at his lordship's express orders." He picked the model up again. The simulacrum led and he followed, with the chair-bearers coming close after them.

"Sir!" Dalbeck turned from the parapet. "They've done it!"

Gard came to the edge and looked out. He saw the swath cut through the Death Zone, and the column of armed men moving slowly through.

He felt a black calm, a serenity like ice. He turned and saw Thrang, wringing his hands. "Inform my lady wife, please," he told him. "And bid her remember."

Thrang turned and ran. Gard looked at the demons assembled there, at Redeye and Balnshik and the others, all those he had called to him and given flesh. "D'you think my armor's black enough?"

"You're perfectly horrifying, darling," said Balnshik.

"I won't be taken alive," he said.

She smiled. "It would be an honor."

"Thank you. Sergeant, take your division down to the postern gate. If they turn that thing on the walls, break out and do your best to take it. We'll cover you."

"Sir!" Redeye saluted and ran.

Gard looked around. "Have we a flag for parley?" Hallock found one and brought it to him. Gard went to the parapet and leaned down, waving the flag.

The simulacrum led the little party along the edge of the Death Zone, until they were well out of sight of the army. It turned its mask this way and that, as though sniffing the air. At last it stopped and clambered down the hillside. It pointed at one particular spot on the steep slope and said, "There."

Quickfire scrambled down. He took aim with the model and bored a passage into the mountain, tall enough to stand in, ten paces deep. "Inside! And again," the simulacrum ordered. "Follow him, soldiers."

They obeyed, half-willingly, watching the hectic sparkle as the back of the passage opened out, and opened out, and led them into the mountain's heart.

Thrang raced weaving between the running troops, threading his way along the corridors to the door in the garden wall. He emerged, panting and whimpering, and came across the quiet lawn and knelt at the Saint's feet. *They are through! Madam must fly.*

Her heart lurched. Grattur and Engrattur howled. They drew knives to cut themselves.

"Stop that," said the Saint, amazed at the steadiness of her own voice. "Jish! You must lead the trevanion. That is a practical instruction, not a mandate for authority. Follow this blue gentleman." She reached out and took Grattur firmly by the hand. "Grattur, take them to the escape route. Engrattur, you will go with us to the nursery. We'll get the children and then you'll show us how to follow the others."

"Yes, Lady."

"Yes, Lady."

"Kdwyr, disciples, anyone strong enough to run while carrying a child, come with us." Engrattur turned and ran and she followed him, heavy, slow, until Kdwyr took her arm and assisted her.

———

"Trespasser," Gard called in the voice he had used on the stage. "Who dares set foot in my dark domain?"

Duke Salting glared up at him. "I, Skalkin Salting! Duke of Silverhaven, Deliantiba, and Port Blackrock! Liberator of Konen Feyy! Owner and operator of Salting Freight Lines! I come for just and bloody revenge and payment in full for all damages, you thief!"

"Be warned and begone, foolish mortal," Gard called back. "For I have sorceries too terrible to name that I shall unleash, to drive you into the dust!"

"Oh, you have, have you?" Salting heard the device being brought up behind him. He turned to glance at it, then turned back, smirking. "Well, you aren't the only one with sorcerous weapons. Behold! Lady Pirihine Porlilon sends it with her compliments. Did you see how we cut through your black maze? That was nothing to what this thing can do!"

Gard stared down at the device, the gleaming darkness on its bright-painted wheels. A diffuse crackle of magic was hanging in the air all around, wafting up like smoke. Some spell was working, grinding away the hours of his life . . . and somewhere his wife and child were racing to safety. How much time might he buy them?

"So," he said, "when did you start calling yourself duke of Port Blackrock? I heard you were afraid of the Steelhands."

"Not now I have this," said Duke Salting, patting the barrel of the device. The captain of the rear guard winced, and some of his men put their fingers in their ears. "Getting rid of greenie bastards like you is only the first thing I'll do with it. The Steelhands are next!"

"Really?" said Gard. "Seems a little cowardly, to me, using a magic weapon to conquer. Yes, I think you're a coward. I think your father was a coward, and his father before him, and all their fathers before them. I'll bet you're even too much of a coward to accept a challenge to single combat. Are you?

"What do you say, Mr. Salting? You and me, one to one, blade to blade, to see who wins here today? You lose, you die, but I'll let your army go home alive. I lose, you can help yourself to my store of treasure. What do you say?"

"That's *Duke* Salting! And what kind of an idiot do you think I am?" shouted Salting. "Single combat! I'm not one of your la-di-da, inbred dueling aristocrats! I've got *brains*! You think I got where I am today by taking foolish risks? You think I'd be so stupid I'd come up here unless I knew I could grind you into powder? Well, think again, Mr. Dark Lord!" He reached out and turned the red switch.

Nothing happened.

Duke Salting turned and frowned down at the device. He flipped the switch back, then forward again. Still nothing happened. He gave the near red-and-gold wheel a kick, and though the men closest dove away from it in terror, the device merely sat there like the plain cylinder of highly polished iron that it was.

Gard tossed the flag of parley over his shoulder. "Kill him."

"Ladies," said Balnshik. "Gentlemen. Fire, please."

The air hummed with the release of bowstrings, the air dimmed with the flight of arrows. The duke was nailed to the ground where he stood and pierced through as he fell. Panic among his unfortunate men, and roars of laughter from the battlements, as Gard's men hurled down stones, and Gard's archers drew for another volley.

And yet the throb of magic was still in the air. Gard turned his head, frowning. Its source was not with the duke, who lay dying. The device sat inert, unspelled, harmless. The duke's men were trampling one another in their haste to retreat down the passage cut through the Death Zone. Where was Pirihine? Why hadn't she, or whatever presence she commanded, been there at the front to gloat over his death?

But she wouldn't have wanted him killed there, would she? She'd have wanted him taken prisoner. *You twisted up old Magister Porlilon's spell, so that now it can only be untwisted by your blood, before they can escape.*

"It's a feint!" cried Gard, but in all the roar of triumph from the battlements, only Balnshik heard him. Their eyes met.

"Oh, that bitch," she said. Then she was gone, running fast as a shadow, down into the house. Behind him, Gard heard a roar as Redeye and his men came boiling out through the postern door, eager for easy slaughter.

"No!" Gard ran to the parapet and leaned down. "*No!* Back inside! The enemy's inside!"

"We must be under the house by now," said Quickfire, panting. He lowered the model and looked around. "But it's not going as quickly."

"I'm a little tired," said the simulacrum, in a wobbly voice. The glow of witchlight it cast about it was growing dim. It held up one hand and tapped its four fingers against the thumb, *clink clink clink clink*. "Perhaps . . ."

Quicksilver nodded almost imperceptibly. He set down the model. "You men! I think we're nearly at the hidden door. Come here and set your shoulders to the wall, and push." The chair-bearers came forward and did as they had been told. They strained and sweated against rock and stone; but nothing moved.

"Set both hands against the wall and shove, then," said Quickfire. They obeyed him. He drew his sword and, smiling, killed three of them in three heartbeats. One man only was able to turn and run, and Quickfire raced after him and cut him down before he had gone a third of the way out.

"Ooooh," murmured the simulacrum, shuddering voluptuously. "Oh, yes! Delicious! Oh, they were *strong!*" Its witchlight brightened to brilliance, illuminating the dead faces of its sacrifices where they sprawled. "Now, dear Quickfire! Again! We're dreadfully close!"

"You must be very quiet," said the Saint, as Engrattur scooped up Bero and Bisha. "Quiet little mice. Can you be quiet little mice?"

The children nodded, putting their hands over their mouths. Kdwyr lifted Fyll in his arms, and Dnuill took the hand of Mish, the most recent foundling. "The rest of you, bring blankets and linen," said the Saint. "As much as you can carry. Move quickly, please."

She picked up Eyrdway, who had been sleeping. He stretched in her arms and pouted drowsily. He opened his eyes and she nearly dropped him, for they stretched forth from his head on stalks, like a snail's; but as soon as he recognized her, they retracted back into his face and he smiled. "Mumma! Way-way mumma."

"Yes, it's Eyrdway's mummy," she said, wrapping him in a blanket. "Come with Mummy now. Be quiet and good." She lifted him to her shoulder and he put his arms around her neck. "Engrattur, lead us."

They moved up out of the nursery and up the corridor, which was deserted now, though the noise of conflict came echoing along the walls from somewhere without. The Saint found herself falling behind, borne down by the weight of two babies, unable to catch her breath. When they came to a turn, Kdwyr stopped and looked back at her.

"Go!" she told him. "Take the others ahead, and then come back for us."

He nodded and turned down the passage. She paused a moment, gulping for breath, shifting Eyrdway to her other shoulder.

Fifteen paces in front of her, there was a sparkle against the wall, like reflected light. A hole appeared there, as the plaster and stone fell away like sand, and a man stepped through. It was a Child of the Sun, carrying what looked like a weapon. He walked out into the corridor and peered around, and saw her.

He grinned. "Well! We're not in the nursery, but I don't think it matters." The Saint took a step backward, feeling her heart beat painfully. "Here they are! Or I miss my guess."

"What?" Someone else—no, some*thing* came through the hole, a thing like a jointed doll of brass, the size and likeness of a woman.

Quickfire gestured with the model. "That would be the mother and child."

"Oh!" The simulacrum leaned forward at the waist, seeming to peer at them. "Yes, how lucky. Just what we'd hoped for! Gard's blood, in a convenient portable container. But you can kill the wife."

The Saint turned and ran back in the direction of the nursery. Fear lent her speed. She reached the door and slammed it, throwing the bolt just as Quickfire struck the other side with a crash. She heard him pounding at it and cursing.

"Eyrdway." She set him in his crib. "Play a game with Mummy. See your toys?" Eyrdway smiled wide and gurgled, pointing at the shelf above his crib.

"We're coming through," sang the male voice on the other side of the door. After a moment's silence, he said something in disgust.

"It doesn't work on wood, you idiot," said the other voice, the woman's voice, sweet and sharp as a sugared razor. "Aim it *around* the door."

"Good baby!" said the Saint. "Be a toy, Eyrdway. Be a toy, for Mummy."

"Ah! Here we go," said Quickfire in satisfaction, as the wall above the lintel dropped away. He trained the model along one side of the frame and then the other, and at last the door fell outward with a crash. Powdered plaster flew up in a cloud; when it dissipated, the Saint could be seen against the far wall of the nursery, staring at them.

"Finally," said Quickfire, setting down the model. He drew his sword and stepped into the room, with the simulacrum floating after him.

The simulacrum clucked in disgust. "Oh, she's hidden the baby. What have you done with the baby, Gard's wife?"

"Gods, she's a beauty. You're sure she's his wife, and not just the nurse?" Quickfire's eyes lit. "I can't pass up the chance to fuck his wife!"

"Yes, you can! I want the child. Where is he?"

"To hell with you and the child," said Quickfire, laughing as he started toward the Saint. She raised her eyes and looked him full in the face. He staggered back and screamed, his hands to his eyes. "Fucking god of the abyss!"

"Serves you right," said the simulacrum primly. "Search the room. Open the chests and cupboards. There's an antechamber there; see if he's in one of those hampers. Do it, or I'll hurt you worse than she did."

"Bitches," said Quickfire, groaning, but he groped and found his sword again and staggered into the antechamber. The Saint could hear him flailing around in there, kicking over furniture as he searched. The simulacrum floated nearer to her. She looked into its eyes with all the white rage of her heart, but the inlaid optics never reacted.

"No, that won't work on me," said the simulacrum, sounding amused. "I am not truly here, you see? My will is here, my senses and hunger are here; but my own body is a thousand miles away, quite immune to spiritual attack."

"Or you have no soul," said the Saint.

"Perhaps," said the simulacrum, shrugging. "Look harder, Quickfire! What a fool he is. Listen to me, Gard's wife: I give you my word I will walk from this place with Gard's boy alive in my arms. Show me where you've hidden the wee one and I'll even let you live, which means your other child will live too. How can you refuse me?"

The Saint shook her head. "I know why you want him alive."

"Do you? Ah, well. I suppose you won't tell me, then. Let's see . . ." The simulacrum turned its mask, as though looking thoughtfully around the room. "You're clearly a woman with a few talents, yourself. Any ordinary baby would have made some noise to give himself away by this time, so . . . I'm guessing you've put a disguising spell on him. Am I right?"

The simulacrum's blank gaze lingered on the toys ranged along the shelf above the crib. "Hmm . . . you hadn't a lot of time before we came through the door. I don't think he's in the other room at all. I think . . ." It reached up and pulled down a stuffed toy, a fat little creature with button eyes. "Maybe this one?"

The Saint did not answer. Watching her face, the simulacrum took one of the button eyes between thumb and forefinger and plucked it off.

"No? No." It tossed the toy aside and reached for another stuffed toy, one with a ribbon around its neck. "What about this one?" It took the two ends of the ribbon and pulled them tight. "Shall I pull tighter still?"

O Beloved, thought the Saint, *wherever you've gone, wake from your silence and please, please help me. My child is innocent of any wrong. In mercy, in compassion, send spirits to my aid—*

A low growl came from the doorway, and the sound of steel being drawn.

The simulacrum swung around, dropping the toy. "Balnshik! You wicked creature. How dare you run away from us?" it said, in tones of sincere outrage.

"Lady, has she harmed the child?" asked Balnshik, moving closer.

"Not yet," said the Saint, ready to weep with relief.

"Quickfire, you coward! Get in here and deal with this," said the simulacrum.

Balnshik smiled, and her face became fearful to behold. "Why, Quickfire! It's been a long time. Do come and play with me, little man."

"Gods below."

Quickfire had no time to say anything else, for Balnshik attacked then like a great cat springing, and his arm was nearly broken blocking her blow. The Saint drew back into the corner of the room, pulling a nursery chair before her to protect herself. Her gaze traveled fearfully to the remaining toys above the crib. The simulacrum noticed.

"So he *is* up there," it said, over the clash of live steel. "I thought as much." It floated a little sideways to avoid Quickfire's counterattack. Balnshik dodged and swung, and Quickfire fell and rolled; he was on his feet again in an instant, but Balnshik lunged and he was barely able to get his arm up in time to beat her blade back.

"Ah!" exclaimed the simulacrum. The Saint looked up and saw with horror that it had at last noticed that there were *two* little wolf cubs of wood, side by side on the shelf.

"Which one would it be, I wonder?" said the simulacrum. ". . . I'm going to say it's not the one with the teeth marks. Shall I toss them both on the nursery fire and see?"

But it was unable to get close enough to reach the shelf. Balnshik sprang before the crib, locked in struggle with Quickfire, who was sobbing for breath.

"You've grown old, Quickfire," said Balnshik in disdain. "You were such a lithe boy in the Training Hall. Slow and old, now." She flung him back against the wall once more and came on, and once more he nearly failed to get his arm up in time. Blade screeched on blade and the hilts locked; they hung there a second, staring into each other's faces, and Balnshik bared her teeth.

Quickfire dropped his free hand to his belt and drew out a knife and plunged it up beneath the mail shirt, into her side.

"You cheating little prick," said Balnshik. She broke free and cut him down, her blade cleaving through his shoulder and into his neck. He fell and died. She stepped back, staggering a little, and drew the knife from her side and looked at it. "How typical," she said, looking at the discolored blade. "Poisoned."

Her skin had gone the color of ashes. She turned to lurch toward the simulacrum, but her legs folded under her and she fell.

"That's what happens to bad slaves who run away," said the simulacrum. "Damn you! I needed Quickfire to get home. No matter." It swung around to confront the Saint. "I can sacrifice you instead. Now, shall I burn your baby, or will you save him that much pain, at least?"

The Saint said nothing, staring steadily into its face.

"The fire it is, then," said the simulacrum sulkily, and reached for the shelf.

A point of steel emerged from where its waist joined its hips. It looked down and laughed disdainfully. "Stupid demon bitch. Haven't I just explained I'm not—"

Gard pulled out his sword, and blood spurted from an unseen source. The simulacrum looked down and gave a little cry. "You brute," it said, as the blood flowed steadily and began to spatter the floor. "You big stinking beast! Don't you know who I am?"

Gard raised his sword and smote off the simulacrum's head. With an explosion of blood in midair, the mask and empty helmet dropped. Then the rest of it came apart and fell to the floor with a clatter of metal limbs, and there was no more blood.

He stepped over the pieces and kicked the chair away. The Saint fell into his arms, before pulling free and grabbing one of the toy wolves from the shelf. "Good boy," she said in a weak voice, as the toy expanded and its shape changed. Eyrdway laughed in her arms. "Mummy's good boy!"

Gard went down on one knee beside Balnshik, who lay on her side with her gloved hand pressed to the wound. Her fearful pallor had intensified, as though heat lightning flickered just under her skin. Her lips drew back from her long teeth. She leaned up to Gard, with difficulty; he leaned down and put his ear to her mouth. She whispered something. Then she closed her eyes and fell. Gard watched a light the color of morning glories flare forth from her body, and fade.

"What did she say to you?" asked the Saint, beginning to weep at last.

"She told me her true name."

I Was the Dark Lord's Passion Slave is carefully edited, painstakingly typeset, for typographic errors can cause so much unintentional hilarity in books of this nature. Suitably lurid cover art is engraved, hand-tinted, and pasted on the cover of the finished product. Copperplate & Sons' jobbers load it into carts and send it off to better booksellers everywhere.

One crate containing twenty-five copies is delivered to a vendor in Gabekria. He offers light reading matter for sale, along with sweetmeats, sun lotion, and other sundries likely to be wanted by persons intent on a relaxing day at the seaside.

The vendor ranges the copies of *I Was the Dark Lord's Passion Slave* on a kiosk, admiring the effect, before his attention is drawn by a small crowd of people coming down over the dunes to the beach.

Watching them he perceives, as he is meant to, a wealthy businessman of his own race, with family and servants. The servants arrange the sun pavilion, as the husband and father busies himself setting up a folding chair for his wife. Though she is veiled against the sun, nothing can obscure her remarkable beauty. The vendor murmurs an oath and indulges in a brief fantasy.

His imaginings shrink, however, as he contemplates the husband, who is big, black-bearded, and looks as though he occasionally sacks cities. Now the vendor notices that the liveried retainers are large, exceptionally ugly, and heavily armed. He shivers and turns his attention back to his wares.

But out on the beach, the black-a-vised man bows his wife into her chair and settles into his own. A nurse—tall, raven-haired, and shapely, but also heavily armed—releases the two little boys, who run down to the edge of the sun-glittering tide and dance back, screaming happily, as it advances. The nurse sets the little girl down and presents her with a bucket and sand spade, growling gently to dissuade the child from eating a fistful of sand. From his basket the nurse lifts the tiny newborn, bringing him to the veiled beauty.

"Little Ermenwyr, Lady."

The beauty receives him in her arms. The infant's feeble shrieks stop abruptly. The beauty smiles down at him, stroking back his limp curls as he snuffles at her breast.

One of the armed retainers goes to the kiosk and, looking over the cheap novels offered there, grabs down a few copies of *I Was the Dark Lord's Passion Slave*. He pays the vendor, unintentionally one silver piece short, but the vendor says nothing. This is surely, he thinks, some gang lord from Mount Flame and his family, on holiday. Best not to complain.

The retainer goes back and passes out the books to his fellows. They open more folding chairs and take up discreet positions around the pavilion, pretending to read. The husband and father leans back. He reaches out to the beauty and she takes his hand.

They sit together, watching their children.